A LOVE MOST BRUTAL

A LOVE MOST BRUTAL

A MAFIA ROM-COM

MORELLI FAMILY BOOK TWO

KATH RICHARDS

Book Cover by Cass at Opulent Designs

Illustration by Sophie Zuckerman (@dextrose_png)

Editing by Elaine Richards

Proofreading by Micah Clemence

For my husband, with whom love is never brutal.

And for all the weird youngest siblings. Sometimes you are the main character.

AUTHOR'S NOTE

Thank you for picking up *A Love Most Brutal*. If you haven't read the first book in the series, *A Love Most Fatal*, you won't be completely lost, but you will be missing information from book one and the plot and events will be totally spoiled.

If you did read *A Love Most Fatal*, welcome back! This book is more violent and spicy than the first and touches on some more serious topics as well. Mary and Maxim are both tortured individuals who have gone through (and done) awful things. Their love story is less bubbly and comfortable than Nate and Vanessa's was —they have to work a bit harder to reach their happily ever after, but I can guarantee they do get their HEA.

In this book you will find depictions of panic attacks, violence (gun, knife, and hand-to-hand), murder, multiple on-page deaths, explicit on-page sex, death of a parent (historical), child abuse (historical), and pregnancy.

If you read on, I hope you like it.

Love,
Kath

PROLOGUE
MARY

I AM NOT SO DELUDED as to think that love makes people weak.

If anything, a person falling in love goes through a metamorphosis into something softer yet sharper. Love introduces new tenderness while enforcing or obliterating boundaries you thought you knew. Suddenly, "I would never kill" becomes murkier, because if you had to, for them, wouldn't you?

You would, I think.

I've studied love for years, watching how it can recreate a person.

Love was the single driving force in my father's life, the glue of my mother's.

Love made my sister more careful, her husband more lethal.

Love has broken my cousin's heart again and again, but he still won't trade it. It's why he keeps reaching into the flame, certain it will burn him, but hopeful each time he might be tough enough to withstand the pain.

I think love is supposed to fill the gaps of what you need most.

Love has never made me tender, though.

Something isn't right about me, everyone can see that much. Love's never made me softer, never given supreme peace and contentment. It doesn't pacify, it adds stress, a constant vigilance, a weight that is ever-pressing and unending. I've asked my sisters if they feel this way, but they're better adjusted than I am.

"Of course I worry about them, they're my kids," Willa told me once while said kids practically drowned each other in the pool with their games. She yelled at them to settle down, then sighed, smiled. "But they're such a blast, aren't they?"

As recently as last week, I asked Vanessa how she could handle being in love with someone as clumsy as her husband.

"How do you leave him alone at all? What if he falls into a sinkhole somewhere?" I asked.

I meant, *aren't you afraid he will die tomorrow?*

"He'd call me," Vanessa said.

"If he leaves his phone at home?"

"He wouldn't," Vanessa assured, and slid a mug of coffee across the counter to me. "And if he did, someone would notice an inner-city sinkhole and get him out. I'm just as likely to fall into a sinkhole as he is. Maybe more so because he drives much less than I do."

That did nothing to comfort me, but I dropped it anyway.

Neither of them are so constantly concerned about death as I am, or if they are, they think the joy of love makes it all worth it.

I have joy in my life, I do, but it's in this joy where I find the most fear.

Love begets connection and allows for hurt, for loss.

Love is unstoppable, as far as I can tell. I've never been able to curb it, not when my sister put a tiny human in my arms, or when my brother-in-law wormed his way into our hearts with his bad fighting and worse clothing. With every person, it weighs on me, another brick added to my shoulders.

I think love has made my sisters lighter, or more sturdy—

assured, like they have a purpose. But what of the inevitable loss?

With every addition to the family, the what-ifs double, then triple.

Loss is inevitable. Life—love—it's a game of who you can keep alive the longest.

So, love has never made me tender. If anything, it's made me into something brutal. A weapon.

1

———

MAXIM

TODAY I'M thirty-eight years old. Well, yesterday. It's past midnight now, so I suppose that just makes it Christmas. It's past time for celebration, anyway. If I felt I had anything to revel in.

Thirty–eight years old, and what do I have to show for it? An empire, plus more money and power than any one man should hold alone. That weight is not something I bear easily. I have no partner, no heir, only a tenuous grasp on a power I don't dare believe I deserve.

And more expensive vodka than I could safely consume in a lifetime, so I guess there's that.

I take a long pull from my glass, the burn sliding down my throat, then place it empty with a clack on the side table next to my chair. There's a fire going in the mantle, but even that does nothing to soothe me. I watch the flames consume the logs, spitting white, then blue, then orange and red licks of flames, crackling and smoldering. I imagine putting my hand in the heat and wonder how long it would take to burn, then consume me entirely.

I wanted to be left alone for the remainder of the night, and in this vein, asked my half-brother to send away any visitors. This was all for naught, though, as he strides into my office.

"You've got a birthday present downstairs," he says. He stops next to me and nudges my shoe with the toe of his own until I turn away from the fire to look at the half grin on his sharp face.

"It's not my birthday anymore," I say.

"Christmas gift, then."

"Tell them I don't want it."

"Even if it's a Morelli girl?"

I stiffen, watching Sasha with a still gaze. He just smirks, hands stuffed in the pockets of his slacks. Smug fucker.

"Which one?" I ask.

"Which one do you think? The little one who's captured your attention."

I roll my eyes and get up, the leather chair groaning as I do. Alexei Orlov—better known as Sasha—is the closest person to me, which has its disadvantages. Namely, he's too observant, and I can never keep a secret from him.

"She hasn't been here for months."

"Well, she is now. Wearing a tacky Christmas sweater, even. More festive than her usual style, but she can pull it off," Sasha says. This image he paints is so discordant from the picture of her that lives in my mind. I almost think he's lying about her showing up here after months away, but my brother is not cruel.

"She's not here for me." I walk toward the window to study the street. It's more productive to watch the cars drive by than it would be torturing myself watching *her*.

"Come on, it's fate she'd show up here tonight right when you were about to put yourself out of your misery."

"I should kill you for talking to me like that," I say over my shoulder. Sasha winks.

"Your mom would be too mad at you."

"And yours would be *relieved*," I mutter, which only amuses him further.

Fate.

Sasha has always been too excitable about things like fate and destiny. Sometimes he reads my horoscope to me over breakfast. I blame his mother, the kindest of my father's secret conquests, and the only one to get a bastard child from the arrangement. God knows our father would have beaten Sasha's fantastical dreams out of him had Sasha been permitted to live with us.

As it was, Sasha's status as the disgraceful Orlov bastard kept him safe from my father's cruelty.

"Fate that I watch her go home with another twenty-something. Best present I could imagine." My voice drips with sarcasm, but Sasha raises an eyebrow, ever aware that I'm more than happy to torture myself watching her until she's danced away with another beautiful young someone. With the new year, though, I ought to put all that behind me. No more watching her, no more thinking of her.

This will be the year I forget about Marianna Morelli. It will be my New Year's resolution.

"I could call her up here. She knows this is your territory, the least she could do is say hello. It's common courtesy."

He's right, and if she were anyone else, I would've demanded their audience on their first visit. But she's not anyone else. She's the Shadow of Boston. The youngest Morelli. A menace to my peace.

"Don't bother. Let the girl have her fun." I sulk across the room to pour myself another drink. She doesn't need an old fuck raining on her simple solace, getting lost in the music and bodies.

I pour Sasha one too, then take a silent sip, glancing one last time at the fire still crackling. Despite promising myself I wouldn't, I lead us wordlessly out of my office, and down the hall to the elevator which deposits us on the second floor.

There's a ringing in my ear as I stalk down the hall, toward the upper balcony of the club, my sleeves rolled halfway up my arms and shirt unbuttoned at the neck. Not as put together as I like to look when visiting The Brickyard, but it is *my* club after all.

I feign casualness as Sasha and I stride past the staff, who do a good job pretending not to look surprised to see me here after I'd retired with strict orders not to be bothered. When I reach the balcony, it takes only a moment to locate her. Even in the throngs of people, my eyes are drawn to Mary Morelli like magnets.

She's not in her typical uniform of tight, short, and all black, instead wearing dark jeans that hug her muscular legs and a multi-colored Christmas sweater. When one of the yellow lights slides over her, she is like a flushed visage, pink cheeks, and a halo of frizzy brown hair.

It's been months since she last came here, not once since last summer when she was almost too late to save her sister. I thought she might have found a different club to frequent, and maybe she has, but tonight *she's back.*

Marianna used to enter alone with her flirty smirks and narrowed eyes, catching every receiver into her web like flies buzzing about her. The bartenders always offered her free drinks —which she never took—the bouncers thrilled to see her and the patrons stared; everyone was weak to the enigmatic pull into her orbit.

I've seen her when she's working. In the light of day, she is hard lines and no smiles, the single best enforcer for the Morelli crime family. She is formidable and intense, but in these walls, she became something entirely different.

In her months of absence from this place, I both yearned to see her and was relieved to be free of her. And here she is again, like she never left.

Just when I'd decided to never think of her again.

She dances with abandon—the freest thing I've ever seen. It's impossible to look away as she closes her eyes and tilts her head back, moving with the music, dancing alone, dancing with anyone who approaches her, dancing, and dancing, and dancing. And from the second story, I watch.

I used to try to look away, but these attempts were short-lived. My determination to forget her this year has already been forgotten as I stare at her now.

I don't know how to look anywhere else when she is here—this strange, vibrant creature.

Marianna Morelli is propulsive and consuming. I am addicted to studying her. It's been four months since I spoke to her last, at her sister's wedding to the math teacher. I saw her again, two months later, laughing with her cousin in a restaurant. I wish I could say I thought of her as infrequently.

"You should go to her," Sasha says.

"Thank you for the input." I'll settle for watching instead. It's probably less devastating than having her laugh in my face when she sees the unquenchable interest in my stare.

I release a long sigh, but my eyes narrow on the place she dances now. She's squeezing her eyes shut, not smiling, maybe not even breathing. She shakes her head, and then her eyes open and land on a dancing pair. She puts herself between them, and it seems all is back to her normal ways of bewitching strangers.

"Could be you down there," Sasha says, but holds his hands up in mock surrender at the glare I point at him.

"Please, Alexei. Go do your job before I fire you."

He chuffs a laugh and claps me on the shoulder. It is the first touch I've had all day.

"Merry Christmas, brother," Sasha says before leaving me to my brooding. Marianna dances on, her arm sliding around a woman's neck while a young man slides his hands down her sides. She kisses her, and then him.

I'm debating how long I'll torment myself here and decide I'll stay until she leaves with them. Then I can drink myself to sleep in peace.

This is when she breaks away from them.

Marianna pushes away from the couple who look on in obvious confusion and longing, and her shoulders rise and fall as she spins, disoriented on the dance floor.

Her face is drawn up, anguished.

I do the one thing I promised myself I never would: I go to her.

2
___

MARY

WHEN MY DAD DIED, I was in a bad way. His death couldn't have been avoided. That's what the doctor said. Even still, I believed I could have prepared us, if not stopped it entirely. Like, if I knew anything about heart attacks ahead of his, I might've been able to warn him to go get a check-up.

I believed him invincible. I was wrong.

And now, for the fifth Christmas Eve in a row, we celebrate without him, and we wish he was here. We sit around the table, laugh, play games, eat sweets until our teeth hurt, and miss him. The people around the table have remained, for the most part, though in the last year, we lost one brother-in-law and gained another.

It's been only six months since a man I believed I could trust almost killed my sister. We all thought we could trust him. He was family, the brother of my sister's husband, the godfather of my niece. The image of his gun to Vanessa's head flashes through my mind as she tells a story now and I wince. His dead body wasn't enough; I needed to know that everyone who was even tangentially involved was dead.

And now, they are.

This wasn't the half of it, though. Cillian had our trust, abused it, then came into our home and placed tiny explosives everywhere. It was weeks before we found them all—under every bed, beneath desks, beneath cars—these eraser-sized, sleeping things, just waiting to destroy us.

He would have killed us all if he lived, and, once again, I hadn't seen any of the signs. I was none the wiser until it was almost too late.

Everyone slept in a hotel while we searched for the bombs. Ten days in an Orlov, the kids loved it, and we found most of the bombs in the first week; he had a list of the general area where each was located. But then we found others, ones tied to a different list.

Contingency plans, if I had to guess.

When everyone deemed we'd sufficiently turned the house upside down, we settled in back at home. But at night, after everyone went to sleep, I would look for them. I searched around the house, in the garage, under every car.

I found seven like this.

Every time I found one it made me want to look for more. In the daytime, when I should have been working, when everyone else was doing something productive for this family, I was searching their bedrooms, fingers roaming beneath their furniture, in their closets, wherever my mind could conjure to look. For weeks, my exhaustion showed in the bags beneath my eyes, the rigid posture, my ever-roaming eyes.

It's been three months since I've found any, but I still look sometimes. When we eat meals, my fingers trail beneath the table in the spot where two had been taped. There's nothing now, only the residue from the peeled-up duct tape.

When I'm out, I imagine a new place where one might be, a dormant thing waiting to kill my loved one. At those times, I press half moon slivers into my palms with my nails until I can think about something else.

It's Christmas Eve, I remind myself, trying to force my mind away from its abysmal thoughts.

I've been having those horrible nightmares again, the ones where my father is still alive and I hug him and tell him how much I'll miss him if he dies. In these dreams I feel preemptively lonely, the kind of dream where when you wake there should be relief, but instead I grieve again.

My shoulder still hurts where I was shot, an ache that persists no matter how much physical therapy Willa insists I do. I massage my fingertips around the pearly pink star-shaped scar. The therapy really does help, but I still feel twinges of pain at odd times; like when I reach for something in the cupboard, or sometimes while I drive. When I train as hard as I used to, I get numbness all the way to my fingers.

I work hard on the rehab though, because the other option is accepting that I've become weaker. It's more imperative than ever to be strong, ready for anything.

The family spreads out around the house after we clear the table, the twins playing cards with their dad and uncles, Mom watching and sipping tea, Vanessa and Nate cleaning up the kitchen and probably looking lovingly at each other, as they are known to do. Vanessa is pregnant. She's going to have a child just six months after Willa has another, so now we're going to have not one but *two* more Morelli babies, and it's when they're babies that they're most fragile.

I sit in the living room with Willa, both of us eating pie, her plate perched on her round stomach. I scrape my fork over the whipped cream, wondering if this will be the thing that takes a small cavity into a problem cavity, or if that's how cavities work at all, when Willa gasps.

My head snaps in her direction.

"Feel," she says, waving me closer until I hold out my palm. She grips my wrist and presses it against her stomach. It's the size of a basketball these days, stretching beneath her maternity couture.

I hold my breath and wait. I've touched my sister's stomach before, felt the little flutterings of movement, but she said the little thing's been really wiggling around now. The baby bumps against my skin once, then again harder—a real sturdy kick—and I gasp.

"Little fighter," I breathe, and Willa grins.

"I hope she's like you." Willa pats her hand on top of mine, then takes another bite of pie like she didn't just say the most tender and devastating thing imaginable.

Vanessa wrangles everyone into the living room for a movie, but my hand still tingles with the feeling of the tiny foot thumping against my skin. We are two months away from the child being a breathing, crying, pooping thing in this world, and I will have to protect it. Her. A baby girl that my sister hopes is like me.

I hope she's nothing like me.

My niece Angel sits next to me on the couch for the movie and lies her head on my lap. She is fast asleep twenty minutes later, and her brother too. They look younger when they sleep, like tall little kids instead of new teenagers.

I comb my fingers through Angel's hair, straight and sandy blonde like her dad's, and that heavy weight of fear settles over me. We'll need to get a bigger couch in a few years, or some bean bags at least, equip the space to fit the still-growing family as my sisters keep adding children to the mix.

How many can they really have? Don't they know our ability to keep each of them safe is stretching thin?

Angel and Artie will start fighting lessons after their birthday, sure, but it'll be months if not years before they're able to defend themselves, and how many years until the next babies can protect themselves? And by then, Vanessa and Nate will probably have a diving team worth of children—Nate *loves* kids, he won't be able to help himself, and Vanessa can deny him nothing.

My heart rate goes erratic, thrumming in my ears, but I sip some water and pretend to watch the movie while Angel drools on the knee of my sweatpants.

The feeling of my lungs tightening is familiar, though still oppressive. I draw a quiet shaking breath through my mouth and gingerly extricate myself from beneath Angel's head. I'm careful not to trip over Ranger still dressed as a tiny, geriatric dog Santa as I tiptoe out of the living room. He cracks an eye open and watches me, like he knows what I'm doing and doesn't approve.

"Mary," Vanessa whispers, and holds her hand out over the back of the couch. Nate sleeps next to her, his own breathing quiet. I take Vanessa's hand in mine and squeeze three times, our code. *I love you. I see you. I'm okay.*

This is enough to appease her and she squeezes back, smiling before returning her attention to the movie.

Once upstairs, I change into black jeans and put on my chest holster under the bright red and green matching sweater that Nate insisted we all wear this year.

I slip on my shoes and leave the house as quietly as I can.

It's freezing outside, and not much is open on Christmas Eve, but I take one of the cars, roll the windows down until I'm shivering, and drive with one destination in mind.

———

THE CLUB IS BUSIER than I thought it would be. I didn't even know that it would be open, I just thought I'd try it, and when I drove past, I heard the beating music through the car's open windows.

The Brickyard's bouncer looks surprised to see me and waves

me in without a cover fee. I've been staying away these last few months, first because my shoulder was still too busted to go out clubbing. But when it was healed enough, I wasn't in the mood to dance with strangers. Too stressed about the non-strangers in my life to humor the idea of meeting anyone new.

Plus, I have more destructive things I can get up to than this, and sometimes *destructive* is exactly the right thing to distract me.

There are fewer people than a normal Friday night, but still a crush of bodies on the dance floor moving to the loud music. It overwhelms my senses immediately, between the lights and the thudding bass in my skull, I start moving on autopilot.

I beeline for the dance floor, not stopping to smile at my favorite bartenders or sip sparkling water while I assess the crowd for my target of the night. I just push through until I reach the middle of the floor and take a few deep breaths.

This has to work. It has to be enough to distract me.

It will.

Even with my shoulder, at least once a week I find myself at Leroy's for a fight; it's impossible to worry about the crushing reality of mortality when I'm trying not to get my ass handed to me by a man twice my size. It's how I used to feel here, when dancing and making out with strangers was enough to occupy my mind for a few sweet hours. It's never enough to make the anxiety go away fully, but sometimes I can pretend.

I don't know if the club's owner is here to watch over me tonight, his heavy gaze following me around the club. I'm not here for him.

I close my eyes and start swaying to the music, loosening my arms and hips trying to get out of my head for even a single moment. When I'm not so tense, I'll dance until I'm dizzy and pick someone to go home with, and by the time I leave their apartment without fanfare, I will feel much, much better.

My family is safe. My sisters are probably in bed now, wrapped in the arms of their spouses. Angel and Artie are surely asleep beneath the Christmas tree with that old dog that owns us. In the morning, Leo and my mom will make something delicious for breakfast, we will open presents, watch movies, sleep, and do a puzzle. It will be just as it should be, and everyone will be safe.

So why can't I get my chest to stop squeezing in on itself?

There's a trembling about my limbs that won't settle, but I jump to the music anyways, as if sheer exertion of energy will cure me from the impenetrable dread that has snaked itself around my lungs.

A man and woman dance together near me, grinding indecently against each other. Her eyes are bright and mischievous when she catches mine lingering on their bodies, and after a few unmistakable glances, she beckons me toward them with a crook of a finger.

They're drunk, or almost drunk, entirely loose and warm.

This is perfect. *They* will be perfect.

I slide over to the pair and fall too easily between them, taking the woman's place, my back against her front and her boyfriend facing me. They're both tall, completely beautiful, and I've never seen them before in my life. They want one thing from me, which I can most certainly give to them. I reach one hand behind me and hold the woman's neck while gripping the man's shoulder.

He tries to yell their names into my ear, but I can't hear them over the music and the still-rushing blood in my ears, and that's just as well. I don't need to know them. They don't need to know me.

One song bleeds into two, and by the end of that one, the woman is kissing me. She tastes tropical, piña colada if I had to guess, and as we kiss, the man's hands run down my sides.

They're perfect, I remind myself; nameless, young, harmless.

Six months ago, I would have jumped at the opportunity to leave with them—a way to blow off steam, have some fun, and escape the weight of everything that lives in my mind.

They should be perfect, but this isn't *working*. There's no escape now, no distraction. I find no loss to the sensation, there is only a pleasant, if sloppy, kiss on a dance floor, my skin too hot, pressed between two too-hot bodies, and the urgent, unending torture of my anxieties.

My thoughts race through an infinite supply of horrific images in my head—one of my family members dying, *all* of them dying, the gun to my sister's temple last summer, my dad's face as his heart stopped working—

I recoil from the beautiful woman's mouth and pull away from the pair's embrace.

I don't know what I need, but it's not this, not here.

If they're disappointed, I don't give them a chance to convince me to stay before I push through the crowd toward somewhere, anywhere.

The lights are too much, the sound, the bodies—there's a sheen of sweat on my skin.

I might be dying.

Before I can reach the edge of the dance floor, I'm dizzy. My chest is heaving, I realize.

Breaths slice in and out of my lungs, and I need to get out, need to do something, anything, need to—

"*Marianna*," a deep voice says into my ear, a man, and even with the music, I hear him clearly.

One large hand wraps around my waist and pushes me forward, off the dance floor, down a hall, guiding me through the club as my vision tunnels until we reach a metal door he pushes open.

Cold air stings my skin as soon as we step outside, and I gulp breaths as if I've just surfaced from drowning. I think I might have been.

I take a few steps into the now-spinning alley, a dim yellow light above us, and promptly fall to my hands and knees.

"Breathe, Marianna," the man says from above me, but he doesn't touch me again.

I cough, and heave, my chest so tight, my eyes stinging with unshed tears. I stare at the concrete that is so cold beneath my hands and knees, and then see his expensive dress shoes.

Massive feet, I think, even through the panic that racks my body.

This happens sometimes, the panic attacks. They've been happening for years, more since my father's death. Usually I can manage it, I could now if I could just get my damn breathing normal, but everything is so much, my thoughts spiraling down and down and down, a dozen horrific what-ifs for every self-assurance that I'm alright, I'm okay, I'm alive, I'm fine.

He drops to his knees in front of me wearing dress slacks that cost no less than three hundred dollars. The backs of his hands enter my line of sight, his palms pressing against the concrete, and my eyes trace up large, tattooed forearms, then broad shoulders until I see his eyes on mine. He's mirroring me, hands and knees in an alleyway, with eyes so full of concern I can't look away.

Maxim Orlov.

Part of me wants to feel embarrassed that the head of the Russian mob is seeing me this way, weak and vulnerable, but I have only the unbridled panic of inevitabilities coursing through my body.

They will die, they will all die, and if they don't die first, then I will die and then who will protect them?

"Close your mouth. Breathe," Maxim demands.

I do as he says, shutting my mouth and inhaling fast, shaking breaths through my nose.

"In your nose, out through your mouth. Yes, like that, good. Longer now, slow them down."

"I can't—" I hiccup and hot tears fall onto the backs of my hand from my chin.

"It's okay," he shushes me, "don't try to speak, just look here." His fingers push my chin up and he points to his eyes. "Breathe with me, I know you can."

I am increasingly certain that I will never feel comfortable nor stable again; *this* is the thing that's going to kill me. I'm going to die on Christmas Eve in front of Maxim Orlov and it'll probably start a fucking war between our families, and I won't be there to protect them.

"Marianna," he says again. I blink, forcing myself to focus on his eyes, forcing myself to breathe in through my nose, out through my mouth, attempting to match him.

His eyes are blue. I never noticed, never had reason to look at his face for long, and never this close.

It's uncanny, this blue, almost unnatural. Nothing frosty about them, I think they could be purple in the right light.

My thoughts slow by degrees as I look at him, this along with the racing of my heart beats and breaths. The cold concrete begins to sting my palms, or maybe they've been stinging, but I've just now begun to feel it.

"Tell me what you need," he says, voice steady. Has it always been so low? So firm?

My mind flips through all the things I need, a slideshow of the faces I need kept safe. My sisters, my mother, my cousin, the babies—God, *two more babies*.

How does Vanessa carry the weight of us? How did my father? No wonder his heart gave out, I—

"Marianna," Maxim says again, and I blink, forcing myself to focus on his eyes.

The debilitating truth escapes me in a rush. "I can't keep them all safe."

He doesn't miss a beat. "Tell me what I can do."

Vanessa was going to marry him. It was to be a political marriage—certainly not one of love, not when her heart belonged so clearly to Nate—allying herself with the head of the second largest mob family in the city. It would have reassured our clan that the Morelli dynasty was secured, but it also would have come with something much more valuable to me: more eyes, more guns, another prayer that we could keep us all in one piece.

I knew he was wrong for her, but she believed Maxim could protect us and I agreed. He was ready to tie himself to us then. . .

I must look bad, panting in the frigid night like this, because he adds, "Anything," and there's pleading in his voice now.

I cannot fathom Maxim Orlov begging, but I couldn't imagine him kneeling in an alley, either, so I suppose the man is full of surprises.

"How old are you?" I ask. He looks confused by the inquiry. He has black hair that's just graying at the temples, a sharp nose and even sharper jaw.

He still looks quite young. Looking at him is no hardship.

"Thirty-eight."

Twelve years.

He can't think of me as a child, can he? I'm closer to thirty than twenty.

"Marry me," I say, surprising us both.

"What?" he asks.

On the street at the end of the alley, a car honks. The winter air swims with our visible breaths between us.

I take a deep breath and set my shoulders before I gracelessly rise from the ground, wipe off my knees and palms, then look down at him. He doesn't move, seemingly frozen there, eyes studying me.

I steel myself, and meet his gaze. I step closer, as unfamiliar with looking down at him as he probably is with looking up at anyone.

"I need you to marry me," I tell him.

3

———

MAXIM

THE DAY AFTER CHRISTMAS, two days after she demanded I marry her, Marianna Morelli calls my phone.

I'm eating breakfast, Eggs Benedict, at the Orlov hotel, sipping black tea and stewing about her so intently that I fear I've conjured her call. I've been trying to convince myself that she really did say what I remember her saying, and in so doing, I've incited a phone call, and now she's going to take it back. She will tell me that it was a lapse in judgment due to a panic attack. A momentary low point that led her to think that, for even a moment, she was desperate enough to marry me.

I told her yes, because in that instant, I had promised I would do anything to help her. She'd nodded, used the backs of her hands to wipe the tears from her cheeks, and then walked past me without saying goodbye.

I almost thought I dreamed the whole interaction.

"Marianna," I answer in greeting before it can ring three times. There's a moment of silence through the line, and then a throat clearing.

"Maxim," she says.

"I hope you had a nice Christmas," I say. It seems better than

23

what I've been thinking, which is, *Get on with it, don't worry about my feelings, they won't be hurt. Tell me I'm an old fuck and you'd never marry me in any universe. I'll understand.*

"Where are you?" she asks. I briefly worry that we established plans I've forgotten, but the concern is fleeting. *I would remember.*

"What's wrong?" I demand more than ask.

"Your doorman says you're not home," she says, annoyed. "Says I'm not on your list, so I can't come up and wait for you."

I don't understand these words; my mind translates them into Russian as if this will help. It does not.

She is at my apartment building, asking after me. She presumably wants to see me, and further, she wants to *enter my home.* Wants to wait there for my return.

I pull the phone away from my ear and send a text to the doorman that reads, "Do what she says, Jean."

She's waiting quietly when I put the phone back to my ear.

"I'm seven minutes away. Please, make yourself comfortable." The drive is more like ten minutes, but I gave my driver, Samuel, the week off, and he's much more careful than I am.

She hangs up, and I rush to the town car parked on the curb, leaving my meal half-eaten on the table with a hundred-dollar bill. I'm impressed that Jean would be brave enough to say no to Marianna Morelli. It's his job, of course, but I don't know that I could deny her, and I have a lot of practice saying no to intimidating individuals.

When I get to the building six and a half minutes later, Jean is flustered and fidgeting at his desk. He rushes around the side, apologizing profusely for his misstep.

"That's quite alright, Jean," I say as I stride toward the elevator. He takes rushed steps to keep up with my gait.

"It won't happen again, I assure you, and—sir, are you smiling?"

"Hm?"

The elevator chimes before opening in front of us, and I waste no time stepping inside. "No, Jean. Happy holidays."

A blur of my reflection reflects on the metal doors and damn if he's not right.

I force my expression in check as the elevator climbs to the penthouse suite.

She's here to call off the engagement. It's probably the shortest-lived engagement in existence. She proposed marriage—well, demanded it, really—barely more than 24 hours ago, and now she's here to tell me that she's come to her senses.

So why am I so excited to see her here?

I resist the urge to call out to her when the door opens into the apartment's foyer, instead stepping inside and looking first to the sitting room, which is empty. I carry on to the kitchen and the wide living room. She's there, arms crossed over her chest, in a maroon sweater and a skirt that shows me too much of her thighs. Knee-high leather boots.

"Marianna," I say, and she doesn't turn around. Doesn't acknowledge that she heard me at all as she peers out the tall window to the city below. I often stand like she does now and remind myself that by some farce of fate that this is my city—the one I own. She and her sisters own Boston just as much as I do, though.

"Why do you call me that?" she asks. I stand to her right facing the glass. "Nobody calls me Marianna since he died."

She doesn't need to elaborate on the *he* in question.

Lorenzo Morelli was a formidable man, one whose soft spot for his daughters should have made him weak. My father certainly believed it did. If it did, Lorenzo's loving them certainly didn't make *them* weak. My father thought it a disgrace to teach your daughters to fight, to let them in on business, and he said as much to Lorenzo any chance they had the displeasure of meeting.

"Marianna suits you." It's the single most beautiful name I have ever heard, rolling over the syllables in my mind. "I never thought Shadow quite fit you," I say of the silly nickname most of the city referred to her as when her father was alive.

She looks up at me, eyebrows raised. "You knew of me?"

Lorenzo used to bring Marianna around with him when she wasn't at school. I remember her trailing the man around town to meetings not fit for a teenager, looking as fearsome and composed as him.

"You were hard to miss." When she was a teen, her near-constant presence around her father confounded me. I resented him at first for putting any child in danger, but especially a young girl. As she got older, though, she proved not to need his protection.

She was his shadow, but by the time she was eighteen, her kill count was the speculation and gossip of low-level gangsters around Boston. It was rumored she'd killed nearly twenty men before she turned twenty herself, her reputation preceding her and making her all the more a notorious mystery.

"The nickname would indicate otherwise," she says.

"Which is why it never suited you. People don't often think about a man's shadow, much less fear it."

She hums, like I've made a good point, then lifts her shoulders in a shrug. "Fear, maybe, but I'm not the Morelli people think about."

I do not correct her, though I have the impulse to laugh at how wrong she is. Vanessa may be the boss of the Morelli family, and the first female boss to grace these streets, but Marianna is possibly the most clever enforcer in the state, if not the entire East Coast.

She looks away from the tall window and meets my eyes. She's much shorter than I am, even with her tall boots, and at this distance, she has to tilt her chin up to look at me directly.

"I came to warn you away from me," she says, getting right to it.

I blink down at her, unsure of her meaning. She doesn't apologize for coming unannounced, at least. A relief because I would give away too much telling her that I don't mind.

"Before you say you'll do it, you have to know what you're agreeing to." Her eyes are lighter with the sun shining onto her face, the warmest brown. Mahogany.

"Tell me. Then I'll decide," I say. It's not as if anything she could say would make me change my mind.

I am reminded of a summer night on a rooftop with her sister last summer, when Vanessa Morelli proposed to me herself and explained the arrangement in no unclear terms: a loveless alliance, a business deal with rings. But Vanessa had been lovesick, shattering her own heart by asking me to marry her when she loved someone else. Marianna looks intense, almost nervous.

I could almost laugh that history is repeating itself with a different Morelli sister, one I fear I would never say no to.

"Vanessa is smart," she starts. "She's reasonable, good at parties, and personable. I am . . . well, my family says I can be a bit of a liability. I have a short temper sometimes, and I can be rude."

I nod, imagining her sisters saying these things about her, likely out of love or gentle correction in social situations. Perhaps these suggestions are well-meaning, or jokes, but I see the weight Marianna carries from them, these so-called truths she thinks she's learned about herself.

"I am violent, off-putting, and sometimes deeply unkind. By no means am I suitable to be a wife, and I'm especially not fit to be a mother."

"Would you like some tea?" I ask, halting her string of self-assessment.

"I—yes, please," she says with a breath, and follows directly behind me while I lead her to the kitchen where I click on the kettle. She continues like I hadn't interrupted her. "People think I would be a bad parent, and I believe them. It's not that I'm bad with kids, I'm just not *maternal*, I think."

I've never heard so many words strung together from her, this list growing longer for reasons she. . . what? She thinks these are enough to make me wish to deny her? If this is the case, I'm not as transparent as Sasha made me fear. Her short temper is the least of my concerns when she could commit heinous crimes in front of me, and I would look the other way—help her dispose of the bodies. They'd deserve it, she wouldn't even have to convince me.

"You're a good aunt, no?" I ask.

"That's different." She dismisses me with a wave. "I am emotionally distant, combative, and impulsive," she lists off while leaning back against the granite counter.

I retrieve two mugs before mirroring her on the counter across from her.

"This is quite the list," I say.

"Oh, there's more." She crosses her arms over her chest and looks up like she's rehearsing the items to share. "I don't sleep well, I'm overly confident, and I am somewhat destructive—but only because I believe that I really *can* get out of any bad situation with brute force and by being smarter than most people I meet."

"Sound logic," I remark. I don't doubt that she is smarter than most people she meets, and not just because she hangs out with gangsters. The kettle finishes boiling behind me, clicking off. "How do you take your tea?"

"I don't know, like with honey or milk or something?" she says, and I take that to mean she'll have it however I offer it. "I'm very good at protecting the people I care about, but—" Mary takes a deep breath, slows her speaking. I pour hot water over two black tea bags. "There are getting to be too many of them."

My chest warms at her sincerity, the obvious concern in her eyes as she imagines each person she cares for. Her family is growing fast, first with Nate, now with the two new babies.

"Can they not protect themselves?" I ask as I spoon sugar into the cups. "I've seen your sisters fight, and your cousin is a force. Nate, too. He killed Cillian."

"He shouldn't have had to." Mary sounds haunted as she speaks this. "And yes all the adults are perfectly capable, but if they keep fucking like rabbits, the kids are going to outnumber us."

I try to withhold a smirk at her derision. I've seen her with those kids; she adores them, and they love her likewise. The two new children will be just the same, and all of the little Morellis and Donovanns that come after them.

"I must be clear that I asked you to marry me for one reason only: security," she says.

I shouldn't be as pleased as I am to hear that she thinks I can offer her security. It's like a hindbrain response to knowing that she thinks I can provide for her. Caveman shit. I hand her the mug of tea, and she eyes it before taking a sip and flinching like she wasn't expecting to burn her tongue on freshly boiled water.

"Christ, that's sweet," she says. I cross the kitchen to the fridge and retrieve a container of lemon slices.

"Vanessa told you that she couldn't love you, but I think after enough years, she probably would have. You seem. . ." Mary squints at my face, and I don't allow myself to wilt under her stare or look away. "Kind."

I blink at this assessment, then squeeze a wedge of lemon into her mug.

"I will never love you, though. I have a limited number of

spots in my heart, which are rapidly filling up. I need you to know that."

I pass the mug back to her slowly, and she looks down at the wedge floating on the surface before taking another sip.

"And what of your own children? Would you have room for them?"

Marianna nods and holds up two fingers. "I can manage two. Any more and I'll be stretched thin worrying about them. It'll be best if I get my tubes tied after that, I think."

She's being serious, no levity or irony, she's thought deeply about this question ahead of meeting with me, and this is her answer.

Love, to her, is like an equation. Like a sack of beans that she can divvy up between a set number of people and no more.

She confounds me.

"I can offer you two children," she starts, "and I will protect them with my life. In return, *you* will protect them, and commit to protect everyone else in my family too. I will live with you, try to look pleasant enough at parties, stay out of your affairs as well as I can, and remain faithful so long as your protection extends to every Morelli and Donovann in my inner circle."

"Romantic," I can't help but remark.

"I didn't say I was offering romance. You told my sister you need a child, and I can offer you that so long as I can trust your people will have my people's backs." She looks me up and down, checking me out. It's not common that I feel heat rising up my neck, but I do now. "And sex is fine. No romance, though."

For the second time this week, the youngest Morelli has rendered me speechless. She drinks another sip of tea, burning her tongue again, before this time setting the mug back on the counter to cool.

"Why are you telling me all of this? It's like you want me to reject you."

"I was going for transparency," she says. I follow the movement of her hand as it pulls at the collar of her sweater before she clasps her hands in front of her, slender fingers interlocking. "If you're going to marry someone as messed up as me, you ought to know beforehand. I can never love you, Maxim."

The words should hurt me. They're not a threat, but a stern promise, a proclamation in no unclear terms. They should dissuade me from this arrangement.

Looking at her now, loose curls hanging around her face, I can't bring myself to care.

"Do you love someone else? Is there a middle school teacher in your favor that you're running from?"

Marianna cracks a smile. Well, a smirk. A slight upturning of her lips. I can't see her teeth, but I'm going to count it anyway.

"There's no one. There's never been anyone," she admits simply.

I think of the dozen patrons I've seen her leave my club with, the ones who would've loved her if she let them, a plethora of pining hearts strewn about the city.

I've never seen her with the same person twice.

"Why?" I can't help but ask, and then take a long sip of my own tea to hide my blatant interest. I don't know that I can achieve any sense of nonchalance around her.

"Dating is a distraction, love is a liability. I have to stay focused."

I watch her for a few too many silent moments. Her eyes remain fixed on mine, unflinching.

"You're right that I need a child," I say. "I'm thirty-eight, and if I died today, everything I've built would go to the wrong person. He'd undo everything. I will not lie to you, I am running out of time."

Mary takes another sip, this one not causing her to recoil. She inclines her head for me to go on.

"You are very young."

"Not that young," she interrupts. "I'm twenty-six."

Hearing this makes me feel only marginally better about my obsession, and only marginally. She's still twelve years my junior.

I am still an old fucking pervert.

"You'd be a young mother, but I can't wait years. I need an heir. You have to know that now."

A flash of concern is there and wiped from her face in an instant. After brief deliberation, she straightens her shoulders.

"If I can't make a child? If I'm incapable for some reason?"

"Are you?" I ask.

"Not that I know of. Everything seems to be in working order. But you never know."

"Well, then we'll cross that bridge when, and if, we come to it."

"But you're saying we'll need to *try* to conceive," she says bluntly. "Immediately."

"After the wedding, yes," I say, though the thought of *trying to conceive* with Marianna Morelli is making my throat constrict. "I'll understand if you need time to think about it."

I cough and drain half of my mug in one hot gulp.

Mary turns away from me. Her fingers curl around the side of the stone counter as she looks to the tall windows in the living room, and a muscle ticks in her jaw.

Her perfume is so subtle, something fresh—lavender, I think. It reminds me of spring, warm weather, and the sun on my skin.

She was sent here to torture me.

"You're a boss, and I respect that title," she finally says after her deliberation. "But I'm a made man just as much as you are, and if you treat me like a little wife, I will kill you."

"You say *wife* like it's a bad thing to be. Do you think so poorly of marriage?"

I always believed her parents to be unique in their love for one another. Her sisters, too, with husbands who never waver. I envied them for this when my father was so insatiable.

"Depends," she says. "Most made men are more likely to be struck by lightning than be faithful to their wives. Sweet things to be kept at home, made pretty with expensive gifts, and chattering with the other little dolls."

"You speak lowly of these wives."

"You misunderstand me." Mary turns her eyes to mine, unrelenting and hard. "They are this way because their husbands keep them this way. While they have their girlfriends, their jobs, their respect, and their street cred, their wives can't complain. They're not truly partners."

"And that's what you want?" I ask. "To be a partner?"

There's an intimacy associated with the word I didn't expect to hope for in this arrangement.

"Well, I'm no good at cooking," she says. I'm momentarily rendered speechless at what I think was a joke. "I know what's expected of a boss, the girlfriends and the mistresses, the second apartments, but if you have so much as a date—and don't think I won't hear about it—your death will be painful and slow."

"I believe you," I say. There's a light amusement in my eyes that I cannot quell.

I want to ask her *how* she would do it. I want her to describe it to me in great detail, but that is neither a normal question nor healthy for me to know.

"And do *you* get girlfriends?" I ask.

She squints like I've made a joke she's not amused by.

"I'm not stupid, Maxim. Either of us having someone else would make the other look like a fool. No girlfriends or boyfriends. Just you."

I smile and shake my head, more certain with every moment that she will destroy me.

"Okay," I agree. "Partners."

Marianna studies me as if to detect my bluff. There is none, though, and she shrugs when she comes to the same conclusion. "Then I accept."

I almost choke on my tea, caught off guard by her easy decision. I suppose I shouldn't have expected anything different from her, straight to the point as she tends to be.

We're just talking about spending the rest of our mortal lives together, no need to sleep on it.

"That's not right." I stand straighter and peer down at her, then clear my throat. "Marianna Morelli, will you marry me?"

Marianna smiles, unmistakable this time, and I am gone for the way it makes her eyes sparkle.

"Sure." She holds her hand out in front of her for me to shake. I hold her palm in my grip, small in mine, and shake it.

Sure. A baffled grin would take over my face if I didn't have such great self-discipline.

When she's satisfied with the handshake, she pulls back and steps away from me. Too soon. "I'll tell my family today," she says.

"Should I join you?" I'm friendly enough with the Morellis, more so since the events that have occurred over the last year, but I worry about how they'll take the news of me marrying their Mary. I don't think she realizes just how protective the rest of her family is of her. She is who each of them has the softest spot for.

"Give me a day to answer their questions. Expect Willa to call you in the next five hours with legal concerns. Vanessa, too. They'll want you to come to dinner, but I'll hold them off until tomorrow."

"I don't mind," I say too quickly. "Any time."

"They'll probably be in better spirits about the whole thing after a sleep. That, or they'll be ready to kill us both." She says this last part with a smile. She couldn't be less afraid of her family's opinion.

She takes another sip, her throat bobbing as she swallows. I watch the movement.

"Tomorrow then," I mutter.

I have a long list of questions yet to ask her, and we could talk about logistics all day, but the fact of the matter is that the woman in front of me has agreed to marry me, among other things. Things I cannot think about in her polite company.

Well, perhaps *polite* isn't the right word.

"Maxim," she says, making me stand at attention. "This is the last time I'll ask; I need you to be sure before I tell them. You can't change your mind."

I search her eyes for any uncertainty and find none. She is solid, none of the panic I saw in that alley as tears spilled over her cheeks. Now, she is the picture of steady determination, looking up at me beneath thick black lashes.

"The way I see it, I have more to gain than you, Marianna, and less time. I won't change my mind."

She squints, looking away from me, then nods. She takes one last long pull from the mug, then sets it in my sink. I watch her walk about my kitchen casually, not like she's never seen it before. She exits to the foyer, and I follow, resisting the urge to help her into her coat.

I suppose we're done here.

"Tomorrow night," she says. "Bring something for my mom. She'll be the weirdest about all of this, but she'll understand eventually."

I think that every Morelli will be opposed to the arrangement of their little princess marrying for duty, but I don't say so. I'll just have to bring gifts for everyone and assure them as intently as possible that I'm not looking to hurt her. In fact, I am much more likely to be hurt by this arrangement.

"You got it," I say.

"Hm." Mary gives one last nod before hitting the button to call the elevator. She turns over her shoulder, and I catch my breath. She really is the most beautiful thing; warm eyes, pink cheeks, a lower lip so plump I want to run my thumb across it.

"My ring size is seven," she says as she strolls into the elevator. "Let's be married before spring."

The doors close on her not-smiling face, taking her down and away from me.

"Fuck." I breathe, take a moment, then start making calls.

4

———

MARY

TWO WEEKS INTO JANUARY, I'm perched on a stool in Vanessa's bathroom while Willa stands behind me. Her pregnant belly bumps against me as she pulls my hair into a braided style that she says will look fancy but effortless, so much so that nobody will be able to tell that it took more than thirty minutes and three different curl taming products.

I sigh and slump my shoulders until my sister smacks me with the comb to sit back up straight.

"We're going to brunch, not an engagement party," I grumble, but it falls on deaf ears. Willa already explained that this brunch is arguably more important than an engagement party, because now that our engagement was formally announced in front of two hundred mafiosos on New Year's Eve, it's time for me to be seen with billionaire bachelor Maxim Orlov in *the press*.

Maxim isn't a regular mob boss; he's got a lot of illegal funds, yes, but he's also got insane business acumen so he's got a lot of *legal* funds too. Money the rest of the world knows about. Basically, he's hot and rich and owns a lot of property in this city, so of course people want to talk about him in newspapers and online news sites. And now they want to talk about *me*, too. Sure.

It's not ideal, and the thought of reporters conjecturing about me and my dazzling personality makes me kind of want to hide underground for the foreseeable future, but I will do what I must.

"You want to look good for his Twitter groupies," Willa says.

"People still use Twitter?" Vanessa asks, sending off an email on her phone. My sister is too busy to use social media, which is for the best. I think it would just piss her off.

"Yes, they make fancams of him and everything," Willa says, then apologizes when a strand of my hair gets caught in her big ass ring.

"Fan what?"

"Wouldn't dinner be better?" I ask before Willa can explain stan culture to Vanessa. "Then I could wear an evening dress instead of whatever this is."

I gesture in the general direction of the outfit which I never, never, would have chosen for myself.

"You're already salaciously younger than him, you need to be photographed in the light of day so you don't look like some torrid love affair only marrying him because of his money," Willa says.

"I have my own money," I say. "I'm a Morelli."

"Yes, but he has more," Willa says.

"More legal money, at least. Jury is out on the rest, we have yet to compare coffers," Vanessa muses before locking her phone and setting it on the lip of the tub next to her. "You think the *famiglia* is intense about appearances, the Russians are worse. You look perfect. Very Jackie Kennedy."

"Exactly!" Willa exclaims like someone finally sees her vision. "The heavy black eyeliner and tall boots always make you look younger. You can go back to that when the whole East Coast isn't trying to learn who has captured the heart of Maxim Orlov."

I sigh but don't protest more.

I feel ridiculous in this plum dress. It's got a high neck, a white scallop collar, and pearly buttons down the front. Willa says it's couture and will be better received than a black leather jumpsuit or whatever the hell I usually wear. I resented this comment because in what world would I be wearing a leather jumpsuit to a Saturday morning brunch? A black sweater? Yes. Jeans? Probably.

The skirt is short enough to not make my legs look tiny, and long enough that I can hide a small handgun in an upper-thigh holster. The new tights are nice enough, too, and I do like the boots. Calf-high, black, and a little retro with a chunky heel.

"You can make me look as wholesome as you want, but I doubt anything will make him look like I've *captured his heart*," I mock.

"You worry about your own face. Maxim will be fine," Vanessa says. She absently rubs a hand over her own round belly, which is past the point of being able to hide, but still not as massive as Willa's.

"You look nice," Nate says from the door, way too enthusiastic. His ugly dog, Ranger, follows in, a loyal sentinel, and when he stretches his paws on my ankle, I lean over and scratch his head.

"Don't sound so surprised, dickwad."

"Dickwad," Nate murmurs before he leans over and presses a long kiss on Vanessa's cheek. "Don't let anyone tell you you're not creative, Mary Morelli."

"She does look nice, thank you!" Willa says, and tugs my hair again as she finishes the braid. "See? Nice."

"Kind of like an American Girl doll," he adds, which makes Vanessa snort.

I glare at Willa in the mirror and she clicks her tongue against her teeth. "Well, usually you look like a Bratz doll, so I'll take it."

After a few more tugs and about twenty bobby pins, Willa steps back and surveys her work. It's a single braid down the center of my back, little thin twists of hair leading into it. My bangs are their normal curly, albeit less frizzy than I usually leave them on account of the mass of taming products. Between the dress, the hair, and the simple makeup, I look exceptionally soft. If someone didn't know me, they might even think I'm sweet, looking like this.

Friendly.

I scrunch my nose at the thought.

The doorbell rings from downstairs. Ranger yelps once, running in a circle before retreating from the crowded bathroom and trotting out.

"Let's get on with it then," I hop down from the stool.

"Wait!" Willa calls. I turn around, already grumpy about whatever additional primping I need, but she just holds up the big ring I'd left in the dish by the sink, the diamonds sparkling.

I take the thing, much too precious and vintage to look normal on me, and slide it back onto my finger. I'd usually wear a stack of silver rings on either of my hands, but today I wear only this. It's a delicate, beautiful ring; shiny yellow gold and a sparkling diamond. Maxim gave it to me without fanfare on New Year's eve, and said it was his grandmother's, so it's probably cursed. Like, his babushka might actively be haunting me.

"*Now* you look perfect," Willa says with a wink before following Nate and Vanessa out of the room.

I am the tail of the procession, clipping down the stairs to the foyer where the whole family is greeting Maxim with shoulder slaps and handshakes. They're obsessed with him, I swear.

Maxim gives each of them a slight, though genuine, smile, but his lips fall when his eyes find me where I've stopped near the bottom of the stairs. His shoulders are taut in his charcoal suit, and huge. I agree with Nate's assertion that Maxim looks like he was built like a refrigerator—the fancy, industrial kind, stainless steel and fit to hold a few week's worth of meals and many sodas.

The collar of his shirt is unbuttoned, showing the base of his thick throat, and it bobs with a swallow. He looks nervous, or like he's just now realizing that agreeing to marry a volatile twenty-six year old with anxiety issues that's been dressed up like a debutante was actually a very bad idea.

Too late to back out now.

I nod at him, and he belatedly nods back, greeting enough for us.

"Willa said I need to look like I have a kid in a prep school if we want the general population to think I'm not a harlot slut trying to seduce you for your fortune," I explain.

"I did not say that," Willa denies. Maxim's eyes light with amusement, which pleases me. At the root of it, he's doing me a favor by marrying me instead of finding someone nice who can love him. Sure, I'm offering to bring life into the world, but that doesn't change that this is a big, life-altering favor.

It's the least I can do to make sure he's not miserable all the time about it.

"Well, you look beautiful," he says. "That color suits you."

I blink in surprise at the compliment, my cheeks heating slightly.

"Shall we?" he asks. I nod before I thud the rest of the way down the stairs and brush past him to the door.

"Have fun!" Willa says, helping me into a thick, pink peacoat that I've never seen.

"Don't flip off the paparazzi," Nate says, and I flip him off instead.

A sleek, black town car is idling in the driveway, and an older man in a suit stands ready to open the door for us. I stop in front of him, eyebrows raised.

"You are fancy," I muse, and the man offers a warm smile. We don't have drivers, but then again, we tend to move in pairs at least. When I can, I make Leo drive.

"I'm Samuel," he says, his Russian accent evident. "Good to meet you, Ms. Morelli."

"Mary is fine," I say, before sliding into the car's back seat. The seats are leather with heating *and* cooling, which is how I know the car is expensive. Plus, there's lots of legroom, but I guess there has to be, because Maxim slides in beside me and doesn't look cramped at all even though his legs are massive.

I wonder how many cars he has. I expect they're all as nice as this one.

"Do you have a yacht?" I ask, and Maxim's nose scrunches.

I bob my head. Knew it.

It's funny that he's embarrassed about his obvious wealth. It's not like I didn't grow up rich—organized crime pays—but so far as the general public knew, my dad was just in charge of a big, successful construction company. They expected him to have a nice house, they *didn't* expect him to wear a thirty thousand dollar wrist watch.

Dad had a boat, not a huge one, but there was a big deck that he entertained guests on sometimes. He liked the boat, and I liked it too. I suppose it belongs to Vanessa now, or maybe my mother, but we don't use it. I think it stings too bad, being there without him. Mom should sell it. Put it into a college account for one of the million babies my sisters are birthing this year.

"Honestly, it would be weirder if you didn't have one," I say, and mess with the row of buttons on the door panel, clicking each one. They lower hidden shades on either of the back windows, then a knob changes the volume of the music.

As I said, very fancy.

"It has its uses," Maxim says. "Certainly better than hosting people in my home. And more private."

"I like boats. Better than planes, anyway." I pause, then look at Maxim who is already braced in anticipation of the question. "You have a plane too, don't you?"

"Not a big one," he says.

I smirk and shake my head. Maxim is in charge of a massive holding company of luxury hotels and clubs around not only Massachusetts, but the entire country. There are even some international resorts, Nate informed me last week after a deep dive into everything he could find on Google about my fiancé.

No one expects Maxim Orlov to fly coach.

I can't imagine why he would care what I think of his money unless he really does think I'm marrying him in an elaborate ploy to take his dirty fortune.

"I agree about hosting. I hate when people come over and put their germs on all of our things," I tell him. I squint out the window (the tint certainly illegal) at the thought of all the old mafiosos who come over and don't even wash their hands before sitting to dinner. They don't even ask if they can help clean up. "We do have a holiday house," I offer about the beach place in Rhode Island. "It's not unfortunate to be as comfortable as we are. But it's okay to be ashamed. Eat the rich, or whatever."

"I'm not ashamed, per se, it's just—my father was. . .excessive," Maxim says. I would like to pry about his miserable father, but the tense set of his jaw tells me that doing so might be like pressing the butt of my gun into a bruise, so I refrain.

We're pulling up to the curb beneath a huge Orlov hotel before he can say any more on the matter, and I shoot him a glance as I inhale, straightening my spine. "Willa says we have to look in love if we want to sell it, think you can manage?"

His throat shifts again with another swallow before he nods.

"Alright. Now, don't look too alarmed," I say.

"Why would I be alarmed?"

I set my shoulders and then attempt a *sweet* smile which feels more like pulling my mouth away from my teeth to show him how great a job the braces did in high school. He recoils slightly, exactly the shock I imagined at my attempt. It makes me laugh, a surprised snort and now he *really* looks surprised.

"Not natural?" I ask.

"Not particularly," he says, and for the first time since we got into the car, he's smiling too. "Just be you."

"I don't think that my resting bitch face is what your public image needs."

"You're perfect," he says definitively before sliding out of the car first and offering me a hand as I follow suit.

Maxim's PR manager worked with Willa to make sure the right paparazzi were tipped off about the public day date of Maxim Orlov and his mysterious, soon-to-be, gold digging, child bride. There isn't a legion of photographers like I imagined, but as we walk down the street and he offers me his elbow for me to slip my left hand into the crook of, I hear the sounds of shutters going off down the street, a cluster of a few men with cameras trained on us. I seek Maxim's eyes instead of looking at them, and he's already looking down at me, searching my face as if to decode how I feel about it all.

I'll give him credit, he looks wholly focused on me, which isn't the "enamored by his bride to be" that Willa thinks we need, but it might be better somehow.

This time when I smile, it's quieter, and when he smiles back, I think this whole sham marriage might not be so impossible.

5

———

MAXIM

I SIT across from my fiancée for another meal. It's the third weekend in a row we've been seen out together, though this time no photographers. She's still dressed up like a young congress-woman, today a soft pink sweater and a complicated hairstyle that leaves little curls around her face.

She looks so different, polished and glowing, exactly the sweet kind of girl my mother would choose for me. There's nothing of the girl I've watched in my club: no devilish light behind her brown eyes, no dark lipstick, no frizzy hair. I'm besotted by both versions of her.

I didn't realize before how much she looks like her sister, the older one, though I see the resemblance to Vanessa as well. They all share features, same slope in the nose as Vanessa, the high cheek bones of Willa. Of all the sisters, she might look most like their mother, Claire, though that woman's face is soft and gentle. Claire could be getting a speeding ticket and the officer might somehow still feel fundamentally *seen*.

Since the local news outlets had their fun reporting on my much younger fiancée, it's only a matter of keeping up appear-ances until the wedding next month. Thus, brunch, then a dinner,

45

and now a mid-week lunch in the nicest Orlov hotel in the state. The Meridian is a great restaurant, but everyone here knows I own it, so the entire staff is attuned to the table, worrying over their boss's experience.

Someone tops off Mary's glass with more water and we haven't even ordered yet.

Today's outfit is doing horrible things to me. I've seen her in far more revealing things at the club, but the prim little sweater over a collared shirt is something in between cute and the sexiest thing my mind could have conjured. I had to put concerted effort to not stare at her muscular legs in black tights—have mercy—and her eyelids shimmer with a warm color that makes her brown eyes bright. She bites her lip as she studies the menu and I once again wonder how the fuck I am going to do this.

How am I going to keep sitting across from this woman once per week until we're married, and then every day for as long as I live? My cards will be revealed eventually, I won't be able to hide my infatuation forever.

She puts the menu down. "Can we get a bunch of appetizers?"

Her eyes narrow, I think this might be a test, though she asked over the last two meals we shared and my answer was the same.

She could get the whole fucking menu if she wanted, she has no clue.

"As many as you want."

She raises an eyebrow as if to test this theory, and I'm pleased that when the waiter arrives—the manager this time, who is exceedingly polite and welcoming, and probably sweating through his dress shirt—she orders three different seafood appetizers and a french onion soup. I get the Margherita pizza, and she adds a slice of cheesecake and a coffee.

"Black tea for him," she says as she closes the menu and hands it to the man.

The exchange thrills me.

Her eyes wander around the restaurant, squinting as she takes it in, but they return to me when I speak. "You love seafood?" I ask. She ordered lobster on our dinner date last week, though the restaurant was loud and we didn't converse much. I did a lot of watching her, and she did a lot of watching everywhere else.

"Do you?" she asks instead of answering.

"I do," I say after a moment. "My mother used to make fish soup when we were sick or when the weather got cold." My mom has always loved fish; caviar, pickled herring, *ukha*, the whole lot. There's a warm nostalgia in my chest when I think about it.

"You know about the feast of the seven fishes?" Mary asks.

I nod. I've, of course, heard of the Christmas Eve tradition, though I've never actually attended one.

"My favorite meal of the year, I think," she admits.

Her eyes look past me, distant, and I imagine that she's remembering the last Christmas Eve, a month ago now, when I crouched with her in the alley and she demanded I marry her.

The silence isn't awkward, though I do wonder if I should be trying to fill it. I'd like to ask her more about the meal, her favorite part of it, if she prepared any of it herself, what her favorite dish tastes like on her tongue, but I don't want to overwhelm her.

She sits up taller in her chair, her face perplexed as she looks out the big restaurant windows.

"What is it?" I ask. Mary blinks, staring out the window for another moment then lifts her shoulder in a shrug.

"Nothing, I guess."

I'm not so convinced, but the waiter is back with our drinks, setting them down as unobtrusively as he can on coasters in front of us.

Mary takes this as an opportunity to change the subject.

"Your sisters are coming into town. Which of them is your favorite?"

My eyebrows stitch together. "You're not supposed to have a favorite."

"Right, right. Very diplomatic of you."

I think of them—Nadia, Vera, and Sofia—all so different from one another, but united in their ability to needle me relentlessly. Father always wanted another son, never mind the bastard son he had, but other than me, my mother only gave daughters. Served him right.

Made my life Hell though, the *only son*.

"They have different strengths." Nadia is closest in age to me, and the only sister that still lives in Massachusetts. She is headstrong and takes absolutely no shit. Mary would like her. In fact, I think she might like them all. Vera and Sofia are loud and creative, both incredibly talented at various arts, both living half of each year with our mother in Russia. I miss their noise when they're gone.

"I like them all," I decide.

"Mhm." Mary sips her coffee, burning her tongue and wincing at the heat. She uses a spoon to scoop an ice cube into the steaming mug, then pours from a small tin of creamer and a spoon of sugar. Tendons dance under the skin of the back of her hands as she performs the ritual.

"Who's your favorite then?" I ask. "I thought every Morelli was as close as the next."

"Leo," she answers without hesitation. "It *was* Willa, but yesterday she was annoying me, and Leo made cinnamon rolls."

My lips fall open, and after another drink of her coffee, her face breaks into a slight smile, signaling another of her dry jokes. I'm dumbfounded and thrilled each time.

"I also love them all," she amends. "Except for Nate, who I hate."

"You're funny." It comes out surprised.

She smirks. "Occasionally."

In the lull that follows, I watch Mary's eyes scan across the restaurant pausing again on the large windows that light the space. Once again, her lips turn down into a frown.

There's usually patio seating, but not until it's warm enough outside. Now, it's empty, only the street and another building beyond.

I turn back to Mary and see that her hand rests lightly around her coffee cup, my babushka's ring reflecting in the light. I feel an undue possessiveness at the sight.

"Do you trust me even a little?" she asks without looking away from the window.

"What's wrong?"

Mary's eyes dart to mine, and then back to the windows.

"I'm going to ask you to do something that might cause a scene."

My hand immediately moves to hover over the gun at my hip. I don't know what she sees, but I trust her instincts indelibly. She is as quiet and broody as she is watchful—it's what makes her so dangerous.

She opens her mouth to speak, just as I hear the first unmistakable pop.

"*Get down,*" she shouts and lunges off of her chair. I follow as the gunshots break glass, shattering into the restaurant and spraying over us. I immediately cover her body with mine, crawling on top of her crouched in the fetal position, and cradle her head against me as a barrage of bullets zip above us through the windows. There are so many shots, and so quickly, I know they have to be shooting Uzis at us. Those damn machine guns are illegal for a reason.

This isn't just some drive by, it was calculated, targeting both me and Marianna.

I hold her tightly, staring at the top of her head until the gunfire stops. It feels like an eternity, but is likely only a few seconds before the restaurant quiets to the gasping and crying of patrons and staff.

I lift just enough to look at my fiancée beneath me. The hairs around her face have fallen out of her braid, and her brown eyes are wide. She's okay, neither of us shot. Neither of us are bleeding.

She's alive.

A strand of hair lies over her eyes and I exhale before I trail just the tips of my fingers across her forehead and tuck it behind her ear. I would never let myself touch her in this way, only a respectable hand on the small of her back, my fingers brushing her palm when I placed the ring there.

But here, when she could've been shot, I let myself, just once.

"Sir, are you alright?" an employee asks, crouching beside us. We both turn to him and, after a moment, nod. He looks relieved, and is talking something at me, assurances perhaps that the authorities are on their way, but I return my attention to Marianna and help her to her feet.

"How'd you know that was going to happen?" I say once the waiter has left us. Her wide eyes harden. "I'm not accusing you, I—"

"The car drove by three times. Dark fucking windows," she explains. She sounds out of breath, rattled even. I watch her brown eyes scan quickly around the restaurant from one damaged thing to another.

My own heart is still racing in my chest, my throat dry, but my water glass was shattered with a bullet so there's no relief there.

"Thank you," I tell her. She swallows and nods.

"Can we go?"

"Of course," I place a hand on her back and usher her beside me out of the restaurant. "Let's get out of here."

6

___

MARY

NATE'S BEEN in hysterics all afternoon, griping on and on about the "goddamn murder attempt" that I endured this afternoon. I admit that the barrage of machine gun fire into the restaurant was a close call, but he keeps asking if I need to go to therapy for the trauma of it all.

"I lived," I mutter, when he asks for the twelfth time if I'm okay.

"This is just par for the course, I guess," he says with a heavy sigh. "My first date with Ness ended in a near death experience too." He pats my forearm absently in what I think is intended to be a comforting gesture.

For once, I do not glare at him for getting too close to me because he was just worried and the mafia is still rather new to him. I'm still not sure how Vanessa convinced him to go from math teacher to part-time mafioso, but he's not so bad. As much as I pretend to dislike him, he's weaseled his way under my skin the same way he has the rest of the family.

I would kill for him, and expect that, if needed, he might for me as well.

Willa and Vanessa were more pissed about the situation than

concerned when I got home. They understand there's no use fretting over what *could* have happened when I am obviously still in one piece. After making sure I wasn't injured, the pair of them immediately started making calls. Maxim had been doing the same since ushering me into his town car, a protective arm around my shoulders. All three of them are trying to get to the bottom of the attack—who made it, why, if they'll try again, etc.

Boring shit.

I make no calls, because that's not in my job description nor particular skill set, but I do go downstairs and punch things until my arms hurt. My hands have been shaking since Maxim loaded me up in his car. I balled them up in my lap then, but now, they still shake.

The punching doesn't help, nor the twenty minutes of stretching, the food I force myself to eat, the shower I take, the deep breathing—none of the usual fixes.

Now, in my bathroom, I stare at my hands in front of me for a moment, steam from my shower still fogging the mirror.

Nate's frantic reminder that I could've died slides around my brain, bumping into the "what if's" that are once again raging there. I could've died, a shot through the brain or neck or chest that would have resulted in a quick death. After all these years of fighting, that would've been it.

This is the thought that keeps me so on edge, this reminder of my mortality.

My sisters would mourn me, my mother would weep over my casket like she did over my father's. They'd miss me and yet, life would move on. They'd each deliver two perfect babies and I wouldn't be there to protect them.

Maxim would find another bride, maybe a nicer one, and have no obligation to the Morelli family.

I grip the stone counter and squeeze my eyes shut, breathing slowly in through my nose and then out through my mouth.

A knock sounds at my bedroom door, distracting me from my impending spiral and I flex my hands at my sides before I go to answer it. I'm taken aback to see Maxim waiting on the other side, still in the same shirt from earlier, but the sleeves now rolled up over dense forearms crossed over his chest. I raise my eyes to meet his. Water drips from the ends of my hair onto my bare shoulders and tank top.

"You're still here," I observe. I thought he'd left hours ago, off to run his own investigations.

"I came back," he says. His voice is impressively deep. Nate always mentions it, and he's right. "I wanted to give you the opportunity to tell me to go to hell."

My face twists into displeased confusion and I take a large step backward, granting him access into my room. He stalks past me, his huge frame foreign in my space. I'm suddenly self-conscious of what he sees; the basket of dirty clothes, the weapons on my desk, the journal on my nightstand that I'm supposed to write in when I feel myself slipping.

"Your shoes," I say before he can step on my green rug. He peers over his shoulder, then down at his leather shoes that are probably twice the size of mine. Christ, why is he built like that?

Maxim kneels to untie them and my mind supplies that this is how he might have looked if he was proposing to someone he actually liked in a different world—one less fucked up than this one.

He stands and leaves the leather shoes side by side on the wood floor.

"I'll understand if you're done here," Maxim says. His face is entirely impassive. I have no idea if he wants me to be *done here* or what he's saying, but it's making my stomach churn. If I'm getting shot at in public, what's to say my sisters won't be next? I need him more than he needs me at this moment.

I step past him, pulling out my desk chair and setting it down facing the bench at the foot of my bed. I drop down on the bench and grip the cushion beside my thighs to hide the way my fingers are still trembling. After an unsure moment, Maxim sinks into the chair opposite me.

"Did you find out who it was?" I ask.

"No, but I have my suspicions."

He won't look me in the eye. His shirt is unbuttoned more than it was this morning, and I see the top of a tattoo peeking from his chest that I do *not* let myself wonder about. Now is not the time.

"I told you I need to have a child," Maxim continues after another quiet minute. "If I don't, my cousin is next in line and, to some, he is the preferred choice."

Maxim always speaks of his legacy like he's part of the royal family—heirs and a line of succession—like Boston is his hard-won kingdom and the slightest misstep will put it in the hands of the wrong king.

"Who is he?"

"Nikolai Orlov."

I recoil, recognizing immediately the spineless Orlov that's not much older than me. He was a senior in high school when I was a freshman—same grade as Vanessa, and he hated our fucking guts. Said it was unnatural to let girls get into what we were getting into. Leo beat his ass once—I'm still surprised it didn't start a war. I guess Nikolai was too embarrassed to snitch about a Morelli beating him in a fight.

"You know him?" Maxim eyes me warily, as if I might favor Nikolai as well.

"He's an idiot. Not to mention a prick," I say. "I knew he was an Orlov, but I didn't realize how closely he was related."

"He is," Maxim agrees, "and his morals are nonexistent in the shadow of his desire for respect and power."

I blink at Maxim's intensity and the disgust on his face. He has the slightest Russian accent, but it's more pronounced when he's angry. "Why would anyone choose him?"

"He's easy to sway. A compliment, a bribe, it doesn't take much. He's a simple man."

"And you think he tried to kill us?"

"No. He's stupid, not suicidal." Maxim rests his elbows on his knees, which brings him fractionally closer to me. He twists the signet ring on his pinky, then flexes his hands when he catches me watching the movement. "I believe it was someone with direct interest in Nikolai taking over."

"Why kill me then? My sisters would retaliate if I died. It would be a mess."

Another reason to take greater care of my life, I realize. Starting a crime war in Boston isn't safe for new mothers nor their new babies.

"Our relationship and short engagement has spurned rumors."

"They, what? Think you already knocked me up?" I must be more tired than I thought because I could almost swear that his cheeks darken at this.

"Yes." He stares at the carpet as he speaks. "They believe it's already too late. I worry this isn't the last move they'll make against us."

If I was anyone else in the world, I might be more worried about this prospect. But I'm not. I've trained for nearly my whole life to be sharp, observant, agile, and deadly. If we can both stay at the top of our games, we will be fine. Maxim needs me; he needs a wife and a baby and someone who stands a chance at keeping that baby alive—but I need him *more*.

I mirror his position, resting my elbows on my knees and leaning toward him. It brings our faces close enough that I can see the light wrinkles around his mouth, probably from too much frowning. We lock eyes, his as blue as mine are brown. Some strands of hair have escaped from his gelled style and hang over his forehead. I refrain from moving them, though the thought returns the phantom touch of his fingertips on my face this afternoon.

"If you're offering a way out to protect me, then forget it. I'm capable, and I'm not going to change my mind," I tell him. I clasp my fingers together to keep him from seeing the shake, how fragile I really feel. I don't need him to see, again, how weak I can be.

"I can't protect your family if I'm dead, Marianna." He looks away, but I can't lose him now. Racking my brain for a way to convince him, I say the one thing I've wondered about the Orlovs for years.

"How did your father die?"

"What?" Maxim asks, not following the abrupt subject change.

"Tell me."

Maxim presses his lips into a thin line. I know the story, and he knows that I know it. But I also know the rumors. "He was very sick."

"Right." I chew on my bottom lip for a moment then release it from between my teeth. "Now how did he really die?"

Maxim exhales. A line appears between his brows, one I've noticed there when he's thinking or worrying, which seems to be almost all of the time. I want to press my thumb against the spot until it's smooth.

"I killed him," Maxim admits.

At the risk of rejection, I reach out and place one of my hands lightly atop of his.

He stills and I take a slow breath. "You did what you had to. I think you would do whatever it takes to protect the people in your circle. I can't protect anyone if I'm dead either, which is why you'll watch my back and I'll watch yours."

Maxim finally drags his eyes back to mine from where my

skin touches his. After another moment where I believe he'll fight me further, he nods.

"Fine," Maxim turns over his hand so that my fingers rest against his palm, then squeezes them. I squeeze back twice.

In two weeks time, we'll be married.

———

THERE'S a gun drop tonight and the load is big enough that I don't trust any of the underbosses to manage it without fucking something up. Having a night to myself is not worth the risk of losing cargo because someone else is careless.

Usually Leo and I would handle it, and if not Leo, then Sean, but both of them are tied up with other work. We have family rules about not doing mafia shit alone, though, so I made Vanessa let me bring Nate.

I pick him up from his school and he throws his backpack into the trunk before he slides into the car, buckles up, and stows his teacher lanyard in my glove box.

"Lose the tie."

"What's wrong with the tie?" he says. There are little space ships on it. I'm sure his students love it.

I don't dignify the question with an answer, only a dark glance and he tsks before tugging the tie loose and tucking it in the glove box with the lanyard.

"Did you bring a gun?" I ask before he can start telling me things about his job I do not care about.

"To school?"

"Don't sound so incredulous, *yes* to school." Nate has all sorts of weapons these days, now that he knows how to use them. He's really improved, but I would not tell him this.

"No, Mar, I did not bring a gun to teach thirteen year olds."

When he annoys me, I want to withhold things from him, like nickname rights for instance.

I refrain.

"Rafael is never far, and he's got a gun. I'm fine," he adds.

We had the young gangster get a job at Nate's school to be a line of defense for Nate and the twins, but it was mostly to keep Rafael out of trouble. I think we all feel responsible for him after what happened to his brother Tony last year.

Rafael considers it a big honor though, and takes both his job cleaning the school and protecting the three Morellis there very seriously.

"Why do I need a gun anyway if it's just a drop?"

"Sometimes drops go bad, stupid." We've just pulled onto the highway when Vanessa calls, her voice coming through the car speakers.

"Did you do the drop?" my sister asks.

"Not yet. Just picked up Nate."

"Hi, angel," Nate chimes, louder than necessary. "Mary's in a pissy mood again."

"Literally not true," I intone. This is my standard mood.

"Do you have your gun?" Vanessa asks Nate, and I raise my eyebrows at him. He sighs dramatically.

"I brought him one." I point to the center console and he opens the hatch to find the pistol I stowed for him there.

"Are you sure you're good? We can push it back until Leo is free if you need," Vanessa says, ever worried about her husband's tender sensibilities.

"Oh, please, he's fine." We watched the man shoot Cillian in the head last year—he'll be okay.

"Yeah, I'm fine," Nate says.

Vanessa sighs. "Alright. Stay safe and stay sharp. I love you both."

"Love you," I say at the same time as Nate gives a "Love you, baby" before the line clicks off.

"Where's Mr. Orlov?" Nate asks. He hates comfortable silence.

"I have no idea." There are still ten days until our wedding, which means ten more days of my own Morelli freedom before I become Mrs. Orlov. After the drive by, he insisted I bring one of his guards or Leo with me everywhere I go, but that would be rather excessive.

"I'm surprised he let you out of his sight. Guy watches you like you're a flight risk."

"I thought you liked him," I say. Nate was obsessed with Maxim last time I checked. He should've married him, then, if he likes him so much.

"Oh, I do. Someone needs to watch you like a hawk. God knows you don't watch your own back."

I only squint in response.

"So how are you liking him then?" Nate asks.

"What do you mean?"

"He's your fiancé, you're marrying him in a week and a half. How do you like him?"

"I don't feel for him at all," I say, though that's not entirely true. I feel mild annoyance when he stares at me like he's trying to decode a riddle written across my eyes. I feel contempt when he indicates that I'm not capable of doing my job without one of his goons at my side, as if I haven't been working for years. I feel begrudging attraction to him and a general pull into his orbit.

"You don't like him?"

"I don't dislike him. He's okay."

"You don't think he's hot?"

I look over at Nate like he's stupid, which sometimes I think he might be. "Of course I think he's hot, you've seen him."

"Right," Nate says. "But you don't like him?"

I shrug. "What do I need to like him for?"

"Mary." Nate pinches his nose like he's already tired.

"Look, I like him fine. He's hot and already way more attentive than I bargained for and I will have his tall babies that will probably destroy me in childbirth from being so broad shouldered. Happy?"

Nate sighs, but doesn't keep on asking dumb questions.

I thought it was obvious that this marriage was not one born out of mutual affection. Maxim doesn't want *me*, he wants what I can offer him. The same can be said vice versa. Nothing wrong with a business deal wedding, and honestly two out of three of the Morelli daughter marriages being out of love instead of obligation is a shock. One of us was bound to have to marry strategically.

"Why are you always so nosy, anyway?" I ask.

"Alright, okay." Nate holds his hands up like I'm threatening him. "I bet he'll worm his way into your cold, cold heart yet."

"Sure," I say, though I know this isn't an option.

I won't let it be.

7

MAXIM

MARIANNA WEARS a deep purple gown the night before our wedding, thin straps and with a low back, hugging her body's every slope and curve, and a slit up almost the entirety of her leg. Pure white heels complete the look and match the delicate white ribbon one of her sisters threaded through her hair. It's striking seeing her in this color; it makes her pale skin look even paler, and her brown hair almost auburn.

I cannot take my eyes off of her, but she, as usual, has no difficulty keeping hers off of me. She scans around the room, eyes bouncing constantly to each of her family members as if counting them in her mind. I'm beginning to realize that she is never relaxed; even now she's too on guard to even enjoy the events of her sham wedding to an old man.

I have lots of valid reasons to look at her tonight, so I don't try to stop myself; first the rehearsal, as she walks down the church aisle to me while the lawyer Morelli directs us like an elaborate production. We are just players here, in this life, perhaps, but especially in this marriage.

Behind me stands Sasha, the one man on my side of the wedding party, and behind him stands Nate, Leo Morelli, and

Sean Donovann. The kind of line up that would make my dad roll in his grave. He would rather have died than see his son marry a Morelli with a Donovann also in the party, and that thought pleases me.

Marianna will have a host of bridesmaids between her sisters and mine. Willa was first to propose the idea of inviting my sisters to the wedding party, and the three of them were all too excited to be involved. Nadia and Vera were with my mother in Russia, and Sofia has been navigating her own, new, loveless marriage arrangement to a boss in Chicago, but they all deemed my wedding reason enough to get together. They're all here tonight and were fast friends with every Morelli.

It's uncanny, my three sisters talking with the three Morelli sisters. The make up of our families isn't so different, but where the Morellis were raised in a home full of love, trust, and respect, we had a monster of a man who preferred fear to friendliness. I'm amazed my sisters turned out as lovely and personable as they have. All thanks to our mother.

Mother didn't make the trip, the city too haunted by her twenty-nine years of marriage for her liking. I cannot blame her.

"Mary, you'll stand here," Willa points to the spot in front of me. "But first, offer your hugs, and at this point, the wedding party will take a seat in the front row." Marianna hugs her mother, who has a mist of tears in her eyes alongside what I believe to be guilt. Grief for her daughter's loveless future, I gather.

The rest of the wedding party sits in the first row and looks up at us expectantly, save for Vera and Sofia who are whispering like teenagers. I stand beside Marianna, Willa still buzzing around us, nine months pregnant but not missing a beat.

"This is when you'll hand Angel the flowers. You can't forget, okay?"

"Mhm." Marianna mimes handing off a bouquet.

"I'll take them and then you'll hold Maxim's hands in front of the priest."

Marianna stands opposite of me, though doesn't take my hands, instead letting them fall at her sides. Beneath the left strap of her dress I see the star-shaped scar from where she was shot last year. I want to run my thumb across it.

"Go on," Willa urges. I think for a nonsensical second that she means I really should reach out and touch the scar, but come quickly to my senses.

Marianna sighs slightly before putting her hands in mine, her fingers warm in my palms. She looks me in the eye, maybe for the first time since the rehearsal began, and my lungs constrict in my chest. I would be concerned if this wasn't how it always felt to be in her thrall.

"Good! Perfect," Willa says. "Then you'll have the ceremony, the kiss, and then everyone will cheer and be so excited."

Willa gives a meaningful look urging us to mime this part as well, Marianna lets out a barely audible sigh. Her heels are so tall that she can't push much further up on her toes, but she leans toward me and offers her cheek. I swallow, probably loud enough to echo in this cavern of a place, and lower my mouth to her cheek. She tilts her head slightly and my lips land on the corner of her lips, instead.

I retreat after the kiss, pretending that something isn't igniting in me at just that touch.

"Make it real tomorrow if you know what's good for you," Willa sing songs just loud enough for the two of us to hear. "Good then! After the kissing and the clapping, you two will walk down the aisle holding hands—Mary, for the love of all things holy, please *smile*. You too, Orlov."

Marianna rolls her eyes, then flashes that wholly unnatural smile from our first brunch. It startles a chuckle out of me, and she smirks, a real smile gracing me like a miracle. Our first, and only, inside joke, something we share that's just ours.

"Yes, like that! Thank God," Willa mutters, and ushers us down the aisle. "You'll walk off first, followed by the wedding party, and you can take like thirty minutes to pose for pictures before we do the reception. Yes?"

"Yep," Marianna says. "I have been to a wedding before."

"Don't be fresh," their mother chides. "She's helping you."

Marianna clicks her tongue and turns back to her older sister. "Thank you," she mouths, and Willa smiles, clicking her pen and closing the notebook she's been carrying around.

"Now I think we should eat something," Willa says.

The wedding party claps, and files out into the reception area, where although all of the tables are already set up for tomorrow, only the long family table is set for dinner tonight, little flickering candles and all. I was told there will be floral arrangements everywhere, hanging from the walls, draped across tables, in little vases, in the hair of my bride, even.

Seeing how beautifully everything is set up, I have a renewed respect and admiration for Marianna's sisters, their mother, and Nate, for planning this whole affair. Leo helped too, apparently, choosing menu items and cake flavors. I have done next to nothing to plan and execute this wedding, other than offer my credit card, stand for a suit fitting, and pretend to every Orlov that I am perfectly pleased and not at all distraught over trapping the young Morelli into marriage.

Not trapping. She chose this.

It doesn't matter how many times I try to remind myself of this, every time I catch a flash of that spark in her eyes, I remember that I'm tying her to a cruel man twelve years her senior.

The thought excites me, followed by an overwhelming sense of self loathing for just how excited I am.

"I agree with the spritely pregnant one, don't forget to smile, brother." Nadia lightly bumps her shoulder against mine. "You only get married once. Ideally."

"Ideally," I agree.

"I hope that's not true," Sofia mutters while dropping into the seat opposite mine. Not all arranged mafia marriages are so amicable. My youngest sister was promised to Dante Delvecchio before my father died, and it wasn't until early last year that he finally called to collect. We thought he'd perhaps forgotten, and maybe he had, but when he came to visit and heard Sofia was seeing someone, he was all too glad to remind me of his claim.

I tried to fight it, but unless we wanted a swarm of Chicago mobsters to come down on our heads, I had to keep my father's promises.

"Such a hardship being married to the hottest man in Chicago," Vera teases and Sofia glares at her in turn.

"Don't let him hear you say that shit tomorrow, he's full of himself enough as it is."

"I like her," Marianna tells me as I take my seat to her left. "You didn't tell me your sisters were so fun."

"What, like I'm not fun?" I ask. Her eyes light with the same surprise they do every time I joke with her. I revel in that look.

It doesn't take long for Sasha and my sisters to start mingling easily with the Morellis. Everyone is all smiles and friendly faces; a wedding is a joyous occasion after all. Claire has been especially welcoming to my sisters, asking with earnest interest about their lives. I think she and my mother would love each other.

I'm glad it's such a small group tonight, just immediate family members. Tomorrow will be enough of a spectacle, and I can't be certain some of the older Orlovs and Morellis won't have words with one another.

The first combined Morelli-Orlov gathering was the failure of an engagement announcement party last summer, when we were supposed to announce the marriage between myself and a different Morelli sister. Instead, Vanessa was abducted by her brother-in-law and the only announcement shared was of the new partnerships and growing collaboration between our families. Some were not pleased and let me hear about it. I let them complain, but only to a point before putting them in their place.

I am the boss after all.

By New Year's, when my engagement to the youngest Morelli was announced, the sentiments had mostly started to soften. Not entirely though. Old habits and the like.

"I'd like to offer a toast," Vanessa says, and stands. Vanessa is also quite pregnant these days, her stomach stretching beneath a crimson dress. If all goes to plan in this arrangement of ours, Marianna won't be far behind them. The thought makes my throat dry.

"Mary and I haven't always seen eye to eye, probably because she's my little sister." I watch a soft smile grace Marianna's lips. "You are incredibly stubborn, worse than me, and hardheaded to a fault."

"I thought you were supposed to compliment me," Marianna protests, grinning now.

"Right, right, okay." Vanessa rolls her eyes, smiling back. Her lip wobbles, eyes brimming with tears. Nate's too, as he looks up at his wife with so much love. "Mary, you have an extreme sense of duty and are the most loyal person I've ever had the joy of being related to. Everyone used to call you his shadow because you're the most like Dad of any of us."

I glance at my fiancée, her own eyes glassy, a rare softness on her features.

"He would be so, so proud of you," Vanessa says. "And Maxim, I know you'll take care of her. You'd hate to see what would happen if you didn't."

The party chuckles at this, but everyone knows the truth

behind the threat. Vanessa holds her glass of water up, and everyone follows suit with their water or wine.

"*Per cent'anni,*" she says, and all the Morellis repeat it in cheers.

Marianna leans closer to me, her low private voice surprising me. "For a hundred years. That's what it means."

"That's a long time," I whisper, and can't help but smile down at her.

8

———

MARY

DESPITE MY PROTESTATIONS, on the day of my wedding, I wear white.

I thought maroon might be good if my sisters wouldn't consider black, or bright red even. A red dress is traditional for some cultures, and I thought I had a good chance with this argument because Google told me that Russian brides traditionally were all about red. Willa and Vanessa said that would be great if I were Russian, but since I'm Italian and this wedding is all about appearances, we're sticking to white. I managed a very red bouquet, at least. And these deep red heels which I like so much I might wear them to every formal occasion for the rest of my life.

They both cried at my dress fitting, pregnancy hormones making them a mess, and Mom cried too, but she always cries, she can't help it. I thought I looked strange, but I've been in Willa's costumes every week since this engagement was announced, so might as well go all the way for the wedding.

In my bright, luxurious bridal suite now, I step into the simple gown and pull the thin straps over my shoulders before letting my mom help with the zipper and the many, many buttons down the back of the dress. The fabric is exquisite, smooth satin that feels too fine beneath my finger tips. I am forced to stand taller as Mom pulls the bodice into place.

"You don't have to do this," she whispers. I look at her through the mirror, and her eyes are on mine. I smile softly at her.

"I know."

"There's still time," she says, even as her fingers still deftly slide every little button into place. "I'd help you."

Once she finishes the row of buttons, she turns me by the shoulders and looks so earnest, so genuine in her promise to help me be a runaway bride if I needed. The nervous part of me craves to take her up on the offer, but that thought is quickly squashed when Angel waltzes into the room wearing her own white dress, hers knee-length with wide purple ribbons tied in bows at the tops of her shoulders.

She's turning fourteen this year, the age I was when she was born, and my chest squeezes at the memory of her tiny head in my hands. She never wanted to be put down, a Velcro baby, and my tiny best friend.

I meet my mother's tearful stare again and offer as honest a smile as I can. "Thank you, Mamma."

She exhales, sets her shoulders, and accepts my decision. I've always appreciated this about our mom, ever-willing to let us make our own choices. She kisses both of my cheeks and squeezes my hands three times before wrapping Angel in her own hug.

"What are we crying about?" Angel asks.

Mom laughs, and gently pats under her eyes. "Your auntie just looks so pretty. I wish her papa could see her now."

"Ma?" Vanessa calls from the door, obviously in transit somewhere else. She and Willa have been scurrying from one place to the next all morning. My job is easy in comparison; I just have to get married. "Can you help with the cake delivery?"

"Of course," Mom says. She kisses Angel's head and leaves

me and my niece in the bridal suite. Willa has already done Angel's hair into a sophisticated braid down her back, but I bend slightly and push some baby hairs behind her ears before I squeeze her cheeks.

"You're going to mess up my makeup," she protests.

"You're the one eating mini donuts, Menace."

"Blame Artie, he got them from Nate!"

"So we should be blaming Nate," I conclude. "Well, chocolate fingers and all, you're stunning."

"You look weird in white," she whispers, and we both break into a fit of giggles.

"That's what I said!" I wrap her in a side hug and then tickle her. She laughs louder, drawing the attention of Willa in the hallway who has planned this wedding like a military operation despite the fact her water could break any day now.

My sister smiles at the scene from the doorway, but then puts on her stern face. "Who gave you those? You are both wearing white!"

I take a step to the left, bringing Angel with me so our bodies hide the offending chocolate donuts on the table behind us. Angel is almost as tall as me these days. She'll be taller than me within the next few months. I suppose that's not difficult, since I'm somehow the smallest of the family by many inches.

Someone calls Willa's name before she can chastise or direct us more and she points two fingers at her eyes and then us before stalking away to deal with whatever else could go wrong.

"Mary," Angel starts. I can tell from her tone that she's about to ask a difficult question. One of the ones with a messy answer.

I give her my attention and nod at her to go on.

"I asked Mom if you love Maxim and she said it's complicated. But you do, right? Love him?"

I blink at the candor of the question. I can see my sister trying to be honest with her daughter without telling her the whole truth. Normal people don't need arranged marriages. *Complicated indeed.*

"I am marrying for love." I don't mention that this is not love for *him*, but for her, for all our family. "Maxim will be a good uncle to you, you'll see."

"But are you in love with him? Like Mom and Dad?"

I open my mouth, then close it. I can't lie to her, she's too sharp. She'll see straight through me; she already has, she just doesn't want to believe it.

"I don't think I've ever loved someone as much as your parents love each other. But that's okay."

She's quiet for a long moment, takes a bite of a mini donut. "Do you think I'll love who I marry?"

I nod too quickly, any other option too abhorrent to me. I don't want her to know how thoroughly that question just knocked me on my ass. I think if she tried to marry someone she didn't love, I'd drag her away to another country to hide out in a beach house. Hell, I'd take her to Italy. We could start a business, fend for ourselves.

"You will," I say, my voice firm. "You'll find a love so big it'll make you dizzy. And you'll drive your kids crazy by kissing at the dinner table, and you'll be so deliriously happy."

She smiles, quiet delight so evident on her face. I pinch her cheek again and she bats me away.

I look in the mirror at us in our white dresses and smile. I will do this for her, so that she can live long enough to have that future.

A throat clears from behind us, and we both jump, turning to see none other than my husband-to-be standing in a crisp suit, all black, with a crimson rose boutonniere pinned to his lapel.

Angel shrieks. "You're not supposed to see her!"

Maxim doesn't respond at first, his gaze preternaturally still on me.

He probably agrees that I look as ridiculous as I feel. He snaps out of it and offers a smile to Angel.

"But if I can't see her, how will I give her my gift?"

Angel's eyes go wide—the girl, like any thirteen year old, *loves* gifts.

"Scram," I whisper. She gives an excited giggle before walking off past him. Then it's just us in the quiet bridal suite, sun casting through the tall windows on the floor between us. I don't step toward him, and after a moment, his strides eat up the distance between us.

"Willa will scream if she sees you in here. She's superstitious."

"And you?" he asks, a smirk tugging up his lips. "Do you believe in bad luck?"

I shake my head.

His eyes flit down again before returning to my face. If I didn't know better, I'd think my fiancée was just checking me out.

"You are very beautiful," he says. I note that he didn't say I *look* beautiful, only that I am.

"And you are very. . ." *handsome, striking, perplexing*, all cross my mind, "tall."

That rare smile breaks over his face, and I find a soft one on my lips as well. "You look very nice," I amend. "Like a groom."

"I brought you something." Maxim reaches into his coat and retrieves a rectangular box. I take it tentatively from his hand and run my fingertips over the leather before sliding over the clasp and opening it.

It's a necklace, a dainty gold chain and a golden pendant with three small diamonds embedded like stars. It's simple and beautiful, and my finger traces over the oval pendant.

"I thought—"

He cuts off like he's at a loss for words when I look back up at him. After a moment, he tries again. "I wanted you to have something to remind you of your home."

I look at the pendant again—three diamonds, one for me and each of my sisters, I realize.

"Will you help me put it on?" I ask, already pulling it from the box's soft interior.

He closes the distance, and stands directly behind me, close enough that I feel his body heat against my bare back and smell his cologne. It's not offensive to me like most colognes. His is softer and more citrusy.

I lift my hair off my neck. Willa tried to convince me to put it into some outrageous updo, but I drew the line at the wide skirt.

My head comes just above his chin in the heels I wear, and I watch in the mirror as he focuses intently on the task of clasping the chain around my neck. When it's secure, his hands drop to his sides and his eyes meet mine in the mirror.

We aren't often alone like this, usually surrounded by strangers, or at least his driver. It's for the best; I'm not sure we really have anything to talk about. But even still, we have an agreement, a mutual understanding of what this is and why we are doing it, and I see that in his eyes reflected through the glass.

In the secret depths of mind, I hope he'll be able to stand me.

He must know by now how unlikable I can be.

The pendant hangs in the center of my chest above the square neckline of the dress, and it really was the perfect thing to add to the outfit. Simple, but beautiful. The kind of delicate thing I would never purchase for myself, which makes me like it all the more.

The ring I wear is far from simple, vintage and gold and with the most massive diamond. Even if his babushka haunts it, I have grown to quite like it.

"Thank you, Maxim."

The thank you is for more than just the necklace. He knows it.

"Of course."

I set my shoulders back and exhale a big breath. "Shall we get married, then?"

9

———

MAXIM

THE CHURCH IS FULL, one half of Russians, the other of Italians and a large handful of Irish clan members, too. They're not all criminals. Some are children, others just *married* to mobsters, some none the wiser or perfectly fine pretending to be oblivious.

Our communities have been friendly enough these last months, a feat considering that when my father was alive it wasn't uncommon to spit as you walked by a Morelli. 'Friendly' might be too strong a word, but there is a cordiality there.

Or maybe a begrudging respect for the decisions of their dons, even if they can't get behind them with all sincerity.

My three sisters sit at the front row on my side, Nadia looking like she is going to burst with the excitement of the event, Vera off in her own world, and Sophia vaguely bored but as put together and polished as ever. Her husband, Dante Delvecchio, an underboss in Chicago, sits by her side, arm slung behind her. They loathe each other, but he knows that hurting her would mean death by me if not by Sophia first.

Now that it's the day of the actual wedding, I'm trying not to take our mother's absence personally. She hates this city, but I'm certain she does love me. Just too many memories of *him*.

Nadia meets my eyes and hers sparkle as she gives two thumbs up. She said that a new person joining the family is the most exciting thing to happen in a decade, and she might be right about that.

When a violin and piano spring to life with a romantic wedding march, and the tall wooden doors at the end of the church open, blood rushes in my ears.

I'm thirty-eight years old, I've never been married, and now —*right now*—I'm marrying someone I barely know, who barely knows *me*. We have no grand presumptions of love for each other, only shared duty and mutual benefit from the arrangement.

That is all.

I've already seen Marianna, just twenty minutes ago when I brought her the necklace. But when she appears down the aisle after each of her sisters, her arm wrapped in her mother's, I am bowled over once again with the sight of her.

She is stunning, as she always is, but I have a unique reaction to her beauty as she is swathed in white, stepping toward me to become my wife. I cannot help but stand taller, stretch my chest wider, lift my chin, flex my hands at my side.

As she approaches, my mind settles on one truth: Marianna Morelli is not a woman, she is a cataclysm. A natural disaster bound straight for me, and I will be as powerless to stop what she stirs up as someone in the path of a hurricane.

Her face is serious, as it so often is, but her eyes contain a multitude of intrigue that I can't tear myself away from. Her mother hugs Marianna first, and then offers me a hug as well, which I accept, kissing the matriarch softly on her cheek and trying to imbue as much sincerity as I can in my expression. I try to assure her that, if her youngest daughter cannot be with someone she loves, she will at least be safe. She will be cared for and cherished, protected and enabled, and our children will be adored and given what they need to thrive in a world that is punishing and cruel.

I try to tell her, with only my eyes, that Marianna is secure with me. I don't know that she gets all that, but she does nod, and squeezes my forearm before ushering me to look at her youngest daughter who stands across from me now, a bouquet overflowing with fresh flowers and eucalyptus clutched in her hands.

Her niece holds out a hand for the flowers, and Marianna startles, realizing she'd forgotten the step and hands them to her.

Now, with both of our hands empty, she meets my eyes once again. After a quiet moment, one side of her mouth lifts into a slight smile.

I offer her one of my hands and she takes it, then the other, and her fingers are cold and mine are too warm and we're holding onto each other before a city of mobsters.

The priest begins his speech, and I barely hear him. Marianna looks at the priest while he speaks, and it gives me the opportunity to study the slant of her nose, slightly crooked like it's been broken once before. She has freckles on her cheeks, ones you'd have to be very close to see, and I want to count them. The dress's straps slightly cover the scar on her shoulder, but not entirely.

"Maxim?" The priest says, repeating himself.

I clear my throat. "Hm?"

"I know she's stunning, but now you have to say your vows," he says with a smile, and a chuckle sounds from the audience.

Even if I wanted to, there would be no going back after this.

I tune into the words the priest has me repeat and, in front of every person in my world and hers, I vow to be faithful and honor her. She does the same, her voice steady and determined.

And then her nephew is at our side, rings in hand, and before I know it, I'm slipping a thin gold band on her finger and reminding myself to breathe when she puts a ring on mine.

"You may now kiss," the priest says with a grin.

Marianna looks up at me from beneath her lashes and tilts her jaw up as I lean down to meet her mouth.

The church feels heavy with silence. Her eyes close as my lips press against hers and I know in this instant I will not be the same again.

I attempt to move away before I fall too deep into the madness that is kissing her after imagining it for so long, but one of her hands comes up to grip my lapel and tugs me back to her, closer this time, and deepening the kiss as the church erupts into loud cheers and applause.

My hands slip around her waist and pull her up to me. We didn't talk about kissing, nor intimacy, only about the necessity of making a child. I don't know if she'll kiss me again for the rest of our lives, but if this is the last she ever offers me, at least it is *this one*.

———

IMMEDIATELY FOLLOWING the ceremony came the pictures, then the food, the line of guests to congratulate us, the cake cutting, more pictures, before, finally, it's time for our first dance as husband and wife.

The DJ announces that it's time for the bride and groom to make their way to the dance floor, dimming the lights as we approach, and Marianna grabs my forearm and pulls so that she can reach my ear.

"Pretend you love me," she whispers. Her eyes are on the table where her family and my sisters sit. "Please. Make it look like you actually love me. I don't want my Goddaughter forever disillusioned by the institution of marriage."

"Yes, wife."

She smirks at my response, and doesn't stiffen when I pull her close to me, one hand on her back and the other holding up her hand. We are still, everyone quiet like a held breath, and then the music begins and I lead her in a dance.

She's in shorter heels than usual, putting the top of her head in line with my chin. Tiny pearl pins are arranged in her curly hair without order, reminding me of the freckles on her chest. I was engaged once, a separate time from my nonexistent engagement to Vanessa, and my ex fiancée was tall, almost six feet. I always *believed* I wanted a tall woman. I had many beliefs about my type; what they should look like, be like, act like.

Marianna fits not a single one of them.

She is brash and violent, a storm of a woman in a very compact form. Her hands are calloused, knuckles scarred, and her arms and shoulders have muscle definition in spades. She seldom smiles, and laughs less.

And yet.

"You're good at this," she says.

"Dancing?"

"Acting."

"Right," I breathe.

"This isn't the first time we've danced like this," she says, like she's just remembered. I wait a beat to nod as if I haven't recalled the weight of her hand on my shoulder dozens of times in the last eight months.

"The Mayor's Gala," I say, and hitch her closer until her chest is pressed against mine. It's all for show, of course. And because, well, this is my only wedding as Vera so kindly pointed out.

"Do you remember what you told me?" she asks.

"Hm." I stall by leading her into a spin under my arm and am surprised to see a light in her eyes that immediately makes me do it again.

She smiles, eyes shining, and I pull her closer to me still.

The night of the Mayor's Gala wasn't the first time I'd seen

Marianna Morelli, but it was our first real conversation. I was just a person on her list, assigned by her sister to seek intel from while the rest of the family did the same with every other criminal in attendance.

My resolve to stay away from her was weak after just one conversation. A five minute interaction and I was ignoring the careful rules I'd set for myself and asking her to dance.

I saw on her face that it was begrudgingly, but she said yes.

"I asked if your sister knows where you like to spend your evenings," I recall from that night.

"And I told you to fuck off and mind your business."

It's my turn to smile, much like I did then, and duck my head. "And then I told you that rumor has it you're as good of a fighter as you are a dancer."

"And *that's* when I thought you might be trustworthy," Marianna says. Her hand travels up to my neck and tugs until my face is close to hers. I think for one mindless moment she might kiss me, but her lips pass mine and press near my ear, sending goosebumps I hope she can't see over my skin.

"Do not make me regret that trust, *husband*," she says, and it doesn't matter how scary she sounds, hearing her call me that makes my stomach flip.

I'm fucking thirty-eight years old reacting like a teenager to my own wife calling me her husband.

"I vow to kill you if you do," she says, and her lips trace over the shell of my ear like a kiss.

I pull back to meet her eyes that remind me of fall; of the sun filtering through leaves.

I smile and press a kiss to her temple. She tenses, just barely, in my arms.

I don't recite my own private vow.

I vow that you will be the very death of me, Marianna Orlov.

10
———

MARY

AFTER TWO HOURS of wedding reception festivities, I thought I might actually start shooting people if I had to receive more kisses on my cheeks from clan members and fake smiles from Maxim's people. Willa, sensing my growing agitation from too much attention, rescued my new husband and me and ushered us to the long family table to eat some of the catered meal. This, at least, was ludicrously delicious.

But the peace only lasted so long before a new batch of people decided I needed to be kissed on both cheeks while trying to enjoy my meal. Then the song and dance of everything else.

Now, all that's left is eating dessert and dancing before we can make our escape.

That cannot come soon enough.

After our first dance bled into a second surrounded by our families and guests, I lied saying that I had to go to the bathroom and escaped into the back hallway, where I've been standing, my back against the wall for the last seven minutes.

The hallway is much quieter, just the sounds of the kitchen staff behind the heavy doors and the live band from the reception hall but dulled enough that I don't feel so overwhelmed by everything.

I can't hide out here forever, I know, and I won't. Just another minute to myself. The ceremony itself was a whirlwind, and my lips remember the searing touch of Maxim's lips on mine. I've suspected that beneath his steady exterior is something less steady. A devouring sort of beast.

Now I know I was right.

I'm steeling myself to go back inside when someone turns the corner, bumping directly into me, then steadying me with a hand on my shoulder. I brush it off without thinking, and when I look to see who I've collided with, it's a man I vaguely recognize.

"Forgive me," he says, and I squint at him. He's an Orlov, I know, but I can't exactly put my thumb on which one.

"Beautiful ceremony, by the way. Congratulations."

"Thank you," I say, and am about to walk past him, effectively ending the conversation when he goes on.

"You know, I was starting to think nobody would be able to put up with that mean cousin of mine. But then came you, the meanest person in Boston."

Cousin rings a bell, and I remember in an instant who he is: Nikolai Orlov. He's younger than Maxim, but still older than me —maybe thirty. He's as tall as Nate, though much shorter than my now husband. Tall-ish. And less broad, almost willowy in comparison to Maxim.

"He's not so mean once you know him," I say. I don't deny my own asserted meanness.

"Yes, well, that's always been his problem. He could serve to be meaner." He winks and smiles like it's a fun joke for us to share. He's calling out weaknesses of my own husband at his very wedding, and to his bride no less. I tilt my head and step closer, about to put him in his place when his eyes go over my shoulder and his smile widens.

"Marianna," someone says from behind me, and I know without looking it's Maxim. No one calls me that but him, for one, and his presence in any room is tangible. His hand settles on my lower back as he stands beside me, and now we are two against his cousin's snake-like one.

"I was just meeting your cousin," I say, though my voice lacks the warmth my sister would say it should for an introduction.

"Ah. Nikolai, this is my wife."

"A pleasure, *Marianna.*"

"Mary," Maxim and I correct in unison. I note that even Maxim knows that my full name is for next to no one.

There's something serious in Maxim's stare at Nikolai, a warning.

"Well, Mary. I'd love to show you around sometime."

"I know Boston," I say. Maxim's hand slides from my back to my hip, pulling me lightly to his side, which is warm against my bare arm.

"Yes, but the Orlov's Boston, I think you'll find, is a touch more exciting than the one you know."

I don't dignify this with a response, nor do I shake the hand he holds out for me. I cross my arms over my chest until he drops it back to his side.

Nikolai mutters what I assume to be his congratulations in Russian before excusing himself to return to the festivities.

"So that's the snake," I say as soon as it's just the two of us in the hall. Maxim sighs and his hand on my waist relaxes before falling away from me entirely.

"Nikolai wants nothing more than for me to die an early death without an heir," Maxim says, his lips set into a strong line.

"And you don't kill him?" I ask as quietly as I can. A waiter with a tray of glasses emerges from the kitchen door and brushes past us.

Maxim nods to the big main room, where I return with him.

Though there are more people here, it's louder, harder to over-hear sensitive conversations. I watch his throat bob in a swallow before he gathers me closer to him. I'm sure we look more like a happy couple sharing a private moment in the midst of the chaos of their wedding than me demanding why he lets a man live.

"It's not so simple. His father was my uncle, and he and my father were close. They ran the Orlov empire together."

"So he was a piece of shit too, then," I say, and Maxim's mouth tilts up in a lopsided smirk.

"Yes. The apple doesn't fall far for Nikolai. He believes not all of my changes were for the benefit of the family."

"Sounds like Cillian," I muse, my blood heating at the memory of his betrayal. After so many years playing the part of a member of the family, he was just waiting for his moment to attack.

"I could kill him for you. Wedding present," I say, and I do mean it. I feel indebted and grateful to Maxim for marrying a volatile woman who has claimed she can never love him, even if he's just in need of this arrangement as I am.

To our left, a flash goes off, the photographer buzzing around us and the party. Maxim brings his mouth very close to my ear, close enough to feel his breath on my skin.

"He doesn't work alone. I need to understand the threat fully before I can remove it."

He drops a featherlight kiss on my cheek then pulls away, that familiar diplomatic smile on his face.

He didn't mean it as a slight, I am certain, but I feel a burn of embarrassment despite myself. Too hot headed, too impulsive, too quick to react. He's strategic, where my impulse is to deftly dispose of any problems we might have before the threat can balloon to something bigger.

"I might prefer a watch," he says. "For a wedding present."

The flash goes off again as we smile at each other. "To each their own, I guess."

———

BY THE END of the night my face is long past sore from smiling so much and is, instead, numb. When I let my face rest at any point, Willa was behind me, appearing from thin air, to tell me to not look so evil.

I did my best.

I'm not used to having so much attention on me—in fact, it's most ideal if the attention is on anyone else. Vanessa and Willa, for instance, are incredibly good at being in the spotlight. My father was also very good at this.

I was not. I suppose it's why they called me Shadow when he was alive.

At least during the ceremony, no one was drunk enough to ask incessant, prying questions about my fast and passionate love affair with Maxim while offering their sincerest congratulations. I saw through them, though. They are all shocked out of their minds that I could be with someone, that someone would want to marry *me*.

Whatever. I'm likable. And hot. And frequently pleasant.

I told Maxim a list of shortcomings in December, and he still said "I do" today.

After the ceremony, everyone stood up and Maxim's side of the crowd yelled something in Russian that made me wish I'd spent literally any time on Duolingo in the last three months. He has never once made me feel like a child, but after enough pointed comments from nosy busy bodies about my age today, I wonder if he feels like I am. Like twenty-six isn't old enough to be a full adult.

My favorite thing of the day, by far, was the cake; chocolate with blackberry jam and little pears cut on top. I don't know what strings Willa had to pull to get such fresh-tasting fruit in the middle of March, but I would trust her with anything.

I yawn into my fist then roll my shoulders back. Maxim, seeing this, bows his head close to my ear.

"It's time," he says. "We've done enough."

I offer one last sweet-ish smile. I can feel a dozen eyes in the room on us, as they've been all night, so I lean forward and press my lips against Maxim's, forcing myself not to overthink it. It's just a kiss between a husband and wife who do not love each other. In fact, we hardly know each other.

I am a great kisser. I know this. For some reason, though, kissing Maxim makes me very certain that I've never actually kissed someone correctly and we've all just been pretending.

Maxim nods at the DJ, giving the signal to wrap it up, and the man does so with ease, cutting off the Black Eyed Peas song early to usher people to where they should start gathering for our send-off in fifteen minutes.

This is our cue, and Maxim follows behind me out of the hall until we're back in the bridal suite upstairs, now vacant of all the light that poured through the windows earlier.

Maxim shrugs off his suit coat and undoes his black tie, leaving him only in his black shirt, now unbuttoned at the collar slightly. The effect is devastating.

Maxim Orlov is *exceptionally* handsome.

I clear my throat and he looks over at me, still standing in my puffy white gown. I point behind me with my thumb.

"Tiny buttons," I explain.

Willa or Vanessa would've come in to help me out of my dress, but Vanessa is stuck in conversations with some of the old heads, and Willa is resting her heavily swollen ankles. I wouldn't dare disrupt that, she might go into labor.

This leaves my options to cutting the expensive gown off of

my body (Willa would murder me) or ask my newly wedded for help.

Maxim holds his breath as he processes the request. I think he might say no when he nods and closes the distance between us in two strides. Now standing very close to me, he has to crouch to reach the buttons that start halfway down my back, and I watch his face in the mirror while he works. He's focused on his task, his attention entirely on the row of three million buttons as his big fingers work over them.

"Why haven't you been married before?" I can't help but ask. "You were engaged, right?"

His hands pause on their work, just the briefest hesitation before they resume.

"When my father was alive, he wanted me to be married. Bothered me incessantly about it. But I didn't want to subject anyone to him." His eyes remain fastidiously on my dress, but I watch his fingers work through the reflection. "He was horrible to everyone, and worse to family."

My eyebrows furrow of their own accord. I am no stranger to vile men, but family has always been the safest of places for me. I forget that this is a privilege.

"He was weak," I say, then mentally kick myself for overstepping. Any tension I expect from Maxim though isn't to be found as his shoulders shake with a slight laugh.

"He was," he agrees, then undoes the last button before pulling down the hidden zipper beneath it.

I immediately let out a huge breath and release my rigid posture. The dress fit my figure perfectly, but had an unyielding bodice.

"After he died, I was engaged to someone named Katerina who decided she wanted to marry someone else," he says simply.

"She cheated on you?" I shrug the thin sleeves off my shoulders and arms, pulling the gown down my body so I can step out of it completely. Maxim steps away and when I look up to him, he's averted his gaze from me.

A gentleman.

Belatedly, I realize I should maybe be nervous that he's seeing me in just my thin white slip. Modesty, though, has never been a strong suit of mine.

"Emotionally, perhaps. I do hope she's happy."

"How generous of you." I step past him for the hanging rack where a deep red dress hangs on a wooden hanger. It's got short, flouncy sleeves and a very loose skirt.

Willa didn't let me have a red gown, but agreed that it was appropriate for a send-off. It's not my usual dark jewel tones, but it feels less foreign than the bright white did.

I step out of my long slip, turning my back to Maxim since he apparently really does *not* want to see my boobs. I pull the red dress off the hanger only to find a different, much sexier slip hanging beneath the dress. It's white and satin with a built-in lacy bra that has a blood red bow in the middle. My meddling sisters have planted slutty lingerie to ensure that I seduce my business deal husband?

"Your dad died a long time ago, though. Why'd you wait so long?" I ask after I shimmy into the lingerie and step into the red dress. I step in front of him again, now bare foot and even shorter. "Zip."

He does as he's told, his fingers deftly pulling the fabric together and tugging the zipper up. "Are you calling me old?"

"Sure, practically geriatric," I say, and he laughs.

"Pretty dress," he says instead of answering the question.

I love the dress, it's leagues more comfortable than the last one, the cool silk swishing against my thighs, and I look, objectively, very beautiful in it. The gold necklace hanging on my chest compliments the low, cupped neckline.

"It is," I agree.

A knock on the door stops any more polite conversation we might make, and it's Nate peeking around the door.

"Hello, happy couple," he sing-songs as he walks in. "You kids ready?"

I look to Maxim, who looks back at me. He offers a tight-lipped smile and a nod, and I follow suit.

11

———

MARY

MAXIM DRIVES us to one of the nicest hotels in the city—an Orlov hotel, of course—and the valet is already expecting us when we arrive. It was a quiet, tense sort of ride, two people who don't love each other wearing rings heavy with meaning on their hands.

"Mrs. Orlov," the concierge greets me first, and I let the name roll around in my brain. It's more abrupt than Morelli, but no less strong.

Marianna Claire Orlov.

"Everything is prepared for you, and your bags are already delivered to your suite," the man says, walking ahead of us toward the elevator.

I stride beside Maxim, my hand in his, not really listening as the man describes a laundry list of amenities available to us during our stay.

When we reach the elevator, the man places a black card in Maxim's hand after swiping the scanner and typing in a room number.

Remaining in the hall, he wishes us a peaceful stay and the

metal doors slide shut in front of us. I let my hand drop from Maxim's.

The metal box is quiet and we stand next to each other without touching. As the elevator climbs, I peer up at Maxim, whose eyes dart away from me like he was already looking down at me.

Is he. . .nervous?

He hasn't seemed nervous even once through the day, a picture of serene composure.

I blink, wondering what it could be that has him on edge now, but as the doors open to the world's most glamorous suite, it dawns on me.

Today was our wedding. Tonight is our *wedding night.*

Do we begin attempting to make a baby tonight? Am I even ovulating?

I suppose we should have discussed expectations on the matter of sex further than "full fidelity" and creating the Orlov heir.

I exhale a breath and step into the suite—though *suite* doesn't even begin to describe the grandeur that is this massive apartment-like hotel room. It opens into a living room not unlike Maxim's with tall windows spanning the walls, only, there's a patio of sorts—if you can call it that. I stalk across the room to investigate this, the exterior lights drawing my eye to. . . Is that?

I slide open the glass door and poke my head out to find, yep, a private hot tub with a perfect view of the city. It's insane, and garish, and even though it's still cold as hell outside, the water is bubbling and steaming. I kneel and feel the water, which is hot, perfect for soaking. Despite my protests, Willa insisted she pack my bag for this little mini honeymoon. She thought I wouldn't bring enough fun outfits, but I think most of my outfits are mostly fun. I can only hope she included a swimsuit.

Maxim stands at the door, those blue eyes impassive as he watches me.

"I've never stayed at an Orlov," I say as I stand, flicking the water off of my hand. "Are they all like this?"

"No, they're not all so ridiculous."

"Hm." I stride past him, my arm lightly brushing his chest as I do. On the marble table in the kitchen, a bottle of champagne sits on ice in a metal bucket next to a plate full of chocolate strawberries. There's a note, too. Handwritten congratulations and a reminder that room service is on call for us at any hour.

I offer the note to Maxim between my index and middle fingers and take one of the strawberries before circling the table, my fingers skimming over stone. There's a fridge with various beverages in glass bottles and fresh fruits, a bedroom with carpet so plush, I kick off my heels just to feel it beneath my feet, and one massive bed.

I stare at it, unsurprised that there's only one bed in this romantic honeymoon suite, but still surprised at the unease of what it means. Of course newlyweds share beds. Of course, so will we.

I hear his leather shoes step slowly through the hall until they stop at the doorway behind me. Even if I hadn't heard him, I would feel his eyes on me, heavy as they always are. His attention is tangible.

I peer over my shoulder. "I've never stayed somewhere so nice," I say, and his eyes dart to the floor, almost as if he's embarrassed, like he'd been when I mentioned the plane, the boat, the car. "I like it."

"Good," he says, and his shoulders relax just so. I stand, waiting for him to talk, but he remains quiet.

I lean against the foot of the bed and cross my arms and ankles in front of me. I am channeling *relaxed, confident, cool* into my every motion and word, though my skin is tingling with the general anxiety that I've felt all day. Part of my mind still works to convince me that Maxim thinks I'm too young, too childish, a nuisance, and now his responsibility 'til death do us part.

"You should take off your shoes," I say after the moment of levity dissolves into silence. He blinks once, and does as I say. Seeing his black socks feels intimate.

It serves to remind me that I've just married a stranger.

"Is the weight of your mistake dawning on you now?" I ask.

"What?"

"Because unfortunately you're rightfully stuck with me now. Before law and God." I point toward the inordinately high ceilings, and he winces.

"No, of course not, it's—" He stands straighter. Maxim *is* nervous, I wonder how many people have seen this side of him, even momentarily. It makes me want to press, to needle, so I step closer. "It's only that I don't want you to think that I have expectations of you. Not tonight."

"Expectations," I repeat.

I know he means sex. He expects that I will produce him a baby, and presumably he knows how babies are created, but I like to see him this way, so I raise an eyebrow and wait for him to spell it out in no unclear terms.

"There's no need to consummate tonight," he explains. "I don't even expect we share a bed—"

"You don't want to share a bed with me?"

"I mean only that I do not *expect* that you share one. Nor do I believe that because you're my wife am I entitled to your body in any way."

"A criminal *and* a gentleman," I remark. "You don't want to consummate our marriage?"

"No—I meant, we do not have to tonight. If you are not ready, I—"

"Are you?" I ask. "Not ready, I mean." He looks stiff as a fucking board, but after a tense moment, he shakes his head.

"I am comfortable," he says, though there is a strain to his voice.

"*You've* had sex before, I presume?"

His face turns perplexed, but a shadow of a smile makes itself known. "I have."

My eyebrows pinch between my eyes, realization souring my stomach. It may not be just my age or his attentiveness keeping him so restrained; I hadn't considered that Maxim Orlov might not want me at all.

I drop my eyes to the ground, embarrassed suddenly—not something I feel often. I don't know how I could have just *believed* that he would be attracted to me, would take no pain in our marriage bed. He could love exclusively blonde women. Models. *Older women.*

He's never said he wanted me, only ever offered intense stares and tight-lipped smiles.

"Where have you gone?" he asks.

I take a deep breath and clasp my hands behind my back.

"I have asked a lot of you. Infinitely more than you have asked of me. I. . ."

My mind rolls over the wrong words, the ones that tell too much, that reveal me too plainly. I am not pathetic, I never have been, but I am not unrealistic. I am beautiful, I am strong, I am good at my job, but I'm headstrong, argumentative, and some-times rude as my sisters are quick to point out.

I am not easy to love. Not even easy to like.

Maxim waits, quiet as he always is, so still and solid.

"I should have considered that you may not want that." I force my eyes to his, though I would rather look elsewhere. "Sex," I clarify. "With me. Unless necessary."

"That's not it, Marianna, I just. . . I want you to feel comfortable—"

I believe that he wants me to be comfortable—he's the type to worry about that type of thing, but I'm not fully convinced that he does indeed want to have sex with me.

"Well, for what it's worth, I think we probably *should* consummate this thing. Don't want anyone discovering my unbroken hymen," I say, and suddenly Maxim looks extraordinarily panicked.

"Kidding, breathe. I think my hymen broke when I was learning to ride a horse as an eleven year old." His shoulders hitch with a surprised laugh. The smile on his face is preferable to the strained seriousness that was there before.

"We can sleep together tonight," I say with finality. "Unless, that is, you want a sexless marriage. In which case, I suppose I do have very many toys."

"Has anyone ever told you that you're a brat?"

I blink, a smile taking over my face at his boldness. *He has no idea.*

"Maybe. But none brave enough to tell me twice."

Maxim chuffs and shakes his head. My husband is perfectly respectful and, it seems, perfectly uninterested in me. I could take his offer to sleep separately, to get my bearings on my own, but why delay the inevitable? He needs a baby, I need his resources, and he probably will be more inclined to lend his support to my family if I am upholding my side of the bargain.

Thus, it's prudent we move forward with the arrangement. Why wait?

I stand and step in his direction, fully aware that if I do not make the first move, Maxim's propriety will keep him from doing so.

"I have no doubt that you are a noble man, Maxim Orlov. I trust that my body is safe in your very large, bloodied hands."

He looks down at his hands, like there may actually be blood on his palms, then back at me, still inching toward him.

"You won't break me," I assure. With one last step, the space is closed between us and that cologne that's already become familiar fills my senses. "I do not fear you."

"Is that wise?" Maxim asks.

"Well, I am a very good fighter," I remind him, my voice just above a whisper.

"You are," Maxim says.

We stand in front of each other, quiet and still, and I guess we are doing this, because I turn around and look over my shoulder. "The zipper."

12

MAXIM

WHEN MARIANNA'S red dress slips from her pale shoulders and falls in a satin pool on the ground, it leaves in its wake lacy white lingerie that could technically be called a dress, but is practically see-through and ends just over the base of her ass, showing me all of her thighs beneath. In refraining from running my palms up her sides, I bite my cheek so hard I almost draw blood.

My cock is already hard in my pants, tenting my slacks like a teenager. Marianna attempts to turn toward me, but I grip her shoulder to stop her.

"Wait," I manage. "Just—give me a moment to look at you."

She does as she's told, which surprises me, and I realize I can't just stand still and try not to pass out from all of the blood in my body rushing to my dick. So I do what my hand is begging for me to do and slide it down her back, then over her hip.

"You're sure about this?" I ask. "You want to do this?"

"I do."

Marianna lifts her hair off her neck and pulls it over one shoulder, revealing the perfect slope of her neck. I drag my index finger down her skin, thrilling to see the goosebumps that rise there.

"I know this isn't real," Marianna says, the reminder like cold water poured over me. "Not real feelings, real newlyweds, but we can pretend. If that makes it easier for you."

I mutter curse words in Russian, hoping that if the language is different, then she might not hear so transparently how desperate I am for her. My hand has tightened on her waist without me noticing, pulling her back closer to me. "Pretend how?"

"You pretend you want me, I pretend to be the wife you wanted."

I attempt to swallow the dryness in my throat. If I tug her any closer, then she will see just how real my want for her is, how there's nothing *pretend* about the heat coursing through my extremities from her presence. Ducking my head low, I press a kiss against her shoulder, and then her neck, inciting from her a gasp that makes me sick with power.

"Like this?" I ask, my voice hoarse.

"Yes."

I wrap my arm around her front, spreading my palm out over her stomach and pulling her against me, boner be damned. I suck her skin into my mouth, then glide my tongue against the red spot I left there.

"Like that," Marianna breathes, resting her head back against my shoulder.

I turn her to face me and roam my eyes over her face, not as guarded as usual now that her cheeks and neck are flushed pink; her eyes betray the desire she feels. I wonder if I reached between her legs, would I find her wet already?

"And like this?" I ask before I lower my mouth to hers, kissing her long and deep, pressing her lips open with my tongue and then tangling it with hers. She kisses me back, just as deep, and her hands raise from her sides to hold onto me, one in my hair, the other clutching the front of my shirt. I lift her off the ground, her legs wrapping around my waist, kissing and kissing as I take us to the bed.

My mouth still moves over hers as I place Marianna on the comforter and position myself over her. My hands want to explore her everywhere, and I can't keep myself from roaming over the front of her, her tits, her stomach.

"Well?" I ask, pulling away from her.

"What?" She's breathless, same as me.

"Is this how we pretend?" I ask. She's quiet for a long moment before nodding. My eyes trail over her body, then do a double take because *holy fucking shit*. I didn't think it was possible for more blood to rush to my dick, but the sight of her nipples beneath the white lace bra ruins me. Her tits are practically spilling out of the cups, laid out as she is, and the red bow between them is what does me in.

I exhale a hard breath and cup one, squeezing until her nipple pebbles beneath my thumb.

"Wedding gift from my sisters," she says, wearing an almost nervous smirk.

"We'll have to send them a card." I pull the fabric down, revealing the dark pink and, in the name of pretending, drop my head and pull the bud into my mouth.

Marianna gasps, arching her back closer to me.

"Perfect," I breathe against her skin. Not to be forgotten, I pinch the other nipple over the bra until she makes a tiny, breathy moan that will sustain my fantasies into old age. She's completely overwhelming my senses, I might come in my pants just from touching her, from having her in my mouth like this.

"Take off your clothes." Marianna pulls my hair until I turn my eyes to her.

"Say please," I tell her, even with her perfect nipple still between my teeth.

She flushes at the command, her neck even more red, and I

store that piece of information for later. I think my little wife likes to be told what to do and hates that she does.

"Maxim—"

I suck her nipple harder into my mouth then release it with a crude *pop*. I crawl back over her so my face is directly above hers. "Say it."

"*Please*, take off your clothes," she says, though she doesn't look happy about it.

I lean back on my knees, still straddling her hips, and unbutton my shirt. She stares at my chest as I do, then as I pull it off, her eyes roam over my shoulders and arms. She tugs up the blank muscle shirt, too, and I do as she bids, pulling the material over my head, and tossing it to the ground.

Marianna wriggles out from under me until she can sit up. I remain completely still as she lightly scrapes her finger nails down my bare chest, my throat, my shoulder, down my bicep, and then my forearm. I wonder what she thinks of the scars that mar my skin, dozens of thin, steady slices from my father's blade. Her fingertips trace them, then circle the bullet scar on my side.

Using her index finger, she traces over the edge of one of my tattoos, and I wonder if she likes them. My skin is as covered in bumps as hers was, and when she slides her fingers above the top of my waist band, I tense and shiver.

She reaches for my belt and starts to remove it, but if she does that, I will make an absolute embarrassment of myself, so I grip her wrist tight to stop her. Her hands are strong, but they look small in mine.

"You're like a bear," she says on a breath. I raise my eyebrows and she blushes like it was an observation she didn't mean to share. "With the chest hair and the hands, I—it's a lot."

I think this is a compliment, if her red face and roving eyes are anything to go by. There is no comparison for her, so I call her what she is. "And you are a brat."

Amusement lights in her eyes and she wriggles in my grasp until she's sitting on her knees too. My eyes pinball between her bare thighs and cleavage, I think this is the single greatest garment to have been created in the history of clothing.

"Are you going to unhand me?" Her cheeks are still pushed into a smile, dark eyes bright.

"I don't know that I can trust you not to use them to make a fool of me," I tell her honestly, which only pleases her more. Slowly, I do let her hands go, and she bites her lip, keeping her hands in her lap and not attacking my belt like she had before.

I unbuckle the leather belt, unfasten the button of my slacks, and stand to strip them down my legs. She watches every movement while I watch her.

Her eyes are wide, tracing up my legs and torso, as if she's committing what she sees to memory. I would be self-conscious beneath her stare, but there is no judgement there, only curiosity and perhaps lust. Marianna crawls toward me on the bed. I meet her at the edge of the bed, and tuck her curly hair behind both of her ears before holding either side of her face and kissing her again, tenderly this time. Less feverish, but every bit as consuming.

"Like that," Marianna says, pulling away from me before kissing me again.

Right. *Pretending*, I remind myself.

Pretending she is what I want in a wife—this inhumanly beautiful creature who cares for her family more than herself.

With my hands behind her back, I push her until she's once again laid out beneath me. I take the chance to stroke a hand up her bare leg, which is as muscular as the skin is smooth. When I reach her hip, I lift her skirt, only to stop when I find panties as silky as the slip. I pull back and stare like a fucking devil at the panties, pure white and high waisted, ruining me completely.

I curse again, Russian or English I'm not certain. I kneel

between her legs and press her knees open until they are spread wide.

"As a wedding present, I'd like you to make me come," she tells me, all confidence, though the lilt to her voice belies her nerves.

"You will come first on your husband's tongue, and then you will come on your husband's cock, do you understand?"

Her cheeks flame crimson, but she still quirks an eyebrow at me. "We'll see."

Taking her words for the challenge they are, I pull her toward me and hook my fingers beneath the band of her underwear before pulling them down her legs, off her ankles, and toss them to where my pants lie discarded. Later I will put them in my pocket and she will never see them again.

"You look like you're thinking perverted thoughts," she muses.

"As you so kindly reminded me, you are my wife, after all." I waste no time dipping my fingers between her legs, then go preternaturally still at the supreme wetness I find there. "*Marianna.*"

"Yes?" She sounds wary, like I've reprimanded her and she doesn't know why.

"I haven't even touched you yet and you're this wet?" I press a finger inside of her without warning and her back arches with a surprised moan. "Have you been with anyone since Christmas?" I ask, maybe to torture myself.

"No," she breathes. "You?"

"No," I answer honestly. It's been much, much longer than that—not since before the first night she stepped into my club early last year, but I do not tell her this.

Instead, I drop my face where my finger resides and start licking her there, long strokes up her center before swirling around her clit. My jaw and cheeks are covered in a light stubble by now, and I'm aware of the scrape it must be against her smooth thighs, but there's no stopping me now. The taste of her makes me unbearably harder.

"Maxim," she moans. I suck her clit hard, brushing my teeth against the sensitive nub and her hands thread through my hair.

"Like this?" I repeat, the refrain like a taunt.

"You're good at that."

I grunt and attack with new fervor, watching her face for signs of just what she likes until she's writhing and gasping beneath my mouth. My cock aches, I could come just from rubbing it against the mattress while eating her like this, but I will not.

My hands travel up Marianna's body, one grabbing a breast and squeezing, the other coasting down her stomach, around the curve of her ass.

When I feel her climbing toward the edge of her release, little halting gasps coming out of her mouth, I press two fingers into her and we both groan, like it gives me just as much relief as it does her in this moment.

I pump my fingers against the soft spot inside of her while I suck and her breathing stutters as she falls over the edge, clamping down hard on my fingers in a way that makes me groan again. I lick her long after her heavy breathing settles.

"Good," I grunt, and rub soothing circles over her outer thigh. She lets out a laugh and lifts her head to look down at me.

"I didn't do anything," she says.

I take one last lick up her center, dipping my tongue into the space my fingers just vacated, before crawling up the bed until my face hovers just over hers.

She lifts her head toward me, imploring for a kiss, but if I kiss her now—her taste still on my tongue—I might perish. I track the movement of her tongue darting out to lick her lips, and it breaks my resolve. My mouth presses firmly against hers, my tongue pressing into her mouth with zero finesse. It's been a long time since I kissed someone new, since I've had to learn what their mouth tastes like. The taste of her, of *all of her*, is better than anything I could have imagined.

She kisses me back with the same fervor and wraps her legs around my waist, trying to pull me closer.

"You took mine off, now yours," she says between kiss after searing kiss. "The boxer briefs have to go."

"What do you say?" My mouth presses long and hard against hers and she pulls back with a frustrated groan.

"*Please*," she mocks. I reach between us to pinch her nipple, not lightly. "Fuck, okay, please, Maxim, take off the stupid underwear so you can fuck your wife. Please."

I pinch her again, but crawl off of her to remove the offending garment. As soon as I do, though, Marianna looks startled at the sight of me.

I think this is a compliment.

She blinks, and I let her stare at my groin. I wish I could read her mind, but she rolls onto her hands and knees and approaches me with a single intent in her eyes, I shake my head.

"Don't," I warn. Her eyes leave my cock to meet my gaze in confusion. "Not tonight."

She frowns, her swollen lower lip pressing out further.

"And why not?" She reaches out and lightly grazes the soft skin of my cock. It twitches beneath her touch and I try not to hiss.

My tentative composure is back in place, but fucking *barely*.

She wraps her hand around me and slides her grip up the length. I suck in a breath through my teeth and a pleased smile lifts her lips.

"*Brat*," I mutter and crowd her until she falls back onto the bed again. As soon as I'm lying next to her, Marianna pushes my shoulder and crawls on top of me, her legs gripping my hips.

"I think a wife should be able to blow her husband," she

muses. She looks about ready to shimmy down my body to do just that when I grip her hair at the nape of her neck to keep her still. "I won't bite."

"And I won't *last*," I say, tightening my hold on her hair just enough to sting.

She blinks at this moment of complete honesty. All pretense of control would be shot if she took me into her mouth now. I fear I've revealed too much in this confession, but she leans forward to kiss me again. Marianna deepens the kiss until we're both worked back up to this never-ending frenzy of groping hands and probing tongues. I haven't felt like this, not as a teenager, not ever.

She's grinding her wet cunt against my length, completely indecent, the stuff I've created in three dozen dreams over the last year but much, much better.

"Hold on—" I try but she grips my chin in a tight hold.

"If you're going to keep stopping me you're going to need to hold the headboard," she says.

I can't help it, the image startles a laugh out of me while also making me impossibly harder. *Marianna fucking Morelli.*

"I have a condom," I tell her. She looks at me like I've just said something strange.

"I thought you were trying to put a baby in me," she says. The image makes my brain empty of all intelligible thoughts. She will kill me, I think. I'm amazed she hasn't already, just from this. "Too soon?"

"No, I—carry on."

She grins when I close my mouth and don't try to stop her again. I keep my hands firmly on her hips while she lines my cock up beneath her entrance. We both hold our breath in the moment before she sinks onto it.

I moan.

Long and indecent, I moan into the room as she wiggles her

hips, adjusting to the size of me as she slides down to fully seated.

"Good Lord," she mutters, squeezing her eyes shut and pressing her nails into my chest.

She is so damn tight around me, and there is no steadying my breathing, though I do try, because if I don't, I will burst in the next fifteen seconds. My grip is bruising on her hips, and when she stays still for a moment longer, I thrust without intending to from beneath. She lets out a high little moan at the pressure.

"Christ, make that sound again."

Before she can even try though, I lift her on my cock, thrusting into her deep, and every move makes a high, breathy sound come from her mouth.

"Yes, just like that. You're perfect," I tell her. She falls forward, her bare chest pressed against mine, and after a moment starts to bounce her hips against me, a delicious friction between us.

"Marianna," I breathe against her neck. She has nothing sharp to say, no rebuttals, just lets me meet her hips thrust for thrust and hold her lower back down to keep her just where I want her. I'm moaning into her ear, chanting unintelligible praises in English and Russian about her body, her voice, my perfect, perfect wife.

I'm almost there, dangerously close, so I flip her over so that I can loom above her again with my legs between hers. My thrusts grow harder, rutting into her as my gaze is fixed on the place where I am joining with her.

Her hand slides over my cheek and into my hair, where she pulls my head until our eyes lock.

"You look at me," she demands. "Look at your wife while you fuck her." Her breath hitches. "You are stuck with me."

In this battle of wills of our first time together, I acquiesce, and keep my eyes firmly on hers. She doesn't look away until I reach between us and rub circles over her clit. She can't help but close her eyes and arch her back closer to me, and then, as if it surprises her, they snap open again as she comes with a startled sound, tightening again on me and sending me barreling after her.

I have no coherent thought, no ability to make sense of what's just happened as I spill long into her.

My wife, my wife, *my wife.*

My hips slow to a stop, but I stay atop of her for minutes while our breathing levels to normal.

"Like that?" I ask of her game of pretend, though there was nothing fabricated about my performance. She furrows her brows at me, having forgotten.

You pretend you want me, I pretend to be the wife you wanted.

"Yes," she says, finally. "Like that."

13

———

MARY

THE DAY AFTER MY WEDDING, I wake to an empty bed and thirty-two texts in the family group chat, most of which are from Willa and Nate asking about my first night as *Mary Orlov*. Those two are worse than the women that my mother hangs out with, nosier and more invasive by double, if I had to give a generously low estimate.

WILLA

Did you sleep with him?

VANESSA

Leave her alone

NATE

Right leave her alone

(but did you?)

WILLA

It's a reasonable question, they're married and Mary is hot! Of course he wants her!

NATE

and maxim needs a baby

VANESSA

they got married YESTERDAY

NATE

and Maxim isn't getting any younger!

SEAN

he is an old fuck

WILLA

Babe don't say that

NATE

not cool, Sean

VANESSA

He's not even forty, aren't you like 35???

SEAN

I didn't say he was ugly, I said he was old.

He is handsome, though. Dude's built like a building.

LEO

Real

NATE

an absolute unit.

MARY

I am blocking all of you.

WILLA

Oh good, you're alive!

LEO

no death by penis

MARY

YOU ARE INSUFFERABLE.

Sean sends a slew of phallic-looking emojis, many eggplants, and baguettes, which I will give points for creativity.

Leo leaves laughing reactions on like fifteen messages, making my phone buzz again with every one.

This is the problem with being this close with your siblings; no damn boundaries.

MARY

You all need to stop thinking about me having sex. it's not normal.

WILLA

right, right

LEO

of course, we're sorry.

Nate sends a row of kneeling emojis, as if in prayer for forgiveness.

VANESSA

(but blink twice if you had sex with him)

MARY

GOODBYE, GOING ON MY HONEYMOON, SEE YOU PERVERTS NEVER.

WILLA

Text us every day!

NATE

send pictures!!!

LEO

take a picture of every meal, literally every one

SEAN

Guys leave her alone.

MARY

Thank you, Sean

SEAN

she has a baby to make!

MARY

I hate you so, so much.

"Good morning," Maxim says from the door of the room, and I jump, dropping my phone in the process, it falls to the ground with a loud thunk.

"Hi," I say. "Morning."

"Something wrong?" he asks, nodding once in the direction of the dropped phone. I play dumb, looking around like I'm not sure what he means. "You got a lot of texts, is all."

I blink. "Right, yeah. It was just my family being. . .well, yeah there was a problem," I lie. "But they took care of it. And I told them never to text me again and I put in my two weeks notice."

Maxim's lips quirk in a smile at my story, and I look down at the metal tray he holds. I sit up in the bed and push my hair behind my ears. I just know it's a damn mess and I would be more self-conscious of it, but he's stuck with me now so he might as well get used to it.

"Is that for me?"

"It is," he says, and crosses the room to the bed, setting the tray down next to me. He's already dressed, and not just sort of dressed—he's wearing his usual expensive slacks and a button-up shirt. No tie, though.

I am woefully underdressed, but it's like nine-thirty and we are technically on our honeymoon, so I think he's the one at fault here.

Maxim takes a metal lid off of a couple of plates and my eyes go wide as I see the offerings. "I tried to order like I thought you would, by which I mean, every appetizer and a dessert."

"You learn quick," I say, then gasp, reaching for a tiny bowl.

"Cream puffs? Everyone should put them on their breakfast menus."

Maxim hums but looks pleased as I stuff a whole cream puff in my mouth.

"Is there coffee?" I ask around my bite, but it's clear enough that he knows what I'm asking for and exits the room before returning a few moments later with two to-go cups.

I take a big sip then wince at the temperature. "How long have you been awake?"

"Not long," he says. "A couple hours."

"Do you always wake up so early?" I pick up a plate of what looks like an omelette covered in mushrooms and cheese.

"Usually. I don't always sleep well."

I nod, too familiar with that struggle, but not willing to go into it. Maxim certainly doesn't want to hear about my nightmares, nor the waking thoughts that haunt me as I try to sleep.

"Well thank you for breakfast. And coffee."

We lapse into silence, Maxim standing casually, one hand in his pocket, the other holding his coffee while he watches me devour two plates of food. I wonder if he's thinking about last night. Even wondering about it brings to mind the torrid details of our consummation, making my cheeks hot.

What even was that?

Best sex of my life? I would say probably, yes. Utterly confusing? That too. Neither of us were supposed to like it *that* much. I wasn't supposed to see a bottomless well of want in his eyes, nor feel it reflected all the way through myself.

There are worse things in life than enjoying sex with your husband. It's not such a horrible affliction, is it? So long as he doesn't start getting any funny ideas. I can have feelings-free sex with Maxim Orlov while we try to make a tiny Orlov.

I'll deal with the stress of actually *having* said tiny Orlov when the time comes.

"So what's with the outfit then?" I ask. "I thought we were on vacation."

He looks down at his clothes, a crease between his brows and lips turned down.

I take another bite of croissant before I speak. "You look like you're going to a meeting. I was thinking, like, swimming."

"You want to go swimming?" he asks.

I halt my chewing, my turn to frown. Is swimming too immature for him? Does the man know how to take vacations?

"This fancy ass hotel has a pool, fitness center, spa—we have our *own* hot tub. It would be a shame not to partake. A waste of money, even."

"We stay for free," he reminds me as if his last name isn't embossed onto the stationary on all of the bedside tables in the hotel.

"All the more reason. It's like a buffet, they should be *losing* money on us." I wipe my fingers on the cloth napkin and crawl out of the bed, the air cool on my bare legs. I slept in Maxim's muscle shirt which he'd slipped over my head after declaring that me walking around naked would be too distracting.

His eyes flit to my legs, and then quickly back up at my face.

So polite.

"Did you have other plans today? Work?" I ask.

"No, we're traveling today."

I stare blankly at Maxim. The honeymoon isn't a long one; just three days, and mostly for appearances, but I didn't think we'd be going back to his home *today*. I thought we'd have time to get facials and what the fuck ever someone does at an Orlov.

"Willa didn't tell you?"

I prop my hands on my hips, causing his eyes to stray downward again before quickly returning to safer, less indecent territory. "She didn't."

"We're going to Mexico," he says. "Three days. You can do lots of swimming."

I blink, processing this news. Part of me wants to be upset at the surprise—I do not love surprises—but I had already written the next three days off of productivity of any kind. Now I'll just be unproductive in Mexico, presumably next to a large body of water.

"When do we leave?" I ask.

Maxim looks down at the shiny watch on his wrist. "We leave in an hour."

———

I SHOULDN'T BE SHOCKED that the beachside Orlov resort in Mexico is even nicer than the Orlov we slept in last night. Everything since we left has been dripping in luxury—the plane that took us here, the limo that was waiting for us when we arrived, the full spread of chilled tropical fruit on our table as we stepped inside the room. I knew Maxim had money, everyone knows this, but to know his net worth and to experience it are two different things.

It's not like we didn't have our share of luxurious vacations as kids, but there is a difference between a nice room at a nice resort and the nicest room at the *nicest* resort, and it's felt in thread counts and included amenities. Even more with every employee knowing us by name, politely welcoming *Mr.* and *Mrs. Orlov* as we passed.

Our room isn't as large as the other was, but it has indoor and outdoor seating as well as its own small *pool*. I'm not tired since I slept most of the flight here—the plane was nice and the leather seats were stupidly comfortable. The flight attendant even brought me a blanket that was so soft I asked Maxim if I could take it with me.

The blanket sits on our second California King bed in as many days while I float on my back in the pool, Maxim reading a paperback in a patio chair beside me.

He traded his slacks for shorts and his button up for a polo, which was more exciting to me than it should have been, seeing his shins and biceps, his detailed tattoos on display for my perusal. Willa packed all new clothes in my suitcase, including three of the sluttiest little bikinis I could imagine. I put one on as soon as we'd arrived and caught Maxim staring at my ass immediately.

Once again, my sisters love to meddle.

My fingers sufficiently pruned, I dunk my head under water one final time before I climb out. My bathing suit is bright purple and probably not appropriate to wear in public spaces, but I look great and it's just Maxim. He saw a whole lot more of me last night.

The sun is setting, beautiful pink and orange painted across the sky over the ocean. I turn over my shoulder to tell Maxim, only to find him already looking up at me. I can't see his eyes beneath the sunglasses, but I imagine they're violent and stormy based only on the firm set of his mouth. If I let my mind wander, I begin to imagine that he resents being here with me. That this is a honeymoon he would've preferred to save for his ex-fiancée. I am sure she was nicer than me.

I say, "I'm hungry again," and it's that simple. The novel is set on a side table, sunglasses tucked into his shirt pocket, and he's listing options of food, either to be delivered or restaurant options. I choose one of the resort's restaurants (if we stay alone in the room for any longer I'll probably get bored and try to seduce him into more orgasms), and make quick work of changing before we're walking side by side there, both smelling of sunscreen.

"You like to read," I say once we're seated. "I just remembered your house was full of books."

Those piles of books stacked on side tables and shelves seemed so strange to me then, so incongruous to the image of Maxim Orlov I'd created in my mind. I think I imagined him perpetually with a glass of liquor in hand, forever brooding in a club, maybe puffing a cigar. I couldn't imagine his legs propped up and brow furrowed while reading sci-fi.

"Yes, I've always liked to read. My father used to say books were the sign of an impressionable man. He loathed them."

"So, obviously, you got your hands on as many books as you could," I conclude and he smirks.

"Exactly."

"When do you find time to read?"

"Probably the same way you find time to play games with your niece and nephew."

We smile at each other. Anyone watching might believe there's real tenderness between us. I don't know that I would go *that* far after three months of this charade, but I do have respect for him, and a general contentment of his presence.

As he orders every appetizer on the menu for me, I'm sure that my choice in spouse was a good one. Not the most romantic of stories, not like my father might have wanted for me, but life married to Maxim will be comfortable. And the added protection of my family will alleviate some stress I carry.

The waiter offers to pour wine into the glass in front of me, but I cover it with my hand and shake my head. "No, thank you. Water is great."

"Apologies," the waiter says, and retreats with a bow.

I avoid alcohol as much as possible, because you really never know when you'll need to be in control of all of your faculties. Only one of Maxim's guards came on the trip with us, and has kept his distance, out of sight and out of mind. By all accounts, I'm probably safe, but I try not to risk it.

"Maxim Orlov?" A deep voice says, interrupting our comfortable quiet.

We both turn in their direction, and a sun-kissed man I am almost confident I've never seen approaches with a much-younger woman on his arm. She's way, way hotter than him, but he's got the rich as sin thing going on, so good for her.

"Maxim Orlov at an Orlov resort, I'll be damned. And I hear congratulations are in order." He's got a southern accent, though not a thick one. He turns to me and whistles. "You're the new Mrs. Orlov? How'd he manage to pull you?"

I scrunch my nose in distaste at the remark, and all geniality is gone from Maxim's eyes.

"This is my wife, Mary. Mary, this is Colton Tenneson."

Marianna for himself, *Mary* to those he dislikes. Noted.

The man's name is familiar and surprises me; Colton Tenneson owns a lot of property in Boston, a couple even built by Morelli Construction. I've never met him, but Willa has had to work with him and his team; says he's insufferable and the perfect example of just how far nepotism can take an unqualified person.

"A pleasure, Mary," Colton says, not bothering to introduce *his* date. I nod at him and smile at her. "I was surprised to hear you were getting married. When was the big day?"

"Yesterday," I say. "We're celebrating."

The woman next to him startles, and Colton lets out a belly laugh.

"Your honeymoon! Incredible. Well, then I better not try to talk business with you, eh?"

"No," Maxim says simply. Colton taps Maxim's shoulder as if they're friends, and the action makes me want to commit bodily harm to the man.

"We'll meet up when you're back in the city. Nice seeing you both," Colton says before, thankfully, making his exit. These days, a mob boss can't just be a mob boss, they have to be respectable businesspeople and have annoying, perfunctory business conversations. It's not all crime and cleanups.

Plates of food are brought out to us, and I really was starving because I'm distracted from asking any prying questions about the disturbance in our evening. I'm about to dish up one of everything when I remember Leo's request to take photos, so I snap and send a photo off to him.

"So you work with that guy?" I ask between bites of the most delicious stuffed mushrooms I have ever eaten.

"No, but not for lack of trying on his part."

"So what, everyone wants a piece of you?" I ask, though I already know the answer. Maxim has worked hard over the last decade to make Orlov Enterprises into a worldwide juggernaut of a company and to make his crime family respected and feared. Of course they want a piece of it. "Speaking of, got any angry exes I should be on the lookout for? I should have asked last night. If they were at the wedding, you could have pointed them out to me."

"None of note. None that you'd need to worry about if there were."

I raise a brow, unsure of his meaning.

"None of them can fight," he explains, and it's a concerted effort to keep from smiling at the hint of praise. I know many men who hate to acknowledge that I can fight because, usually it means they know I could beat them. Maxim has no such concern for his perceived strength or masculinity, as he's made clear on multiple occasions.

"And what about you?"

"No exes," I dismiss quickly.

It's Maxim's turn to pause over his food, but instead of a raised eyebrow it's a knowing smirk.

I wave my fork in the general direction of his face. "What's that look about? You know of an ex I'm omitting?"

"Only the shattered hearts of a dozen patrons of my club," he says, and puts a bite of chicken in his mouth.

"Yes, well I wouldn't call drunk hookups exes."

"You were never drunk," Maxim notes, and I still. Noticing my pause, he leans across the table and lowers his voice.

I imagine we look like two lovers, leaning close to converse over our candlelit dinner, not two practical strangers who now share the same last name. His eyes drop to my lips and back up with a challenge. I force a closed-lip smile.

"It was never about the drinks for you. I don't know what kept you coming back to my club—I don't flatter myself that it was the ambiance—but in all of your time there, you never drank anything but water."

He nods at the empty wine glass, a punctuation to his observation.

"So why did you pick my club?"

I look away, uncertain or unwilling to answer. At first, I went to his club because of the distance. It was a good place simply because no Morelli or Donovann clan members were there to see me. But then it was something different, that I struggled to admit even to myself. It was Maxim.

He was never a discreet observer of me, standing on his perch of the second story staring into the crowd. I never tried to convince myself that he was looking at someone else, I could feel his eyes on me, and a part of me craved that attention. He never looked at me with knowing condolences or concern for my health and well-being.

He looked at me like I was interesting, not dangerous.

That's what kept me going to that club instead of to another fight night; his eyes, and the promise of a meaningless hookup at the end of the night.

"Good DJs," I lie. "I never went home with anyone more than

once, so you have nothing to worry about. No one would fight you for my attention."

Maxim leans back in his chair and gives me a long look, so long that I fold and take a sip of water to look away from him.

"You don't know," he says. "Do you?"

My skin prickles, unsure what he means and not liking the feeling of being seen in ways I don't see myself. It makes me uneasy.

"What?"

Maxim smiles, shakes his head. "I should have been paying you commission, Marianna. You took those guests, first timers some of them, and with one dance, one kiss, one night alone with you, you made them regulars. They came back, mooning eyes looking for you, distraught to see you with someone else. There is no shortage of women and men in Boston who would loathe me to know it's my ring on your finger."

I blink at the image he painted, strangers lusting after me, pining for more than one night. I know he's wrong.

I am a catch, sure, but no one would want me for more than a hookup unless there was something in it for them. The promise of a child, in Maxim's case.

"You're lying," I say.

Maxim's face is serious, but there is still a glint to his eyes, like he knows a secret. His dark hair is slicked back, per usual, but some strands have fallen loose over his forehead. At his temples, a slight dusting of gray hair mixes with the black. He is striking.

This time, I don't look away.

"For someone as perceptive as you, you sure don't realize how people perceive *you*."

I do, though. They've always made it very clear; I am frightening, off-putting, surly, rude, brash, short, nightmare fuel for small children and nerdy math teachers. I am not approachable, nor particularly polished, not like my sisters. I am the youngest daughter, the runt, the one who's never been *quite right.*

"Well at your club, I was always just pretending," I say. "Nobody would covet me as a wife."

His face turns to shock and then concern, and he's about to say something else, something that will make me feel completely naked before him, and I don't want to hear it, so I stand abruptly.

"I'm tired. Please have them send my meal to the room, I'll eat it later." I leave before giving him a chance to urge me not to.

14

MAXIM

WHEN I FIND my way back to the room a half hour later, after a short walk agonizing about another completely fumbled interaction with my wife, I find her submerged in a bubble bath, her hair piled on her head in a bun. The sight of her naked shoulders above the surface of the water is enough to necessitate adjusting myself in my pants. She makes me feel seventeen, or like an animal, want bubbling about me and making me tense. I've never had the particular urge to run through the wilderness in pursuit of a person until meeting Marianna Morelli. Marianna *Orlov*, now.

"How is it?" I ask. She doesn't startle, just closes the paperback I was reading earlier and glances over her shoulder at me. As I approach, I see a hickey I left above her collar bone and the necklace I gave her still around her neck.

"Boring. Too much sand worm, not enough kissing. You should read books with more sex."

"Noted."

She gestures to the large, jetted tub. "Do you have one of these in your house in Boston?"

"What, a bathroom?"

Marianna cracks a smile and it is my personal victory of the day.

"Why, do you want one?" I ask. She shrugs, the movement lifting the tops of her breasts just out of the water. I would buy her as ridiculous of a bathtub as she wanted—I'd get her multiple, even. I would buy her a house—a whole building—full of tubs this size if she asked. Whatever she wants.

I don't know what possesses me, maybe lust or an unconscionable desire to be close to her, but I toe off my shoes and strip off my shirt before climbing into the bathtub facing her. Even with the size, my limbs are long enough that there's still some maneuvering of her legs between mine before I can settle.

If her bright, wide eyes are any indication, I think I've surprised her and much as I have myself. I told myself that I wouldn't seek intimacy with her again, at least not until I could get my thoughts under control where she is concerned. Easier said than done.

It's only that I have an unending need for her, worse now that I've tasted her, and she's made it very clear that there is not, nor will ever be, anything as tangible as love between us. I saw her desire, though. I felt it.

Maybe desire can be enough to sustain me.

Under the water, I stroke a line up her calf and revel in the pink that rises on her cheeks.

"Maxim?"

"Hm?"

"You're not supposed to wear clothes in the bath," Marianna whispers.

I stare into her brown eyes for the space of a dozen heartbeats before I push a lock of curly hair behind her ear. Her words feel like a challenge, if not an invitation, so I stand and unbutton my shorts, pulling the soaked fabric down my legs until I'm bare in front of her, evidence of my arousal unmistakeable between us.

I sink back down into the hot water, the suds rising to almost the tops of her shoulders as I sit.

"About last night," Marianna starts, then glances away from me. "It was—fun, but I know sometimes, for some people, sex can be. . .more than just sex."

Willing my jaw to relax, I nod for her to continue.

"It's not for me." She looks vulnerable, concern on her face, like I might be angry at her for this after she's promised me multiple times that she can never love me. "Just because it appears we are *compatible*, doesn't mean something more."

As much as I would love to hear about our *compatibility* and her inability to love me, I can count about a dozen things I would rather do instead. I reach under the surface and grab her hips, tugging her in one motion toward me, disrupted water splashing over my chest and some over the edge of the tub onto the tile.

Her face now just inches from mine tilts up.

"I thought we were pretending," I muse. I lower my mouth until I'm just a breath above hers, then wait for her to close the distance. Her eyes flit down to my mouth, and she's about to when a loud buzzing pulls her attention from me. She looks to the ledge where her phone is lit up and vibrating with a call. I want to tell her to ignore it, to kiss me instead, to let me pull her body against mine and pretend again for the rest of the night, but when she sees the name on the screen, her face turns from confused to concerned. She answers the phone and puts it on speaker.

"Sean?"

I glare at the screen as if her brother-in-law might feel my ire through the phone for the interruption.

"How's Mexico?" Sean asks, his Boston accent thicker than the rest of the family. "Am I interrupting something?"

"What do you want?" Marianna says instead of answering either question.

"I wasn't going to call you, since you're honeymooning and all, but Nate said you would poison me if I didn't."

"Sean," she starts, her tone a warning.

"Willa's in labor," Sean says.

Mary stands from the tub immediately, sudsy water sliding down her naked body as she steps out of the tub and reaches for a fluffy robe.

"Is she at the hospital?"

"Yeah, we just got checked-in."

Relief shows briefly on her face before she goes on, all business. "How far is she?"

"That's the thing, the baby never flipped the right way, so they have to take her back for a C-section."

Marianna stops moving and stares blankly at the floor, processing this news. Her eyes are wide, her face draining of color. I stand, too, and pull the drain on the tub.

"Mare?" Sean asks. "You good?"

"Yeah," Marianna shakes herself and pulls the robe tight before securing it around her waist. "I'm fine. We'll be back as soon as we can."

"What? No, you don't have to —"

Marianna cuts the call short before he can protest more, and when Sean tries to call back a minute later, she rejects the call. Her eyes track around the room, her breathing sped up as she seems at a loss for what to do. With a towel wrapped around my waist, I place my hand on her cheek and force her to look up at me. She does, her chest rising and falling like it did on Christmas Eve when I found her in the club.

"Breathe," I command. I take a deep breath through my nose and release it out my mouth for her to follow. She does, and after four of these, she appears less frantic. "Willa's going to be okay. Now you go pack your bag. I'll make the calls. Okay?"

Marianna nods and whispers, "Okay."

I squeeze her shoulder, wanting to pull her into me and make her feel better, but I know what will make her feel most at ease is getting back to Boston. So, less than twelve hours after arriving, I make the calls to take us home.

———

SEVEN HOURS LATER, we are back in Boston and Willa is recovering in a hospital room after the delivery of a new baby—a girl—who, Sean assured over text, is healthy and bonding with her mother.

I got Marianna to eat on the plane, though she was too tense to eat her usual amount. The flight was less than five hours, but she didn't sleep, instead opting to pace around, check her phone, read a couple pages of my book, and pace around more.

The nervous energy in her body is palpable as we stride through the hospital. The only clothes she had were the items Willa packed for her, so even though it's below freezing outside, Marianna wears a short, pink sundress with one of my sweatshirts over it, the sleeves cuffed three times to fit right. I have a sick pleasure in seeing her in my clothes again, and idly wonder how I can manage to keep her wearing them as often as possible.

"She's okay," I remind her as the elevator makes a slow climb to the sixth floor. Marianna blinks to attention, as if her mind was elsewhere. "Both of them."

"I know, but—" Marianna shakes her head, a curl falling onto her forehead. I refrain from righting it. "I used to think everyone would die if I wasn't there to make sure they didn't. She could've."

I inhale to tell her that this wouldn't have been her fault if Willa had been hurt, but the elevator doors slide open and Marianna is off down the hall. Is that what she carries? Why she insisted her family need more protection? Because she holds the pressure on her own shoulders?

When we reach Willa's room, she's awake, sitting propped up in her bed. Vanessa and Claire are there brushing and braiding Willa's hair while Sean and Nate stand in the corner both looking at a bundle I assume is the new baby. The room is larger than most hospital rooms I've seen, but the addition of myself would make it crowded. I lean in the doorway and watch as Marianna reaches the other side of her sister's bed to the shock of all three Morelli women.

Willa exclaims that we should have stayed in Mexico, but all of the Morelli women have tears in their eyes as Marianna hugs her oldest sister.

"You're okay?" she demands.

"Oh, Mary," Willa says, and squeezes Marianna tighter. "We're alright."

Claire rubs Marianna's back and Vanessa wipes her cheeks, smiling, but when she looks at me, I see a sadness in her eyes. Vanessa kisses both of her sisters on the head, then nods at me, which I assume is a command to wait for her in the hall. Already feeling like I'm overstepping on the family moment, I am quick to retreat down the hall to a small waiting area where I can watch the morning sun rise in the sky.

"Sorry about your honeymoon," Vanessa says behind me a few minutes later. She's not in her usual sharp attire, instead casual and soft in a way I know she seldom gets to be in her position. She'll soon have a baby of her own, the bump obvious beneath her sweater.

"Some things are more important."

"Thank you for bringing her," she says, quieter. I feel a second, heavier message in her eyes, one that confirms what I already believed: Marianna's need to be here was about more than just the new baby. "I'm sure you've noticed our Mary is. . .a sensitive soul."

Sensitive isn't a word that I'd guess anyone other than her family has ever dared use in talking about Marianna Morelli. I understand it, though. Christmas Eve, I saw it as she fought to regain control of her emotions in the alley behind my club, and again last night when she got the call.

"She's always been nervous—superstitious, even—but after our dad died," Vanessa trails off as she looks back at the sky beyond the window. She drops her voice to just above a whisper. "Be patient with her."

"I will."

"I know," Vanessa resets her posture and smiles, a habit I've seen from all the Morelli sisters. Recentering and putting back on the masks they think they ought to have. "I'm not stupid enough to think that I can control my sister's decisions, but I wouldn't have let you near her if I thought otherwise."

Vanessa's faith in me feels unfounded, and she'd probably be less confident if she knew how deranged I feel when it comes to the youngest Morelli sister, but I appreciate the gesture all the same.

"Now come meet your new niece."

———

WE STAY at the hospital for a couple of hours before Marianna offers to spend the rest of the day with the older kids at Vanessa's house. She says goodbye to the new baby, whose name, we learned, is Clara, and Marianna squeezes Willa's hands for a long second before leaving the room.

I follow her around like a dog—my schedule is cleared for the next two days after all—but when we get to her sister's house, my phone rings with an incoming call from Sasha.

"Miss the beach yet?" he asks.

I don't tell him that we didn't even get to see the beach in our few hours in Mexico. He knows.

"What is it?" I ask.

"Colton Tenneson called. Said he heard about your restaurant getting shot up and offered to buy the building before you take on repairs."

My eyes narrow at the memory; Marianna saving us by observation and intuition alone, the stomach churning fear I felt imagining another bullet slicing through her body. The scar on her shoulder is a reminder that she was lucky last year.

Renovations on the restaurant are already underway with Morelli Construction, set to be completed in the next couple of weeks. The hotel has lost a good amount of money from the incident, but not enough that I'd be willing to part ways with it.

"On my honeymoon? He's relentless."

"He thought marriage might make you more agreeable. Opportunistic son of a bitch," Alexei mutters.

"He was wrong. Did he tell you I saw him in Mexico?"

"I'll be damned, he did not." Alexei whistles. "He still wants to talk about the place by the water. Brought it up after I said you probably weren't interested."

"Absolutely not."

I'd excused myself to take this call, but I can hear Marianna's animated voice as she plays a game on the TV with her niece and nephew. They adore her plainly and completely.

"What's his deal with that place anyway?" Alexei asks. "How many times can you say no before he gets it?"

Colton Tenneson has been asking after that property for two years now; it's an abandoned textile factory that's more of an eye sore than a prime investment. As friendly as he may seem, he resents my footprint in this city. Resents that I won't work with him more.

I have no clue what he wants with the factory—perhaps he wants to gentrify another neighborhood—but I'm sentimental about the place. My dad used to use it as storage, and it's there where he ultimately met his demise. I don't wish to part with it.

"Tell him we're reconsidering parts of our portfolio this summer and can get back to him then." It's not completely a lie, though I know I will never sell to him. The man isn't involved in organized crime, but he might as well be a criminal, slimy as he is. I've never liked him, though that may have more to do with the fact that my father loved him, and as a rule, I usually hate the things my father loved.

"Done. So, how was it, newlywed?" Sasha asks.

"What?" My mind goes first to the sex, and I won't speak of it with him, but my mind supplies that if that's what he wants to know, then the answer is that it destroyed me—I am an inhuman version of myself, remade into something much weaker and more feral because of it.

"Your first night married to the shadow. Does she snore? Does she even sleep?"

"She sleeps." Marianna sleeps hard, sprawled on her stomach, curly hair fanned around her head. "I think you'll like her."

"I already do. You seen her fight?"

"Yeah, I know. I'll check in tomorrow," I tell him and say my goodbyes before hanging up to spend the rest of my afternoon off with Marianna and her two favorite thirteen year olds.

15

———

MARY

BY THE TIME Maxim pulls his massively expensive car into the underground parking garage and the private elevator deposits us into his—*our* home, it's late and I am thoroughly exhausted. I hated feeling the way I did today, hopeless and guilty, as if the baby was in the wrong position and a week early by *my* doing.

I do fear it was the wedding that sent her into labor, but as Willa explained multiple times, the baby really was all cooked up and ready to come into the world any day now. I thought the wedding should be earlier, but they wanted more time to plan (*Two months is already an insane turnaround, and if we wait any longer, Vanessa will be the one indisposed*). So it was decided: a wedding ten days before Willa's due date.

I kick off my shoes and hold them by the backs as soon as we step inside, the floor looks spotless and shining. Our bags were already brought inside, so Maxim doesn't carry anything as he holds back a few steps behind me while I look around.

My new house.

It's so different to the home I grew up in, this modern penthouse atop a building. It's perfectly clean, and I would be shocked if Maxim had anything to do with the choices of the luxury furnishings and art pieces around each room. The space isn't devoid of him, though. Built-in bookshelves line two walls in the living room, not filled with leather-bound first editions and decorative encyclopedias, but instead with the colorful spines of novels, many well-worn.

Movement from the corner of my eye puts me on the defensive, but when I snap my gaze in that direction, I am more shocked to find a stretching, grey ball of fur on the loveseat.

"Is that a cat?" I ask, though it could be nothing else. It stretches into an arch before looking up at me and emitting the scratchiest, smallest meow I've ever heard.

I approach the cat slowly, and it does not scurry away, even as I kneel down in front of it. It's got blue eyes, kind of like Maxim's, but sea blue instead of the middle of a storm.

"Oh, yes. I should have asked, are you allergic?"

I hold out a hand to the cat who sniffs it for a moment before pressing the top of their head against my hand.

"I'm not," I say. "Just surprised you have a pet. It's friendly."

"Her name is Greta. My sister Nadia left her with me as a kitten. I couldn't get rid of her," Maxim explains. The cat jumps to the ground, opting to rub her fluffy body against Maxim's legs until he picks her up. She's a tiny thing, made to look even smaller in his arms as he scratches under her neck.

"I thought you might have a pet snake," I say, standing and facing him and the cat. I step closer to him to scratch her head.

"And why's that?"

I look up at him and his eyes are already on my face. I swallow and grab his wrist, sliding his shirt sleeve down his forearm until his detailed tattoo is displayed. It's a snake, beautiful and detailed, wrapped around his arm with flowers. Forget-me-nots, I think.

"You don't have a Greta tattoo," I say.

"Not one you've seen, at least."

I think he's making a joke, but I can never be certain with him —his humor is rare and subtle, delivered with as serious a tone as his normal conversation. Greta meows between us, squeaky still but louder, affronted that we stopped petting her, I think.

I didn't realize I'd stepped so close to Maxim. I put some distance between us before he lets the cat down so she can rub against our ankles.

"Can I have a tour?" I ask. Now's as good of a time as any, and I have to see our room one way or another.

"Of course." Maxim clears his throat, then leads me through an efficient tour of the downstairs. I've seen much of the public spaces, the entryway, the kitchen which looks on to the living room with the tall windows over the city, but there's a hallway that leads to a gym. It's smaller than the one at home, but I suppose that's to be expected, especially if he trains here alone. He doesn't have a horde of Morellis training together most days.

I feel an errant pang in my chest at the reminder that I won't be training with them like I have for most of my life. When Willa moved out, I missed her in our daily sessions, but she came back to train with us at least once a week, though after she was pregnant with the twins, that training turned to lounging in a reclining chair our dad brought down for her, reading or doing coursework on her laptop while she did.

Maxim opens the door across the hall and I peek inside.

"Guest room," he says. It's completely inoffensive. "Full bathroom there, and then another guest room." He points to the final door.

"Do you often have guests?"

"Not often," he says. "But my sisters, at times."

I hum in acknowledgment. I didn't get much time to talk to his three beautiful sisters, each tall and perfectly polished. Like

Willa or Vanessa. His sister Sofia, at least, looked mean, which made me like her more.

Maxim leads us up the stairs next, and the first door is already open to his office. It's nice, cozy. There's a dark wood desk, a matching side table, a leather couch, and a loveseat. I suppose he entertains meetings here on occasion. Hopefully not too many.

I don't love strangers skulking around the house, especially the upstairs. It's egregious enough that the elevator opens directly into the home; there should be some sort of rule about guests not venturing upstairs.

The next room is large with an en-suite bathroom and a bed I'm sure is quite comfortable. It's the least decorated of any room we've seen. When I peer into the closet, I see familiar luggage and bins.

My stuff.

"This is your room," Maxim explains, and I lift my eyebrows.

"Why is it so empty?"

"I thought you may want to make it your own." He puts his hands in his pockets, belying his nerves. He wants me to like it?

"And where is your stuff?"

Maxim looks surprised by the question and stands in a dumb-founded silence. Greta meows again before she leaves for the hall.

"My belongings are just in the room next door."

I blink, processing this news, then cross my arms over my chest. I am mostly astounded that not once in the past two months had I considered that Maxim wouldn't want to share a room with me. Have I been stupid to believe even sham marriages have some requirements, shared rooms and sex being two on the list?

"Is the room. . .alright?" Maxim asks.

"What do I need my own room for if there's a gym?"

"I thought you'd want your own space."

"Do you? Want your own space?"

Maxim frowns, unsure of my line of questioning

"As in, do you not want to share your space with me? Your room."

Maxim is rarely flustered, but at this moment, I swear he is.

"I would not *mind* sharing space with you, I only thought this would be more comfortable. For you."

The concept feels something like a king and queen—separate quarters, what so he might have his own concubines? A separate space where he'll visit me to make a baby and nothing more?

"Do you not want to sleep next to me? Are you a light sleeper?"

"I thought you'd *want* your own bedroom," he repeats.

Is it my age? Does he not want to share a room with me because he thinks I'll be messy? I admit I'm naïve to many things regarding marriage, but does our arrangement require that I be relegated to a life-long roommate?

He looks at a loss, though, not frustrated like this is something I should understand. Maybe he thought it would be a nice gesture, giving me my own room—a show that he doesn't expect anything from me. Well, aside from the baby. Or maybe he'd prefer not to share a bathroom, shower, closet, or any of the other intimacies that might come with a marriage I chose.

"Show me yours," I demand. His mouth snaps shut and without a word, he does, backing out of the room and leading me next door to a room which is slightly smaller, though no less nice. Much cozier, little piles of books perched on floating shelves and surfaces.

I stalk barefoot around the perimeter of the room (the carpet is damn nice) and I survey his most personal items. If he's uncomfortable, he doesn't show it, only leans against the wall with his arms crossed as I make my perusal. His closet is huge, but not full. I have lots of clothes thanks to my sister's shopping addiction, but they would all fit here.

I drop my shoes in a corner of the closet before I return to the room and prop my hands on my hips. I'm still wearing his sweatshirt over the pink dress I pulled out of my suitcase when we were about to leave Mexico. It's cozy and I've already decided I will co-opt it for myself.

"I like this one better," I determine. "I'll stay in here with you."

He rushes to assure me that I *don't have to feel beholden to this*, but I cut him off. "I'm not a porcelain doll, Maxim. Don't treat me like one. A wedding ceremony and a new house isn't going to break me."

I cross the wide room until I'm standing directly in front of him, I have to look up to meet his eyes, but I offer as hard of a glare as if I could sneer down my nose at him.

"Do you think I'm a weak woman?"

Maxim huffs, his collected veneer chipping and giving way to the frustration beneath. It lights me up inside, seeing his stony facade crack. It's why I preferred him on our wedding night and then again in the bathtub.

"No, Marianna."

"You didn't seem to think I needed coddling when you fucked me—"

"Christ, you're difficult," he breathes, and it takes everything in me not to grin.

"Born this way, I think." I don't know why needling him is so fun, but seeing this big, bad mafioso flustered brings me almost as much joy as meeting my new niece for the first time today.

His tone softens. "I was only trying to be mindful of you."

I drop the glare and nod before speaking. "I think, if we are going to be married, make a baby, and raise a baby, we should at least know each other. And sleeping in different rooms and masturbating alone in the shower doesn't seem very conducive to knowing each other."

Maxim swallows, his Adam's apple giving away his discomfort. He gives a jerk of his head in response. "You're right."

I'm surprised he gave in so quickly, acquiescing instead of fighting further. I think I would like to fight with him.

Between our feet, Greta meows, alerting us to her presence. I crouch and scratch her head for a second before I stand again.

"I'll get settled and showered, then."

16

MAXIM

USUALLY I DON'T OPERATE on a whole lot of sleep, but my wife, it seems, goes on even less. Nadia used to go on and on about how women need more sleep than men when I told my sisters to wake up before ten, but if this is true, Marianna does not feel so inclined.

Her side of the bed is empty when I wake up, save for Greta who's curled up in a ball beneath the pillow. The sheets are cold, like she hasn't been lying there for a while. It's not even 6:30 AM.

This, I've learned, is common for her.

It's been two weeks since we returned from our honeymoon, if one can even call it that. Two weeks of her sleeping in our bed, showering where I shower, sleeping in little more than T-shirts and underwear, and we have fallen into somewhat of a routine. There has been no more sex. First because she started her period and said *no use having sex if we can't make a baby, right?*

I think she was testing me, she had that teasing lilt in her eye just asking for me to deny this and admit I crave her desperately. But my heart can only take so much.

"Whatever you wish," I said. Fool. She licked her lips and I think she took that as a challenge, waiting for me to approach her again, because two weeks later, we don't so much as touch unless she's brushing past me for sugar in the kitchen.

It's no use thinking about it. She knows the importance of trying to make a baby, and so do I. I'll bring it up tonight and will be completely composed, no inkling of the number of times I've had to fuck my hand to avoid touching her or just smelling her hair, anything to be closer to her.

I climb out of bed, dressing quickly for a run and peer around the house as I make my way downstairs. No sign of her in the bathroom, office, living room, or kitchen, and the security system is still set, so I know she hasn't left yet.

After pulling a bottle of pressed juice from the fridge, I finally find Marianna on a mat in the gym, pieces of her curly hair stuck to her forehead and neck from sweat. She wears a bra and shorts, and I know I've seen her naked on multiple occasions now, but her body all flexed and sweaty is a different vision than her splayed out on a bed. My workout will not be productive if I keep my eyes on her body, though, so I shuffle around the perimeter of the room toward the cardio equipment.

"Morning," I say, and she nods, only speaking once she's finished her set of twists. Moody music I don't recognize plays from the sound system in the room.

"Hi," she takes a sip of water from the bottle next to her. It's one of the reusable ones from the kitchen, and it pleases me to know she's already started to make herself comfortable. "Am I in your way?"

"Not at all." The only person who's ever worked out in here at the same time as me is Sasha, who I have not ever had an issue with being distracted by, unless he's yammering on about something or other. The man loves to talk.

Come to think of it, he and Nate really would get along if they had the chance. Marianna and Sasha already get along much easier than she and I do; Sasha has always been better at jokes and friendly conversation than me.

Mary reaches for a pair of wireless headphones. "It's okay," I say. "I don't mind the music."

She takes another drink of water and resumes her workout as if I'm not here watching her from the corner of my eyes and through the wall mirrors, even when I try not to.

If someone asked me what I thought Marianna Morelli listened to, I might have said club music exclusively. That's the only thing I've heard her listening to, and she dances to it so well, so I'm surprised that her playlist is a mix of R&B, old rock, and songs that move from moody to screaming.

When I reach two miles, I slow the machine down and wait until she drops from a plank to speak again.

"I've been meaning to ask, what do you like to eat?"

Marianna's eyebrows pinch together. "I'm easy. All of the places we've gone are great."

"Yes, but our chef Elise is back from her vacation and wants to know how she can adapt the menu for you." I'm not entirely used to saying *our* anything, not after so long of everything being mine alone.

Elise didn't ask for Marianna's food preferences exactly, though she did ask me if my bride had any allergies she should be aware of. She's been making the same meals for me for the last five years, but I'm ready to shuffle the entire menu if need be.

"Oh." Marianna stretches her arm across her chest, then behind her head. Her chest glistens with a sheen of sweat. "The usual stuff, what you like is fine."

I raise my eyebrows and wait for her to give more information, and after one song rolls into the next without budging, she presses her lips together and thinks about it. "Chicken parm," she pauses, "fish, eggplant dishes. Thai food—curries of all kinds. Soups."

I retrieve my phone and jot the items into a text message.

"What kinds of soups?"

"Brothy ones with beans. Ones with kale. Zuppa toscana. Normal stuff like pizza, enchiladas, pasta. Salmon and quinoa. Like I said, I'm easy."

I type the rest of the items into the list then send them off to Elise to incorporate into the upcoming schedules.

"Elise comes Thursday and Sunday and leaves meals for the rest of the days. I'll let her know what you prefer."

"Oh, we eat at my sister's house on Mondays," she says. "Well, I do. If you're busy, you don't have to. But Nate will bother you about it if you're not there for his pizza dip or whatever abomination he's testing that week."

"He always cooks?"

"No, thank God," she mutters, smirking. "I'm not one to talk though, I'm worse than him. Be glad you didn't request cooking in this arrangement of ours."

Marianna's phone rings, and she picks it up without looking at who's calling.

"Yeah," she says. I can't hear who's on the other side, but what I can hear is decidedly feminine. One of her sisters, if I had to guess and be nosy about it. "How many?" she asks. "Yeah, be there soon."

She hangs up and looks up at where I'm staring on my unmoving treadmill. Very cool. Casual.

"Work already?" I ask, because I am nosy.

"It's always something, I'm sure you know how it is. Plus we're down a man with Sean out with the baby."

"I'll go with you," I say before I can think better of it. My assistant might develop a permanent eye-twitch when I tell him to move my meetings, but I'm deeply curious about what keeps Marianna busy when we go our separate ways during the day.

"Don't you have a job?" she asks. "Like, work to do?"

"Sure, but it's early. Most of my meetings today start after the typical workday ends," I lie. I have an extremely busy schedule this morning, but Marianna does not need to know that.

"It might get. . .messy."

I try not to look fazed as I step toward her. "Messy how?"

Marianna squints at me, debating her response if I had to guess. Fine with whatever she sees apparently, she shrugs. "I hope you actually have a strong stomach."

———

AN HOUR LATER, we've picked up a box of donuts at the bakery down the street and are driving through morning traffic to the Morelli estate. Sasha drives us, he and Marianna going beat for beat debating about some movie I've never seen. After the shooting, Sasha started attending every outing, keeping close watch of our surroundings and looking all-around menacing. Because Marianna is an enigma and he loves to make friends, my half-brother never bothered to keep from asking her lots of questions until she'd finally acquiesce and tell us something new about herself.

He and Marianna like a lot of the same things—they get along. Talking for them is much easier than it is for me, maybe because Sasha is closer to her in age and more social, at large. The guy loves to gossip, which is one reason he's so good at his job, and even though Marianna doesn't know about half the people he talks about, she listens intently and says all the right things to egg him on.

"You're full of shit, the *Oceans* movies clear those by a mile," she says, leaning forward in her seat, eyes lit up with amusement.

"I didn't say they weren't better, I said they were less *fun*, less charming."

"You are insane for that."

"Brother, you hear this? She's calling me names, even though I'm right," Sasha says. "Control her?"

Marianna laughs and raises her eyebrows at me. "Well, Maxim? What punishments will you dole out to your rude wife?"

"She can be as rude as she wants," I say. "Especially if it's to you."

"Man," Sasha says, but he's laughing too as he pulls through the gates to the Morelli home.

Marianna climbs out of the car first, forgetting the box of donuts that sit between us, so I grab it and follow after her into her sister's home.

"Yo," Marianna calls when we get through the door. Vanessa calls out from down the hall a response that I don't make out, but we follow the sound into Vanessa's office where Vanessa and Leo sit across from each other at the table.

Vanessa looks surprised to see me and Sasha trailing behind her sister.

"Bring Your Guy to Work Day?" Leo asks.

"Morning, Orlov," Vanessa says, indicating I take a seat in one of the three chairs across from her.

I do, Marianna dropping into the one next to me after giving her sister and cousin kisses on their cheeks.

I place the box of donuts on the desk and Leo reaches for one.

I don't know her cousin well, but I know his father was Lorenzo Morelli's right hand and a widower, so Leo was raised with the rest of them. He's strong, well respected, and would be as feared as Marianna if he wasn't seen as her more reasonable counterpart.

"What do you have for me?" Marianna asks.

"Hugh Sullivan," Leo says, and his expression is grim. "Third strike."

"What'd he do this time?"

Vanessa clears her throat, her eyes flashing momentarily to

mine. "Almost killed an Orlov. Said it's bad enough Cillian couldn't take me down, now we had to go merge families again with," she reads from a paper on the desk in front of her and sighs, "the *little psycho girl.*"

Marianna whistles before reaching for a donut.

"Why haven't I heard about this?" I ask. I might have taken him out myself if I heard he'd said that.

"I heard about it," Sasha says, reaching between Marianna and me for a chocolate sprinkle donut himself. "Dmitri beat the shit out of the man for threatening him and talking shit. Score seemed settled."

"Maybe for you, but this isn't his first infraction," Vanessa says.

"And if he was Cillian's side like that? Well, that's just one step too far," Leo says, and I completely agree. Cillian attempting to force Vanessa into marrying him last year secured his death. He should've died sooner, but nobody knew he was responsible for Marianna being shot.

"Sean knows?" Marianna asks.

Vanessa nods as she rubs her pregnant belly absent-mindedly. "He made the final call."

Marianna sighs and takes the last bite of her donut. Sean's rise to head of the Donovann family was unexpected, and the weight of the last six months has probably aged him a few years. He's looked tired since taking over, but wears it well. He's tough and sharp.

I'm rooting for him, more than I had his traitor of a brother. It's difficult making decisions like this one—it's not easy killing someone you thought you could trust, even after said three strikes.

"Alright. I'll handle it," Marianna says.

My gaze snaps to my wife. What does she mean she'll *handle this*?

"Handle it how?" I ask. Both Vanessa and Leo look a little uncomfortable at the question.

"I'll take him out," Mary says, like it's the most casual thing in the world. I blink, processing this. We are here at nine in the morning because they want Marianna to do a *hit*? Like she's a fucking unmade lackey?

"Why would you have to do that?"

Marianna squints at me. "My job?"

"Christ," Sasha mutters behind me.

"Why would you ask this of her?" I direct this at Vanessa. She and Leo look at me with some amount of pity, but also like I might be speaking Russian.

"Probably because Sean's with Willa and the baby? This isn't some dealer. Hugh Sullivan is a low-level general for the Donovanns," Marianna says, and Vanessa nods. "You do know that this is my job, don't you?"

"That's the problem." I've heard all the rumors, but I didn't realize that I would feel this way when actually faced with the truth of her actually out on the street as a hired killer. I turn to Vanessa with my indignation. "You'd have your sister do this grunt work? Like some reaper?"

"Oh, boy," Leo mutters. Suddenly Vanessa and Marianna's faces ignite like I've said the completely incorrect thing by asking something so reasonable.

"It's what she wants, *she* asked for this despite countless pleas to do something else. And I respect her decisions. Plus, Mary's the best at the job," Vanessa says. "You knew when you married her that she wouldn't just quit working."

"Yes, but why *this* job?"

"What is your problem?" Marianna asks. "Talking about me like I'm not here. You act like I've never killed someone."

"I just don't understand why you have to be the one taking out hits," I say.

"Maybe you don't need to understand everything," Marianna snips. I close my mouth and meet her stare, a battle of wills that she could win every time.

I take a breath and get my tone in check. "How will you do it?"

Mary looks to her sister before answering. Vanessa looks to Leo and they both shrug.

"Up to her how she does it," Leo says. "Sean just said it needs to be today."

"We don't make this choice lightly, Orlov. We've given him more chances than he deserves, more than any of our fathers would have," Vanessa defends.

"I'm not questioning your decision, but you'd let her do the work?" I ask, my voice's volume increasing without my intending.

Marianna scoffs next to me. "Don't talk about me like I'm some kid."

"That's not what I meant, Marianna. You shouldn't have to be out there killing common criminals."

"I don't think that's any of your business."

"I think it became my business as soon as we got married."

"Well what's not your business is how I run mine," Vanessa interjects before Marianna can fume hotter. "Mary knows the moment she wants another job, she has one. She doesn't have to do this if she doesn't want to, but, frankly, when we need something done right and done quietly, she's the best for the job. Now are you done?"

I overstepped, I recognize this, but I still can't help but feel like when it comes to Marianna, there is no such thing as me overstepping to keep her safe.

"But you want this? You choose this?"

"You're acting like you've never killed before." Marianna

asks. "What, are you learning your wife's not moral enough for you? Grow up."

She stands from her chair, the last part spat under her breath like I'm the exasperating one here.

"Where are you going?" I ask, as she retreats from the room.

"To do my job," she says without turning around.

After a silent moment in the office, I exhale through my nose and follow her out, waving at Sasha to join us.

17

MAXIM

IT TOOK some convincing that I wouldn't be a dick bag (her words), but Marianna finally acquiesced to Sasha and I joining her on this hit of hers. For safety. She grumbled about how I shouldn't be slacking off from my job while she threw various items into a duffel bag in a hidden closet in the Morelli basement.

She insisted on driving, said our car was too fancy for trying to do secret illegal things, and now drives us in a black sedan, Sasha's long legs folded up in the back seat while she drives.

He's looked entirely amused through the whole of this. *Prick.*

Marianna makes a few calls, succinctly issuing orders to the people on the other line, never having to repeat herself nor explain further than her few-word requests. She speaks with a brutal efficiency that would be hot if she wasn't actively orchestrating the death and clean up of a man.

Honestly, I hope Sasha is taking notes. He takes far too long on things like this, drawing out hits when they ought to be quick. Maybe that's why he and Marianna get along so well: they're both comfortable ending lives.

By the time we get to where we're going, we've made three stops and we're an hour out of Boston in fucking Swansea. Marianna maneuvers through residential streets until we park in a quiet suburb. She waves at a woman who jogs by, and the woman smiles back, nodding as she jogs down the road.

"In the middle of the morning like this?" Sasha asks, awe tainting his voice. "What about the witnesses?"

"I'm not doing anything sketchy," she says, and opens the trunk to retrieve the bouquet of flowers we picked up. "Just bringing flowers and an early lunch to the family. Get the sandwiches."

I do as she says, retrieving the take out bag from the back seat and follow her up the walk to the house where she rings the bell.

"No one is like her," Sasha mutters to me as we follow. "*No one.*"

An Italian man lets us in, giving Mary loud kisses on both of her cheeks before handing her off to his wife to do the same.

I'm on edge, but they're perfectly nice. The man is her great uncle, it turns out; her own father's godparents. They were at the wedding but in the hubbub of the day were only able to greet us briefly.

"The flowers are nice, *bimba.*"

"Well you only turn seventy-four once, *Zia*," Marianna says as she retrieves a set of plates from a cupboard before handing them to me. "Set the table."

"Yes, ma'am," I muse, setting the plates on top of the pink place mats that match the pink and red candles down the middle of the table. A remnant from Valentine's day, maybe.

And then we do the damndest thing. Marianna sets half a hoagie and a bit of chips on all of our plates, her great uncle retrieves bottles of seltzer water, and we eat a meal.

Twenty minutes bleeds into thirty while the old couple tells us about the various dramas of their neighborhood, all completely mundane; no mention of illegal activities of any kind, and when they ask about our honeymoon, Marianna kisses my shoulder over my suit coat and it shocks me into stillness.

An act, I remind myself. *Always just pretending. For appearances sake.*

"We were in Mexico but then Willa had her baby. Do I look tan?"

"Not at all," her aunt says, and laughs.

"Too much time in the bedroom," her uncle muses, and I have to drain my water to keep from choking on my bite, wincing at the bubbles.

"Guilty," Mary says before leaning over the table and retrieving everyone's empty plates. Sasha protests, standing to clean up, but her uncle directs a question at Sasha, keeping him at the table. I follow Mary into the kitchen.

"What are we doing here?" I take the plates from her before she can load them into the dishwasher herself. "You're going to kill someone here? In her lovely home?"

"We're eating lunch, Maxim," she says like I'm stupid. "Now we're cleaning. Then we're gonna play a few rounds of cards. Then we're gonna pose for a few photos my auntie will want to take on her iPad and then we'll go."

I blink at the explanation, speechless not for the first time today.

"Why? You got somewhere to be? I told you this would take a while."

I load the rest of the plates and watch as she breezes back into the dining room, deck of cards in hand.

The next forty minutes go on just like she said, even the pictures on the iPad, Marianna and I posing on the old leather couch, my arm around her waist while I'm unable to look away from the gentle smile she wears for her family, no hint of what we're supposed to be doing today.

"Beautiful," her aunt says. "I'm going to change the background on these on Facebook, you're going to love it."

"Can't wait. Next month will you make pierogis?" Marianna asks, and then makes a scene clasping her hands in front of her chest. "Please, Zia, please."

Her aunt laughs, always laughing at Marianna, and agrees. She pulls my wife, then me, and then Sasha in for tight hugs. Business isn't mentioned, Marianna gives no hint to our plans, we just leave after ninety minutes of visiting. And then we're off down the road the way we came.

Halfway back into Boston, though, Marianna brings the car into the parking lot of a butcher next to a Dunkin'. She stops for a coffee first—one cream, three sugars—and tells Sasha to get the cooler from the car. In the butcher's shop, the man working is Irish, and greets Mary warmly, yelling that it's been too long and just who the hell has she been getting her guanciale from if not him.

She hands him the fresh coffee. "I haven't been cooking! Didn't you hear I got a rich new husband who follows me around and has a private chef for us?"

The butcher looks at me as if just noticing I'm here, sizing me up. "She eating right?" he asks me.

"Of course," I say. "Whatever she wants."

He can respect this, mutters that she'd better, and offers a sturdy thud on the shoulder as we pass him to go to the back.

We pass through the back of the old, tidy shop, and I think we're going to go old school and find ourselves in one of the freezers, but Marianna leads us out the back door and up a set of exterior steps to an apartment, opening the door without fanfare.

Three men sit shooting the shit at a table, and one of them pales when they see Marianna.

If I had to guess, that's our guy.

"Shadow," he starts after clearing his throat, trying to act cool.

I've never met the man, but he can't be that much older than me. "What brings you to these parts today?"

"Ms. Morelli," another man greets.

"It's Orlov now, Ronny." She wiggles the fingers of her left hand, her ring impossible to miss. I feel an absurd urge to preen at her correction, though she was just calling me an idiot this morning.

"Have you met my husband?" She nods in my direction and I nod at the three sitting around the table. "I wanted him to meet my uncle. Thought I'd stop by here after."

Mary takes her cooler into the kitchen like she owns the place, and the quiet that follows is unsettling. Two of the men at the table look at the one who's now sweating, their faces grim. If I was a betting man, I would bet his name to be Hugh Sullivan.

The man puts his cards down after tapping them on the table a few times.

"I think I should be going. Duty calls and all that."

"Nah, Hugh, I just got here," Marianna calls from the kitchen. "Sit."

His eyes flash, terrified, and he looks to where Sasha stands with his back against the front door, arms crossed over his chest. Sasha smirks at the man.

"I, ah—" Our Hugh stands as Marianna reenters from the kitchen, four short glasses in her hands.

"Sit the fuck down," she says, nothing friendly about it, and he does. Mary takes her time sitting at the folding table after setting the glasses down. She slides one to each of the players, then chuckles to herself and switches two of them.

A bead of sweat slides down the side of Hugh's forehead.

"Baby, why don't you sit down?" she says to me, standing from the chair so I can take her place. As soon as I do, she sits on my leg, shocking the hell out of me, doing so like she's done it a hundred times.

Nobody touches their glasses, and Marianna snaps like she's forgotten something, retreating into the kitchen only to return with a bottle of Vodka. She sits back on my lap and my arm snakes around her waist settling on her upper thigh.

The man across from us watches the movement.

"I didn't get to congratulate you," Hugh says. "I heard it was a beautiful wedding."

"It was," Marianna says. "You know, I worried people would be mad about it. Maxim's such an eligible bachelor, he's got so many ears and eyes around the city, and well, I'm just—what's it we heard recently?" she asks me.

My lips part and I answer, "A little psycho."

The words burn coming out of my mouth, no matter if it's part of her game. She doesn't act like they hurt her, but after hearing it enough times, it's bound to. Marianna grins and snaps.

"That was it. But people have been really supportive. Blending families is nothing new around here."

Mary unscrews the cap and pours a shot's worth into each glass.

She hands hers to me instead of drinking it herself, and nods at the man across from her to pick his up. He does just that, reluctantly, though, like he'd rather be doing anything else.

"I'm not really drinking these days," he says, but it's weak.

"Today you are. For the happy couple," she says. "To our ever growing family."

The two men on either side of us lift their glasses, faces grim while they drink theirs. I drink mine too, the burn familiar down my throat. Still, Hugh sits unmoving.

Marianna leans forward, the only sound in this apartment the creaking of the table as she leans her elbows on it. Her ass on my thigh is distracting, but the tension is so high in the room that I could drown in it.

"Drink," she commands, and with a shaking hand, he does.

The taste of the vodka seems to offer him some relief, and his shoulders relax slightly as he puts the glass down. He even smiles.

Marianna's face remains blank.

"You scared me, Shadow. Coming in here acting all crazy."

Marianna lets out a breathy laugh, and he laughs too, much too loud, before he cuts off with a sharp inhale and a cough.

"You could've had a very long, very comfortable life," Marianna says. "I want you to know that. You really could have."

"What?" he says, but he's breathless, and his face is turning red.

"It's not that hard to fall into line. We ask so little of you, Hugh, and we take *such* good care of you."

His hand claws at his chest, pulling the neck of his shirt as if it will offer him any breathing room. Nobody speaks.

My hand tightens on her leg as the man fights for breath across from us.

"Look at me," she says, but he can't. She slams a palm on the table. "Look."

He does, eyes wide, almost bulging from his head.

"You are a weak man, Hugh. I am not a shadow. I am the grim fucking reaper, and this is faster than you deserve."

The man falls from his chair then, shaking on the ground as the other two men look sadly on. They knew what was coming, knew there was nothing to be done to stop it, but probably have known him most of their lives, and that loss stings, deserved or not.

When his shaking and choking finally comes to an end, the sound of the heater clicking back on radiates through the apartment, and Mary takes a deep breath. My hand on her thigh finally loosens.

I've heard rumors of this version of her; the stories of the ruthless shadow of Lorenzo Morelli, a demon in her own right.

Seeing it first hand is completely different, it's sickening and magnetic all at once. She's impossible to look away from like this, but lethal enough that looking feels like a great danger.

And she is mine.

"Take care of him," Marianna says to the man next to her as she stands.

"Of course," he says. She puts a surprisingly gentle hand on the man's shoulders, and he pats hers in return. They both understand.

Sasha no longer leans casually against the wall, now standing ramrod straight while he watches the scene, his eyebrows low. He looks like I feel: transfixed. Possibly horrified.

Marianna retrieves the cooler and his glass before brushing past and out of the apartment without any theatrics or discussion. When we get back to the little shop, the butcher offers Marianna a serious nod, one that says he knows what he has to do and will make sure he does it. Then he trades coolers with her, replacing hers with an identical one.

"Good to meet you," Sasha says.

"We'll be seeing you." The butcher nods at us, and it's like a peace offering, a promise that he won't make the mistake the other man did. He knows what would happen if he did—who would visit him.

When we get in the car, there's a stony silence as Marianna backs us out of the parking lot and off toward Boston. She clicks on the radio, old jazz playing through the speakers. Sasha speaks first.

"Remind me not to get on your bad side, Mary."

She smirks.

"Noted."

18

MARY

THE CAR RIDE home isn't quiet, on account of Sasha never *really* being quiet, but Maxim has a tense, brooding sort of energy about him—more than usual, and that's impressive since quiet brooding is kind of his whole thing.

We swap cars at my sister's house before driving back to the apartment to clean up. I expect that Maxim and Sasha will just leave me there, but I'm surprised when Maxim follows me inside and up the elevator in silence.

He won't even look at me, and that guy is always fucking looking at me.

"What's your deal?" I ask when we step inside the penthouse. Greta pads down the stairs and stretches at my feet until I scratch her head.

"Nothing," Maxim says, but his shoulders are stiff and he looks pissed so obviously it's not *nothing*. I'm mentally rewinding through the day to see if I said anything egregious to him, but come up blank. Until I remember this morning, him acting like Vanessa asking me to do a hit was the same level as asking me to dispose of a body or something.

And that just rubs me the wrong way.

I stalk into the kitchen behind him. "You know, as far as hits go, that was as clean as I possibly could have made it. Thought you'd be pleased."

He scoffs. "Yeah, a real master class."

"Oh, come on, Maxim," I say though it comes out more like a taunt. "You knew about me."

"I did," he says. He pulls open the fridge door and retrieves a glass water bottle. "I just didn't know you were still doing grunt work."

"Well someone has to do it, and if it's me, at least we know it'll be done right." Maxim looks pained as he takes a swig of his bottle. "Can you really not stand that I might be good at my job?"

"No one should be good at *that* job."

"What, you'd rather I be sloppy? An emotional mess? Do you hear yourself? That man was a bad apple, one that would've gotten to others if left to rot. He thought Cillian should've killed my sister, you think he should live?"

"No," he snaps, too loud, and we're both surprised by the volume of his usually level voice. He takes a steadying breath. "Of course not, but you—"

He looks away from me while searching for the right words, like he can't even meet my eye.

The realization that big bad Maxim Orlov might be disgusted by me is more of a kick to the stomach than I could've anticipated.

"It shouldn't have to be you who does it," he says, quiet and level once again.

I press my lips together tight and count to fifteen in my head before stepping around the kitchen island until I'm directly in front of him. I move my head until he can't look away from me, and force his eyes to mine.

What I see there surprises me into silence momentarily—not disgust, but something else. Something hot and familiar, the same thing I saw on our wedding night, when we consummated this loveless legal entity. It's hunger and guilt and a fire that smolders behind the storm gray of his eyes. Seeing them now, I don't know how I ever thought they were *just* blue.

I laugh, an ungenerous sound, and grab Maxim's jaw so he can't look away from me.

"Oh baby, you're as sick as me. I just don't feel bad about it," I say, the endearment mocking even to my ears. "You liked watching me kill him, and you hate that, don't you?"

"I don't want you doing hits," he says, disregarding my words.

I lick my lips before I step closer, pushing our bodies flush together. Sure enough there's a stiff length between us, pressing into my stomach. I smile before I push away from him.

He doesn't like me doing hits, or he doesn't like how seeing me doing hits makes him feel? Either way, his indignation pisses me off.

"Where are you going?" he asks, voice still strained.

"My sister's. I don't want to see you until dinner tomorrow."

Maxim curses behind me and calls my name, but I ignore him. When I get into the elevator, he doesn't follow, though his eyes stay locked on mine. Before the door closes, I wink, and swear I hear him curse again.

———

I DRIVE AROUND for a long while before going to my sister's, and by the time I get there, everyone is already in bed. I walk barefoot through the house, looking at every room with new eyes. It hasn't even been a full week, and yet the house already feels different.

I hover my hand over my doorknob, but am overwhelmed with a sense that it doesn't feel right to sleep there. I can't shake it, so I crawl into bed with my mom, waking her gently to not startle her into cardiac arrest when seeing me.

She doesn't ask questions, maybe too tired, only tucks the comforter in at my sides like when I was a kid. She rests her head back on her pillow and smiles slightly.

"Making your escape already?" she asks sleepily.

"Maybe," I whisper, but she's already fallen back to sleep.

Sleep doesn't come for me, and I stare at the ceiling until my eyes burn.

Two weeks. Not even a *month* of sleeping in the same bed as Maxim, and I'm already noticing the lack of him—the way he smells, his shins warm against my cold feet, the soft puffs of his breath.

After an hour with no luck, I determine a snack might help. Maybe some tea.

When I pad down the stairs, I find a light on in the kitchen. It's almost enough to make me want to turn around and go somewhere I can do my own brooding in peace, but I skipped dinner and my stomach wins out as I venture into the kitchen.

It's Vanessa sitting at the counter looking at something on her phone while eating cake directly from a Tupperware.

"Mary," she says, her mouth still full of icing and chocolate cake. She wears little blue gel patches under her eyes and her reading glasses. The sight makes my heart ache for home again, which makes little sense because first of all, I am already here and, second, I haven't been away for very long.

"Grab a fork." I do as she says, taking a big bite of cake before pouring us both glasses of water. "Why is this stuff so good?"

"I think Leo puts something in it. In no world is this just a regular cake, I don't care what he says. It's sugar, butter, milk, eggs, flour, and a mystery ingredient that's probably illegal."

"And chocolate," Vanessa points out. "Cinnamon too."

"Cream cheese and vanilla," I add about the frosting.

"He's probably not spiking cake children are going to eat, right?"

"Well, he might."

Vanessa laughs and pats the stool next to her. I finish chewing my bite before rounding the counter to sit next to her. As soon as I do, I drop my head on her shoulder.

Her arm comes up to my back for a squeeze. Sitting with her like this reminds me of being a child and having a bad day at school. Another fight, another argument with a teacher, another call home to Mom and Dad; I was never good at controlling my emotions, and it was so frustrating then. It still is, but at least now I'm better at hiding it.

"Do you want to talk about it?" Vanessa asks, and I know that if I say no she will drop it. Willa is less that way, she loves to pry and weasel answers out of us.

Instead of explaining what happened, I start with a question. "Does Nate ever try to stop you from doing your job?"

Vanessa laughs, and the sound startles me to sit up straight.

"All the time!" She licks her fork clean. "More since I got pregnant. To him, the perfect world scenario is me working from home in a secure fortress. He offered that we spend this summer in Connecticut, can you imagine?"

"Doesn't it annoy you?" I ask. "You're more than capable."

"Of course I'm capable, and he knows that. But it's not annoying to be cared for."

"Sure, but you can take care of yourself—you don't need him telling you what you can or can't do."

"Yes, but—" Vanessa looks away as if trying to find the right words. Like when she tries to explain a big topic to one of the kids. "In the same way, it feels nice to know you've helped some-one, it feels good to be taken care of sometimes."

"You've gotten sappy," I murmur. She smiles before

stretching her arms above her head. Her stomach is rounder now that she's five months pregnant. A girl.

"Is Maxim being cruel?" she asks instead of justifying her softheartedness.

I scrape my fork over the last of the frosting while I consider the question. I've seen cruel, and Maxim is not it.

"He's being unreasonable."

"Hm." Vanessa pulls her lips down into a frown to hide a smile. I hate her amusement, mostly because she sees something that I do not and it makes me feel obtuse. "That sounds unlike him."

I will admit that maybe a core tenant of Maxim's personality is his level headed surety and ability to think through problems rationally. It's why everyone I've met loves working for him and with him. It's very antithetical to his role, and the complete opposite of his father.

"You heard him this morning, he doesn't like when I do my job," I explain. Once again, her face shows no sympathy.

"He can join the club," she says. I've heard the argument from her before, the pleas that I choose anything else, but that's different. She's family. He's just—well, my husband. "You are very good at what you do Mary, and I respect that you want to do it, but you know I'd rather you work in an office like Willa. Or on job sites with Sean. Dad felt the same."

"Who would do all the illegal stuff, then?" I ask, though the answer is still all of us. We all are doing illegal stuff, Willa and Vanessa just don't have bruises to show for their work.

"Lackeys?" Vanessa offers. I can tell she's not actually pushing the argument, just talking about it casually.

Lackeys are fine, but none of them are that scary. It's not all that hard, what I do, beating on people. I've always said I do it because I'm the best, but I don't say what's harder to admit; I don't believe what I do is particularly difficult, only that I don't know if I'd be good at anything else.

Vanessa yawns. "It's time to sleep again."

When she stands, the metal jangle of Ranger's collar tells that he's ready to follow her upstairs. She takes the container and drops it in the sink before squeezing my shoulders in a tight hug.

"Is Maxim coming to dinner tomorrow?"

"Yeah. I'll go back with him after."

"Okey dokey," she says. It took no time at all for her to be infected by Nate's dorky ass way of speaking.

She kisses the side of my face, loud and a little slobbery and laughs when I tell her that's gross and try to push her off. Vanessa smiles, lingers at the doorway. "There are worse things than having someone worry after you."

"Goodnight, Ness."

Vanessa nods and trudges sleepy toward the stairs, Ranger's collar jingling behind her as he follows.

19

———

MARY

THE BASEMENT HAS ALWAYS BEEN a place for me to blow off steam. When I was a kid, my dad sent me here to work off my excess energy and anger, and, still, exercise is the best way to keep me level-headed. Endorphins, whatever.

Training the next day consists of Leo, Nate, and I sparring while Vanessa does some weight lifting and walking on the treadmill. She still works out since being pregnant, but no fighting.

"Trouble in paradise?" Nate asks while I take my turn on the punching bag.

I kick the bag with extra force. "What gave you that idea?"

"I think you should give him a chance," Nate says.

Even though he's gotten pretty fit after a year of training with us, he still sweats like crazy every workout. I think he might just be a sweaty person, like it might be in his nature, alongside annoying optimism and general nosiness.

"I've *given* him a chance. The ultimate chance, I fucking married him."

"Yeah but have you given him a chance since?"

I stop my combo and drop my arms to hang at my sides.

"Get to the point, Nate."

"He's asking you how big of a bitch have you been to Maxim since the wedding," Leo calls from where he stretches on the mat.

"Why would you think I've been a bitch to him? I'm perfectly nice," I defend.

Leo and Nate both say nothing, and when I look at Vanessa, she's still looking down at her iPad, but she's smiling, so I might guess she's just pretending to be reading. No damn help.

"I once told you that your form was messed up and you didn't talk to me for a day," Leo says.

"You were wrong," I say. "You deserved it."

"Even if I was, you shouldn't punish me for not knowing," Leo says, sounding *way* too much like Nate. I should've seen the writing on the walls with these two. Leo ditches me for a new best friend and suddenly he's a well-adjusted individual trying to diagnose my mental and emotional shortcomings. He was fine before.

"Can you all stop defaulting to believing that I'm in the wrong here? Maxim isn't some perfect man."

Leo and Nate share a look that tells me they really don't believe this assessment.

I punch the bag hard one last time. "If you like him so much, you should've married him," I mutter. Wrong thing to say because Nate and Leo peel into laughter, not to be stopped by the cool glare I set on them.

"Look, if Maxim laid a hand on you, you'd kill him. Hell, if he was really as much of a dick as you're acting like he is, he'd already be dead," Nate says.

"You've gotten too comfortable talking to me," I tell him, and he laughs again.

"You're my sister now. It's my duty to be real with you."

Vanessa sends a look so sweet and loving at Nate that my molars hurt from the impending cavity.

"I would treat Maxim right," Leo says. "You're right, maybe I should've married him."

I am about to leave without further engaging in this asinine conversation when the basement door opens to reveal none other than the object of my ire. He steps tentatively down the stairs and I think I would recognize his figure and gait anywhere. It's incredible how quickly you learn a person.

My mom trails behind him smiling, and when they reach the bottom, she addresses me. "Mary, sweetie, your husband is here."

"I can see that," I say, but she goes on undeterred.

"Maxim was just telling me about the hotel in Mexico. He said we can all go for a vacation."

Maxim turns to look at me and his blue eyes roam over my body, which I know is covered in sweat. Not something I'm usually self-conscious about, but I idly wonder if he can smell me from where he stands.

"Marianna," he says in greeting. He doesn't come closer, and neither do I, but I nod in return.

When I look back at my mom she is communicating with her eyes that I need to get over my shit and be nice to my polite, handsome, and very tall husband.

I present the single peace offering I can muster. "Would you like to spar with me?"

He startles. "What? Now?"

"Yep. Since you think I'm so defenseless." So, okay, not so much a peace offering as a throwing of a gauntlet, but as we all know, I have room to grow as a person.

"I don't think that," he defends.

I raise an eyebrow, but don't recite from memory his intense assertions that I get a new job and never complete a hit again. Mom clicks her tongue and pats Maxim's thick shoulder.

"I'll leave you to it," she says, and retreats up the stairs.

Once she has, I point to Leo's abandoned boxing gloves on the mat behind me. Maxim shuffles under my challenge.

"We shouldn't," he says. He's in his business clothes, after all.

Slacks, button-up, leather shoes. I resent that he looks hot while I look like I've been working out for the last hour.

"You scared? We've never sparred before and I think we should," I tell him.

"I think that too," Nate says, and I shoot him a quick glare.

He just lives for the drama.

"We need to shower for dinner," Vanessa calls to Nate. Her eyes are saying *leave them alone*. I can tell he wants to object, but after second thought, he sighs and follows Vanessa like the puppy he is.

Leo whistles and follows them, leaving me alone in the basement with my husband.

I squint at Maxim. I might be projecting, but he looks tired, too. His jaw is unshaven and his eyes are a dead giveaway to his lack of rest last night. We're like a mirror in that way.

"Spar with me," I say again. "I'll forgive you for being an ass if you do."

The tension is his shoulders releases as if he's giving up the fight against this, and then he shrugs off his suit coat. I try not to look as delighted as I feel. It feels like bees buzz in my stomach, and something really must be wrong with me because the thought of hand-to-hand combat with my husband makes me more excited than any expensive date he's had to take me on in the last few months.

He tosses his coat over the arm of a treadmill, pockets his cufflinks, and rolls up his sleeves revealing that snake tattoo that I sometimes have to resist outlining with my fingertips. His forearms are thick and my hands tingle remembering just how warm and sturdy they are.

He rolls his shoulders back as he approaches the mat. He's much larger than me; in my sneakers I'm almost a whole foot shorter than him and I've seen him naked—the man is jacked. Even still, I could probably take him, I think. I've fought many large men and more often than not, I have something they lack: cunning.

Or speed. Sometimes both. Big guys are sometimes absurdly slow.

Maxim is smarter than any of the men I fight at Leroy's though. It's so obvious in his assessing stare, in the way he speaks. I wouldn't have married him if he was stupid.

"Did you have a good day?" he asks once he's got the gloves on.

"Peachy," I lie. I was tired and irritable the whole day, a real joy to have around according to Leo who was sick of my attitude before lunch. "You?"

"No," he says simply. "Shall we get on with it?"

I smirk at his honesty then get into my fighting stance, knees bent, feet light, fists up in front of my face. He lowers into one of his own and I thrill to see him poised as he is instead of his usual, stiff, businessman posture.

He nods, I nod back, and then we begin circling one another, slow steps on the mat. He's wary of fighting me, trepidation so clear in his blue eyes. I take the opportunity to strike, jumping forward and punching straight for his face. He huffs and blocks, but leaves his side open, so I kick his abdomen, which is pure fucking muscle.

I knew it was, but feeling it with my bare hands on our wedding night is not the same as in a fight. An image of me sliding palms up his torso, down his ribs, down further fills my mind unbidden, and it distracts me enough that I almost let Maxim trip me.

I right myself and attack with a flurry of blows—none hard enough to actually hurt him, but hard and quick enough to keep him from being able to do anything but block.

When I finally let up and jump back, he throws a half-hearted punch in my direction and I duck from it easily.

"Stop holding back," I spit.

"I'm not."

I punch his right side, harder this time; he grunts and lets out an incredulous laugh. "I'm not going to *hit* you, Mary."

"Mary now?" I taunt before I kick him, this time a good hit on his thigh that might bruise if I'm lucky. He deserves it for treating me like I'm a delicate thing. "Good to know the full name is reserved for when you deem I'm being a good girl."

He drops his stance in surprise and I take the opportunity to kick him again. He groans this time, and shuffles back a few steps to recover, but I don't let him. I run combination after combination at him until we're both panting and there's sweat dripping down my back.

"Come *on*," I yell again.

He shakes his head. "Fuck it."

Maxim surprises me when he lunges. He's faster than I gave him credit for and as fast as I can blink, he grabs around my waist and takes me down to the mat with a loud thud. The breath isn't totally knocked out of me, but I'm startled enough that I can't get free before he pins my legs under his. He uses his forearm to press my wrists above my head before I can really retaliate.

In less than a minute, I'm completely pinned. His face is so close to mine, that Maxim's panting breath mixes with my own.

"You can't help but be a brat, can you?" he asks. "I want to protect you and you act like I'm a misogynistic devil."

He pushes my arms harder into the mat, and I glare at him. He uses his teeth to undo the velcro on his right glove and pulls it off to free one of his hands.

"You might be. Jury is still out on that," I bite.

His eyes dart down to my mouth when I speak and it reminds me that, while he may have bested me like a damn amateur, I'm not entirely defenseless.

I arch my back to press my chest against his. He laughs, but the sound is mirthless.

Using his free hand, he holds my jaw and makes me face only him. No matter my wriggling or fighting, he has me completely pinned.

"You got too cocky when you needed to stay fast on your feet," he says. I arch further bringing my chest up to meet his body. My tits glide across his chest and he stiffens. "If I had a weapon—"

"You'd what? Have already killed me?"

"What would you do, Marianna?" he asks instead of humoring my taunt. "How do you get out of this?"

"I break his nose with my skull," I say. He moves his hand from my jaw down to around my throat and lightly squeezes.

"If he holds your head down?" he asks, breathless.

My thoughts race as quickly as my pulse beneath his fingers. I can't think clearly when he's touching me like this, his presence overwhelms my senses entirely, and it is a dangerous thing.

"You wouldn't come for me?" I ask.

"I would always come for you."

I lick my lips and the slightest groan escapes his throat as I do. Pressed between us, I feel him getting hard and it makes me grin. Even though he's right—pinned as I am, I would be in horrible danger—I feel I've still got a leg up in this fight.

He lets go of my throat and his eyes betray him when he glances down at my mouth again for a too-long moment. His throat bobs with a gulp. I look at his lips.

He hasn't touched me in a private, intimate way since his hands skimmed up my legs in Mexico—in fact, he hasn't even seen me naked unless accidentally walking in on me changing and quickly walking out of the room. I think he's been aiming for chivalry, letting me settle in before really going to town on the baby making. How polite.

I lift my neck to bring my mouth closer to his, and he looks at me with surprise. His eyelashes are long and dark, he's so intensely handsome it boggles my mind sometimes.

I give him a tentative nod, permission to close the space between his mouth and mine.

The firm pressure on my arms loosens and his free hand slides lightly down my side, leaving goosebumps in its wake. Slowly, he readjusts his legs, freeing mine.

"You win," he murmurs. "You are a good fighter."

"I know," I whisper. And then he brings his mouth down to meet mine.

Kissing him is dizzying; his lips are so soft and warm, I could lose myself in them easily. His tongue presses into my mouth and it shocks me into granting him entrance. He still has my arms above my head, but only half-heartedly keeping me there while his mouth moves skillfully over mine. His non-gloved hand slides around my neck and tilts my head back farther so he can deepen the kiss.

I usually hate kissing when hooking up. It's not that I'm not good at it, only that it allows too much time for my mind to wander. This feels nothing like the usual kisses with strangers, this—*just this*—I could do for hours.

His five o'clock shadow rubs my chin in a way that really does make me feel lightheaded, and I worry that my mom will come to retrieve us for dinner and find us here like horny teenagers.

I thought I would use my feminine wiles to seduce my way into winning this fight, but now I find myself considering how I can get his clothes off of him, and that is *not* the energy I need when I'm supposed to be mad at him. I *am* still mad at him.

I gather the remaining shreds of my sanity to get a damn grip and use my body weight to push him over. He doesn't fight me—I suspect if he wanted to he could keep me beneath him very easily, but he lets me roll him, my mouth still on his while I move to straddle him.

I push away from him quickly, and scramble to my feet to not give in and kiss him again. He lifts on one of his elbows, bewildered, and his erection is obscene in his slacks. I take three big steps back and remove my gloves, depositing them on the counter in a rush.

"I have to shower," I say, backing toward the stairs.

And then I leave my husband there, still laying out on the mat, and retreat upstairs to my bathroom.

20

MAXIM

THE DONOVANNS and their three kids have arrived by the time Marianna comes downstairs with her hair dampening the shoulders of a cranberry red sweater. Seeing her niece across the table from me, my wife walks directly to us.

It took me fifteen minutes before I'd calmed down enough to rejoin the family upstairs while she showered. I still don't feel fully recovered.

Seeing Marianna fight is one thing, but fighting *with* her, being the sole focus of her attention like that—I fear it's too much for me to handle.

"Hi, little," Mary says to Angel, but she stops by my side and squeezes my shoulder. I remember her plea that I *look in love with her*, for her niece's sake, and follow her lead, turning to kiss the back of her hand. She smells clean, and like the subtle perfume she wore on our wedding day.

With one steady look of affection, we're the picture of a loving couple. Her siblings and their spouses freeze, watching the exchange, and pink tinges Marianna's cheeks.

"Hi," Angel scurries up to Marianna's side and gives her a hug. She's nearly as tall as her.

The boy is taller, and he gives Marianna a side hug too before sliding in his socks across the wood floor back to the living room to resume the video game he's been playing with Leo.

"Maxim was teaching me Russian words," Angel explains. Marianna raises her eyebrows and leans against me.

"What have you learned then?" she asks.

"She learned hello," I say.

"*Privyet*," she supplies and I nod.

We go through the other handful of words like this, me saying them in english, Angel repeating them back in Russian; *baby sister, thank you, ice cream, art.* She's written them all down in her drawing notebook, and I'm impressed at her pronunciation. Charmed, too. I haven't spent much time around teenagers, and I'm not sure if they're all this way or if she is just a particularly nice one.

"Oh, and he taught me this," she looks up at her aunt with a grin and haltingly recites the phrase from her notes, "*Ya lyublyu tyebya.*"

"And what's that one?"

Angel looks at me expectantly, still smiling. I clear my throat and am all too aware of my grip on Marianna's waist.

"I love you," I say, and then repeat the phrase in Russian.

Angel repeats it again and yells it to her mom in the kitchen, who says "Good work, hon!" not tuned in to the conversation at all. Marianna has stilled at my side, her torso under my hand suddenly tense. I look up at her, her eyes already on me, and then she lets out a breath and smiles at her niece.

"You'll get your teenager card taken away if you keep being so sweet," Marianna says.

"Don't listen to her!" Willa says as she enters the room. This is the first I've seen her, though Marianna has been visiting most days to help with the baby. Two weeks after her Cesarean, she's in better spirits than I'd expect after an abdominal surgery. "Just because you were a devil, doesn't mean all teenagers are."

"Yeah," Nate agrees, coming in with a stack of plates. "Only most of them."

Marianna extricates herself from being pressed up against my side, charade over, and I feel the absence of her heat immediately. Getting a good night's sleep without her last night was not a possibility. I told every guard and Jean to call me if she returned and spent the night sulking around in my office above the nightclub.

I slept for a short two hours in one of my chairs and woke with a dry throat and a twinge in my neck. Miserable. That's how I would describe myself without Marianna Morelli after two fucking weeks. She's turned me into half a man without her.

She looks tired, too, gray under her brown eyes, but I won't let myself believe that this is because of me. Marianna has made her lack of affection clear. There is friendship between us at the best of times, disdain and scorn at the worst, and chemistry only when we're having sex or making out in her sister's basement. The rest is a farce.

From her carrier, the little baby starts fussing and Marianna is closest, so she rubs a pump of sanitizer on her hands before she scoops up the newborn and rocks her a bit. She looks at the baby with such tenderness it makes my stomach ache.

"Are you hungry, Miss Clara?" Marianna coos, and lightly swipes her pinky over the baby's forehead.

"She's always hungry," Willa groans. "Huh, tiny girl?" She leans over her baby in her sister's arms, and both of them talk to the baby in light voices for a moment before Marianna hands her off.

This is how the Morelli house always is; comfortable, soft smiles and laughing, warm food, teasing over a table, quick jokes and quicker comebacks. It's a delight to be with this family. I don't believe any Orlov guest could say the same about mine.

Marianna sits to my left at dinner, and Angel to her left. The two of them mutter quietly about things I can't hear during the meal. It's like they're friends, not an aunt and a teenager. It endears me as much as it intrigues me, and I wonder what I would have to say to a thirteen-year-old girl beyond the novelty of teaching phrases in a different language. I think she would tire of me quickly, the bore that I am.

When I asked Marianna what the kids knew of the business, she admitted that it was very little, but an increase every day. They'd kept them mostly sheltered all their lives, but after the events of last year, figured they had to start teaching them.

I don't remember a time when I didn't know about my father's crime dealings, but then again, I was a very poorly adjusted child. Marianna, too, if I had to guess, which is probably why she's so protective of these children.

"So you're like our new uncle then?" Artie asks me. I halt mid-chew; with all of my siblings still childless, I've never been called uncle in my life and the sentiment surprises me. Nate speaks for me.

"Yes, he's just joining the party late," Nate reaches across the boy and grabs a basket of rolls, depositing one onto both of our plates. Nate pretends to lower his voice, "But you're not allowed to think he's cooler than me, I am the cool one here. Obviously."

Little laughs snort around the table and conversation carries on comfortably between us.

All the while, Marianna sits at my side and I sit by hers, ever aware of the fight that lies unaddressed between us. She plays nice for the children, but does she plan to stay here again? I idly debate on staying here myself if this is the case, but determine that would be too clingy of me.

Lord, I'm so out of practice dating that I don't even know how to navigate a disagreement with my wife.

"How old are you?" Angel asks.

"Angel, don't be rude." Sean scolds.

"It's alright. I'm thirty-eight," I say, and it's excruciating to admit. If they're disgusted by our age difference, though, the kids don't let on.

"So four years older than Mom and Dad," Artie says.

"Did you go to school together?" Angel asks.

"No, but I believe they know my brother Alexei." I'm relieved they didn't follow the line of comparing my age to everyone else's.

Sean nods. "Good guy."

Conversation veers to topics more interesting than my age, and before long, Willa returns with the baby now fed. Nate scoops her out of Willa's arms so she can eat, and I'm reminded of what Marianna said in passing after visiting her sister last week. A *baby hog*, she called him.

When the table is cleared, the kids waste no time rushing back to the living room, and Sean, Vanessa, Marianna, and I are left sitting at the table, tea and coffee steaming in front of us. Marianna's chin rests on her fist, her eyes somewhere beyond us as she's lost in that mind of hers which is so unbearably unknowable to me.

"Your cousin is a fucking piece of work," Sean says, only to be met by a stern *"Language,"* called from the other room. Sean sighs and lowers his voice, repeating the sentiment again, this time while pressing his pointer finger against the wood surface for emphasis.

This snags Marianna's attention. "Nikolai? What'd he do?"

"Nothing, but that's the problem. With the new alliance, new lines have been drawn all over town, and today he's still giving lip to one of my guys about staying on our side of town."

"Nikolai is. . .spirited," I agree, holding back from my own choice words I have for him. "I'll speak with him."

"I offered to take care of him," Marianna says, not exactly words *to* me, but I still count it as a step forward.

"Nah, his goons will claim it was unprovoked and cause a riot," Sean says. My sentiments exactly.

"You think they'll have any muscle with him dead?" Marianna asks. "And whatever, I'm bigger than them."

Vanessa snickers.

I say, "They don't know what they want, or who they stand behind. They're idiots. They don't care that it's him leading, so long as it's not me."

"What did you do to earn all that?" Sean asks.

"Probably the same thing your family did to earn your brother's ire."

"Marry a Morelli?"

"No, clean up shop." Everyone bobs their heads in understanding. From what I heard, Cillian was just biding his time, playing good criminal until he could get Vanessa under his thumb and start back into the kind of shit that makes me sick to my stomach. Little did he know, Vanessa Morelli was not one who could be kept.

"Nikolai feels entitled to lead," I say. "Thinks I shouldn't have been the one to inherit."

"How do you plan to deal with him then?" Vanessa asks.

"We wait him out," I say. "He'll mess up, preferably very publicly. We will make an example of him."

"A baby would probably help with the whole line of succession thing," Sean says, and everyone shoots him a look, but he's right. It would help and we all know it.

Marianna tips her mug back, drinking a large gulp of her tea before she stands and grabs my own mostly-empty mug from in front of me.

"I still think we should just kill him," she says with a shrug before retreating into the kitchen.

Vanessa and Sean share a look before they offer empathetic smiles. Sean stands and thumps my shoulder with his palm. "Good luck, brother."

When I look back, she's standing in the doorway with a canvas bag over her shoulder. I'm equal parts relieved and apprehensive. More relieved that she wants to come back with me at all.

"Let's go home," she says.

Home.

I waste no time following behind her.

21

MARY

MY ATTEMPTS TO go straight to bed when we get home are stymied by Maxim leaning against the bathroom door frame as I finish my skincare routine (it's like two steps, but it's a routine nonetheless).

"I want to talk about yesterday," Maxim says. Of course he does. He's an adult, and adults *talk about their feelings and disagreements*. Gag.

He's wearing the gray long sleeve that's so soft and light, it must be a decade old.

"If I can wear that, I will talk," I bargain. His lips quirk in that surprised lilt I'm growing accustomed to seeing. He stands to his full height and pulls his shirt up over his head in that slutty way that men do, then tosses it to me. He put it on less than twenty minutes ago and it already smells like him.

And good Lord, naked Maxim torso. He's broad and dense, undeniably muscular without being chiseled. Like, he works out six days a week minimum, but also still really likes pasta. A big tattoo of a fully-bloomed rose bush covers his ribs next to a traditional dagger and other sweeping designs. I want to study them closely, but his alarmingly hot body is distracting me from being mad at him. Instead, I put on the shirt, unclasp my bra, and pull it from the sleeve before tossing it in a hamper.

Much cozier.

"Talk." I brush past him into the room, careful not to touch his bare chest as I do.

"I overstepped," Maxim says. "I was unfair when you were doing what had to be done."

He clicks on my bedside lamp and unfolds the soft blanket I like from the bottom of the bed. I rub lotion on my legs for something to do that isn't looking at him.

"I apologize," he tacks on. With the bedding turned down for me, he retreats into the closet. I glance up as he puts on a new shirt, effectively covering the distraction that is all of *that*.

I sigh and rub my forehead. "Thank you."

I can sense that this little conversation is not yet over, so I sit on the side of the bed and wait for him to go on. Maxim walks toward me and I think he'll sit next to me on the edge of the mattress, but instead, he crouches down in front of me, putting his eyes a few inches below mine for once.

He pulls my socks off and replaces them with the softer ones I always end up kicking off halfway through the night. I let him.

"I want to understand you better," he admits.

"Why?" I ask.

"I—" Maxim cuts off and sits back on his heels. "It will help me protect you better if I can understand what you do and why you do it. Let me."

I take a big breath, processing the request. He has a point; it's easier to keep track of someone you know. I suppose this isn't so different from me asking to share a room, I was the one who said we should probably *know* each other. I just didn't think that meant unpacking all of our old baggage.

But we've already come this far; he already knows how I take my tea in the morning, the socks I like to sleep in, my deepest fears.

As he said so eloquently before tackling me earlier, *fuck it.*

"My dad used to bring me around with him," I start. "I was a really nervous kid, but I liked being with him. I had these nightmares a lot, so um, I didn't want to sleep. I was always trying to sneak out of my room and find my parents, get them to play another game with me, watch another movie. It worked, sometimes.

"There was one night, though, I had a nightmare. Just the usual horrifying shit my little brain came up with, so I went to see if my dad was awake in his study and I heard noise coming from the garage." I chew on my lower lip, remembering. It was so long ago, almost twenty years, but I can still picture it, the fluorescent garage lights, the way I was surprised blood was in fact *that* red. "He was there with my uncle, Leo's dad, and they were. . .dealing with someone." I raise my eyebrows at the euphemism and Maxim winces.

"How old?" His voice is grave.

"Seven. It—" I close my mouth, not sure how to admit this thing I've never spoken. Not even to my sisters, but they knew, I think. They had to. "The dreams got really bad after that. I wasn't sleeping, I was angry or scared all the time, I couldn't cope."

I raise and drop my shoulders in a shrug. Maxim stays quiet, though there's an intensity simmering behind his eyes. Sympathy, too, I think. For once, it doesn't grate on my nerves.

"Therapy wasn't really—Dad didn't think that was an option. That's when he started teaching me to fight. He hired instructors and they taught all of us. It helped, actually, having something to channel my feelings into instead of letting them simmer in my body."

I remember my little fists hitting a punching bag for the first time. I was so scared of everything, scared I would hurt myself, or hurt the bag, or that when I did hit it, it would break and seep blood so red it was almost purple.

And then, as is the case with anything you practice repeatedly over any length of time, I got better at it. Go figure.

"I wasn't so scared all the time, my dreams were less frequent, training and fighting were really good for me."

Whether too stunned to speak or aware that the story doesn't end there, Maxim stays silent on his knees in front of me. His eyes never leave my face, even when I can't meet his. I lean my elbows on my knees, heels propped on the bed frame.

"My dad wanted one of us girls to take over. Willa was almost fourteen and she was such a freak, she already knew she wanted to go to law school. Vanessa has always been *so* level-headed, she was the perfect choice, but she didn't have the stomach for violence, really. He started bringing me around with him."

"His shadow," Maxim recalls, and I nod.

"I think all of it kind of made me," I search for the right word, "weird."

Maxim leans forward and the move brings his face so near mine that I want to retreat, to regain any sense of control after telling him something so raw, but I don't want to look weak, not after I just told him all that.

"He was a good father and he really, really loved me." My voice breaks and I have to clear my throat before I go on. "He was just trying his best with the resources he had, I don't resent him. But that's why I do what I do. To protect them, and—" I exhale through my mouth and can't speak above a whisper. "Because sometimes I think I'll break if I don't."

Maxim's lips part with a breath and he tentatively reaches out for me. I'm not one to easily accept a peace offering, but maybe I'm feeling sensitive. I drop my arm and let him hold my hand in his. It's warm, a comfort I didn't expect.

"You're not strange, Marianna."

I scoff and give a wry laugh because I am strange, and he fucking knows it. His lips quirk in a smile, but he lowers his head to meet my gaze again. "You're resilient and loyal, and your dad knew you were strong. He wouldn't have brought you around the most dangerous men in Boston otherwise."

"He was a little crazy for that, wasn't he?"

"Absolutely mad," Maxim laughs, and we're both smiling. "Do you still get the nightmares?"

I almost lie, tell him I haven't in years. But his candor is infectious and once you start spilling secrets, others have a habit of following.

"Yes."

I don't tell him that before I found him and demanded he marry me, they were the worst they've been in years. How they've quieted some in the last month.

"Wake me," he says. "Next time, please wake me."

His grip tightens on my hand, a long squeeze. After a quiet moment, I squeeze back.

"I have something for you," I tell him before I lose my nerve. I go directly for my underwear drawer in the closet and retrieve the red leather box I stowed there last week.

I steel myself for a moment before I return to where he now stands with a question on his face. It feels more familiar facing Maxim standing, looking up at him instead of directly into his eyes. I hand him the box before I can think better of it.

"Open it," I nudge after he stares at the fine leather for a beat too long.

He does, shifting the clasp and opening the lid to reveal a gold watch with a leather band. The face is not plain, but dark blue, with tiny diamonds to look like stars behind delicate watch hands.

I study him with apprehension, searching for a sign that he despises it.

"It's a wedding present," I explain. "Since you didn't want the one I originally offered. Sorry it's a little late."

I press my lips into a line while his middle finger traces the edge of the band, the watch face, the buckle. I fiddle with my own wedding present, the gold necklace still resting around my neck, where it has every day since we were married. I seldom want to take it off.

"It's exquisite," Maxim says.

"I know you already have one—"

"This one is better," he says immediately. He sits on the side of the bed, still looking at the gift. "It reminds me of my grandfather—my mother's father."

Stopping my fidgeting, I sit next to him and hold out my hand for him to pass back the box. He does, and I pull out the watch. He takes his old one off while I do, and offers his wrist for me to secure the new one there.

"What was he like?" I ask.

"He was kind. Hated my father more than I did. He had a leather and gold watch with my grandmother's name inscribed on the back. He wore it until he died."

I can't help but smirk in surprise at the description. Pausing before I can wrap the band around his wrist, I turn it over and let him look at what I had engraved there.

Per cent'anni

A reminder that for better or worse, he's stuck with me.

For a hundred years

His thumb rubs over the engraving before he offers his arm for me to secure the watch on him. I do, and his skin is warm beneath my fingers. When it's on, I stare down at it, both of my hands holding one of his.

He can't see the tiny tracker installed within. I won't tell him about it, won't tell him that I felt completely out of control when

Cillian took my sister last year, and can't stomach the thought of feeling that way again. About him this time.

"Thank you, Marianna," Maxim says.

"Your present was more thoughtful." I roll my eyes with a smile. "You gave me something to remember home. This is just to keep you on time."

"I love it," he says and his serious tone makes my throat dry. I swallow and squeeze his hand again.

22

MARY

SUNDAY, I sleep in. It's the damn black out curtains, they lull my body into thinking it's eternally 2 AM and if I don't set an alarm, I can sleep forever. When I finally wake up, it's past ten and I'm sprawled in the middle of the bed, my head on Maxim's pillow instead of my own and the cat asleep on my stomach.

We had a pet cat when we were young, a huge orange cat fondly known as Tiny Devil or Tiny for short. Greta is much more cuddly than Tiny was, but I try not to let it go to my head. I'm just a warm body for her to sleep next to when Maxim is doing God knows what.

Maxim, of course, is nowhere to be found. He doesn't sleep past seven, even when he can.

I open my mouth a few times, dry from the sleep, and displace the cat (she meows in protest but resettles in the warm space I leave) before I drain the rest of the water Maxim left in a cup on his nightstand last night.

There's chattering of some kind downstairs; sounds like Sasha being noisy, and a woman's voice that I don't recognize. I take as quick a shower as I can manage before getting ready. I'll train tonight.

It's a cold morning; I can tell because the apartment is extra cozy. I pull down a thick knit sweater of Maxim's that hangs like a dress halfway down my thighs.

I could buy my own oversized clothes, or have my sister do it for me, but conveniently I share a closet with a massive man who wears suits most days and likely won't miss a black cable knit for a day.

When I get downstairs, Maxim is leaning on the tall bar counter, listening to Sasha who is talking with his mouth full of what looks like soup. The kitchen smells delicious, savory aromatics bubbling from a big pot on the stove, and from the pantry bustles out the source of the female voice I heard in the form of a woman. I've never seen her before; she's got soft blonde hair (the kind that doesn't require anti-frizz cream) pulled back and a light pink apron. She's smiling at the story Sasha is prattling on about but jumps when she sees me standing like a ghost at the base of the stairs.

"Oh!" she says, and Maxim and Sasha both turn to look at me. I clear my throat and pad the rest of the way into the kitchen, stopping next to Maxim, who gives me his usual morning appraisal, his gaze making my neck heat.

"You must be Mary," the girl says. Well, woman. She looks around Vanessa's age, and a good four or five inches taller than me. She holds out a hand and I offer mine, letting her shake it in hers. She gives me a smile that's way too warm and kind for this early in the morning, but I try to reciprocate in my way. "I'm Elise."

Ah, the chef.

"Right," I say. "Nice to meet you. The food you make is really good."

Elise's smile grows bigger, and her front two teeth have a slight gap that makes her impossibly sweeter to look at. Her voice is light and oh-so cheerful.

"How'd you sleep?" Maxim asks, in a voice low enough that only I can make it out.

"Good, yeah," I say.

"Mary, you gotta try this. Zuppa toscana," Sasha says, absolutely butchering the pronunciation, and I'm sure my shock shows on my face.

"I'd love to." I take a seat on the stool in between where Sasha sits and Maxim stands. The tall chairs make me feel less like the shortest being in the room, but not by much.

Elise ladles a few scoops of soup into a bowl for me, grating some parm over top before placing it in front of me with a genuine smile. I swear, the girl kind of looks like a Disney princess. Like she might start singing beautiful melodies that call forth vermin and woodland creatures to do her bidding.

Maxim's fingers on my wrist pull my attention from the chef, and I look down to see him deftly cuffing the sleeves of the sweater I stole so that it doesn't hang so low over my hand. I offer my arm for him to do the other as well, and as soon as he's done, he's back to listening to Sasha like nothing happened at all.

The soup is delicious, absurdly so, and I listen as Sasha tells a story about people I've never met, Elise cutting in with questions or charming laughter every few minutes while she chops various vegetables on the island.

"Are you an Orlov, Elise?" I ask. It's clear that she and Sasha work in the same social circles. Elise flushes, like the question embarrasses her, and her eyes flash to Maxim.

"No, I just grew up in the same building as this one," she points the tip of her knife in Sasha's direction. "We went to school together."

"Do you know my sister? Willa?"

Sasha, Willa, and Sean all graduated high school together, at which time Maxim would have been finishing college, and I was, well, ten.

"Sure do," she says. "Haven't seen her in years though. How is she?"

"As sickly in love as she was then," Sasha says. "Now she's got three kids, though. Hot shot lawyer."

"Hot shot," I repeat with a laugh. "You are so right about that. Are you married?"

Elise looks down at her chopping board where she deftly slices an onion.

"No, much to my mother's agony," she says. "Max was nice enough to help me find work after I finished culinary school."

Max?

I turn to my husband who's already looking at me, watching me eat like he does. Freak. He smiles before looking back down at his phone.

Now, if they're so friendly, does Elise know this is a sham marriage? Two people who barely know each other thrown together to make a baby and play house?

Does he confide in her?

The thought is unfathomably uncomfortable to me, the image of him making friendly conversation while she cooks meals for him twice a week for who knows how many years? And now for me too?

I'm suddenly not hungry, but I drain the last of the broth and stand from the stool. Maxim abandons whatever email he was sending and looks at me expectantly.

"I told Angel and Artie I would take them out today. Time away from the baby," I say by way of explanation.

"I'll come with you," Maxim says, once again brazenly including himself in my plans without invitation. It's bold, I'll give him that. "I'll drive."

I'm about to tell him he doesn't have to, but Elise is watching the interaction, and if I tell him to stay, he'll just be here with her and Sasha, being friendly and chattering on in the kitchen while she cooks.

"Okay," I say instead, and find a coat and boots.

———

IT'S rare that we get to drive alone together, but with Samuel having the day off to attend an event for his son, and Sasha off to take care of business at one of the clubs, it's just us. Maxim drives and I pick at my cuticles.

"Elise is very nice," I say before I can stop myself. I keep thinking of her gentle hands and straight hair. She's like Rapunzel, I think. Or Cinderella.

I, on the other hand, am often more goblin than girl.

"Why didn't you marry her?"

"Marry Elise?"

"Yeah. She's. . ." I trail off, not sure how to finish and simultaneously hoping he will fill in the blank with something other than *perfect*.

He is no help, waiting quietly for me to go on, and when I sigh, I swear he's smirking.

"Well she's beautiful, good at cooking, and single. Plus, I think she likes you. *Max*."

I wasn't wrong, he really *is* smiling, mirth dancing in his eyes, and it kind of makes me *want to die*, so I scoff and look out the passenger window.

"Forget it."

We're pulling up to Willa's house anyway, and I'm about to flee from the car when Maxim locks the doors and grabs my forearm. I stop but don't look at him. I'm being childish, but it was a fine, reasonable question and he laughed at me.

"Are you jealous of Elise?" Maxim asks.

I sputter and offer my most indignant stare. "Should I be?"

Maxim leans across the center console and there's nowhere for me to escape when one of his huge hands slides over the side of my neck and jaw, keeping my face pointed toward his.

"Elise is very nice and very pretty, is that what you want to hear?" he asks.

"I'm just saying, if you knew her for so long why didn't you marry her? She'd have a baby with you, I'm sure of it."

"She didn't ask."

Before I can think through what I'm saying, I demand, "So you would have if she did?"

Very chill. Very not jealous sounding.

Maxim laughs again, the fucker is *laughing* at me, and it makes me want to hit him or maybe break one of his toes.

"I didn't marry Elise because I never considered her. I don't think we're compatible, even if I had. She's too. . ." Maxim's fingers trail through the hair around my ear, "blonde."

His eyes flicker to my mouth, and mine to his, not because I want to kiss him again, but because his face is close to mine and really the only other place to look is his eyes, which make me uncomfortable with their intensity.

"Are you done worrying about the chef?" he asks, voice low. He's brought his mouth even closer to mine.

I'm about to close the distance, not because I want to kiss him, just to remind him that even if he had considered the chef, we have a deal, but a string of three knocks on the passenger window startles us away from each other.

Maxim curses something in Russian and I try to calm my heart rate as I see Angel and Artie standing outside the car, giggling in their coats. Behind them, Willa stands in the doorway, holding the baby, eyebrows raised at us.

Maxim unlocks the car doors with a click and I wave at them to get in, only slightly mortified about the whole thing.

If they were younger they'd be singing about us sitting in a tree, but since they're almost fourteen, they just snicker while they settle into the car.

"Were you kissing?" Artie asks, because he likes to be a shit sometimes.

"Oh my gosh this car is fancy," Angel says.

"I know right?" I say, and point at her brother. "And no, we weren't kissing, I was checking his teeth for spinach. Now put your seatbelt on."

"You said you're our new uncle so do we get to call you Uncle Maxim now?" Angel asks. "I didn't think we'd get another uncle."

"What do you call Nate?" I ask.

"Well we used to call him Mr. G., but now we call him Nate," Artie says.

"Then you can call him Maxim." I shrug. "Or Uncle Maxim if you really wanted."

"There's a seat warmer back here," Artie whispers to Angel and they both gasp, clicking buttons much the same way I did when I first sat in the Orlov town car. "Auntie, are you richer now?"

I turn around to tell them not to be rude, but Angel speaks first. "Of course she's richer. Maxim is a CEO."

"Nessa is a CEO," I remind them.

"Yes, but she isn't in the tablets," Artie objects.

"The *tabloids*," Angel corrects.

"She was in *The Post* last year," I point out. "We had a party about it."

"But Maxim is richer," Artie says definitively. "Dad says hotels are lucrative."

"Very lucrative," Maxim muses.

"Okay fine, yes!" I say, exasperated, but I grin, part of me thrilled by their banter. I haven't seen them as often since the wedding, and I've missed them. "I'm rich now, maybe the richest person in the world."

"*That* is not true," Angel says, and we all laugh. When I look back at Maxim, he's smiling, too.

"Since you're so rich now, can I get two books today?" Angel asks.

"And chocolate croissants?" Artie adds. My two favorite little shits.

"Bleeding us dry," Maxim sighs, and my eyes light up like they do any time he makes a joke.

"We'll see." I turn and give them an exaggerated wink that I know looks stupid because they both giggle.

I don't think of the chef again.

23

MARY

"YOU WERE RECKLESS," Nate says for the third time as he drives us through traffic to my new home. I wince as I press the bag of frozen carrots to my cheek that Nate grabbed from a corner store in a huff.

I can only hope that my dear and ever-nosy husband is still out visiting one of his clubs, because if not, I will get no peace this evening.

As it is, I'm getting none now.

"What were you *thinking* going in there alone?" Nate asks again. "You don't *think* sometimes."

"Stop yelling at me," I grumble, but he is right. I should have waited for him and Leo to get to the drop point before going in on my own. They were on their way, but they were taking a long time and I was getting antsy.

Davini drops are usually harmless; we provide large sums of weapons, they move said weapons wherever they'd like, marking up the cost on their end, and give us an additional cut of that.

Easy peasy.

There were a number of unfortunate events that led to tonight going so horribly and the first of these was that the Davini family decided to send Johnny D.

The Davinis are a key partner from New York; not the top family, but beloved underbosses which translates to: no way in hell can I kill one of them without causing an *incident*. Knowing this, Johnny has gotten too comfortable.

Johnny D is around my age with a fragile ego and probably CTE from all the concussions he's had. I beat his ass bad at Leroy's last year and he still isn't over it, but I am an adult, as is he. I believed we were past that, and if we weren't, that we'd work it out in the ring next time.

Simple mistake on my part.

Nearly the moment I approached, Johnny D told me he wanted a rematch. I laughed, which, in retrospect, was the next mistake of the evening.

He got defensive, puffing out his chest and taunting me like my *fear* was the reason I wouldn't fight him in the middle of a business transaction. It's unlike me to deescalate a situation, though, and today was no different.

I ran my mouth, he got angrier, and all the while, some common thieves that had been trailing Johnny busted in to try to nab the shipment.

This is why you don't go alone.

One of the men got the jump on me, smashed his fist against my face—hence the swollen, throbbing cheek now—and was about to do it again like a fucking maniac, but I swept his feet from under him before proceeding to shoot him in the chest. The second man, seeing the fate of the first, ran before I could get him.

Meanwhile, Johnny D was hiding behind the crate like a coward, willing to let me face off against two men *alone* to save his ass.

Nate and Leo showed up before I could beat Johnny to a pulp for being a little bitch.

They managed to deescalate the situation (Nate's strong suit), but by then, the damage was already done. Though I'm sure there's nothing broken in my face, there's not a world where I don't have a nasty bruise across my cheek and under my right eye for a couple weeks.

"Johnny wouldn't have been able to really hurt me, why are you freaking out?"

"He *did* hurt you, Mary! And now your monster husband is going to kill me, and—you know what? I'm going to kill you first."

I chuff. "You couldn't."

"I've killed before," he reminds me, which is true enough. He landed the fatal shots to Cillian last year and earned my forever respect for it. Hasn't killed again since, though, and I hope it can stay that way.

He's got a tender heart, he doesn't need it all sullied by so much death. It's why we keep him as back up on drops to show him we value his help in our illegal endeavors without putting him in too much danger. Usually very little to go wrong.

Today was an anomaly.

An avoidable anomaly, I will admit. Johnny wouldn't have pulled that shit if I had the guys with me and if he hadn't, we would have been on our guard to get the punks who wanted a quick payout.

"It's like you have a death wish. Do you really care about your life so little?"

"*Nate*," I snap, loud enough to halt his rant, but his shoulders are still hitched up to his ears like he's pissed. He was worried, I know. He was scared. I hate being scared, too.

I soften. "I'm sorry. Okay?"

He doesn't accept my apology, but he doesn't yell at me any

more as we pull up to the curb in front of the building. I can see the night doorman, Jean, through the glass doors at his desk and sigh thinking about him inevitably messaging Maxim the moment he sees my face.

I'd call him a traitor, but he's worked for Maxim for years. I'm the new one here.

"I'll be more careful," I promise.

"No more going into shit alone," he says, and I nod. "You know better. You don't have to do everything on your own."

"Yeah."

Stiffly, I reach out and pat his arm. Nate and I have spent lots of time together in the last year, even more since he and Ness got married, but we do not hug. I don't hug many people, and especially not Nate.

But he's obviously distraught, so I offer a lopsided sort of smile that I hope looks assuring but believe probably just looks like a wince.

"Okay, I'm going," I say, cutting the moment off and getting out of the car. I'm about to shut the door behind me when Nate calls my name. "Hm?"

"You're not invincible, okay? You don't have to be." The first part is obvious, the shiner on my face affirms the fact, but it's my instinct to reject the latter. It's a luxury to believe that you can be fragile, that someone will be there to pick you up if you break.

I wave and click the door of Nate's Prius shut.

As expected, Jean smiles pleasantly at me, and then does a horrified double take when he sees I'm holding a bag to my swollen face.

"Goodnight, Jean," I say, before he can ask about it, and rush to the elevator. The whole ride up I close my eyes and say tiny prayers to whoever might listen that Maxim won't be home, but, of course, he is, waiting with his phone in hand in the entryway of the apartment, a stricken expression marring his perfect face.

Maxim doesn't even say goodbye to the person on the line, just hangs up wordlessly as he takes me in. He looks so distraught by the state of me that I feel a foreign wobble about myself. That's the only way I really know how to describe it, an unsteadiness in my chest as he bridges the short distance between us and takes my face so tenderly in his hands. He gently swipes his large fingers down my forehead, under my chin, searching for the extent of the wounds.

There's a burning in the backs of my eyes, and I blink hard until it subsides.

"Darling thing," he whispers, and pulls me into his chest, careful not to press against the injured side.

My body is acting on its own accord, probably a result of the blunt trauma to my cheek, and three hot tears escape my eyes, unbidden and as unfathomable to me as Maxim's shock and concern.

I can't even explain why, only that as he holds me, I cannot keep from crying.

"I'm okay," I say, but don't pull away from his embrace. It feels nice, and I can allow myself something nice every now and then. When I'm tired. "It was just a misunderstanding."

I sniff and try to wipe away the tears falling, then whine when I press too hard against my sore cheek. He startles at the sound and pulls back enough to look down at my face. He's standing so close I have to crane my neck to look up at him. The concern bleeds into a sort of frantic anguish and rage that flickers in his eyes, the flame hardening all of his features.

"Who did this? God, Marianna you're crying."

"I'm not." I swipe the skin under my eyes, gentler this time, though still wincing at the pain. "It just hurts is all. I need some Tylenol."

"*Who was it?*" he asks again.

"It was my fault," I say, and start pulling myself away from him, despite wanting to stay a while longer. I shake him off and stalk into the kitchen toward the cabinet with the low level pain killers. Maxim gives off increasingly furious, off-putting vibes as he grabs a glass and fills it with water from the fridge. He trades the bag of carrots still in my hand with the glass, then tosses them in the trash before getting a towel and a gel ice pack from the freezer.

I take the pills and lean back against the counter, too tired to tell him not to fuss about it. Fuss he does, ushering me out of the kitchen and into the living room where he pulls me onto the couch facing him. The cat jumps onto the couch behind me and rubs her tiny head and body against my hip.

"Tilt your head back," he commands, and I close my eyes, doing as he says. The ice pack pats lightly against my cheek, and it feels nice not having to do it myself. "Tell me what happened."

There are no pesky tears trying to worm their way out of my eye ducts now, which is a relief. "Kinda seems like you'll kill him if I tell you, and we really, really need you not to kill him."

Maxim is silent, and when I crack my left eyelid open, he looks like he's barely containing his rage, but is making the attempt nonetheless.

"Depends what he did."

I sigh and lean heavy into the side of the couch.

"I had a weapon drop, but Nate and Leo were taking forever, and I've done a million of these, so I thought it would be fine, but the guy they sent has a grudge against me so he was trying to pick a fight when two punks jumped us for the shipment."

Maxim says nothing, but I swear I feel this creepy, intense energy radiating off of him in waves.

"I killed the one that did this, but the other got away because the guy we were meeting was too chicken shit to fight." I hoped that Maxim would be calmed by the assurance that death was had for the man who actually hurt me, but if anything he seems to grow even more still with each piece of information. "If it's any consolation, no way did the buyer actually *want* me dead."

"It's not," he says.

"Right, sure." I agree. "Leo broke his nose on the way out, so I think we're even."

Maxim doesn't agree or disagree, but he does push my hair behind my ear, such a tender motion for someone radiating *murder, death, murder, revenge*, etc.

"But I am very, very tired." And a tad dizzy, but I don't mention that part. The throbbing in my cheek has radiated through my skull, making for an exceptionally uncomfortable evening.

"Okay," Maxim whispers. I'm about to push up from the couch when he reaches around me and picks me right up like I weigh nothing, cradle carrying me up the stairs and down the hall to our bedroom.

No use fighting it. Not when he looks so murderous at the thought of me doing my job. Maybe he's worried about the optics of his wife having a shiner—what reason should a polished little bride have a huge bruise on her face?

When we get to the bedroom, it's completely dark save for the light coming from the hall. He sets me on the edge of the bed and clicks on the side lamp.

"Thank you," I mutter, and rub my eye on the safe side of my face.

I should shower, wash my face, but all I can do is take off my boots. I'm about to lie down right on top of the covers when Maxim tuts.

"Arms up."

I obey, lifting my arms so he can pull my shirt over my head leaving me in just my bralette and tight black jeans. He retreats into the closet and I let my shoulders slump for a breath before I reach for the large t-shirt he slept in last night and left abandoned on his side of the bed.

He reemerges with pajamas for me, and pauses when he sees me in the shirt, but nods and waves for me to stand up. I do as he says and try not to blush as he retrieves my gun and pulls my tight jeans down my legs.

I'm not mistaking the heat that flashes in his eyes when he looks at my bare thighs, but it's over in a second and he's on to helping me step into sweat pants. It only sort of makes me feel like a small child.

He stands, my eyes following his up until he's his usual head above me.

"Nate already yelled at me for being reckless."

"He cares about you." Maxim picks up the gold pendant from where it rests on my chest. I take it off to shower and exercise, but otherwise I've grown quite attached to it. It's shiny, and pretty, and reminds me of my sisters. I don't have anything else as delicate as this. He wears the watch I gave him just as often.

"Rest," he says while setting the pendant down softly.

He pulls back the comforter and sheets for me and I crawl into the bed. It smells like him.

Maxim rests the ice pack on my face and I roll over so it's wedged between me and the pillow.

"I'll come back in twenty minutes to take the ice off."

"Maxim," I mutter before he can retreat from the room.

He doesn't respond, but I feel the bed dip behind me where he sits down on it. "I didn't do it to embarrass you. It really was my mistake."

He sighs and one of his hands makes soft circles on my hip.

"Go to sleep, Marianna," he says, and I can't help but listen.

24

MAXIM

I WANTED to do this without making a mess, but my right knuckles bleed and will most certainly be bruised tomorrow.

It is what it is.

My fist slams again into the man's face and his shoulders go slack.

"Please, man, what the fuck," he whimpers and hiccups. He's crying. Really.

"You're fine," I spit on the ground before throwing him onto the concrete.

"Doesn't look that fine," Sasha mutters behind me, and I breathe a heavy sigh through my nose. The man does look bad, but not all from me. Leo had already broken his nose, I just came to mess up the rest of his face.

I did also break his wrist, and many ribs.

He'll live. Probably.

I crouch to bring my face closer to his line of vision. When he opens his eyes to see me there, he recoils.

"I'm not going to kill you," I say. I do really want to, which is a feeling I hate to have. "You will never touch my wife again."

"Okay, dude," he moans.

"Say it."

"I won't touch her!" he yells and tries to scoot away from me until his back bumps against the concrete wall of the basement of the Brickyard. The club is closed by now, all the staff gone home as the sun is soon to rise. I haven't slept. First I had to wait until Marianna fell asleep, had to call her cousin to learn who was responsible for this. Leo was tight lipped, said Mary told him she'd hurt him if he spilled, but Nate had no such compunctions.

"Don't kill him," Nate said before I could hang up. "Mary didn't think he needed to die and we'll be in hot water if he does. She's right that it would cause more trouble than he's worth."

"Fine," I bit out.

"Plus, you know, she's tough but I think all the death wears on her. Just a hunch."

I thanked him before hanging up.

Sasha was sleeping when I knocked on his door, but opened it groggily a minute later. Behind him, a woman I'd never seen was sprawled in his bed asleep. A common occurrence.

"Come on," I grunted and he was dressed and ready within two minutes, no explanation needed.

"You look like a demon," he'd said when he met me in the car, and I gave no response.

Now Johnathan Davini whimpers before me, scared and bloodied. I'm filled with supreme loathing, beating him hasn't made me feel better—violence rarely does—but I am less murderous than I was two hours ago, which isn't nothing.

"I swear I won't touch her again," he cries. "Not even at the fights."

My eyes narrow at this. I glance over my shoulder at Sasha who shrugs like he's not all that surprised to hear my wife still fights for sport. I knew Marianna used to fight—in fact, one of the first times I saw her after her father died, she was twenty-two and knocking out men twice her size in an underground ring. I, foolishly, believed she was beyond those events now.

"If I find out again that you had the chance to protect her and so much as hesitated, I'll call your father and make him understand why your death was a slow one."

Him trying to pick a fight with her is almost less infuriating than him hiding when shit hit the fan. Cowardice of that level is not something I can forgive, especially since it could've gotten my wife killed.

"She was nice not to kill you." I spit on him, he whines like a sad dog. "Next time I won't be," I promise.

I accept the strip of cloth from Sasha, wrapping it around my fist as we stride out of the room. There is only one place I want to be now that this is taken care of, and I cannot get there quickly enough.

"Feel better?" Sasha asks.

"Not really," I say. Impromptu beatings in the middle of the night are far from my usual, but Sasha only wears a knowing smirk as we exit the club. He might have beat the man himself if I told him what happened.

The image of Marianna's eyes filled with tears is seared in my mind, her cheek swelling and already purple.

In general, I try to keep a level head, and for the very most part, I can. I have a supreme determination to not give into the parts of my father that reside within me, and I haven't slipped in a long time. It's what makes me good.

My father was hot headed, volatile, and extremely violent. He wasn't often stood against, because when he thought there was inkling of a threat, he cut it off at the head, usually by literally cutting off heads.

I am not afraid of killing my threats, especially when they get out of hand, but I make less enemies than he did; I'm more logical, thoughtful, and have more mercy than he ever did. I'm a good leader, like Vanessa is—people largely *like* to listen to us. Cillian Donovann was like my father, and I believe that's where he failed.

It's too soon to see how his brother will fare, but I anticipate great things from him.

Beating up Johnathan Davini wasn't especially cool headed and will likely create a grudge between his family and mine, but the kid should have known better than to touch her. His father would understand if I explained it to him. He would probably punish the boy himself.

For this, I'm not worried about retaliation.

"How's your little brawler look anyway?" Sasha says once we're on the road.

"Looks like my mother used to," I say, and understanding shoots over his face. My mother's bruises were usually beneath her clothes, but toward the end of his life, some showed on her face more frequently. I thought he would kill her. I wasn't ready to take over, but I knew I was out of time.

"The guys got Johnny dropped outside his place," Sasha reports from a text as we pull into the parking garage. "Clean your hand good before you go to bed, yeah?"

"Yeah," I agree. We're quiet in the elevator to his floor and then to mine.

I shower the small remaining splatters of blood off of me, the hot water stinging the broken skin on my knuckle, but it's not bleeding any more. A small split. I dress it after anyway, and slide into bed across from Marianna. Her mouth is slightly open as she sleeps, Greta tucked against the curve of her legs. The gel ice pack is lukewarm and discarded next to her, so I toss it off the side of the bed, and the movement wakes her.

"Maxim?" She blinks sleepily at me.

"Shh," I soothe, and smooth my palm over her hair.

"What took you so long?" she asks, and threads her feet

between my ankles. I don't think she would do this if she weren't half asleep, but I won't push her away. "I had a bad dream."

"Do you want to talk about it?"

"No. I see it wasn't real."

Her eyes drift shut again and then a moment later she inhales, fluttering them open as she tries to keep herself awake. "Did you go out?"

"Errand," I say.

"Did you kill Johnny?" she whispers, eyes already closed again.

"No." I lean forward and press my lips to her forehead. She hums, and her breathing turns even, back to sleep already.

My chest aches, completely lost for her.

25

———

MARY

MY BRUISE IS BAD, but it also looks kind of badass—emphasis on *kind of*—so I'm not too mad at it. It's exceptionally tender, though, and my head still hurts like a bitch. I forgo my usual workout and sit at the kitchen counter nursing my injury back to health with another ice pack instead.

The intercom rings, startling me from my near hung over state at the kitchen island. I meander to the box and click the button.

"Max?" A cheery voice says over the intercom. Elise. It's Thursday, I realize. Makes sense since there was no green juice for me in the fridge when I came downstairs.

"Sorry, just Mary," I say, and press the button to grant her access to the apartment. I try not to let her use of Maxim's friendly little nickname bother me—I have no reason to be bothered, literally no reason whatsoever.

Elise pulls her little cart full of groceries into the apartment, unwinding a pale pink scarf from around her neck as she does. When she finally looks at me, she stops in her tracks, an expression of horror marring her pretty face.

I can say with abject certainty that she has never had a black eye in her life.

"What happened?" she asks, eyebrows arched together in concern. "Are you alright?"

I smile, but only enough to not hurt my cheek, and I know it doesn't reach my eyes.

"Got into a fight. The other guy looks worse."

Maxim chooses this moment to brush downstairs and into the kitchen.

"Good morning," he says. He stops briefly at my side to kiss the top of my head, indicating to me that Elise isn't in on *all* of his secrets if she doesn't know I'm only his wife by arrangement. I slide him the cup of tea I made him when I got mine ten minutes ago, and he brings it to his mouth for a sip. He takes way too much sugar in his tea, but I must've gotten it close enough because he smiles. "Thank you."

This is when both Elise and I see the state of his knuckles at the same time, undoubtedly bruised in a way they were *not* last night.

I *knew* he went to see Johnny.

Elise looks horrified as her eyes swing from my face to Maxim's hand, and I can't help but snort a small laugh. Maxim looks at me with a question, but I don't explain, just stand and pat Elise's shoulder as I pass.

"You should see the other guy," I say.

At the top of the stairs, I hear her ask Maxim something, but he's already following behind me, his own steps coming up the staircase.

I sense a capital C Conversation coming on, so I head for his office instead of our bedroom. Sure enough, the door clicks shut after he follows me in. Maxim's desk hosts stacks of papers, a leather notebook that I would just love to snoop through, and another pair of those reading glasses he has.

"Did you kill him?"

"You already asked me that," Maxim says instead of answering. I do not remember asking him this, but I have a vague recollection of him getting into bed last night, so I don't call him a liar.

"And what was your answer?"

"No," he says, but he doesn't meet my eye.

I cock my head to the side and plant a hand on my hip. He runs a finger over the spines of books stacked on one of the tall bookcases.

"I can take care of myself," I remind him. His injured fist flexes at his side and my eyes narrow on the movement.

"I am well aware."

"And why does it sound like you just *hate* that little fact? Don't think women should be able to defend themselves? Be good at their jobs?"

When he finally looks at me, I see my words have had the desired effect of lighting that frustrated spark behind his eyes. I recognize that I shouldn't needle, but he's the most honest when that damn stoic mask is broken.

He's in front of me in two strides of those long ass legs and his voice is low, probably to keep our gentle guest from hearing, but the brutality behind it is still there.

"Why is your job fighting nobodies like Johnathan fucking Davini? You're a *Morelli*—and moreover, you are my *wife*."

"And God forbid a woman has a life outside of being a wife."

I resent having to look so many inches up to meet his eyes.

The muscle in his strong jaw ticks as he visibly attempts to put a cap on his reply. When he speaks again, his voice is low and level. "Do you know how this looks? When you go places with cuts and bruises on your face? It looks like—"

"Like you're not so different from your father?" I ask. He stutters to a stop, and I recognize hurt mixed with the shock in his eyes. "That's why you killed him, right? Don't pretend this is about your concern for my safety as much as it is your concern for your image."

I am being cruel, I know I am, but when I get like this, there's no stopping me. He opens his mouth to speak but I step closer and cut him off with a pointed finger on his chest.

"I might embarrass you, but nothing hurts more than someone believing you're no better than your father. Do I have that right, Maxim?"

"This isn't about him."

"Isn't it? Isn't like your whole thing trying to show just how different you are from your dad? Or are you past all that now."

Looking down at me, Maxim blinks, the anger now gone and replaced with something hollow. I hate myself for putting it there, but at this moment, I hate him more for bringing up this stupid argument again. For acting like I should change who I am to fit his image, when I've been bending over backwards to do just that!

The clothes and the smooth hair and the pleasant smiles, I am far from the perfect Orlov wife, but it's not like I'm not *trying*.

"What you do isn't safe," he says, not addressing my vitriol.

"This life isn't safe. I'm used to it. I can take care of myself."

"You shouldn't have to."

I scoff and back away from him. "And you should've married the cook if you wanted a princess."

Maxim presses his lips into a tight line then drags his palm over his forehead and eyes. Exasperated. That's what I do to him, what I do to everyone. I warned him of this, though. He knew what he was signing up for with me.

"People will compare me to my father no matter what I do, Marianna," he says. He looks through the window someplace distant. The sun is out in Boston, shining through the glass onto the dark wood floor. "I do not like to see you hurt."

The admission is spoken so solemnly I must believe him. It startles the mocking expression from my face.

He goes on, still not looking at me. "Thinking about you in

danger makes me feel. . .out of control. Off balance. Do you know that feeling?"

He's well aware that I *do* know that feeling, at least where my family is concerned, but it's not just for anyone. I don't spiral when I think about injury befalling someone I don't care about, if I worried about everyone like I worry about them, I would never have any peace. As it is, I barely find peace now.

"Why?" I ask.

His head turns in my direction and he looks incredulous. My confusion only deepens.

"Do you fret after all of your investments like this?"

He laughs a mirthless, startled sound. "*Investment*?"

"Business arrangement?" I supply, but that doesn't feel quite right for what we've become. No longer acquaintances, something like friends, maybe? I care for him, I know, and I have appreciation for him and this arrangement. I'm attracted to him, and I respect him, usually, when he's not being an ass. But, ultimately, isn't a business arrangement what we are?

Maxim stares at me like he's completely at a loss. Like I'm stupid, and not understanding something fundamental in this conversation.

He shakes his head and heads for the door ready to end the conversation just like that.

"Wait," I say when his hand touches the doorknob. He halts, but he doesn't look at me. This is for the best, because I've got my eyes screwed shut while I try to figure out how to salvage this. Maxim just told me that, for whatever reason, he worries about me. That seeing me hurt is distressing to him. It was ungenerous of me to question that. "Look, I—"

I release a big breath. His shoulders stay tight and pointed away from me.

I've never been good at letting people in, even the ones I'm closest to. I hate when people worry about me because *I'm the one who is supposed to be okay.* I want to keep everything together, everyone safe, in line, things in order.

"I can't promise that I'll never be in trouble, but I'll try to tell you, okay? Beforehand. Where I'm going, and you or Sasha can come with me, or if you can't then I'll make sure I have Nate or Leo and I will try really hard to be safe."

He looks at me finally, and I pull my upper lip between my teeth and shrug.

"I'm sorry you were scared," I say.

"Thank you."

We stand in silence for a moment before I speak again, already grimacing at how I anticipate he will react. "Now, in that vein, I have plans tonight that you are *really* not going to like, but I'll bring you if you promise not to freak out."

Maxim's eyebrows tuck together, but he nods.

"We leave at 10," I tell him.

26

MAXIM

JUST AFTER 10:30 PM, we stride side by side into a seedy building—a closed-down parking structure—before descending three flights of concrete stairs. The walls are covered in layers of brightly colored spray paint and before we even make it to the main event, people are scattered everywhere, standing in the parking lot, smoking against the wall, making out in the stairwell. There's a cacophony of sound some distance below us, cheering and thumping rap music. It's not so different from one of my clubs in this way, except, even the more salacious of my clubs are respected establishments, whereas this is decidedly not.

Mary walks in front of me, her hair in two tight braids that sway lightly over her back, and Sasha follows behind me carrying the backpack she brought. Mary pushes open metal doors that have LEROY'S painted in neon green across them, and it takes all of five seconds for me to understand just where we are.

A Garza fight night.

The plan Marianna didn't want to tell me about was the fucking underground *fighting ring*.

The crowd is full of young people with mismatched beers and red cups in their hands, some smoking cigarettes, others pot, and I know the stench will linger in our clothes after we leave. At one glance at us, people begin to move out of our way. They look with a sort of reverent awe at Marianna and surprise at me. I do illegal shit as often as anyone else, and of course I've been to a handful of fight nights that the Garzas put on at different locations around Boston, but not for years now, not since the first night I saw the Morelli Shadow all grown up.

The thought of her frequenting these ever since should be less surprising to me than it is.

I wrap an arm around my wife's shoulder, tugging her closer to me, and she acts well enough that this doesn't bother her, even snaking an arm around my waist. She wears a black cropped T-shirt and spandex shorts. Not her usual going out clothes, but—

My breath catches, realizing too late what she's planning to do.

I lean to her ear. "What are we doing here? Do not say you are fighting."

"Okay, I won't say that." She surprises me by pressing her lips to my cheek. I would love to read into the action, but that train of thought stops as I see just who we are walking toward.

In clusters of chairs, smoking and drinking, I see big heads from the Garzas, and my eyes narrow on *Nikolai*. My cousin sits looking all too chummy with gangsters he previously claimed to hate, and a woman that is most definitely not his latest girlfriend perched on his leg.

His eyes darken when he spots us.

"I need you to follow my lead," Marianna says.

"Orlov!" Garza shouts with a drunken sort of cheer. He is always cheerful, and it makes the bastard all the more terrifying. He'll tell his men to slash X's into necks with a smile, and is powerful not just in Boston, but all over the East Coast. "It's been too long since you joined us here."

"All work and no fun, you know," I say and look down at

Marianna, who isn't smiling but has a pleasantness about her face, which is more than can be said usually. "You've met Mary, I presume."

"Of course," Marianna nods. "Good to see you, Garza."

"My congratulations are in order. I hear from your sister that it was a beautiful wedding," he tells Marianna.

It shouldn't surprise me that Vanessa works with the Garzas. She is social and clever, eager to build bridges instead of stomping on the ashes from bridges long since burnt.

"Would be hard not to have a beautiful wedding with such a . . .charming bride," Nikolai says, and Marianna does something worse than glare at his obvious insult: she ignores him completely, softly smiling instead at Garza.

"It was wonderful, thank you. And thank you for having us."

"I don't remember seeing your name on the list, cousin. Are you fighting?" Nikolai asks, though it's obvious neither of us are fighting tonight, him in his garish couture outfit, and me in my usual business attire.

"I invited them," a man says from behind Garza. I recognize him as the youngest Garza boy—Santiago? He winks at my wife. "Hi, Mary."

I pull her tighter to my side.

"Good to see you, Santi," she says, a smirk pressing up her cheeks now, the kind she gives out to so few.

Santi? Winking and nicknaming with him? He's the prettiest of all the Garza boys, and probably the same age as Marianna. They obviously know each other, but in what capacity I don't wish to infer.

"Who's fighting next?" I ask to head off any more conversation between those two. No one misses a beat.

"Nikolai's best guy against mine," Garza says, his chest puffed up and grinning. By Nikolai's best guy, I assume he means Ivan, who Nikolai has pulled rank on and used more as a punching bag than a friend since they were teens. Ivan is massive and *mean*. He won't fight fair nor clean, especially not here.

"That's what I came to tell you," Santi cuts in, "Carlitos got hurt, he can't fight."

Garza's excited face instantly falls into anger. He throws his hands in the air. "No!"

"I can fight," Marianna chimes in before he can fume too much, and my heart plummets into my stomach. I must have gone rigid because Marianna pinches my side hard while still looking at the group.

Garza gasps at the idea and stands. "Morelli's princessa out of retirement? For me?"

"It wasn't retirement so much as. . .injured reserve," she says, the most outwardly charming I've *ever* seen her. She's a natural. And *princessa* is new. Garza has a fondness for Marianna, probably because of all the money she's made him here.

"Wonderful!" He booms and laughs.

I am ready to offer myself or Sasha for the task when Nikolai has to open his damn mouth.

"You'd let your woman fight?" Nikolai demands, the woman on his lap discarded. He sounds disgusted but the look on his face is apprehension. He knows my wife's reputation then.

If I had my way, I most certainly would not let her fight, but I won't let Nikolai make her look foolish. Plus, if the last month has shown anything it's just how little control I have over any of her whims.

"Afraid she'll beat your best man, Niko?" I taunt, and the group whoops and *oohs* at the gauntlet thrown down with my words. "She can more than handle herself."

Marianna stands taller, her smile reaching her eyes.

"My champion," Garza says, and practically shakes with excitement. "Let's begin!"

AT THE SIDE of the ring, the place is absolutely buzzing. Santiago Garza got onto the mat and in all his charisma and bravado, announced the change in the lineup, urging people to place their bets in the next few minutes before the fight begins.

Music thrums through speakers, overstimulating my mind which imagines my wife injured *again*, this time with an audience jeering. I *knew* she would be the death of me, I just didn't anticipate that death to come from stress and heart failure.

Marianna deftly twines her hands with the black wraps she pulled from the backpack Sasha held for her. On the opposite corner, Nikolai stands with Ivan, who jumps on the balls of his feet and shakes his head like a feral beast preparing to attack. Sasha meets my eyes over her head, quietly concerned.

"Look murderous all you like, but do *not* look surprised when I win," she says while rolling her neck side to side.

I will murder Ivan if he hurts her; the man hurts for sport, this would be just the reason I need.

"I would say I can't believe you would do something this reckless, but that would be a lie," I say, just for her ears. It was unkind, almost cruel, but she anticipated I would be angry at this plan and she was correct. "How am I supposed to keep you safe if you keep willfully putting yourself in dangerous situations?"

I am careful to not look like I am scolding her, the last thing we need is for me to look like I don't support her in this.

Santiago's voice booms over the speakers asking who is ready for fight, met with the crowd's excitement.

Marianna swings her arms back and forth while jogging in place. With her shirt discarded, her tight muscles are on display along with the scar from where she was shot last year. "I need you to pretend you trust me. Kiss me and look a little less like you're going to kill him, husband."

She pulls my neck down until my lips fit over hers in a brief but searing kiss. It's not enough to distract me, but it grounds me enough to get my expression in check.

"Better," she says. She's about to pull away from me, but I hold both hands on her shoulders before unclasping her necklace and letting it fall into my hand. She watches me stow it in my shirt pocket where she deposited her diamond ring, and nods. "Thank you."

She takes the mouth guard from Sasha's palm and fits it over her teeth. Safety first for at least her dental health, I suppose.

Sasha helps pull her gloves on and slaps her bare shoulder in encouragement. She grins as wide as she can with the flexible plastic beneath her lips.

Nikolai's fighter has joined Santiago in the ring and the energy in the room ratchets up audibly as Marianna climbs up to meet them. Ivan laughs a theatrical belly laugh at the sight of her, but Nikolai's eyes betray him once again. He's seen her fight.

I don't sit next to Garza and his people, instead keeping my place next to the ring with Sasha.

"Did you know about this plan?"

Sasha zips her bag. "I didn't, but she scares the shit out of me. I trust her."

I need you to pretend to trust me?

Do I?

Santiago roams around the ring introducing Ivan who holds his hands up like he loves and deserves the attention, both cheers and boos from the attendees. Bets are hurriedly being placed and I'm sick thinking of them hoping for Marianna's failure.

"And fighting for our gracious host, for one night and one night only, *Marianna Orlov!*" Santiago shouts, and the room erupts, largely in cheers. "*Who. Is. Your. Champion?*"

Marianna looks back at me and winks. I can't bring myself to return the gesture, so intense is the turning of my stomach. If Ivan hurts her, I don't know that I'll be able to keep myself in place.

All too soon, the bell rings, starting the fight, and Ivan underestimates Marianna so clearly, hardly taking a fighting stance, still smirking like this is going to be an easy fight. She shuffles her feet and lands a hit, but it doesn't faze him. He laughs, like it's cute, and takes a swing of his own. It lands to the already bruised side of her face, sending her head sideways.

The crowd cries their displeasure, but something is strange about the way Marianna is fighting.

I've seen her before, she is a flurry of speed and energy, but now she moves almost slow.

He lands one more hit, this one making her fall to the ground. I inhale sharply, but her eyes flash to mine, mischievous almost, and it gives me pause.

While she's down, Ivan is a fool not to further his attack, instead taking the moment to gloat, circling the ring with his arms above his head like it was a two punch knockout.

It was not.

Marianna pushes up from the ground in a flash, her movement so graceful and sharp as she jumps onto Ivan's back. He staggers, not dislodging her fast enough before she's got him in a headlock, her legs squeezing tight around his sides.

It's in this moment I feel I can exhale for the first time since she volunteered for this errand. In my distress, I had forgotten that Marianna is the single best fighter in every room she enters.

Ivan tries to shake her off of his back, and when he's almost gotten her loose, she uses one of her legs to kick the back of his knee, dismounting before he can crush her in his fall.

Marianna doesn't make the same mistake he had, instead kicking his side immediately and with a force I know from experience can break bones. Even in the roar of the din, I swear I hear a rib crack.

Ivan's got red hot rage boiling in his eyes. He wants to murder her, and he rolls to his feet with a shout. She shuffles away from him, letting him get his bearings before they circle each other. She glides so easily on her feet, like she's done this a thousand times before and her body moves on muscle memory.

Ivan lunges for her, but she's faster, dodging him and planting a punch on his side. I'd guess it's more embarrassing than it is painful, because when he rights himself, Ivan immediately charges for her again, faster this time and with a furious fist flying through the air.

It's almost comedic how easily she dodges him, her speed making him look slow in comparison. When her back isn't to me, I see mirth in her eyes. She's *laughing,* enjoying this. This is *fun* for her.

Marianna plays with him like he's a mouse she's just waiting to kill, albeit Ivan is a mouse that's twice her size and could probably snap her bones if given the right opportunity.

Her body is muscular, thick legs and toned shoulders; she is small, but she is not the tiny thing Ivan believed he had nothing to worry about.

My pulse jumps in my neck when she lands a solid hit on his torso, the side she'd kicked before. The fear I've felt for her morphs into something warmer in my body, anger receding, giving way to the constant desire I've felt since laying eyes on Marianna Morelli in my club last year—the desire that's only gotten worse since having her in my bed, in my home, since being able to call her *mine.* She's not mine like I want her to be, but mine by name, at least. Here she is mine, she is Marianna Orlov, my bride, a beautiful anomaly. And I crave her desperately.

He lunges once more, this time jumping for her, sloppy in his desperation to regain control he never had. He falls to the mat and before he can get up, Marianna's foot makes contact with his jaw in an impressive strike. She is relentless and faster than him, on his feet, but especially on his back. She kicks and punches and one blow lands squarely to his nose. Blood erupts from his face.

The crowd is going completely ballistic, the parking structure seeming to shake from their noise alone.

The man acting as referee doesn't stop her—this isn't a regulation fight after all, but when Ivan groans and looks otherwise knocked out with Marianna's knees pinning his mammoth biceps, Santiago counts down from ten into the microphone.

"She's incredible," Sasha yells as the number passes five. I can only breathe a disbelieving sound that's muted by the shouting around me.

A loud buzzer rings out when Ivan doesn't stand before Santi reaches the end of his countdown.

Mary climbs off of him and lets Santiago hold up her arm as every person in the room screams for her. They can't even be mad that it was such a short fight, not more than one round, because the spectacle of it was too great.

She is their champion, Ivan's blood on her gloves and arms to prove it. Garza is cheering as exuberantly as the people around him. Beside him, Nikolai claps reluctantly, starting at Marianna with an icy loathing that makes me want to crack *his* nose. Maybe I'll have my wife do it.

Her eyes find mine and though visibly tired from the effort, her expression is nothing but mischief and determination. It's an "I told you so" and a reminder not to underestimate her. She spits her mouth guard into her glove and yells, spurning the crowd on more.

I'm still upset that she orchestrated this, that she would willfully put herself in danger, but I can't help the smile that takes over my face, especially as she climbs through the bands and jumps into my arms, wrapping her legs around my waist.

She's sweating from the fight and Ivan's blood smears on my button-up, but I kiss her anyway, a show of a deliriously in love couple for the Garzas and my cousin alike. In the elation of the moment, her safe and victorious and in my grasp, I almost let myself believe this is a real celebration and not a piece of her elaborately sketched scheme.

"The fastest fortune I've ever made!" Garza exclaims as I set Marianna down in front of me.

She uses her teeth to pull one of the tabs of her gloves and I remove the other. Sasha takes them both to stow in her bag.

"People prefer a longer fight, but they go *nuts* for a Mary Morelli fight, no matter how many rounds it goes," Santi says, lightly punching Marianna on the shoulder twice in a mock combo.

"Like old days," Garza says, and the image it invokes of Marianna getting battered at fights before winning makes me almost wince. To my surprise, I'd let myself forget why I was angry.

"Always a pleasure," Marianna says. It feels urgent that I get her out of here immediately before she gets into more trouble, winning or not.

"Now if you'll excuse us, we have to get to our own celebrating," I say. I shake the men's hands, and Marianna does the same before walking with her fingers laced in mine through the crowd of people that cheer her on and wave their earnings at her as she walks by. She's a celebrity here, the best thing any of them have ever seen.

We're handed a black cloth bag by a Garza as we exit, and I eye it warily.

"It's not drugs," Marianna mutters as we enter the stairwell. She hands it back to Sasha, who puts the sack into her backpack. "Cash. My winnings."

"Is that why you did this?" I ask, unable to keep the frustration from my voice. Marianna scoffs and presses a fingernail into the back of my hand, not enough to break the skin, but enough to warn me to drop it.

When we get to the car, I open the door for her, and she brushes past me without making eye contact. She's icy now, the smiling, electric girl who was kissing me minutes ago nowhere to be seen.

She's a brilliant actress for someone whose anger usually simmers so close to the surface.

"Marianna—"

"Later, Maxim," she says, a demand. I meet Sasha's eyes in the rearview mirror and then nod, driving us home without saying another word.

27

MAXIM

IT WAS A SILENT DRIVE HOME, followed by a silent elevator ride. She would've gone straight to the bedroom if I hadn't called her name and pointed to the kitchen. Now she sits on the counter, a bag of ice against her cheekbone. The skin under her previously uninjured eye has already started to purple, and the sight makes my stomach roil.

I say nothing, only make two cups of tea, a squeeze of lemon in each, and lean back against the counter across from her, arms crossed over my chest. If I speak, I might yell at her, and if I yell at her, she will get defensive and yell back, and we've already fought once today. This marriage is a balancing act. It's neither of our natures to default to empathetic patience, particularly me when it comes to her safety and particularly her when it comes to her autonomy. Winning combination.

"Loyalties in this city are shifting," Marianna finally says by way of explanation.

I still want to shake her, to hold her, to fuck her, to yell at her for putting herself in Ivan's murderous path in front of a blood-thirsty crowd, but we both know how poorly that will end the evening, so I stay quiet.

"Cillian's betrayal showed the big heads of the city that they need to know who they can trust and who they can count on if that trust is broken."

I'm not following how this relates to her fighting a man twice her size until she's broken half a dozen of his delicate bones and cartilage, so I wait for elaboration.

"Garza *likes* my sister, but he thinks she's too moral. They have a tentative alliance, but he wants stronger insurance. He knows Ness hates parts of his business, he wants someone who doesn't."

She means skin trade, a favorite business of my father's which I've worked hard to root out over the last decade.

"I don't—" I start to say, but she cuts me off with just a wry glance.

"I know you don't do that, Maxim. So does Garza. But your cousin is on a fucking political campaign and if Garza gets to thinking that he's the right Orlov horse, he'll back him."

"You think Garza would help Nikolai stage a coup?"

"Depends on how appealing the alliance would be for him with Nikolai in charge. Either way, it would leave all of us vulnerable."

She moves the ice to the other side of her face, wincing slightly as she presses it against her skin. Her cheek is bright red from the cold. My brows knit at these seemingly disparate pieces attempting to fit together.

"Me offering to fight for Garza was a huge goodwill gesture. Friendly. Champion fights already make the most money, but people bet recklessly when I'm in the ring."

"And what if Ivan had won?" I ask.

"He might've if he was fighting Carlos. I've fought him before. It would've been a well-matched fight, and probably a long and bloody one."

I grip the stone counter instead of demanding she tell me

about every man she's fought in that building, the detailed outcome, and their first and last names.

She goes on. "If Carlos was fighting, it would be a win-win for Nikolai. If Carlos beat Ivan and Nikolai was a good sport about it, it would do a lot in growing Garza's amity toward him. And if Ivan won, it would've earned Nikolai some respect."

I let out a breath finally understanding. "You orchestrated the absence so the goodwill could be for you instead."

She nods and takes a sip of her tea, not burning herself this time thanks to the single ice cube I dropped in. She never waits for it to cool down, a horrible habit, always searing her tongue.

"For us," she says. "I'm an Orlov now. I wanted to remind Garza which Orlov was the better pick when Nikolai won't even fight his own battles."

"How did you know to do this?"

"Santi called Leo. Leo called me."

"And you decided this was the best path forward? For a small bit of favor?"

"It couldn't have gone better. Most battles are won through little victories. This was one of them."

I have to admit that this is true, it's a scheme I never could have come up with, but I'm still irritated to have been left out of it. "Why didn't you tell me?"

She jumps down from the counter and looks up at me defiantly. "Because you would have tried to stop me, and we needed this to work?"

"I could've listened."

"You *wouldn't* have, Maxim! You have made it very clear that I'm a jewel that needs protecting, your fragile little thing—"

"I don't think that," I say, though of course I think she needs protecting. She is precious to her family, to me, and she doesn't begin to know how dear she is.

We've stepped closer to each other in our disagreement, me

leaning a hand on the counter to get as in her face as she's in mine.

"You told me once I was a good fighter, but now I'm pretty sure you think I'm only good for incubating Orlov babies in your penthouse."

"Stop *doing* that."

"What?"

"Twisting everything! I know you're capable, that doesn't mean you should have to put yourself in harm's way, you deserve peace and tenderness."

"I don't mind being in harm's way! I can handle it, Maxim. I have been handling it for *years*. Last summer you supported us when we went guns blazing to take down Cillian. You had no concern about me putting myself in danger then, but what, now it's different because now I'm about to be your womb to protect?"

She spits this last bit and I reel away from her like she's slapped me.

I blink, and her face falls from anger to something almost like remorse for the second time today. She shuts her eyes for a moment and turns her back to me.

"I didn't mean it," she says, voice so quiet now. "I know you—"

I what? What does she think she knows? That in one month married to her I have come to adore her? Cherish her beyond every worldly possession? That I think of every person I've ever encountered in this world, she might be the most unique and splendid of all of them?

She cannot know this, but then again how can she not? Is it not in my every glance, every action, every thought of her?

How could I have misstepped so horribly to make her think she means nothing more to me than a vessel to grow a child? Where, in trying to erect some emotional barriers between my flayed open heart and her walled up one, did I make her think she was not invaluable to me?

I step behind her and lower my mouth near her hair. My hand hovers over her hip, but I think better of it.

"Forgive me for being a brute," I plead. Her breath hitches when my fingers fall on her upper arms. "I am not ungrateful for your cleverness. I need you to know that I am on your team. When you act alone, I don't know how to protect you, but if you'll be patient with me, I believe we can be stronger for working together."

I gently spin her around to face me again. Her lips are pressed into a tight line, but she nods.

Retrieving the ice pack from her hand, I press it lightly against her cheek for her.

"Thank you for your help," I say.

Marianna puts her hand over mine to take the ice, her cold fingers like a live wire against the back of my hand. Her eyes drop to my mouth, and I think she's going to kiss me again. I could never stop her.

She presses her mouth into a line and hardens her expression once more.

"I never promised you tenderness, Maxim," Marianna says, her shoulders tugging back, chest puffing up as she stares up at me with defiant eyes. "I promised you a child and a wife. So I'll fuck you, and I'll come to your parties and I'll smile like a doll, pretend I've never killed anyone, like I'm the wife you've always dreamed of having. I'll give you a baby, and I'll teach it how to fight too. And that will have to be enough for you."

She waits for a response instead of storming off in her normal fashion. I scan her face, the frizzy little curls around her forehead, the bruises on her cheeks.

Is that all this is, really? A business deal?

I've always looked for love where it wasn't, trusted too read-ily. At least she is forthright about her feelings and expectations. There's no deception with Marianna.

"Right," I agree, and her eyes darken into something unreadable.

"I need a shower," Marianna says. She doesn't look at me again before stalking out of the kitchen and upstairs to our room.

I heave a heavy breath in her absence, the quiet after the storm she is, the tornado she's been in my life, whirling about me, bringing up all of my long-buried insecurities and feelings and twisting them around.

I pour vodka into a short glass, hoping a drink will lessen the tensioning my shoulders and chest. In all the months watching Marianna in my club, I never imagined she could be mine, that she could make my blood boil and make me crave her while possessing her, my own wife, but not close to *mine*.

The glass shatters in my hand, little shards flying over the counter. My fist clenches and unclenches at my side as I breathe through gritted teeth.

I walk to the sink and thrust my hand under the faucet to wash away the small amount of blood. I take the moment alone to lean on the counter and hang my head, wondering how one man can fuck a sham of a marriage up so royally?

28

MARY

TWO DAYS after I beat Ivan Morozov's ass, the swelling is down and the bruises on my face are totally coverable with some makeup. Just in time, too, because we have to attend a charity event that's so obnoxiously expensive, I determine immediately that I can take no-one seriously. It's long and boring, but I look exceptionally hot in this deep blue dress that shows, like, my entire fucking back.

Willa, despite the infant baby, still insisted she pick my outfit and coordinated with Anette to come to the penthouse to do my hair into an updo that's still curly but absent of the usual frizz. Miraculous what can be done with enough products.

She also got Maxim a matching pocket square, and I'm humble enough to admit that together we look like an *exceptionally* handsome pair.

It's been tense between us, probably thanks to me avoiding any and all serious conversation and alone time with him like the plague. He's been moody, too, it's not just me grumping about all the time, he does his part.

But here, we've put on the usual display, the one that tells strangers we love each other with our quiet glances, his hand on my back, our heads ducked toward each other as if sharing a secret.

"How often do you have to come to these?" I whisper after the final speaker leaves the stage to polite applause and a live jazz band.

Amusement lights his eyes and he pulls my chair closer to his and puts his mouth close to my temple. "Too often."

"Should I pull a fire alarm? We can pretend I'm drunk off the open bar."

When he laughs, I feel the light huff of breath on my face and have to bite my lip not to smile too wide myself.

When he's not being overbearing, it's easy to fall into comfortable company, private jokes, and a shared king size bed at the end of each day. We haven't had sex since our wedding night —haven't come close since the day in my sister's basement. I haven't pressed and he hasn't asked, ever respectful.

I think he's waiting for me to remember that this bargain has *terms,* but the last time was . . .intense. To say the very least. I'm not used to anything beyond a one night stand, and it makes me uneasy.

But I've become familiar with the feeling of Maxim's hand on my lower back, thumb swiping back and forth absentmindedly. I've slipped into complacency, too quickly getting accustomed to the smell of his skin after he sleeps, or his aftershave, or the way he looks reading before bed, these little glasses on his nose.

When we're not arguing about my autonomy, I am comfortable with him.

That—that feeling of *ease* is what scares me more.

"I think we've given enough time and money to warrant an early escape," he says and I could not agree more.

Samuel drove us in a short limousine tonight with Sasha as security in a second vehicle. When we slide into the back seat after rushing out of the hall, Maxim's hand on my waist, the privacy divider between us and him is already up.

"The politicians will be sad you didn't say goodbye," I say.

"Maybe. But most of them were looking at you like they wished you were their date instead of mine, so I think they'll understand."

I laugh, but he raises an eyebrow and looks down at my body like this was not a joke at all. I cough into my fist and reset my posture.

"Can we call a truce?" Maxim asks, surprising me.

"This must be a really nice dress," I remark.

"It is."

My lips part, but I have no sharp quip in response to his earnestness.

"I'd like that," I say. "A truce, I mean."

He offers his hand for me to shake, and after a moment of looking at it, I take it in mine. It reminds me of shaking his hand in his kitchen the day after Christmas. When we set our terms to begin with.

"I suppose we need a truce to make a baby," I say without thinking. I would close my eyes in embarrassment if I didn't think it would look weak. For Maxim's part, his eyes have nearly ignited, a quiet smoldering behind the blue that makes my mouth dry.

"I suppose," he echoes. His hand is still wrapped around mine, keeping them aloft.

Maxim leans closer, and I don't realize I've done the same, my face near his. He looks at my lips, and I cannot begin to read the expression on his face beyond *want*. I shiver remembering his hands on my body, his mouth on my neck, and have to swallow the new dryness in my throat.

"You were the most beautiful person there tonight. Every night," he says, voice measured and low.

"I know," I say. I lean closer, matching his slow slide toward me.

If he was just any man, I would kiss him, roam my hand over his length until he was a panting mess, and then I would have him, and I would never have him again. But this is my husband, the only person I will ever have again, and I've already had him once. I already know what those hands feel like on me, what his cock feels like, how he would make sure I was taken care of.

My breath catches as his lips ghost across mine, the barely there touch making my lips tingle.

It's not bad, having my husband. I will need to have him, and have him a lot to make a baby. Then forever more, he and me, the man I can't love and I.

"I think everyone who met you was charmed by you," he whispers.

"Can I record you saying that for my family? Or better yet, you tell them yourself, we'll pretend it's unplanned."

"Of course," he says, though his eyes are on my mouth, like mine are on his. I've been fighting this, the desire to kiss my own husband again, but sitting here now, the reasoning behind the resolve becomes flimsier. "Marianna—"

I seal my lips to his before he can say something too sappy and serious, and he groans into my mouth, his hands are quick to go to my waist, pulling me against his chest. I deepen the kiss, pressing my tongue into his mouth and he meets me beat for beat.

"Fuck, you're—"

"Shh," I mutter as I climb onto his lap. I need him to stop with the niceties, the praise, the hints that he cares for me at all—he needs to remember that this is sex, a loveless marriage, an arrangement, nothing more. I straddle his waist, my dress bunching at my hips as I roll my front flush against his.

His hands are roaming and his kisses feverish, no ounce of his usual composure present. He is so effortlessly undone by want, I wonder if he's like this with all of his lovers. I selfishly hope he isn't.

His hands stop on my ass, squeezing as he moves my hips over the hard ridge in his pants. Both of us exhaling as he does.

"You're not real."

"Careful," I warn, groaning as I grind again on him. "You're starting to sound like you like me."

"I do." He bites my lower lip hard enough that I know it'll be plump for the rest of the evening. "You're pretty."

I help him undo his belt and pants, pulling his cock free while he tugs my dress further up my hips until my satin thong is exposed.

He groans something in Russian at the sight, and slides two fingers over the damp center, startling a gasp out of me. He pulls the fabric to the side and wastes no time pushing those two fingers into me and pumping twice. "Are you always this way? So wet and ready for me?"

"Yes," I say before I can even think to lie or withhold that truth. Maxim hums at the admission and sucks the fingers into his mouth, licking them clean. I can only watch the movement, limbs useless.

"Unbelievable."

I flush further, heat spreading over my whole chest now. I am losing control rapidly, beginning to wonder if I ever had any to begin with.

I swallow, steadying myself somewhat, and line myself up over his dick. His hands are so wide on my hips, hot like a brand on my exposed back. The tip of him presses barely into me, and then I halt my movement. He pants, his brows lowering in confusion at my sudden stillness.

"You're getting too attached," I say. "I have to remind you that we're just pretending."

Maxim shakes his head, my words not fazing him. He slides

the thin strap of my dress down my arm until one of my breasts is exposed to him and he presses open mouth kisses all over it. I grip his hair and pull before he can suck my nipple into his mouth, all too aware that doing so would make me forget what I need to tell him.

He whines in protest, but meets my eyes. His hips thrust lightly beneath me, but I sit higher to keep him from sinking further in.

"I can never love you," I say. I intend the reminder to be a gentle one, but I'm so horny and feverish for him, my hips rolling on their own accord that I sound more intense and angry than I meant to. "I don't want you getting hurt forgetting this."

His face changes, mouth closing, that vein in his wide jaw twitching as his eyes narrow. If he's hurt, I can't let myself worry about it. It's better if I redraw this line in the sand, remind him of my promise.

"I know," he says. "And while it's so considerate of you to care about my feelings, may I remind you that you are *my wife*. I have the papers to prove it, nothing *pretend* about it."

Bastard. I tug his hair harder, pulling his head back and kneeling above him to look down at his mouth. "I need you to say it, Maxim. Tell me you'll never love me."

"I never agreed to that." My mask must slip for just a moment because he smirks, as if he's the one in control here, the one gripping *my* hair forcing *my* gaze to his. "You can pretend all you'd like, but if I want to love my wife, I will."

"Even if she'll never return your affections?"

One of his big hands snakes around my back until his arm is wrapped entirely around me. With one move, one single thrust, he flexes his hips up and pulls me onto his full length, making me yelp and moan. My eyes close when I mean for them to be staring sternly at him. It brings our mouths practically together, him breathing into mine.

"Up to me to decide," he says.

He keeps a steady, intense pace, thrusting into me from below while I hold onto his shoulder and hair for dear life, both of us breathing heavily against the other's mouth.

"My wife is difficult," he says, and I want to talk back, say she mustn't be so bad if his erection is any indicator, but I can only get out these breathy moans. "She is stubborn, and ruthless, and so fucking reckless sometimes it drives me insane."

"Yeah?" I ask, but it sounds much more like I'm spurning him to continue. The car drives on, but it must be shaking from the intense fucking happening in the back. Maybe limos are made for such activities.

"She's too young for me, and never fucking listens."

The car hits a bump and jostles us, landing him even deeper within me, and we both groan.

"She doesn't sound lovable," I say. "Doesn't even sound tolerable."

"She's exceptional," he says, and the strain in his voice tells me he's as close as I am, my pleasure ratcheting up with every shake of his hips, the bite of pain from the tightness of his grip.

I couldn't help it if I wanted to, I worry I'll never be able to help it, this way he makes me feel when we're together like this.

"And I will love her if I love her," he says, and then presses his lips to mine, claiming and consuming me as he fucks me over the edge until I'm gasping and keening right into his mouth, my pussy clenching around him as he finishes too.

It's ludicrous, the way it feels so good, like it's never been before, never for me, maybe never for two people on this earth. It wrings me out, and minutes later, we're both still breathing heavy, my forehead resting on his shoulder as his hand trails light lines up and down my back.

"Take it back," I say, when I finally can. "Take it back. What you said."

Maxim's chest rumbles with a laugh, shaking my head slightly. "*Malyshka.*"

"Take it back," I say again, weaker.

He slides my dress strap back up my arm and over my shoulder. My skin feels electrified.

"I won't. But you can pretend."

29

MARY

MONDAY AFTER THE CHARITY GALA, I am still going through absolute mental gymnastics to convince myself that Maxim's unhinged dirty talk accompanying the constant sex over the last three days is just that and nothing more. The man is an enigma, guarded eyes and intense stares one moment and then feverish Russian phrases and muttered endearments in my ear while fucking me the next.

Whatever control I was trying to gain by jumping on him in the limo is now completely out of my hands. When it comes to sex with my husband, I have decided that bets are off. He may never have my heart, but so long as he has my hand in marriage, I might as well offer my body.

Because *holy shit* he knows what to do with it.

And so long as I can convince myself that he is not doing something stupid like *actually* falling in love with me, setting himself up for a lifetime of hurt and disappointment, then I can really just enjoy it. When Samuel dropped us off after the gala, the night was not over. I showered, he showered with me. I laid on the bed naked, he also came to bed naked. Things progressed, and then progressed two more times, and neither of us woke up before seven.

I thought it might be a blip and we'd both get a lid on it by the following evening, but I was wrong. I've kept being wrong, in fact, five times since then.

I tell myself it's because he's getting serious about making a baby, even when he's giving me orgasms through decidedly non-baby-making means. It's all part of it, I reason.

This morning I woke up with his hand beneath my underwear and his mouth kissing up my neck. Again, *because he is getting serious about making a baby,* not because he likes hearing me come, as he said. It's the baby thing, really.

That's it.

The whole "*I will love her if I love her*" was just, like, something he said without real meaning. We all say things we don't mean. That was certainly one of those things.

It's the middle of the afternoon, and, in an attempt to *not* think about the sex-filled weekend with my husband, I meet both Leo and Sean on one of the sites. They make me wear a hard hat and glasses even when we're just walking around not even really close to any of the action. Sean's job at Morelli construction is especially boring, full of logistics, planning, and monitoring situations. Not even juicy situations, either, like today he's been trying to determine if the employees taking too-long of lunch breaks is actually a positive investment because they might be doing better work when they come back.

Riveting stuff.

Leo is halfway through explaining why this job site is the most interesting of all of our current projects (I do not care nor am I really listening) when my phone buzzes with a call from Nate. He should be in school, so I pick up right away.

"What?" I'm already imagining the worst of things that can happen in a school.

"Aunt Mary?" a soft voice says through the phone. I stop walking and wave on Sean and Leo who I think are glad to be rid of me so they can do their jobs.

"Angel? What's the matter?"

"Will you come pick me up from school?" she asks, sniffling.

"Are you okay?"

"I'm fine, but please?"

I blink for a moment, glance over at her dad standing twenty feet away from me.

"Give me fifteen minutes."

———

THE SCHOOL LETS me check out Angel without incident or parental approval since Willa put the whole family on the kids' lists. Nate brings her up to the office and she looks unhurt, though also unhappy. Her eyes are puffy like she's been crying; she takes after her dad in that her pale complexion hides nothing.

I pull her into a side hug. She's already as tall as me, probably taller in her platform sneakers, which is startling.

I nod at Nate who gives me a meaningful glance, the meaning of which I cannot decipher beyond "godspeed."

"Should we go to my fancy new house?" I ask and she smiles. Not her gap-tooth grin, but I will take it.

"Yes, but Artie is going to be so jealous, we have to bring him later."

"Deal."

She throws her backpack in the back seat and sits with me in the front, grabbing and unlocking my phone from the console to put on a playlist. "Who told you my password?"

"It's my birthday, it's been your code for a million years."

"A million," I agree, and don't point out that it's Artie's birthday too. "So, do you want to talk about it?"

The song is almost halfway over before she gives a heavy sigh. "It's stupid."

"I bet it's not."

"This guy in my science class was talking about how probably none of the girls in the class would be owners of big companies, and I told him that Vanessa is a CEO and my mom is a lawyer so, like, obviously that's not true."

"Obviously."

"And he said that she probably only *got* to be CEO because of nepotism and that Mom would probably quit being a lawyer because she just had a baby. But, literally, that's so dumb because she became a lawyer when she had *two* babies and—" Angel throws her hands up and makes a frustrated groan. "I told him that he's an idiot and should stop listening to his sexist senator dad and his golf partners and pick up a book for once. And then he called *me* sensitive and told me I couldn't take a joke."

I give her a sympathetic look and shake my head at the bull headed confidence of a kid so obviously repeating after his parents. Kids aren't born misogynists.

"I hate when people say that." In fact, when I was in high school and people said that I couldn't take a joke, I was getting suspended for fighting. So it appears Angel is at least more level-headed than I was. Her mother is to thank, I think.

"Me too! Gah, it's like," Angel looks out the windshield, searching for the words, "sometimes I get so mad and I don't know where the feelings should go. I almost started crying in there, so I just left the class and he was acting like I was so unrea-sonable for calling him out for being an asshole."

I don't chastise her for cussing because her mom's not here, plus, I also think he sounds like a little asshole.

"Nate didn't have a class so I went in there and he let me use his phone."

We've reached the end of the story, and I am quiet while I

think hard about what to say. I don't want to rile her up more because it's obvious to me she's feeling big feelings. It was always my impulse to channel big feelings into rage, and that got me into trouble. In fact, it's *still* getting me into trouble.

I pull up to the apartment and scan us into the parking garage beneath the building before turning my shoulders to face her.

"I'm sorry, Little. That sounds really, really shitty," I say, and her shoulders sag a little.

"Thanks," she says, but isn't looking at me. She looks so beaten down, my heart hurts for her. "I think I was embarrassed."

I squeeze her arm three times. "Come on." She follows me out of the car, quiet while we make our way to the penthouse.

She's confounded by me having to use a key to even hit the button for the top floor and her jaw drops open when the metal doors slide open into our foyer.

"The elevator opens *into* your house?"

"I think that's weird too," I admit and lead her inside, letting her gawk at the tall ceilings and huge windows.

"Grandma's house is fancy, but this place is like. . .different fancy."

New fancy, she means. Shiny walls and white counters and lots of light flooding the space.

I head straight for the tea kettle, a habit I hadn't realized I'd picked up until I've already pulled down two mugs while Angel walks around the house unabashedly looking at everything. This must be how I looked at first as Maxim stood still as stone watching me invade his space.

"Maxim reads?"

"Yes, what did you think he did?" I ask. She giggles.

"I don't know—" She gasps so loud and dramatically I let a spoon clatter to the ground in my move to see what's wrong. She's just discovered the cat.

I catch my breath while she coos over the fluff ball. "You got a cat?"

"Maxim's cat. Her name is Greta."

"She's a *baby*," Angel drops to the ground in front of the couch and pets Greta who, while not in fact a baby, looks thrilled to preen in front of someone who will lavish her in attention. Dream come true for the little creature.

"Do you want tea or hot chocolate?" I ask.

"Do you have soda?" she asks. "Mom stopped letting us get soda."

There were three cavities between her and Artie last time they went to the dentist, but I do not remind her.

"I have green juice?" I offer and she looks excitedly into the kitchen.

"I want that, it sounds weird."

I nod and pour us both glasses, the mugs forgotten on the counter. She winces and scrunches her face at the first taste, but immediately goes back for a second and looks like she likes it a bit more this time.

"Kinda sour."

"She puts lemon in it," I explain.

"Who?"

I lower my voice. "Elise. Our chef. She is very nice, and very blonde."

"Is she your friend?"

I think about the question for a moment instead of defaulting to no. I don't call many people my friends, all of my friends are my family. But I suppose Sasha has become friendly enough, and something about Elise makes me loathe myself, but she is very sweet to me.

"I don't have many friends," I say simply. Angel takes a bigger sip, leaving a green rim of juice around her upper lip.

"Nate is your friend," she says. "Mom told me you guys hang out all the time."

"Nate doesn't count," I deny.

"Are you friends with Maxim?"

"Maxim is my husband."

"But mom always calls Dad her best friend. I asked her if Nate and Vanessa were best friends though and she said no because Nate is *your* best friend."

I laugh out loud at this, and she joins me, her giggle still as sweet to me as it was when she was a tiny baby and laughing at anything.

"Then yes, they're all my friends, except for on the days Nate annoys me. Then he's my enemy."

Angel smiles, takes another sip, but then her smile slowly falls as I assume she remembers her sour mood. It's tough being a teenager, I don't think someone could pay me enough to return to that time of my life.

I take a big breath and try to parse through the words I want to tell her, the assurances I wish I had then.

"When I was your age, I was really. . .angry," I start. "But when guys said stupid shit, I would beat them up and get suspended, and then your grandma would ground me for a week, and sometimes that made me even more mad, because I felt like maybe they didn't know how hard it was to be in high school."

Angel nods like she might know what I mean and agree with me.

"It's okay to get mad. People are annoying sometimes," I admit, and Angel snorts. "And crying is okay, too. It's okay to feel things."

"You sound like Mom."

"Yeah, well," I smirk. "She is a lawyer, so. She's pretty smart."

I'm not the best at consoling, probably because people don't usually turn to me with their emotional woes. Not many people would say that I have particularly good coping skills, but then again, not many people know how quickly my brain summersaults from one horrifying what-if to another. So, I probably have more to contribute on the topic of managing emotions than they think.

I spin my wedding ring on my finger. "Sometimes when I'm feeling really overwhelmed and I don't know what to do with my feelings, I run. Or hit something. Or I convince Nate to fight with me so I can hit him."

She rolls her eyes, smiling, and my heart squeezes. I used to think I hated kids, but then these two came to be. If every kid was like them, they wouldn't get such a bad rep.

"Dad says starting this summer we need to start learning how to fight."

I nod, having been involved in those conversations. Like Vanessa, I was in the camp of keeping these two as far away from fighting as possible, but the safest thing for them isn't keeping them in the dark.

"How do you feel about that?" I ask.

She thinks about it, chewing on her bottom lip, just like her mom does when she's thinking, just like all of the Morelli girls do.

"I want to get good at fighting. In case something like what happened to Aunt Ness happens again." Her chin wobbles a little, the memory still too tender. We were all betrayed by Cillian, but the kids were the most blindsided by the whole ordeal. They got a much abridged version of the events, leaving out some key details. For instance they know their uncle Cillian died, not that Nate shot him through the brain. They know that he was trying to force Vanessa to marry him so that he could take her company, not that this company is also tied to a massive crime conglomerate. This was their first foray into the truth that their families are . . .well, criminals.

"I want to learn," she says decidedly, braver than she knows.

I drain the rest of my juice and set the glass down on the counter with a clack against the stone. "Should we start today?"

Angel gives her big grin this time.

30

———

MARY

AT SOME POINT in the middle of the night, I wake to the sound of the bathroom door softly clicking shut and a light switch being flipped on before sink water starts running. The cat meows on the other side of the door, the same way she does when Maxim comes home later than she deems reasonable.

"I know, I know," I hear him mutter softly, like he's assuring an upset child.

I rub the sleep from my eyes and slide my arm across the cool bedding, ensuring that it's still cold. Maxim wasn't here when I went to sleep, the last sign of life was a text from Sasha that said "making rounds".

Maxim isn't much of a texter, and I loathe to admit that when he's not around, I worry. It's not that he can't take care of himself, but we were attacked in broad daylight in the middle of a restaurant, so it serves to reason he might be in significantly more danger at night in one of his clubs. Particularly the ones below board.

A couple of weeks ago I asked Sasha if he'd give me updates sometimes, little check ins, and then I told him I'd break his fingers if he told Maxim I asked. So far as I know, he hasn't told him, and on the rare occasion Maxim isn't here reading in bed next to me, I get a text from Sasha assuring me that they're fine.

I hear a noisy clatter and a string of Russian curses from behind the bathroom door. I climb out of bed, dizzy for only a second before I push the door open without knocking.

My mouth falls open at the sight I'm met with, first the too-bright bathroom light, then the fucking *blood*.

I take in the spots of crimson on the tile floor and counter, and then his strong back as he leans over the sink, his palms on the counter as if holding him up. In the mirror, I find him looking at me with a cloth pressed to his head. Beneath it, blood stains his face, neck, and across the chest of his white tank top.

Greta is on the ground, still meowing, and looking as concerned as I suddenly feel.

"What happened?" I demand, rushing toward him.

It's not a towel pressed to his face, but his white button up shirt, and it's completely destroyed by the amount of blood it's soaked up.

I reach for his hand to pull the shirt away and assess the wound, but he leans away from me.

"It's fine," he says. "Go to bed."

I can't help the incredulous laugh that bursts from my throat.

"Maxim, you're covered in blood, and it looks like you have a black eye. You're not *fine*."

"I can handle it."

I see now what made all the noise; the contents of a first aid and suture kit are spilled over the counter amidst drops of blood.

"Don't be stupid. Your hands are shaking," I say, and he looks surprised to see that this is true. Then, because I'm trying to be nicer, I lower my voice. "Please, Maxim. Sit down."

His resolve cracks and his shoulders slump before he steps past me to sit on the side of the bathtub.

I prepare some sterile pads, gauze, and reach for a clean towel. I step to him, and he's just below my eye level like this.

"Show me," I say, and with a wince, he pulls his shirt away from his head. I squint at the wound, a small but nasty gash on the corner of his forehead beneath his hairline. That would be why there's so much blood. Head wounds always bleed more, the drama queens of injuries, but this one luckily doesn't look exceptionally deep, but butterfly bandages aren't going to cut it, he's going to need a few stitches.

"Why didn't you call your doctor?" I ask. I toss his shirt into the bathtub and press my fingers beneath his chin until he tilts his head back.

"I've dealt with worse."

"On your forehead? In a mirror?" I ask, but don't let him answer. "You need stitches."

"I'll do them."

"Maxim," I start, exasperated. I raise my eyebrows and prop my hand on my hips waiting for him to realize how he sounds. He smirks and huffs what's almost a laugh through his nose.

"Alright."

I roll my eyes and almost laugh, despite the open wound on my husband's forehead. Placing a wad of gauze against the wound, I have him hold it in place while I put up my hair, put a still-meowing Greta in the other room, and wash my hands thoroughly. I'm not the best at stitches, but I can hold my own. I know things need to be sterile at least. Last thing we need is the cut getting infected.

I pull my sinus rinse supplies from under the sink and mix a couple of the saline packets into the bottle, shaking it until it's all dissolved. I hate nasal rinses, but my allergies are shit sometimes, and in instances like this, it's handy enough.

Maxim doesn't ask what I'm doing, only watches my movement. He looks pale, like, I don't know, he's been bleeding from a head wound for at least twenty minutes?

The first aid kit has multiple pairs of gloves, so I put a pair on and peel the bloody cloth from his head. "Let's get it washed."

I push his shoulder back until he's leaning over the bathtub and pour the saline solution over the cut. He grunts at initial discomfort, but otherwise makes no show of pain. For balance, his hand holds my side and I feel his grip loosen as I keep rinsing the wound.

"Here," I tap his knee with mine, nudging his leg open wider so I can stand between them to get a better look at the wound. It's really not so bad now that it looks less like a bloodbath; I've fixed up many worse cuts on Leo, and once on Sean while Willa tearfully watched, holding his hand and scolding him for not being more careful.

"Deep breath," I say to him, but really it's for me before I get to work stitching him up.

He doesn't complain the whole time, doesn't make a sound while I tie off each suture which is impressive since I know from experience that stitches without anesthetic hurt like hell.

"What happened out there?" I ask after tying off the third stitch. Only a couple more to go and he'll be fine. His palm is warm and grounding where he holds my hip, so I don't tell him to move it.

"Drunk, belligerent fuck threw a bottle at my head when I was otherwise engaged in a conversation."

"Did you kill him?" I ask, no judgement in my voice. I think I would have.

"No. He's a fine man that's gone through something horrible. It wasn't meant for me. Sasha did snap his arm though."

"Good."

I focus on my task, pulling the line through his skin before tightening like my dad taught me. When I tie it off, Maxim's other hand reaches up and fingers the hem of the shirt I was sleeping in. It's another one of his, this one a worn New York Knicks tee that fits me like a short dress. Sean would probably disown me if he saw me wearing it.

"Where did you find this?"

"Your drawer," I lie. It was in the basket, at the top, barely worn. Hardly even dirty. I don't tell him it smells like him, and that I have a hypothesis that the scent of him is the only thing that lets me sleep a whole night through.

"I like it on you," he says. His fingertips skim across my upper thigh, sending goosebumps across my skin and up my back. I pause.

"Stop distracting me," I grumble. "You've lost too much blood, you'll probably pass out if you get a boner right now."

Maxim's eyes fall shut and he lets out a light laugh, one so soft, and so foreign in this gruesome scene it makes me smile and let out a huff of my own.

"Focus, *darling*," I chastise. "We're almost done."

His hands return to their place on my hips, and I think for a moment of the many ways he's used them on me in the last few days.

No.

Not the time.

I force my attention at the job in front of me.

"You're good at this," he remarks.

"Hold your assessment until you see the results," I say, but I admit that they look pretty clean. I once gave Leo stitches so bad on his upper arm that we still laugh about it ten years later. I had to learn somehow, I guess.

"Who taught you?"

"My dad. I was fourteen, he was giving stitches to my uncle."

"Leo's father," he says.

"Yes." I pull the knot a little too tight and he barely winces. "Sorry."

"What happened to his parents?"

"Car crash," I say. The memory still makes my chest ache—my aunt and uncle were a formidable pair and as involved in my life as I am with my sister's children. We live such dangerous lives that it's almost more of a shock to die in as common a way as a car accident or a heart attack. "It was their anniversary."

"How old was he?"

"Seventeen."

"That must've been hard for all of you," he says.

I pause my work for a moment, remembering that time. It was a huge loss to us all, and Leo the most. He was an only child, though always felt like our brother. He moved into the guest house and hasn't left since, which is how we've all liked it.

"Do your sisters also know how to give stitches?" he asks.

"Just Leo and me. And Sean. Willa hates wounds. Vanessa is better at snapping orders and buzzing about while Leo or I do the tending." I cut the thread for the last time and tilt his head left and right to survey my work. I soak a pad with hydrogen peroxide and rub it lightly over the newly stitched wound. "The last person I stitched up was Cillian."

Maxim stays quiet, but his eyes darken at the mention of him.

"I should've let him bleed out," I add.

"I'm sorry he betrayed you," Maxim says. He'd said something similar the day we stormed the church where Cillian nearly forced my sister, bound and bruised, to marry him. I drove there in a car with Leo and Maxim, my arm still in a sling from the gunshot wound.

Maxim was already calling his men to meet at the church, and I remember that I was shaking with adrenaline and rage, urging Leo to drive faster. I'd been picking at my nails, and cursed as I pulled too hard and one started to bleed. Still on the phone, Maxim handed me a handkerchief without missing a beat.

I still have it.

"Me too," I admit while pulling away from him to retrieve a q-tip and my tube of Aquaphor. "I would've killed him slower."

"You would've been within reason."

"I think so too." I gently swipe the gel on the line, then cover it with a bandage. We'll have to wash the blood out of his hair, and then I'll bandage it again.

"How does it feel?" I ask.

"I'm fine," he says, and when I glare at him, he amends. "It feels like my head got cut open and then stitched back up."

"So, could be worse," I conclude.

He smiles again, a sure lot of smiling for someone who was just bleeding all over our very clean, white-tiled bathroom thirty minutes ago.

His thumbs trace paths up and down my side.

"You need to shower. You're not coming to bed like that." I try to step back, but he holds me close to him.

"Kiss me," he says. "Please, Marianna."

It's gotta be the blood loss, the worn off adrenaline, that's making him this way.

"Shower first."

"Kiss first."

"Your lips have blood on them," I say, and he frowns. "Shower first."

He does let me step back then, and pushes himself to stand, slightly staggering. I rush to his side and wrap an arm around his waist.

"Alright, big guy." I lead him to the shower and reach in, turning the knob before helping him strip out of his crusty tank top. Shirtless in front of me now, my eyes scan over the botanical and traditional tattoos on his chest covering rows of neat scars. I trace a finger across one of the raised lines and he takes a sharp inhale.

"My father's favorite punishment," he says by way of explanation. I've never asked about his scars, the dozens of straight parallel lines cut into his skin in places his clothes always hide. My heart constricts at the admission, and I lean forward and kiss one beneath the tattooed dagger.

"Pants off," I command, and he helps me shuck them off of him along with his briefs. I look pointedly away from his penis— see, I am polite and respectful—and usher him into the shower, the water soaking us both.

"Now you," he says. I roll my eyes before removing the shirt, and tossing the wet garment over the glass door.

"You just want to see me naked," I say.

"I always want to see you naked," he agrees, and his hands roam over my body. I push his shoulders until he's sitting on the shower bench, which unfortunately just puts his eyes closer to boob level. They fix fastidiously on my chest; easily distractible, he is.

"Tilt your head back."

I grab the detachable shower head and spray his hair, lightly rubbing his scalp until the water runs clear. His eyes fall shut, still a hint of that smile on his usually stern mouth. I'm careful to avoid the wound as I lather and rinse his face, his neck, his chest. He doesn't offer to help, just lays his head back against the tile while I wash him clean of his blood.

His cock is hard, jutting between us, and I've done a good enough job ignoring it, but now that he's clean, I take pity on him, dropping to my knees on the tile and bringing him into my mouth.

His eyes snap open. "*Marianna*," he hisses, like an admonishment. I take him deeper, though, and his head falls back with a groan.

Part of me is worried that he really will pass out, but he's looking very much alive and well now as I stroke and lick up his length.

"*Malysh,*" he moans, moving his hands from my head to my shoulders, urging my head up and off of him. "Please, let me come inside of you."

"For an heir?" I ask, breathless. He squeezes his eyes shut in tandem with his tightening grip on my arms then shakes his head as if to clear it.

"Sure," he says, not fighting my rationalization for once with sweet and filthy words.

I straddle his hips on the bench before sinking down on him, and Maxim gives the longest moan as his hands grip my hips, guiding me in shallow strokes up and down his cock. I gasp when I take him to the hilt and fall forward to press my lips against his. His tongue is hot and presses immediately into my mouth. I can't help the breathy moans as I ride him faster.

I feel his hips start moving beneath me and I tut. "Stop trying to exert yourself, you're injured."

Maxim sucks and bites on my neck. "I had a good doctor."

"You're insatiable," I murmur.

"You make me this way, don't you see that?"

I kiss him to keep him from carrying on talking like that; he gets carried away easily, traipsing too close to what feels like a confession that I don't want from him. I can't have it, not when I don't have room in my heart for him and never will.

"Marian—"

"Quiet," I command and grind harder on him, inching toward my release until it takes over me. Maxim is right behind me, his strong arms wrapping around my back pulling my chest as close to his as he can while he spills inside of me.

He repeats that Russian word into my wet hair, *malysh, malysh, malysh* as we catch our breaths. I'm sure it won't always be like this. After I'm pregnant, he won't want to have me so often, so intensely.

This is what I tell myself as he peppers soft kisses up my throat, my jaw, my forehead, my eyelids. Our marriage may be an arrangement, a business deal, but we can at least enjoy it for now.

Out of the shower, I dress the wound again with dry bandages, put on another of his shirts, and then tuck myself into bed next to him where I'm certain we'll sleep past our alarms.

31

MAXIM

IN THE WEEKS since the wedding, I've spent much more time at home than I ever have. When I used to spend most evenings in my office above the club, I now try to be wherever she is. Some nights, though, it can't be helped. Last week, for instance, when she had to patch me up. Tonight, too.

Marianna had another drop tonight with Nate, one she swore would go better than the last, and I got a call that someone was caught counting cards at the casino. By the time that was dealt with, it was past 1 AM. A thick exhaustion has set over me, making my spine feel heavy. I used to be better at all this running around late at night; now I'm feeling every one of my years above thirty like a weight on my shoulders and eyelids.

The elevator whirs as it brings me to the apartment, stopping with a soft ding when I get to the penthouse floor.

When it opens into the apartment, I see that most of the lights are off save for the one in the kitchen. There's movement, too, like pans being picked up and moved, deliberate clanging around as if someone decided to organize at two in the morning.

When I reach the kitchen's entryway, I don't see her, but I hear her soft murmuring. I walk farther in until I find my wife on the ground, wearing one of my sweatshirts and a pair of shorts, quickly removing glass bowls and serving dishes from the cabinet and depositing them on the tile. She has a sheen of sweat on her face and neck, the sleeves of the sweater rolled up her forearms, and a frantic look in her eyes.

"Marianna," I say and she yelps, recoiling so hard that she thuds her head on the counter's bottom ledge.

I curse and step over the kitchen supplies, trying not to step on them or her limbs, and kneel beside her.

"You scared me," she says. I replace her hand with mine, lightly rubbing the spot on her skull. I don't feel a bump, but her eyes still have a panicked quality about them.

"What are you doing down here?" I ask. She gulps and looks away from me. I touch her cheek and tilt her head back toward mine, but she's reluctant to meet my gaze. "What happened?"

"I—" She rubs a hand over her eyes and pinches the bridge of her nose hard. I don't know what comfort she needs, but she is out of sorts, so I stroke my thumb lightly across her cheek.

She shakes her head and pulls back from me, scooting a few inches away. Her hands shake.

"Marianna," I say, a plea for her to not suffer alone.

She takes a heavy breath and lets it out through her mouth. "You'll think it's stupid. You weren't supposed to come home yet."

I drop from my knees to sit fully on the ground, my back against the cupboard across from her. I'm too large to sit comfortably in a space as tight as this one, but I bend my legs in front of me and rest my elbows atop my knees as I wait for her to go on.

"Did you know about the bombs?" she asks after we sit in silence for a couple minutes. Something about it is familiar, but I can't recall exactly how. "When Cillian took Ness, he'd planted dozens of these little explosives, about the size of a quarter, all over the place. The dining room, the gym, our bedrooms, the office, our cars, on Leo's motorcycle. They were hooked up to a remote detonator so he could set them off any time if he wanted."

I recall something Vanessa had mentioned in passing after Cillian's death. A couple weeks when she and her family needed to stay at one of the Orlov hotels. She didn't give details, and I didn't press, just gave her the rooms they needed. *We'll be dealing with Cillian's mess for a while,* she'd said.

"We found and disarmed all of the ones hooked up to his list, but these things are tricky. If one is close enough to another, it doesn't *need* to be hooked up to the detonator to go off, so long as the first one did."

Mary squeezes each of her fingertips on one hand, then uses that hand to squeeze the fingertips on the other. She does this twice before she goes on. "There were a hundred and forty bombs between Vanessa's house and Willa's. We looked for days, and just when we'd thought we'd found them all, there would be another tucked behind a headboard, or beneath the silverware holder in the kitchen."

She flexes her fingers, before sliding her hands beneath her thighs to keep from fiddling with them more. I stay silent, waiting to hear more about this living nightmare.

"This went on for weeks. We thought we got them all, would think it was clear, but I kept dreaming about it, these damn dreams," she mutters. "So I would wake up and look some place else. Every night for weeks, I was picking apart rooms in the house looking for these fucking bombs. They're weapons that *we imported here.*"

"Did you find more?" I ask, my voice barely above a whisper.

"Mostly no." She bites her lower lip and I'm overwhelmed with how very beautiful she is. Happy or anguished, laughing or fighting, she is so beautiful it makes me ache. "Twice I did, though, and that was worse."

I put my palm on her knee.

"I know there aren't any here, like, *I know*, but I woke up and you weren't here and I couldn't help thinking about what if, you know?"

My stomach twists imagining her anguish. How long has she been at this? Her mind racing over possibilities she knew weren't probable but not able to let up on them?

She squeezes her eyes shut. "I think something is really wrong with me."

"Why?" I ask, fighting my impulse to pull her to me and mutter assurances that she's perfect as she is. She very well may be perfect as she is, to me this is true, but this is a rare moment when she's so freely speaking these hidden parts of her mind I crave to know, and I'm desperate for her to continue.

She releases her lower lip from between her teeth. "My thoughts get so loud. Like even if I know they're absurd or disturbing, I can't ignore them. Logically I know there are no bombs here, but then I think what if there are? And if I didn't look and they went off when you or Sasha or Elise was in here, that would be *my* fault for not warning you and not looking, and maybe I should've listened to this anxiety." Marianna's shoulders slump further and she rubs her forehead. "I don't know. I'm just. . . It makes me so tired."

She is the most capable creature I've encountered. Marianna is so strong and relentless, it doesn't matter how small she is, she demands respect in every room she enters. *The Morelli Shadow*. I watched her take out a man two times her size and kill someone who threatened her family without flinching.

And here she is, quietly confessing to me the hauntings of her heart, the chaos in her mind. She is so, unbearably wonderful. All of her broken pieces held together by sheer will and her unending love for her family.

And she's mine.

"I'll look with you, if you'd like," I say, and her gaze jumps from the ground to mine. "Only tonight, to show you that we're safe here. Sasha would help too, if we call him."

Marianna's eyes well with tears and she squeezes them tight before they can spill over. She shakes her head.

"Thank you, but let's just—" She takes a shuddering breath. "Can we try something else?"

"Anything."

She steels herself a moment longer, then moves her legs, my hand sliding down her calf as she maneuvers to kneeling next to me. After a few more adjustments, she's right next to me, her face a breath away from mine.

I don't stop myself from brushing the stray tear that spills onto her cheek.

"Close your eyes," she says, and I do. She could ask anything of me and I would do it.

Her lips brush over mine, so light, but I feel it like a shock.

I keep completely still until her lips return, this time firm as they press against mine, and I'm there to meet her. She deepens the kiss and a breath escapes me, my hands moving on their own accord to pull her across my lap as her hands hold my face so tight while she kisses and kisses me.

I don't know if there are words in English or Russian that can describe the feeling of her hot lips against mine, her heavy breath in my mouth, her fingers sliding through my hair. Maybe in Italian she has the right phrase or word for this, or a different language neither of us know. I only hope the memory of this feeling courses through me as I die, like my life flashing before my eyes, but instead just *this. Kissing Marianna* through every nerve ending.

I will keep my hair long if she promises to always run her fingers through it like she does now, I'll never leave her side if it means she might kiss me like *this* again.

Marianna, Marianna, Marianna.

She slides her knee over my lap until she's straddling my waist. The space is too short to extend my legs out straight, and the bend in them forces her closer to my chest.

My hand slides beneath the sweater she wears, and her soft skin is searing against my palm. I trail up her body, fingers roaming up the bumps of her spine, her ribs, stopping at the star-like scar on her back where the bullet tore through her skin.

I hold the back of her neck and pull her closer, as close as she can possibly be and still be kissing me.

My heart aches thinking of her alone searching her family's home and garage for little bombs, searching our kitchen because I wasn't here to hold her, or help her look. She has so much care in that heart, that big, walled-off heart she pretends is hard.

Marianna breaks our kiss, her lower lip lightly caught between my teeth. When I open my eyes, her lips are slightly swollen, her chin and the skin around her mouth red, scratched from my stubble.

"That worked, thank you."

My forehead scrunches before I remember what she'd said about wanting to try something.

Right.

I have no idea what the purpose was if not to make all of my thoughts and brain cells move down to my dick, but I manage to jerk my head in a nod. I try (and fail) to keep my eyes off of her mouth.

"You're welcome," I whisper, voice hoarse.

Her hands still sit atop my shoulders, and she kisses my cheek before standing and offering me a hand up. I take it, not actually using her weight to pull me up. Though, after how much weight I've seen her sling in the gym, I know she probably could.

"Let's leave these," I say, and nod to the assortment of pans on the floor. "Task for tomorrow."

"Okay," she agrees. She doesn't drop my hand as I lead her

out of the kitchen and up to bed where Greta is already asleep in a tight ball.

In bed, I study the slope of Marianna's nose, her eyelashes, her neck.

"Stop looking at me like that," Marianna says, though her eyes are closed.

"Like what."

"Like you really, really like me."

"I do," I whisper. "Really, really."

"You shouldn't," she reminds me. She doesn't have to add her usual refrain: *I'll never love you back.*

"I know," I say and pull her across the bed and against my chest. She sighs, but this time, it's content.

Her words cut less than they used to, less now that I know she worries about me, that she frets for me at all. She may not love me, may never love me, but her care means more than she'll ever know.

For now, this is enough. Nights in a shared bed, mornings in a shared car, dinner together, catching her drifting to sleep on the couch and placing a blanket on top of her.

Any bit she will give me.

32

MARY

IT IS with no shortage of huffing, lingering, and hovering, that Maxim finally agrees to leave for the day. *Just a stomach bug, I've been telling him.* When he demands we call the doctor to check on me, I lie and say it was my period.

My period, which is a full ten days late.

Shit.

His eyebrows pinch together and I reach up and smooth the line there with the pad of my thumb.

"Stop worrying. I kill people for a living, I think I can handle a stomachache."

"My sisters never threw up on their periods." He presses a hand to my forehead. "You feel warm."

"Ever heard of basal temperature? It goes up on your period." I don't know if that's true, but Willa is always saying shit about her basal temperature to track her cycle, so I think I am maybe mostly right.

Right enough in guessing he didn't know anything about basal body temperature, though, because he looks reluctantly convinced.

He presses his palm to my damp forehead one more time, then

the side of my neck, and I'm almost annoyed at the pesky comfort that comes from his touch. I close my eyes for a second and lean into it until he pulls his hand away.

"I'll be back this evening. Sooner if I can."

"I've been dealing with a menstrual cycle since I was twelve. I'll be fine."

Sasha knocks on the door frame in gentle reminder of their pending engagements.

"Go," I say.

Maxim halts for another moment, then squeezes my ankle through the comforter before leaving.

As soon as I hear them exit the apartment, I bolt to the bathroom and promptly retch over the toilet for another five minutes.

Nausea and vomiting has never been a premenstrual symptom of mine. Ever.

When I can finally stand without feeling like I'm going to heave, I make my way to the closet and go through the pockets of my long black coat until I find the three pink packets that Willa had made me take home after last week's dinner when she said it was obvious we were *fornicating again.*

I stare down at the pregnancy tests, the wrapping covered in little smiles as if pregnancy is a thing everyone celebrates. Squeezing my eyes shut, I try to remind myself that this was *always the goal.* Marry the Russian, tie him to my family forever by providing him an heir. Simple.

But the thought of actually having achieved that goal is nauseating for a whole different reason, one I don't want to confront.

Shaking off the thought, I waste no more time before dashing to the bathroom and peeing on one of the tests. I turn it over so I can't see the display and pace back and forth in the bathroom waiting for the timer to go off. Five minutes.

I belatedly remember not to bite on my hangnails, but I'm too late and have accidentally pulled too hard. Blood glides around the edge of my thumb's nail bed.

I curse and run it under cold water, pressing on it to stop the bleeding of the tiny wound.

A positive test would be a good thing, I repeat in my mind again and again, though each time it sounds a little less convincing than the last. It would be good, and Maxim would be happy, and then . . . What? We've achieved our goal and can be celibate until we need to make another child?

Maxim loves sex with me, I am certain. If I said that we should keep it up like we have, we would veer directly into the path of *real feelings*, and that path leads in the exact opposite of my intention to never develop anything beyond fondness for him.

The timer goes off, and I exhale a breath through my mouth while the overturned test stares menacingly at me from the counter. It's taunting me, I think. Greta has been sitting on the edge of the bathtub watching me, probably judging me too.

I put Neosporin and a Band-Aid on the bleeding hangnail before steadying both hands on the cool countertop directly next to the test.

I force my eyes to the mirror as if my own reflection will look steadier than I feel. My lips are pulled into a line and there's a crease in the middle of my forehead that's not unlike the one Maxim often has.

I also look like I've been puking. So basically, I'm looking just terrific.

I nod at Greta, making her my co-conspirator before I flip over the test.

I blink at the little stick, turn it over, and back again. The result is the same.

Two lines.

"Fuck," I breathe.

My heart races, not like I've been exercising, but like I've just woken from one of my dreams again. I stuff the test back into the foil wrapper and immediately retrieve Maxim's glass from his bedside table. I down the rest of his water before filling it up in the sink and draining it twice more.

My stomach jerks, and I almost heave again, but I close my eyes and take shallow breaths through my nose until it subsides. This is all too much commotion for the cat, apparently, who abandons me to work through this on my own, co-conspirator be damned.

An hour later, all three tests are used and stuffed back in their wrappings, each the same intensity of result as the one before it.

I feel different than I expected I would. For as long as I've believed I would be a bad mother, I don't worry about that now. I have no acute anxiety, no impending doom, none of the horror I thought I would feel, but also none of the peace my sisters have always talked about.

I feel exceptionally queasy, and my heart is still too loud in my ears. I feel like I am on the brink of losing something I quite want to hold onto, even while these three tests are proof that I gained the one thing I promised: an heir.

I gather the tests and head downstairs to bury them in the bottom of the kitchen trash can. The one in our bathroom is too small and Maxim will see them and then we'll have to confront what comes next.

We don't need to do that yet, there's still time. Nine months, even. Or as many months as it takes for the growth of life happening in my body to become visibly apparent. I have a few weeks, at least. Maybe more.

I am almost to the kitchen when I'm startled to find Elise setting up. I yelp, and she's just as surprised by my shock as I am.

"Elise," I say, and my brain detangles the image of her at the island wearing an apron, a slew of fresh ingredients in front of her. "It's Thursday."

"It is," she says, and her smile is as kind as it's always been. Her eyes catch on the packets in my hands and she gasps.

"Are you—"

"Covid tests," I lie. I force something of a smile. "Negative, no worries." I stow the tests into the trash can and trust that she will believe me. If she doesn't, I trust that she will have *discretion*.

I'm sure I look a mess. It's 10 AM and I'm still wearing just one of Maxim's shirts and a pair of thick socks. She doesn't usually see me this way, but she doesn't act affronted by it. For her part, Elise looks as soft and polished as usual.

"I didn't realize you were under the weather." Elise sounds regretful to hear this. That fucking perfect, lovely woman.

Maxim should've married her, she would be a graceful pregnant woman. She'd probably record herself telling him the exciting news, both of them with happy tears in their eyes. He'd spin her around in a hug. She'd post it on Instagram and she'd probably have a million followers because she's a private chef married to a billionaire. Content gold.

"Would you like soup for lunch? I'm about to make some."

There's a rotisserie chicken on the counter that she points to with the tip of her knife, but the thought of eating it sends my stomach tumbling into the pits of Hell again. I put my hand over my mouth, and swallow back the bile that threatened to make an appearance. I haven't even eaten anything, so it would just be more heaving.

"Sorry," I say, and focus for ten seconds on getting myself in check. "No, but um. More green juice would be great. Extra—"

"Extra ginger, extra lemon," Elise recites with a soft smile.

"Thank you."

From the base of the stairs, Greta lets out a long, squeaking meow, and we both turn to look at her. She blinks slowly at us, her fluffy tail rising and falling against the step.

"I'll be upstairs," I tell Elise as I head toward the cat. I'm a few steps up when I pause and look over my shoulder. "Thank you, Elise. For all your work."

When I get back upstairs, I manage a shower, but do not feel well enough to go through the usual dealings of the day and decide that today I will let myself sit out. I send off a text to Leo to go on without me today and he sends back a series of question marks.

MARY

I'm sick, leave me alone.

LEO

You pregnant or something?

MARY

fuck off

LEO

Defensive much?

MARY

goodbyeee

I pull the blackout curtains closed and shut the bedroom door until it's sufficiently cave-like in the room. Greta doesn't seem to mind; she sleeps constantly, except for the 2 AM cat-witching-hour where she sprints through the house like a demon is chasing her. I crawl under the covers on Maxim's side and close my eyes, forcing my breathing to slow until, eventually, I drift to sleep.

———

WHEN I WAKE SOMETIME LATER, I'm substantially less queasy than I was before, but now I'm starving which is a different kind of stomach discomfort. My phone shows that I've been asleep for three hours, which is as long of a nap as I've taken in years. Elise should be done or just about done by now, so I venture downstairs to find something in the fridge.

When I make it to the kitchen, I step on something that squishes underfoot. I pause, slowly lifting to find a green smear on my sock. A pea, I think. I take off the sock, because wet feet is a sensory experience I never enjoy, but as I step into the kitchen, I pause. There wasn't just one pea on the ground, but a whole cup's worth spilled.

It's not like Elise to make a mess, and much less like her to leave one. I look around for more signs of her and find her purple sleeve of chef's knives still rolled up on the counter.

I still, listening, but it's silent so far as I can tell. The fridge clicks on, humming in the kitchen, and the sink drips. I twist the handle until the dripping stops.

I retrieve my phone and text Elise, the only other message in our thread from when I asked her a few weeks ago to bring ingredients to make extra juice for Willa.

Mary: you left your knives, I think.

I send the message, then hear a ping from the living room.

"Elise?" I call, but again there is nothing.

I shuffle to the couch where her purse is laid out on the cushion next to her coat. Right where she always puts it when she comes to cook.

Bathroom, maybe? Or she took a trip to her car?

Sufficiently tense now, I set my shoulders and inch back into the kitchen. The security alarm isn't usually armed when Elise is here, but Jean would call if someone was coming up. For as startling as I thought it was that an elevator opens into our home, the building is quite secure.

It's probably nothing, but the hair on my neck and arms is standing on end, and until I can confirm all is well, I know I won't settle.

Starting with the kitchen, I head for the pantry, but my foot catches on something, nearly tripping me. I realize too late that it's a shoe, a bright pink Ked, and as I catch my balance, I see Elise laid out on the ground unconscious. There's no blood, but when I shake her, she doesn't rouse.

I press my fingers to her neck where she does have a pulse, and then sigh, relieved that our private chef didn't *die* while I was upstairs taking an uncharacteristic nap.

An ambulance seems dramatic, so I text Maxim to send his doctor to help me with her. I reach for a fresh towel to put under her head, but while I'm doing this, I spot movement in my periphery. It's slight, but I watch the unmistakable toe of a black shoe as it slowly slides out of sight.

As casually as I can muster, I stand and take a step back, holding my phone to my ear. Maxim picks up on the first ring.

"What happened?"

"Hi, yes, my name is Mary Orlov." I try to put on my most polite voice, like I'm talking to a stranger who I need to help me. "I'm at the Glastonbury. Penthouse apartment. My chef is passed out cold in the kitchen, and I don't really know what happened, but I'm really worried about her. Can you please send an ambulance?"

Maxim is quiet on the other side of the line.

When he speaks, his tone is lethal. "Is someone there?"

"Yeah," I say while I untie her knife sleeve. I pull out one of the big ones and creep back toward the wall with the pantry. "I just came downstairs and found her like this. Please send someone as soon as you can."

"Marianna, you need to get out of there. Can you make it to the elevator or the stairs?"

I flicker my eyes in that direction. I would have to turn my back to the pantry to get there, and I don't know for certain that there's no one in the entryway or front room. Maxim curses and says some feverish demands in Russian on the other side of the line.

"Thanks so much, I'll stay right here with her." I lower the phone to the counter, though I can still hear Maxim's frantic speaking on the line. I won't hang up, because if it seems like I'm about to be overpowered, I will go *Taken* on their asses and call out every defining detail I can.

When I turn the corner, I pounce. I have surprise on my side, but the intruder has about a hundred pounds and ten inches to his advantage. He's dressed in a blue jumpsuit, like the ones I've seen the window-washers wear.

He lunges for me, and yelps when I land a slice to his bicep with the knife. He grabs my wrist, holding tight enough to make me drop the knife between us, but I take the opportunity to punch him with my other arm, my palm colliding with his nose to sickening effect as the cartilage breaks.

"FUCK," the man yells, but only attacks with a faster fury, grabbing for me as I retreat into the kitchen for another weapon. There's an empty cast iron pan on the stove and I test the weight in my palm, flipping it once before swinging up and bringing it down on the man's head.

Between the broken nose and the thunk I just gave him, he stumbles. I'm about to take the opportunity to knock him out when another man rushes into the kitchen in a matching uniform.

The second man dives for me, and I just barely slip past his grubby paws, dropping the pan with a clatter as I slide over the kitchen island. Maxim would tell me to run, but then these men would be in our house where they could *do* anything, *hide* anything—maybe they already have—and they'd be alone with Elise. All of this is unacceptable, so I rush to the hall and unstrap a gun from beneath the side table. I'm about to unload a round into the second man's chest, when he leaps for me, grabbing my wrist and making me shoot upward instead, the bullet landing in the ceiling and raining down drywall dust.

I grapple with him, but the fucker is *huge,* and it's a battle of strength to turn the gun toward me.

I change my footing, twisting and putting my bare feet between his, tripping him enough to break his hold on the gun, but his other hand grabs my bicep hard enough to bruise. I land an elbow hard enough into his chest that his grip loosens enough for me to break free.

I twist and shoot him in the chest twice. He falls like a lead weight in the ocean, choking on his own blood, just in time for his buddy to jump out, broken nose and all, wielding a huge knife.

I dodge the blow he meant for my head, and aim the gun, but slip on Thing 2's blood, throwing off my balance enough to catch his blade in my forearm.

My arm zings with white hot pain as the gun slides away from me.

Blood already drips down my arm and it hurts like hell. Thinking fast, I drop into a fighting stance and use my other fist to punch his stomach, surprising him. I knock the knife from his hand. I waste no time before I dive for the abandoned gun.

"*Bitch,*" he spits and catches my ankle.

The intruder grips my leg hard enough to make me cry out, but I kick with a fury, another blow to his already bloodied face. This one lands on his jaw and only serves to make him angrier.

I make another reach for the gun, but he yanks me across the polished wood toward him and crawls over my body, pinning my thighs under his knees.

Blood from his broken nose drips onto my cheek and I fight like hell to get out from under him, but the man is *massive,* nearly as tall as Maxim and just as muscular. The trick to beating men his size is never letting them get the upper hand like this, and as his fingers clamp around my throat, I realize he has.

I try to claw at his face, his neck, any part of him that I can reach, but he just squeezes my neck tighter, cutting off my air entirely.

My fight weakens as black spots grow around the edges of my vision and all I can think is that I'm going to die here. Maxim is going to come home and find my dead body in the hall. I wonder if he'll try to resuscitate me, if he'll find the man who did this, if the scratches I left on the man's jaw will make it easier for Maxim to locate him.

And then, it stops.

The man is ripped away from me, and he's gripping my neck so tightly that he pulls me up with him before finally releasing me. I double over and cough, sputtering and choking while I try to get air back in my lungs.

Meanwhile, I hear a loud roar before a sickening crack. The man's body drops to the ground next to me, his eyes still open but now unseeing. His neck is broken, and sits all wrong, but before I can really ingrain his grisly visage in my memory, a red-faced Maxim drops to his knees in front of me.

"Marianna," he says, voice breaking as he runs shaky hands down my face, my shoulders, my upper arms, and then back up.

"You killed him." I point out the obvious, but my voice sounds like a croak. I want to thank him, but Maxim crushes me against his chest and holds me tight.

He holds my face in between big hands and kisses my forehead hard.

"*Malysh*," he says, like he always does. I looked it up after the second time. *Baby*, he's saying.

"I'm okay."

"All clear," Sasha reports as he comes in from checking the rest of the floor. He points to me. "She's bleeding."

Maxim's eyes go wider still and he looks between us to the arm that's hanging limp at my side. The long gash left by the attacker's knife is bleeding heavily now, blood flowing onto my bare legs and onto the wood floor.

"What happened?" Maxim demands as he strips out of his expensive suit coat and presses it to my wound. I wince at the sting of pain up my arm.

"I'm fine."

"Lev is on his way," Sasha reports of the family doctor.

From the kitchen, I hear a gasp and we turn in the direction automatically. It's Elise viewing the scene, a hand against her head where a bump is forming.

Before I can say anything, she faints again, her body hitting the kitchen tile with a slap. Sasha rushes to her side, tending to her, but Maxim keeps his place directly in front of me, fussing and fretting.

"Maxim, I'm okay," I repeat. "Call your cleaners for these two."

"What happened?" Maxim says, louder this time, almost yelling as he grips me like I might not actually still be alive in front of him. His eyes are crazed, wild, and his hold on my upper arm is tight enough to bruise.

He's terrified, I realize.

I lift my uninjured arm and touch his jaw.

"Maxim."

"Who—"

"*Maxim,*" I repeat, and he stops talking, his eyes still searching my face for a sign of fatal injury. I lightly touch beneath his head wound that's still healing near his hairline. "I'm okay. It's just a cut. Like yours."

My touch on his face seems to ground him and he settles marginally.

"You're hurting me," I say quietly and his breath hitches as he realized how tightly he holds me. I don't mind the pain, but this has the desired effect of bringing him back from his stricken, panicking state. "It's okay, I'm okay."

I pull his head down until his forehead rests on my shoulder. From where he kneels in the kitchen, Sasha watches us with a sad understanding.

In this position, my face is close to Maxim's ear, so I lower my voice and murmur that I'm alright, I fought them and I won, and isn't it so good that he married such a strong fighter?

"Lev is downstairs. Cleaners are on their way," Sasha says. Maxim takes a big breath before he stands to full height, pulling me up with him. He wipes from his face the intense panic that had just been there.

I meet his stare and give a slow nod.

I don't protest when he leans down and scoops me up in his arms. I let him carry me to the dining room and sit me in a chair where Lev meets us and makes quick work of my arm.

Elise has come-to again, and I hear Sasha comforting her there.

I think about the three tests in the trash can. About how there will never be a good time to tell Maxim if I want nothing to change between us. About the way I never want to see that fear on his face again.

"We'll get to the bottom of this," Maxim vows.

I snatch his wrist before he can leave my side.

"I'm sorry I killed him," I say. He goes completely still. "We could've questioned them."

Maxim leans down and presses a hard kiss on the side of my head.

"Never apologize for protecting yourself," he murmurs.

When he wraps his arm around me and holds me against him, I have to admit, if only just to myself, that there's no escaping the change in our relationship into something much messier than I planned. Not when that change has already taken place in me.

33

MAXIM

I SIT in a chair watching the slow rise and fall of my wife's chest as she sleeps. Her lips are slightly parted, her still-damp hair strewn in a mess about her pillow.

It's been three hours since Marianna called me. Three hours since my world tilted, since I raced through this city with infinite imaginings of her death playing behind my eyes.

She almost died. *He almost had her.*

Earlier, after Lev finished sterilizing, stitching, and bandaging Marianna's forearm, she stood up only to immediately get dizzy and stumble back into the chair she'd just vacated. She then dry heaved into the trash can that held her bloody gauze.

Elise gave a startled yelp as I held Marianna's stiff and shaking shoulders. It wasn't more than a minute of this before Marianna composed herself and wiped the saliva and bile from her mouth, sitting up straight in my arms. She was tired, despite the way her face tried to telegraph she was okay, and I felt her lean into my chest.

"I need to eat something," she said, which is easier than what I was thinking which was—I don't know, hospitalization? She looked to Elise. "Can I have one of the green juices? Maybe some toast?"

"Of course," Elise said, her eyes still glassy from the trauma she just experienced herself.

"Thank you," Marianna said, and then, finally, her brown eyes turned back to mine. I still held her against me and whatever she saw on my face made her sigh. "I think I have a stomach flu after all, but I'll be fine."

"Food, rest, and rehydration will help get her where she needs to be," Lev said as he closed up his suitcase. "I'll be back tomorrow to check in on the stitches, but the best thing you can do today, Marianna, is lie low."

"Will do," she said, already sipping on the bottle of green juice Elise brought her.

"Sasha, will you have Samuel drive Elise home, please?" I asked.

"Yes, sir."

One by one they filed out of our home, our home which has been violated, intruded upon, proven unsafe for Marianna, and all the while I held her to me, her weight still resting against my chest while she finished her meager food.

She didn't protest when I picked her up in my arms again, only rested her head on my shoulder; perhaps she was too tired to pretend she was well enough to walk.

In our room, I removed her blood-stained clothes and sat her down in the bathtub where she didn't speak as I washed her. I was careful to avoid getting her bandaged arm wet, and then dried and dressed her in the long sleeve she always steals from my drawer.

She fell asleep within moments after I laid her down, exhaustion evident in the pallor of her skin.

I wanted to take us to the Orlov, but that doesn't feel safe, either. I settled for posting more security around the building and Leo downstairs.

As I watch her now, I know it could've been so much worse. She's alive and breathing—*my fighter*—and I have failed her.

How many times, and in how many ways will I fail her before one of us dies? Because isn't that just the way of this life? Failing upwards until someone knocks you from your position? The only way out is death; there is no witness protection for us, no escaping to a quiet island where we won't be found, only her hands covered in blood alongside mine.

I let her sleep for a few hours while I handle today's disaster to the best of my ability.

The men entered through the balcony; they were on the side of the building under the guise of cleaning the windows. The real window cleaners for the building are scheduled for tomorrow, so the day manager wasn't surprised that they wanted to do the job a day early.

The security records note only that Elise entered in the morning, ventured briefly to the balcony to make a call, then came back inside to finish her meal preparations. She *had* slid the padlock back when she stepped inside, but it hadn't gone all the way, and this offered the single vulnerability that was needed to let the intruders into the apartment. One fucking lock.

They knocked Elise out, and it could've been much worse for her, but she got away with a bump on her head and a slight concussion that she'll monitor tonight. Sasha found a black backpack in the pantry with a crude handful of tools and knives along with zip ties and rope. Ostensibly, they planned to restrain and torture Marianna—for what, I do not know. She is sure that they would have killed her if she hadn't killed them first.

They made the remarkable mistake of underestimating her, one I imagine whoever sent them will not repeat after today.

I'm staring into the fire crackling in the fireplace when she pads into my office yawning. The color in her face is livelier than it was when she went to sleep, and that's a relief.

She surprises me by not lying out on the couch like she usually does, but instead nudging my knees apart and dropping into my lap, her head on my chest. She must be feeling really unwell to seek such closeness, but I wrap an arm around her waist and pull her closer still then take a deep inhale with my nose pressed into her hair.

I think this is for my benefit more than hers, but the way she sighs and rubs her face on my chest tells a different story.

"Vanessa says we can stay with her if you'd feel safer," I say, though the thought stresses me nearly as much as the thought of staying here.

Marianna yawns again. "Seems like they were after me specifically, so no, thank you."

I pull her closer, like she might disappear if I don't hold onto her.

"I'm sorry you were scared," she says. "Those men weren't good fighters, only large."

She doesn't say what I know we're both thinking. How one of them almost had her, and a ring of bruises has blossomed on her neck to prove it.

"You are a good fighter," I agree. "I just wish you didn't have to be."

"Everyone should know how to take care of themselves," Marianna says. I say nothing, stewing in the anguish that's been bubbling in my empty stomach and making my whole body tense. She pushes off of me to look at my face, and I won't meet her eyes, though I feel them on me. "Are you...angry with me?" she asks.

"Not with you," I say. "You shouldn't have to defend yourself in our home."

"I didn't have a choice, it was me or them, would you have rather I—"

"No," I say so definitively, and so loudly that she recoils. "Of course not. You almost—" I cut off and shake my head. "It shouldn't have happened."

Her eyes narrow and I know that in this I have somehow said the wrong thing again. Common practice for us. Her posture stiffens and she crawls off of my lap to stand. I feel the loss like a punch to my gut.

Doesn't she see how I'm dying here? How this is my fault for putting her in danger at all?

"Do you resent me?" she asks.

"Never."

"All I've brought you is frustration."

The crackling fireplace to her left is no match for the flame consuming me. I lean forward, elbows on my knees.

"How could I resent you? When it is me who cannot keep you from this? In our own home, Marianna." My face cracks, and I feel a welling behind my eyes that I haven't in so long. Like the anguish in me is seeking release through my tear ducts.

My throat burns and I swallow the lump there.

Marianna blinks, her posture changing from defensive to concerned. "I never expected a different life. I am under no illusions of safety."

"But don't you see that it destroys me? How much I hate the cruelty and the games we all must play? The posturing, and the killing? And that for all I've done to get where I am, it hasn't been enough to keep you safe," I speak so loud, I feel like more beast than man. There are hot tears welling beneath my eyes, and if my father were here he would beat me for them.

I curse him, that man, whose inheritance was only blood and hurt.

"I hate that I cannot give you a quiet life, and if not quiet, then one that is secure. You should not have to fight, or be attacked in your own home, you have yoked yourself to a broken man in a world that, obviously, will *never* truly be safe for a child."

I want her to be angry with me, to blame me, to understand that despite it being she who asked me to marry her, I feel that I've somehow tricked her into this, maybe by manifestation alone. I thought of her too much, craved to know her too often, and the universe took pity on me, forcing her into my path when she was vulnerable.

And I *couldn't protect her*.

I've failed Marianna. I almost lost her, the margin of error was wafer thin, ninety seconds later and she could have been dead. It would have killed me, losing her.

She's in more danger now than she ever was before, a new target on her back that I was naive to think I could keep her from. She married me for protection, for her, for her family, and I have proven many times now that I cannot adequately protect her. Useless, useless man.

"You should've picked someone else."

"Oh, Maxim." Her voice is more gentle than I deserve. I cover my eyes with my hand for a long moment and scrape it down my face. When I open my eyes again, she's watching me with her lower lip pulled between her teeth. I want to reach up and release it, but I won't touch her.

She opens her mouth but then presses her lips together, stopping whatever she was about to share. I look down to her hands, where she spins her wedding ring on her finger.

"When I realized there was someone in the house, I could have done a lot of things," Marianna says. She's looking down at me, so serious, any trace of confusion or anger gone from her expression. "I think a few months ago I might've just tried to deal with it myself."

The idea of this makes me feel ill, but I don't look away.

"I would've died, I know that." She bites her lip again and comes to sit to my left. For a silent moment, she watches the fire.

"I could've called anyone, I didn't even know if you were nearby."

It was damn lucky I was. I had a meeting with Colton Tenneson at the Orlov. He tried to convince me to sell the hotel to him again. I hated sitting through it, but am grateful for it now.

"I called *you*, Maxim, because I knew that no matter where you were in this city, you would come."

"Of course I would," I whisper. I want so badly to touch her, to kiss every part of her, to make her see how deeply I feel for her, even if she will never reciprocate.

"I know." She meets my stare, her eyes completely capturing me. "That's what you're not getting. I trust you, I *knew* you would come."

"And if I was late?"

"You weren't, Maxim."

"But—"

She cuts me off with her mouth on mine, a tender press of her lips that renders me speechless. Marianna pulls away, and holds my stare.

"You got here. I feel safe with you. I trust you."

I exhale a sharp breath and kiss her again, longer this time, but just as gentle. It's not a kiss for sex or to bring her down from a thought spiral; it's comforting and warm and so intimate it makes my heart feel like a fragile thing.

The weight of my affections for her are so heavy, it's as if my sternum will break beneath the weight of them. Being with Marianna always feels this way to me, heady and consuming and like loving her will burn up my very organs. It might.

I lift my palm to her neck, sliding my fingers into her hair. I kiss her nose and both cheeks.

"I adore you, Marianna," I say, and pull her forehead against mine.

"Don't be dramatic."

"Am I ever?"

"Constantly," she says, laughing. Closing her eyes tightly, she sighs. "You shouldn't."

"I do." I see the guilt she carries, the unspoken *"I can never love you back"* on her tongue.

"I know," she says instead. When she tries to pull away, I wrap my arm around her and haul her back up to me, pulling her again into my lap. We watch the fire burn together, our breaths synchronizing until hers slows further, asleep and alive with her head on my shoulder.

34

MARY

THREE WEEKS HAVE GONE since the break-in, and Maxim's hovering has been impressive. He insists that I join him for his work, or that he joins me for mine and I don't mind his company. In fact, I am strong enough to admit that I've grown to quite like the companionable car rides, the touch of his hand on my back as he guides me from one place to the next, the way he listens so intently to whoever is speaking that they feel they ought to say the right words as to not waste his time.

The problem is that I am still so fucking *sick*, and though I'm not vomiting more than once per day, the nausea is like a silent sniper waiting at any moment to bowl me over.

He's worried, and I still can't get myself to tell him that I'm pregnant. I am just about out of lies to why I am always looking a little pukish, though.

But every time I'm about to tell him, he does something sweet, like kiss up the side of my neck, or make me come with his tongue, or draw me a bath, wash my hair, be an exceptionally good and thoughtful husband at every turn.

It's not that I think he'll stop when I tell him. He'll be *worse,*

I'm sure. *More* doting, *more* careful, *more* longing stares than I know what to do with.

I don't know that I will be able to do what I need to do. It's hard enough now, this resisting *falling in love* with my damn husband.

The battle is uphill and increasingly fruitless with every whispered Russian endearment, every tiny thing he does to make me feel cared for.

I'm pretty sure he believes that my nerves are frayed from the break-in. I couldn't care less about what happened, but I still would love to know what those fuckers were after.

I've left that for Maxim, Sean, and Ness to worry about as I've been otherwise occupied trying to secretly get a grip on what appears to be a fetus growing in my abdomen. I haven't told my sisters, nor my mom, nor a doctor; only Greta knows and that's because she follows me everywhere in the house, including into the bathroom where I vomit or pee on more positive pregnancy tests. Elise knows too, I think. She hasn't said anything, but she's doubled the green juice recipe and keeps saying things like, "You'll tell me if you want me to change the menu, right? I want to make sure you have food you like."

Nice and innocuous enough, but she gives these meaningful looks when she says it, like she wants to make sure there are meals adequate to meet my pregnancy cravings, of which so far there have been none. At least she hasn't said anything about it to Maxim or Sasha.

I wish I could tell my mom, at least, but I can't be sure she would keep that secret until I'm ready to share it. It's not that my family wouldn't be helpful—probably no one could be more of help than the heavily pregnant Vanessa and recently postpartum Willa, but when I think about telling anyone it all becomes very real, and I'm not ready for that.

I have time.

I need to get a hold of this sickness, but Google is nebulous, each proposed remedy accompanied by five other blog articles that explain why *that* remedy is actually horrible. The only thing I've landed on without issue is using a whole lemon's worth of wedges every day in my water, which I do think has helped somewhat. Sometimes.

It's exhausting.

Maxim has been so intensely protective that I can't be sure that he won't flip his top the moment I tell him and whisk me away to some cabin in the wilderness for the next thirty to thirty-four weeks.

I am at my wit's end after not being able to sleep through the nausea of the last two nights. So, this morning, I was supposed to go with Maxim and Sasha to some breakfast with rich Russians, but I claimed a migraine and convinced him that it would be okay if he left the house without me. There's still extra security downstairs, I'm well guarded.

In determining who to ask for help, my sisters are out of the question. They have loud mouths—my whole family does. None of them can keep a secret to save their lives, at least not from each other, but one of them is easier to bully than the others. I pick up my phone as soon as Maxim's car drives away and call Nate.

He picks up on the second ring.

"Hello," he says, but he makes it stupid by saying it like "yellow".

"Come over," I say. I'd go to him, but I'm too queasy to drive and Jean would probably text Maxim that I'd just left. "Bring bagels."

He makes protests on the other side of the phone, but I don't let him finish. "Come alone," I say, and then hang up the phone.

He rings back two times in a row, the first one I send to voicemail, but the second I actually miss because I do have to go throw up the meager breakfast I tried to choke down this morning.

He shows up thirty minutes later after Jean calls to ask if I approve one Nate Gilbert to come upstairs.

When the elevator doors slide open, revealing him, I pull him immediately by the arm into the kitchen. He looks around the same way he did the last two times he's visited, like the place dazzles and surprises him. If I didn't feel the unbearable weight of a secret about to boil over, I would maybe admit that, yeah, I like the place too.

"Good morning to you too, sunshine," Nate says. I retrieve the toaster from the pantry and a bottle of green juice from the fridge. It's the only thing I can reliably keep down.

"I need to tell you a secret. But if you tell anyone before I do, I will tell Maxim that you're annoying me and he will never look at you the same."

"Harsh," he mutters. "What's the matter with you?"

"Can you keep my secret or not?"

"You know I have to tell Vanessa, she's—"

"Your wife, your muse, whatever, I get it. You can't tell her. Just for like a couple of days."

"Mary." He sounds exasperated.

"I'm pregnant," I confess. He's the first person I've said the words to, and in the silence that follows, he looks as gobsmacked as I've felt about the whole ordeal. He goes through no less than four emotions in less than a minute; confusion, then shock, he almost looks excited, but then it's back to the shock.

"You are?" he whispers.

"Yes," I whisper back, though it's just us here.

"Have you told anyone?"

"Yes," I say, and he looks relieved. "You, just now."

The stress returns to his face in an instant. The toaster pops up one of the bagels and Nate jumps like there's another attacker.

I hand him a plate and a butter knife.

"Please be chill about this, I am too nauseous to fall victim to one of your anxiety attacks."

"You're sick? Like morning sickness?"

"Yes, like morning sickness, stupid."

"Is it Maxim's baby?" he whispers again, as if my husband might hear us from across the city.

I pinch the bridge of my nose. I want to hit him, but I want him to help me more, so I hold back.

"Obviously."

"I knew it. You *did* have a hickey on St. Patrick's Day."

"Nate," I warn. I forget, at times, that my brother-in-law is the single most intrusive person on the planet once he feels like he really knows someone. "Whatever. Yes, we had sex at least one time, yes, it was a hickey, yes, his penis is massive, yes, he is a generous lover. Now are you ready to focus on the problem at hand?"

Nate's mouth snaps shut and then he nods solemnly. The toaster pops up with the second bagel, and he retrieves it, burning his fingers immediately and cursing.

"What's the problem? The baby? Like, what, you don't want it?"

"No." My hand covers my stomach as if to protect the cluster of cells from thinking that. "That's not it."

"How many weeks are you?"

"I think seven."

Nate gets out his phone and taps at the screen before sliding it to me. I see a pastel colored app, a beating number 7 at the top of the screen and a blueberry below next to what looks kind of like a tadpole.

Baby is the size of a blueberry! it reads. My eyebrows cinch in the middle of my forehead. I was envisioning something much more abstract, less like a tiny creature.

I exhale and put the phone face down on the counter before I can get distracted reading the information the app offers about the little thing growing in me. *Focus.*

"The problem is that I can't keep food down. But when I'm hungry, I feel even more sick, and it makes doing anything very difficult."

"I'm sorry, Mary," he says, completely sympathetic. "Ness was sick the first trimester, too."

"Only the first trimester?" This gives me hope.

"Yeah, after that it got a lot better."

"How many weeks is in a trimester?"

The question seems to surprise him, but he wipes the look off his face before I can snipe at him that I can't know everything about pregnancy like he apparently does. "Twelve."

I groan, dropping my head into my hand again. "Five more weeks of this?"

"It seemed to go fast," he says. I think he's lying by the tilt in his voice and general wince. "But I wasn't the sick one."

"I need your help to make me not feel so sick. Symptom management, if there's nothing we can do to heal it completely."

"Why didn't you ask Willa? She's the go-to for this stuff."

"Because she would tell Vanessa."

"Who would be the perfect person to know because she is actively pregnant!"

I should have known he would be unreasonable.

"No, because she would get all intense and call Maxim, telling him he needed to do more to protect me or she'd kill him."

"You haven't told *Maxim*?" he asks, voice too loud.

"No. I need a few days to figure some things out."

He blinks at me, one hand on his hips, the other holding his bagel with his usual dramatic flare. "For instance?"

"For instance, not being so sick. He's already stressed about my safety, if he knows I'm this sick, he'll be even more of a menace." It's a half lie, but it's better than admitting I'm avoiding that there is something else growing in me that's oddly shaped like big, unwieldy feelings.

"God forbid a man care about his wife's health."

I glare at him, regretting my choice to bring him in on this. I could probably have gone another few weeks with the lemon wedges and scheduling in my fifty-five minute naps every day, but if this lasts beyond the first trimester, I might actually go mad.

"Just give me four days before you tell her," I beg. He gasps, affronted by this very reasonable demand.

"Two," he counters.

"Three."

He pulls that face he has, both eyebrows raised, eyes wide like he's warning me not to push it. He remains the least threatening living thing on the planet, though, so I am *always* inclined to push it.

I slump my shoulders. "Please, Nate," I say, voice little, because I'm fucking queasy *again*.

"What have you been able to keep down?" he asks, resigned.

I slide the bottle of green juice in front of him and he eyes it.

"Just this, basically. Saltine crackers are okay but then I eat too many and throw up. Fruits on their own make me feel very, super bad, and meat is a no go. Yesterday I ate three tortillas throughout the day and felt mostly fine but I was too fatigued to train, and then I threw up anyway."

Nate unscrews the lid and smells the drink, not displeased with what he finds. He gets a glass down from the shelf and pours me a glass, rifles through a few drawers as if he owns the place, then sticks a metal straw in it before putting it in front of me.

"If you can eat, you should. Whatever you can keep down is good, have you been Googling things?"

I nod reluctantly. "Everyone has something to say."

"And yet everyone is still different. Willa didn't get sick really, but was fatigued the whole pregnancy."

"She was?"

How did he know this? Why didn't I notice? I wear my unwell-ness on my skin, in the form of greenish pallor and plum circles under my eyes. I look like death, which is probably another reason Maxim has been hovering so much.

"There's medicine for this, Ness was on it. Go to a doctor, you need to be able to eat and sleep so the baby can grow. The medicine will help you."

"She still has some? Pills?"

Nate takes a bite of bagel and nods.

"Great, can you bring them to me?"

"I think sharing prescriptions is illegal," he says.

I stare unblinking at him until he's done chewing, and the irony of what he said dawns on him.

He rolls his eyes. "Right. You don't care."

Greta makes her sleepy appearance, jumping onto the counter and meowing at Nate who just melts for the cat, scratching her so enthusiastically that her fur ends up floating in tiny clumps around them as they fall to the shiny countertop.

"I promise I'll go to Dr. Judd," I say. She's Willa and Vanessa's doctor, a completely lovely woman. Not Italian, but she's family enough by now. My dad trusted her. "But not yet, okay? Soon."

"You have three days before I tell your sister, and that's generous."

"Asshole," I mutter. Three days is generous, though. He can't keep secrets from my sister for shit. He told me and Leo he was planning something great for a proposal, but the day he picked up the ring, he got too excited and proposed as soon as she got home.

"So can we go get the drugs? Like now." I nod down at his car keys. He's still driving that old banged up Prius, though he promised my sister he'd upgrade to one of the bigger, safer cars when the baby is born.

Nate looks at Greta like she'll be sympathetic to what he has to put up with. She rubs her head on his cheek and he melts all over again.

"Nate," I snap. He sighs and gives the cat one last loud kiss on the head before taking his keys and half of his bagel with him in the direction of the elevator.

"If you throw up in the Prius, I'll never forgive you."

35

—————

MARY

THE MEDICINE IS CALLED Zofran and it helps immensely. By the time Maxim came home to share dinner, I was able to eat for once and did not fear I was going to throw up. I was still tired, though, from all the not sleeping I've been doing, so when I sat down on the couch next to a reading Maxim, I fell directly to sleep. When I woke, I was alone on the couch, but now with a pillow under my head, a blanket tucked in around me, and Greta two inches away from suffocating me on my chest.

It was darker, the house quiet, and there were no signs of Maxim who, last I remembered, I had been using as a pillow.

On the coffee table, I found a note written in his surprisingly neat cursive that read, *Dealing with trouble at the Brickyard. Sleep well.*

And, reasonably, since I haven't felt this healthy in three weeks, I grab the keys to one of Maxim's cars and head straight over. I'm still wearing his shirt and a pair of bike shorts, so by no means club attire, but the bouncer doesn't bat an eye before he lets me in with a polite, "Good to see you, Mrs. Orlov."

I don't find Maxim in his office upstairs, but as I'm trekking back down to the main floor, Sasha finds me at the bottom of the stairs. His sleeves are rolled up, shirt unbuttoned a few times, and his hair mussed, too.

"Hot date?" I yell loud enough for him to hear over the music.

"I wish."

"Have you been fighting?"

"Something like that." He jerks his head toward the hall next to the bar and I follow him there. It's the same way Maxim led me on Christmas Eve when I was having a panic attack. I'm calm now, collected, albeit curious.

Instead of the back door to the alley, we turn left and descend two flights of stairs and Sasha opens a thick metal door using a code I don't see him enter but am sure he would tell me if I asked.

I've never seen this room before, but I know right away that Nate would call it Maxim's murder dungeon or his demonic torture chamber. Really it looks like a storage room, some walls of shelves, a concrete floor slightly sloped to a drain, a big sink in the corner. There is a man strapped down to a metal chair in the middle of the room, and *that's* what gives it away, really.

There is also blood dripping from his jaw, so that really seals it.

The restrained man catches sight of me and laughs. If I squint, I can almost recognize him. Low-level Orlov crony, if I had to guess.

"You called in your bitch to finish the job?" The man asks, and I recoil, but smile. This just got a *lot* more fun.

Maxim looks over his shoulder seeing me with Sasha, and his posture goes rigid before he turns back to the man and unleashes a fierce slap that sends more blood and probably one of the man's teeth onto the floor.

I tut and waltz up to the scene, stopping at Maxim's side with a hand on his shoulder. He shakes lightly, perhaps from the beating he's been giving, but more likely from rage barely kept beneath the surface of his skin.

"Who's this?" I ask.

The knock made the man dizzy, but he rights his head on his neck after a few moments of saliva and blood dripping from his lip.

"Mikhail Kozlov."

"He looks old," I say.

"Not much older than your husband," Kozlov taunts, and I grin.

"My husband wears it much better," I say. I turn my attention to Maxim. "What did he do?"

The man must've really pissed him off for Maxim to be here bloodying his knuckles instead of at home softly snoring on the couch. Beating up a mobster in a murder basement feels like it toes the line of the enforcer work that Maxim seems to think he and I are so far above, but duty calls.

"Nothing!" Kozlov shouts. He spits, blood and saliva landing on the ground next to his chair. "As I was explaining, it was just business."

My eyebrows jump in amusement. *It's just business*, being said by anyone other than the boss is a sure way to tell that they were getting up to shit they shouldn't be.

"So you're an entrepreneur," I say. I wrap an arm around Maxim's waist and rest my head on his bicep. Every bit of him is tense, practically vibrating with the anger twinging through his body. "Cute of you."

The description annoys the bound man, but he has some desperate hope in his eyes while he talks to me, like I might take his side and convince Maxim to take it easy on him. Like *I'm* the merciful one of the two of us.

"It's a good opportunity," he explains. "I swear I was going to tell you—I just had to try it out first to make sure it was viable."

"And what was this little start up then?" I ask. "And don't say crypto."

"*Selling. Girls,*" Maxim spits through clenched teeth. My stomach drops, though I don't let it show on my face.

"What kind of girls?" I ask.

"See?" Kozlov's face alights with more hope. "That's the thing, they're not even from the states, we bring them in."

"How old?"

"Twenties," he says, then amends, "most of them at least."

Kids, is what he's saying.

Facing *children*, ripped from their homes and brought to another country without their families so that rich men can do God only knows what with them. It makes me feel sick all over again.

Vanessa confessed that Cillian was mad that we were too virtuous for those markets and that we were wrong to think weapons were any less dangerous than selling real humans and their various body parts. There's money in that, but as Dad always said, "The cost of such business is your very soul."

"You told him no?" I ask Maxim. His eyes meet mine, a slight question in his and I nod just barely, imploring him to trust me. "Could be good money."

"Money we would of course give you your share of," Kozlov says. His tone of spitting and calling me a bitch has changed now that he thinks of me as a potential ally.

I've never gotten to play the good cop before, usually just my face inspires fear, but this man doesn't seem to know me. For once, my reputation really does not precede me other than the wife of a powerful man.

"Give me the financial spark notes," I say, and he does, listing sums well in the eight figures over the next six months. The prospect makes me want to gag, but I just keep my hand on Maxim's waist, squeezing ever tighter as the man goes on. "Quite the ordeal. And complicated. Who do we have to thank for this operation?" I ask.

The man looks nervous at the line of questioning, bites his lower lip then winces remembering too late that it's busted. There's blood on his yellow teeth.

"Tell her or I shoot you," Maxim demands.

"Colton Tenneson," he confesses. Maxim's shoulders move with a quick inhale. He's surprised to hear this, and so am I. Last I saw or heard about Tenneson was our brief stay in Mexico. The man is clean as far as I know. Well, as clean as a multi-millionaire can be. He's got money to throw around, but he's not tied to a crime family. At least not the Morellis or the Donovanns, and I didn't think he was under the Orlov's protection.

"Quite the extracurricular," I murmur. "What team do you propose for this?"

He names three men I've never heard of, but when I look back at Sasha, he inclines his head, familiar with them. "They're ready to start, and I promise we weren't trying to cut you out, *Pakhan*."

Oh so *now* he wants to be respectful.

"It's what your father would've done," Kozlov says, sounding so solemn and righteous about it. "We honor him by trying to grow the wealth of the *Bratva*."

"Well, in that case," I say with false cheer, and retrieve the pistol from the holster on Maxim's shoulder, aiming at the man and firing without hesitation.

My ears ring from the sound, swimming in the room which is otherwise quiet. Maxim's mouth has fallen open as he looks at the now dead man.

I click on the safety and return the gun. When Maxim still hasn't looked away from the gruesome sight, I raise a palm to lightly touch his cheek and urge his gaze toward me.

"Hey," I whisper. "Take me to your office?"

Maxim is no stranger to death, I think he was about to kill the man himself when I arrived, but he'd gone preternaturally still when Kozlov spoke of Maxim's father.

"Come on."

He nods and leads me away from the dead body, not the way we came, but the opposite direction to another stairwell which we scale three flights until he pushes open a door which turns out to be attached to a bookcase in his dark office.

He immediately stalks over to the fireplace and flips the switch to light it, kneeling briefly by the flames and staring into them. I don't know what solace he finds in fire, if it's a comfort he feels from watching the dancing burn or a craving to succumb to the chaos.

Unbidden, an image of him thrusting his hand into the fire flits across my mind and I squeeze my eyes shut for a moment in an attempt to clear it.

It does nothing to make the image go away, so I cross the room to his side and put a hand on his shoulder to comfort him as much as it is to appease my own anxiety that he'll do something I know he wouldn't do.

He's wearing the watch I gave him, and me the necklace he gave me.

"Are you mad?" I ask.

"Yes," he says.

"At me?" I clarify, and he gives an almost-laugh. There's no levity to it.

"No."

Maxim stands, my hand holding his shirt's fabric as he does, still gripping him as he towers over me this close. "If not you, I would've done it. Probably sooner. I wouldn't have gotten those names."

"You can't catch a break," I say. "Was your life this dramatic before you married me?"

His eyes soften for a moment before whatever haunts him resurfaces with a vengeance, his face paling as he side steps me and crosses the room. I don't follow.

"We'll take care of it," I assure him. "He'll be an example not to get into business without your approval. I can call Nessa's girl at the feds and leave a tip about Tenneson, and then we can forget all about it."

"He was right," Maxim says, not facing me. "About my father. It's what he would've wanted. It makes me sick."

"He's gone," I say. "What he would've wanted doesn't matter."

"He won't *die*." Rage bubbles over on Maxim's face before he launches a half filled glass against the wall closest to him.

We both watch it shatter, my gasp loud in the heavy quiet of the office. He looks down at his hand like it's foreign to him, horror showing on his face. I rush to him and take his shaking hand in both of mine.

"It's okay," I soothe, unsure what torrent of emotions races through his mind, only wanting to ease the thoughts which I can almost *see* spiral him some place darker. He looks haunted at the broken glass on the floor. "We'll clean it up."

"I'm like him."

"You're not," I say, firm.

"I am, he raised me to be just like him, he made me do awful things, Marianna, I am no better than him."

"You are better than him. Better than me, even. He never would have aligned himself with my family, he probably would've tried to kill Vanessa ten times over by now."

"I've killed plenty." He sounds desperate, whether for me to understand or for this to not be true, I don't know, but I hold his hand tighter.

"*So have I.* Just now! I didn't think twice about it. We've all had to do horrible things to survive, to protect ourselves and the people we care about. It's not like we do this for fun."

"What is the reason for all of this? This killing, people selling other people in our own city, my wife having to fight and to murder to protect this bloody fucking empire?"

"It's not the empire, it's *you*," I say without forethought, confessing too much. "It's you I want to protect, Maxim. Like you want to protect me. That's why we do this, because we don't have another choice. If we don't, that's it. The end of everything."

His face, normally so stern and solid, has twisted in anguish as he studies mine.

"I hate myself for who he made me. Hate that this was the inheritance I had to take," Maxim whispers, and my heart aches for him. I pull the hand I've been holding to the side of my face, and he holds on like I hoped he would, sliding his fingers through my hair.

"I don't hate you," I say. "Your father would've killed me if I'd spoken to him like I've spoken to you. And still you treat me like I'm something precious."

The very thought makes the cocktail of treacherous emotions on my husband's face even stormier. "You are."

"He's dead, Maxim. Stop letting him hurt you."

Maxim takes a shaky breath and lets out a huge exhale before pressing his forehead against mine. I close my eyes and hold onto his wrist as his thumb swipes against my cheek in a way that's become too familiar, too comforting.

"You're *good*, Maxim. You're not all rotten."

After another moment of our heads pressed together, he exhales again.

"Careful. You're starting to sound like you like me," he echoes. I can't help my lips curving into a relieved smile.

"Only sometimes. Only a little."

"Oh, Mary." Maxim shakes his head against mine. Somehow, after calling me Marianna for so long, the nickname feels foreign and all the more intimate coming from his lips. "Don't you ever tire of the work it takes to pretend you care so little?"

"I don't care much," I say, but even now I'm thinking of how I can help him feel better. How I can convince him that his monstrous parts don't make up a treacherous whole. That he's fine exactly how he is, wonderful, even.

I can feel his breath on my lips, so it's not a jump for me to close the distance and press mine to his. This helped me when I was spiraling in the kitchen, kissing him in the all-consuming way that we tend to. I'm hopeful the same can be true for him now.

He lets out a sound almost like a whine, and deepens the kiss, using his other arm to tangle me closer to him, lifting me a few inches from the ground as he does. The front of his shirt twists in my grip while he turns, depositing me on the desk, where I part my legs to let him closer.

"Darling." He exhales, and kisses me deeper still, his tongue intense in the fight against my own.

"I know," I say, my voice coming out way too high and needy. I don't know, actually, only that it's always this intense with him, always consuming and enlivening—the kind of thing I used to fruitlessly seek in his club. I wanted to escape my incessant running thoughts and feel alive in my body, but it was hollow then.

With him, it's different. Like every time we are together like this we are discovering something the rest of the world hasn't yet.

So I do the thing we do best. I slide my hands between us and fiddle with his belt and button until his pants are open.

"Stop that," he growls, and grips my wrists.

I try to free my hands, but he holds tighter, pulling my hands behind my back.

"Why?"

"I need to tell you."

"You *don't*." I try to kiss him again; if I can just kiss him, it will distract him from whatever he's on about, but he keeps just out of reach of my mouth.

Slowly, he walks me backwards, and I don't resist as he lies me back on his desk. Once my head is on the wood, he presses my hands above me, and trails one callused palm down my arm, stopping once he reaches my chest and squeezing before carrying on.

"I love you," he says.

The words cause panic to course through me, but his grip tightens on my wrist, pinning me where I am stretched out beneath him.

"You don't—" I say, and I mean *You can't. I can't.*

Our lower bodies are pressed together and I feel his length against me through the thin spandex of my shorts. It would be so easy for him to pull them off my legs and slide into me in the name of trying to reach a goal we've already achieved. *That* is familiar, *that* we know.

"You don't know me." I attempt to speak evenly, but I'm still breathless and my voice wavers on the last word.

"I do." Maxim brings his face so close above mine that I can look nowhere else. His breath is uneven, too. "You crave control in every situation and when you can't have it, you lash out. You pretend you hate everyone because you are afraid of them getting too close to you. You are so insanely stubborn and so fucking brave."

"Maxim," I choke, but he's just getting started.

"You are *terrified* of real intimacy because you can't stomach the thought of anyone being close enough to see you. To open yourself up to hurt. But you love harder than anyone I've ever met. You care so deeply."

"That's not true," I deny, but my throat feels tight, my eyes glassy as he goes on without relent.

"What have you been doing if not caring for me, Marianna?" He speaks with an urgency that makes me feel fragile. "Wearing my clothes, thinking of me, killing for me, taking care of me in your quiet and thoughtful ways? You may never love me, but you care, and you know I've loved you."

My breath hitches as he speaks. I can almost see how I must look in the reflection of his eyes; like a scared and cornered animal. It's how I feel, any shred of control I thought I had in this conversation completely eviscerated.

"Don't cry," he mutters so gently and wipes my cheeks. "Call it whatever you'd like, but I am yours. I love you in a way that is intense and overwhelming. I think I'll die from the presence you have in my chest, from the worry that something could happen to you when I'm not there."

"No."

"I *do*. I have, For months now, probably since before the wedding—since you came into my life like a tornado, tossing everything up and spinning it around. Of course I've loved you."

"I hate you." My voice breaks, and I close my eyes tightly. I pray he believes me while I also pray he sees right through me to the truth I cannot voice. That I've never hated him, never been able to. I never stood a chance in the fight against falling for him.

Maxim only exhales and touches me with that same tenderness, his thumb tracing the line of my jaw then my lower lip.

"You can hate me," he says. "Just hate me from here."

Idly, I do wonder how many times I must push him away before his resolve breaks? Is that what I've been testing in constantly needling him? Pushing into his feelings like a bruise to see at what point I become so insufferable that he'll see what I believe about myself? That only those bound by blood are capable of loving me, or tolerating me?

I am desperate for him to stay, to call my bluff, but I don't know how to admit this, how to tell him how much I want him to stay.

Maxim releases my wrists and rubs them where he'd been holding them in place. His other hand cradles my skull, pressing my face to his shoulder. I sniffle against the black fabric that smells like him and even smells like me now.

"Hate me from our home, our bed, our kitchen over tea—hate me all you want. You never have to love me."

"I cannot keep you safe if I love you," I admit. "There's no room."

"I wouldn't ask you to. I watch your back and you watch mine. The entire world doesn't have to be on your shoulders. You can share the weight."

I bite my tongue, not ready to say anything more, but nod again and wrap my arms around his neck. He lifts us and holds me tight against him for long minutes, until my eyes are dry and the music downstairs has died for the night.

36

MAXIM

I LEFT for work before Marianna woke this morning. I placed a note next to where she drooled slightly onto my pillow and pressed a long kiss to the side of her head. Greta meowed softly, so I scratched her head and kissed her too before leaving them to sleep.

Marianna's been tired lately, dark circles under her eyes and an uncharacteristic downward slope to her shoulders. I'm not going to be the one to interrupt any extra sleep she can get.

I already texted Sasha that he's with her today, whatever her plans are, and now drive to meetings downtown in the back of the town car. Samuel brought me coffee this morning which is a rare, but not unheard of, generosity.

"Sir," Samuel says while I press send on an email on my phone. I slide it in my chest pocket and look to the front of the car.

"Yes?"

"I promised to keep Mary safe," he says, with all the gravity in the world in the sentence. I tilt my head, meet his eye in the rear view mirror before his flick back to the road. "The day I met her you asked me to protect her no matter what, and I intend to keep that promise to you."

I soften and nod. I would guess she has become as dear to him as she has to Sasha, to Elise, to anyone who lives for any time in her closest orbit.

"Thank you, Samuel."

I smile before reaching for the cup of coffee and taking a long sip. I used to pretend that Samuel was my father instead of my own, this nice quiet man who's been a steady presence in my life for decades now, driving me from one place to the next in my young adulthood through now. He was much younger when I first met him, somewhere in his thirties.

The coffee is sweeter than usual, but doesn't bother me. The city slides by outside the tinted windows.

I watch cars move on the bridge beside us and realize we're going in the opposite direction to the hotel I'm supposed to be at in twelve minutes. How long have we been driving? Thirty minutes almost?

I take another gulp of coffee.

I must've told him the wrong location, but now that I think back, I am certain I didn't.

"Samuel?" I say, but my tongue is thick in my mouth as I speak. I clear my throat and try again. "I think we're meant to be headed west." My words sound slurred, not as sharp as they are in my head, and I'm unsteady in my confusion.

The car makes a sharp turn and a tire dips into a hole, jostling me. The coffee slips from my hand, falling to the floor of the backseat and spilling, but when I try to reach for it, my arm is too heavy, my hand not flexing.

"Pull over," I slur, something very wrong. My head is spinning, vision tunneling as my thoughts race over the situation.

"I will protect her, sir," he says. "Believe me that I will."

I try to look at him in his mirror, but nothing is where it should be. Before I can call for help, reach for my phone, tell him something is wrong, I'm tumbling headfirst into a heavy blackness.

308

37

———

MARY

MAXIM'S NOTE promised he would be out past dinner, so I took Sasha to my sister's house where everyone was gathered for an early pasta dinner. I maybe wouldn't have invited him if he wasn't sworn to permanent guard duty since the little home invasion episode, but everyone likes Sasha. He can gossip with the best of them, and he and Leo run in similar circles. He went to school with Willa and Sean, too, so they always are thrilled to have him around.

Maxim doesn't call or message, not during dinner, nor when Leo unveils a cobbler he made, nor when the credits roll on the new superhero movie that Artie insisted we watch before he fell asleep halfway through.

I feel Maxim's absence from my side or line of sight. In all his hovering since the break-in, I haven't felt smothered. He's a nice presence to have around, mindful of me, eyes watching, making me another cup of tea when mine runs empty, slathering too much butter on a piece of toast before bed.

Sasha drives us home after another serving of cobbler heated up in the microwave, but my phone is still quiet. It's nearly eight.

"Has he messaged you?" I ask.

Sasha's brows furrow. "He hasn't messaged you?"

"No."

We stop at a light and he glances at his phone. "Nothing."

We sit quiet for a moment, rolling through the night time traffic.

"Meeting should've been over by now," Sasha points out, and dials Maxim, whose phone sends him straight to voicemail. I try too, and am met with the same.

Sasha calls Jean who answers on the first ring.

"Jean here."

"Hi, you seen Maxy?" Sasha asks.

Jean is quiet on the other side of the line for a moment, then, "Not since he left this morning." We hear clicking of his keyboard through the car speaker. "No scans into the apartment since you and Mrs. Mary left."

"Hm," Sasha says. "Thank you, Jean."

He calls Samuel next who doesn't pick up on the first or second try.

We sit quietly in the car, stewing on the radio silence from Maxim.

"Should we check the Brickyard?" Sasha asks, already turning left down the street to take us in that direction.

I chew on the corner of my thumb, but then remember the germs and clench my hands in my lap to stop messing with them. I squint out the windshield and run through the situation instead of panicking. He didn't go alone, he had Samuel nearby. It's not unheard of for him to be out late—so much crime happens under the shade of night for a reason—but not messaging either of us isn't his way.

I gasp, remembering that I have a way of knowing exactly where he is.

"What?"

"The watch," I say, already pulling out my phone and navigating to the tracking app I've yet to use.

"What watch?"

"The wedding watch," I say like this should be obvious. "I put a tracker in it."

Sasha looks flabbergasted by this, but whistles a long low tone. "You're nuts, Mary. Brilliant, but nuts."

"Please, Maxim would've done the same if he thought of it first."

"He did," Sasha says, and shoots a quick pointed look at my chest. I scrunch my nose but follow his gaze to the gold necklace Maxim gave me, his own wedding present. "You're made for each other."

I hold the warm pendant for a moment in my palm. I should feel betrayed, or hurt, or slighted like he didn't trust me, but I feel only softness in my chest for the gesture.

"Well?" He nudges when I've been sitting sappy for too long.

I drop the pendant and look back at the little map on my phone, scanning until I locate the blue pulsing blue dot. I zoom in, confused by what I'm seeing.

"It says he's by the East Shipyard. Did he say he was going over there today?"

"No," Sasha says, hands tightening on the steering wheel as he turns the car in a U-turn to change our route. I sit back in my seat and watch the blue blinking dot, unmoving on the screen.

"Fuck. Is it a building he's in?" Sasha asks, no shortage of concern evident in his voice. "Zoom in further."

I plug my phone into the car and turn on the navigation. Seeing where it's leading us, he curses again.

"That fucking building. Did you call your sister's guy at the CIA about Tenneson?"

"A woman," I correct. "Yeah, I sent a note last night. Why?"

"How did you send it?"

"I sent a guy to give her the note on her morning run. Why?" His intensity about this makes me feel like there's something I really should know but have been left out of.

"And was it actually delivered?"

"Yeah." I chew on my lower lip. Last I heard, she did get the message, but that's usually as far as our communication goes. It's not safe otherwise. It's up to her now what she does with it. "What is this place anyway?"

Sasha's hands tighten on the steering wheel as he speeds up. "It's an old textile factory."

SASHA DIDN'T EVEN NEED the blinking dot to lead us to the abandoned factory by the water. I don't see any lights in the building from where we sit in the quiet car up the street, but I can see some cars parked on the far side of it.

"I've got a very bad feeling about this," Sasha says.

"Me too." I pick at a hangnail and click my tongue against my teeth when I pull too far and start to bleed.

Every part of me is itching to rush in there guns blazing, but I remember the creature in my abdomen that my app has informed is now the size of a kidney bean. Nate's lecture about not doing things alone bumps around my brain.

Because I indeed *can* be taught, I force a calm exhale and dial Leo. He answers on the third ring. It's loud as hell through the line, though, so I know he's out somewhere.

"Give me a sec," he says and I try my best not to snap that I don't have a sec and wait.

"Where are you?" I ask when it grows marginally quieter on his side of the phone.

"Just got to Leroy's, why?"

"Have you been drinking? I need you to come to the textile factory by the East shipyard. I think there's trouble."

"Shit," he mutters, but I hear footsteps and the beeping of his car so I know he's already on his way. "Did you call Sean?"

"No, I need you to. I'll call Ness."

"Where's Max?"

"That's the problem," I say. "Get here."

I hang up before immediately calling Ness, whose phone rings all the way to voicemail, and Nate's is the same. They're probably already sleeping because they're boring and go to sleep early. I call Nate's phone again, and on the second try, he answers.

"*Yellow*," he says in that way of his.

"Where are you?"

"Bubble bath," he says, and I can't tell if he's joking or not. I'm suddenly gripped with fear at the prospect of telling him the situation. He's so good, the best Morelli, I think, or at least the most wholesome. He's so excited to be a father, he's such a baby hog as is, it's going to make his whole life. And Vanessa is *pregnant*, for Christ's sake. More pregnant than me. I shouldn't bother them with this.

It's not safe for them. It's—

"Mar?" Nate asks. I blink, closing my mouth and swallowing. Sasha looks at me with ducked eyebrows.

The entire world doesn't have to be on your shoulders. You can share the weight.

I take a long breath. Nate's about to hang up when I finally speak. "I'm sending you an address, I need you to get there as soon as you can. It might be nothing, but—"

"Should we call in more guys?" he asks without missing a beat.

I take another breath. "Yes."

"Drop the location," he says, and then mutters an abbreviated form of the message to Vanessa. "Okay, I'll be there soon. Love you," he says before the line goes dead.

I sit in the quiet for a moment before looking to Sasha and giving a nod. Backup is already on the way, from the two I called and the messages Sasha sent. Maxim is probably in there having a meeting and it will be fine, no drama, no dead bodies, just a normal Sunday night.

I lower my window and force myself to relax in my seat. "Now we wait."

We are a solid fifty-five seconds into anxiously waiting when the unmistakable sound of a gunshot goes off in the direction of the building.

"*Shit*." I'm already pulling open my door, and Sasha is doing the same. No more time to wait.

He leads the way down the block and I peer around his big shoulders, my hands holding my gun ready and pointed to the ground. He keeps one hand on the Glock at his hip.

This part of the street is quiet, mostly industrial buildings, not even ones with apartments on top of them. A street light flickers pale white light as we approach the lot. A segment of the chain link fence has been unlatched and lies on its side, flat on the ground. We step carefully around it to not rattle the metal chain links.

My stomach roils, remembering this time last year when instead of an old factory, Nate, Leo, Vanessa and I approached a half-built office building in the dead of night. I was shot that night and the scar almost burns at the memory.

We are always getting ourselves in fucking *situations*.

It might be nice to have just a single month with zero situations; no crises for us to handle, no empty buildings to crawl around in the middle of the night, no weapon drops resulting in black eyes.

All of the lights appear to be off through the broken factory windows, but we hear voices around the far side of the building. It would be too risky to just waltz over there, so we find what was once a tall window and climb through the opening.

The factory floor is dusty concrete with various detritus strewn everywhere. Moonlight shines into the space well enough that we can make out a clear-ish path to the far side of the space where a hallway and offices reside, both empty so far as I can tell.

"Maxim is going to fucking kill me," Sasha mutters, and I roll my eyes. I also feel stressed about Maxim's worry, but it's not in my nature to let on.

Plus, I figure if he's in trouble, he'll probably forgive me for saving him. Might not forgive Sasha though.

"Yeah well he can't kill you if he's already dead, can he?"

"Don't say that."

I flex my fist at my side, no more keen than he is to imagine my husband dead.

We walk quietly on, heel to toe keeping in mind not to stomp over the abandoned pieces of wood and metal on the ground. There's a set of metal stairs we climb, trying to be slow, but they creak anyway, making us tense with every step. On the second floor overlooking the factory, there's a row of small offices and closets, along with a short hallway.

We can now hear the voices from outside through a metal door at the end of said hall, warm light filtering through the crack at the bottom.

This feels like we're in a haunted house, just waiting for something to jump out at us at any second. I'm strung so tight, I'd probably shoot first, ask questions later.

There's an office to our left, one with an old desk and the kind of vintage chair that I know Willa would love if only it was in good shape and priced way too high at an antique shop. Behind the desk is a big window looking out over the factory's garage, and as I inch slowly inside, I can see more of the lower level.

There's a group of six men, most of which I do not recognize. As I look longer, though, I realize with a sinking in my gut, that there are familiar faces among them.

"Motherfuckers," Sasha spits, still whispering. He gets out his phone and sends off a series of texts while I squint down at the faces. Nikolai, most notably, stands with his hands in his pockets. As unfortunate as it is to see him here, it doesn't surprise me. It's the face next to him that has me gasping. *Samuel* sits in a metal chair, elbows on his knees looking uneasy.

"Samuel—"

"He wouldn't," Sasha says, and he sounds so sure. The concern clouding his eyes speaks a different story, though.

"What are they looking at?"

They're all facing something under the lip of the balcony that we can't see, watching something unravel with smug satisfaction, though it looks like it's turning Samuel's stomach.

"We can't go this way. They'll see us," I say. "Best thing we can do is retrace our steps, wait for backup, and enter via that door." I point to an exterior door in the far right corner, all of their bodies pointed away from it.

Sasha agrees, sending off a text to his people while I do the same in a message to the family group chat. Leo and Sean like the message in response.

"Let's do it then," I say, already backing out of the office, when the metal doors at the end of the hall bangs open, footsteps sounding with them. Sasha and I both freeze, still concealed mostly in the office, but my leg is sticking out of the door.

As silently as I can, I pull it back into the office, trying not to breathe or make a sound.

"I told you he was made of steel," a man with a heavy Russian accent says.

"Everyone has their limits," another voice says, this one feminine.

Sasha and I make startled eye contact, both recognizing the voice.

"He will quickly reach his when we find *her*," she says. She sounds calculating and confident, so much so that I could almost pretend it's not who I'm certain it is.

"She still hasn't shown up at the penthouse," the man says. I'm startled to realize they're talking about me.

"Did you check her sister's?" Their steps and voices are exceptionally close to the office now and I'm afraid I'm going to have to shoot them if they try to come in here. They halt at a door across the hall, pulling it open with a squeak.

"Which one? Both of them scare the shit out of me," the man confesses. "Plus, all those guard dogs."

I am guessing he means Leo, Sean, and maybe even Nate—which I will never tell him because his ego would be through the roof and I don't think he needs that.

"The boss. Vanessa. If Mary's not at home, I am almost certain she's there."

"I'll make a call."

"Do," the woman says, and shuts the door she'd just opened. A closet, if I had to guess. "Now, Logan. Have you ever tried waterboarding?"

I would laugh at how outrageously and casually evil the question sounds if I didn't think it had lethal intent for *my* husband.

They shuffle back down the hallway to the metal door they came from, and once it closes behind them, I let out a shaky exhale, Sasha doing the same.

"Was that?" He sounds distressed.

"It was her," I confirm, certain.

"But she—" Sasha trails off, then shakes his head. "*Fuck.*"

I stop myself from saying something insensitive.

Elise is *dead* is what she is.

I don't care how many times she's made delicious meals for us, or laughed over the kitchen island, Elise will die for this.

The thought makes me sadder than I'd like to admit, a loss I don't typically feel alongside these determined feelings of rage and vengeance.

It's betrayal. Something akin to what I felt when we found out about Cillian. But he was family. Elise, well, she and I weren't as close as she and Sasha and Maxim, but I had fondness built in the penthouse over weeks of Thursdays and Sundays.

"Come on," I tell him. I'm ready to stride right back where we came from, only to be startled to a halt at the resounding pop of a gun near me.

I duck and look around, eyes landing at the end of the hall where Elise stands holding a pistol up, a half smile on her face. Her eyes are wide and elated, that bright blonde princess hair braided over her shoulder.

I lift my own gun to shoot, but she screams, "I'll kill him!" and I freeze. I'm not sure who she means, but my mind stutters on the thought of her killing Maxim.

She nods to my left and I glance in the direction of her pointed gun. Sasha is there on the ground, groaning in a growing puddle of his blood. My stomach drops at the sight, and I want to go to him, but Elise might kill me or him or both of us if I do.

"I'll shoot him in the head, Mary. I really will."

I want to call her bluff, say she isn't that good of a shot, she'll miss and I can get her down first. The door opens behind her before I can, bright light flooding the space as another man holds a gun in our direction. I could take out one of them, I know it, but then they might shoot Sasha and even if I can't see where the bullet landed, his lack of fight on the ground tells me another shot *would* kill him.

"Drop it, Mary," Elise calls, her voice sharp when she says my name.

Sasha coughs next to me.

"Shoot her," he says in a pained voice. I can't let him die, I will not, so I turn on the safety and let the gun drop to the floor. I like Sasha too much—another person I didn't mean to care for —and even the thought of Maxim hurting like I did when Vanessa was taken is enough to make the decision without hesitating.

"Kick it behind you," the man commands in the same heavy Russian accent as before. I do as he says, using the toe of my boot to kick the gun behind me.

Elise gives a sweet smile. "He's going to cuff you, but if you give him trouble, I *will* shoot Alexei. Do not test me."

I nod, knowing I could best the Nate-sized man in fifteen fights, but not sure how to do so without first getting Sasha killed.

"Don't listen, Mary," he says through labored breaths. "Get the fuck out of here."

"I'm not leaving you, little fucker," I bite through gritted teeth.

"Maxim will kill me if she doesn't first," he says, and the pleading in his voice is so heavy it makes my eyes water with his sense of self-sacrifice. I stay firm in my decision and lift my hands higher in surrender.

I look up at Elise and nod again, doing as she says, gritting my teeth while the man stalks toward me and pulls my hands into cuffs that he clips too tightly on my wrists.

He pushes between my shoulder blades and I stumble forward before righting myself and walking on ahead of him. Sasha groans behind me and I can only pray that someone will come find him in here—one of the people we called.

God, please not Sasha, Maxim's only brother and best friend. My heart aches leaving him here, but I go forward anyway.

"What's in this for you, then?" I ask her.

"Simple," Elise winks at me. "I get to be married to the boss."

I give her a look that I hope encapsulates me with equal disgust and confusion. "Maxim?"

Elise laughs, her sweet musical laugh, but it's poison now. "No, Mary. You ruined him."

She leads me across the threshold into the garage area, and Elise whistles, drawing all eyes from the lower level to us.

Samuel pales when he sees me, and he drops his face into his palms. Nikolai smiles.

"Maxy, you got a visitor," Nikolai yells. The man shoves me not-so-gently forward, and we descend the metal stairs, my hands bound tightly behind my back.

The six men I saw before are strewn in a semi-circle, some standing, others sitting in rusted metal chairs. They all have guns, except for Samuel who just has his apparent despair. Nikolai winks at me as I walk past him and I spit on him, earning me a firm shove from the man behind me.

When I can finally see what the previous position hid from view, my stomach lurches.

Maxim, my Maxim, is slumped in a chair, his arms and legs restrained, his head lolling to the side. Next to his chair is a short folding table, the kind of set up I would recognize anywhere. They've been torturing him.

There's a lot of blood, too much, I think, because any amount of blood outside of his body is too much. There are two slices down the side of his face, straight lines that leak blood down his neck and over the unbuttoned collar of his shirt.

A pained whimper escapes me, a sound I didn't know I could make. I pick up my pace and cross the space between us until I can drop to my knees beside him. I duck my head to try to meet his eyes, which I find closed. I wish I could touch him, feel for his pulse, hold him close to me, stitch him back together, but I can only nudge his thigh with my shoulder and say his name over and over until he opens his eyes, the deep blue wells looking lost before they train on my face.

He looks confused, but relieved. And then, perhaps realizing the situation I've found myself in, he looks absolutely overcome with sadness.

"No," Maxim whispers, his voice so hoarse.

"It's okay, you're okay," I mutter quickly. "We're okay."

None of this is true, and he knows it, pain awash over his beautiful face. But he is breathing and that is enough right now. Broken as he looks, he is alive, alive, alive. I don't see any gunshot wounds, or otherwise massive injuries. Mostly topical.

A long, loud laugh bursts from behind Maxim, from the space I didn't even care to look after I'd found my husband, but I now see a man wearing a suit, laughing like the scene before him is hilarious. A man I last saw in Mexico.

Colton Tenneson.

"She came right to us?" he says through laughter. "How did you find us? No really, tell me."

My nostrils flare as I take him in; luxury suit, hair perfectly slicked back, teeth that are just too straight. If Vanessa's friend in the CIA was going to move, it wasn't fast enough. They're never fast enough over there, way too much tape and paperwork.

"God, they were right, you do look scary," he says, still grinning. "Like a little feral chihuahua. Now really, how did you find us?"

I meet Maxim's eyes then look down to where his right hand is cuffed down to the chair, his wrist stained a rusty red from fighting against the bonds. His watch sits on his wrist not ticking, the glass broken.

"I tracked him," I admit. If the situation wasn't so dire, I'd think Maxim almost looked soft at the admission that I'd planted a tracker in his watch, the same way he'd put one in my necklace.

"Trust issues, Ms. Morelli?" Tenneson muses.

"Orlov," I correct, and his insidious smile grows wider still.

"You told me it was a sham marriage," he addresses Elise where she stands behind me, her arms crossed over her chest watching the scene unfold.

"It was. For her, at least. For a while."

"You keep making this easier for me, little Mary," the man says and closes the gap between us in three quick strides of his long, scrawny legs. He lifts the toe of his leather loafer and presses it into my bad shoulder until I fall back on my heels, nearly collapsing to my ass. Maxim thrashes fruitlessly against the handcuffs, yelling, but Colton's movements are slow and deliberate. He smiles and pulls a gun from his waist before raising it to Maxim's head.

"What are you doing?" I ask, but Colton Tenneson looks unfazed.

Maxim closes his eyes in grief and agony before opening them again to look at me.

"Stop," I cry, my voice breaking.

If I could hold out my hands, I would do so in surrender to get him to stop. I am not above begging; I think I would do anything to see Maxim live through this night, anything. I'd kill, forfeit a finger, a hand, anything.

"The codes to the safes, Maxim, or your little wife watches you die."

"I won't," Maxim says, and I whimper.

"What codes? Maxim, please just—"

"Marianna," he says, his tone an apology.

"Wait, wait," Nikolai shouts from behind me. "You didn't say anything about shooting him. You said he lives."

Colton looks over my head at Nikolai. "Well, Niko, plans change."

"You need him," Samuel shouts, desperation evident in his voice. "If you kill him, he'll never be able to tell you."

Tenneson pauses, considering this, before he clicks his tongue and changes his plan, holding the gun to the next nearest skull: mine.

"*No*," Maxim roars, and Tenneson cocks the gun.

A chorus of "Woah, woah"s and "Hold on"s sing from the group behind me, but Tenneson is unyielding.

"Tell me, or I'll kill your wife."

"And don't forget the baby," Elise says, an obvious smile in her voice. I glance at her with as much derision as I can hold, which is a lot.

Maxim's face washes with shock at this news, and I wish my eyes could explain everything, how I was going to tell him, tonight even, if only he'd come home.

"A baby?" he asks, and I nod just barely.

"Yes."

"I'll tell you," Maxim says, and the room falls silent.

After a moment so tense and silent, a dozen breaths held, Tenneson smiles.

MAXIM

I'VE FELT my share of grief in my life: grief for the life my mother could've had, grief for lost family members, even grief for myself. My sister Vera got a degree in psychology and another in social work just to tell us that life is about grieving. I believe that she's right about this.

Never, though, did I know that my very soul could experience agony like this. There's a sense of grief so intense that I'm drowning in it. Regaining consciousness to find myself in the same dire circumstance, only now, my wife here with me, I felt something in me shatter. It was the thing that kept me strong, firm in my decision to not give in to corrupt men and their horrific dealings. It was her.

I believed I would die, and even still, my body is telling me that I will, but I lost any chance of it being a noble death the moment I saw her, tears staining her cheeks as she rattled me awake.

I would do anything, give anything, to keep her alive. They found the one person who, above all else, I need to survive.

And then they told me she's pregnant. I don't know how Elise knew, but really I don't know how I didn't realize it sooner. Her sickness, the fatigue, I didn't dare believe we'd actually done it. Now, the life I craved for us is dissolving rapidly in front of me.

My wife. My child. My family.

"Get that *fucking gun* away from her. I said I would tell you."

Colton's lips are twisted into a smile that turns my stomach, the kind of evil I thought died with my father. I should've known this bad would always exist on this earth, no matter how nice of a pocket I found for myself in the quiet moments holding Marianna in our bed.

"Was that so hard?" he asks. My shoulders relax marginally as he lowers the gun from her head. Behind her, Samuel slumps in relief. Nikolai even looks unsettled by Colton's display.

"Did she come alone?" Colton asks.

"Alexei was with her," Elise says, sounding almost bored. "Probably bled out by now."

My soul breaks impossibly further, and I meet Marianna's eyes which are already staring back at me. Hers say a thousand apologies, her pain reflecting my own, her concern for my sorry state and hers, her own agonies.

Colton wants one thing, and it is *everything*. He's lost his patience waiting for me to agree to work with him, to sell him properties one after another. Our killing of his inside men last night forced his hand.

After waking here this morning, he was very clear about his demands; first, he wants every deed to every property I own. He wants my will changed, transferring everything to Nikolai, who Colton knows he can use as a puppet boss. He wants to kill me and Marianna and make it look like a tragic accident.

Then he'll bring the Orlov empire to what my father used to promise him: this bloody, invincible beast for him to wield quietly behind Nikolai.

What I can't comprehend is where Elise fits into this. Or Samuel. Both of whom I trusted so thoroughly.

"I love you," I mouth to Marianna, in case I don't get to say it again.

Marianna inhales and looks at Colton.

"More are on their way," she says. Elise smirks like Marianna's admission was a mistake. I don't know why she said it, they might've been able to help us, had they gotten the element of surprise. But then again, the man I've trusted my whole adult life betrayed me in this, so who can say how many Orlovs are *really* on their way to help.

"Let me call them off," she pleads. "You don't need more bodies to clean up tonight."

Colton thinks about it, squinting at Marianna, and then turns to Elise who nods like cleaning up a lot of corpses would be more of a headache than they need.

"Call them. Now. Try anything funny and I'll cut off Maxim's ear."

Marianna nods quickly, looking full well like she believes him, which is a good impulse. The man has sliced thin lines down my jaw, side of my neck, upper chest, and biceps, cuts crisscrossing the scars my father left. A steady, lethal hand for a fucking business man.

"My phone is in my back pocket," she says by way of explanation, her hands still cuffed behind her. Elise offers a long suffering sigh before stalking over to us and pulling my wife up by the armpit and retrieving her cell phone. She holds it in front of Marianna's face to unlock it.

"Call Nate," Marianna instructs, and Elise goes through the short favorites list before it starts ringing. Nate picks up on the third ring with a hello that's cheery as ever. Sweet, strange man.

I'm surprised that Nate is the one she would call first for backup when usually she frets about him being able to protect himself.

"Hey, are you on your way?"

"Yes, traffic's a bitch, they're doing construction on the bridge," he starts, but Marianna cuts him off.

"Well, you can turn around," she says. "It was a false alarm."

A beat of silence on the other side of the phone, before he can say anything, she goes on. "I think it's, you know, the pregnancy brain. It's making me fucking crazy. Paranoid. You were right when you said it's just an old textile factory and Maxim is probably out, like, screwing around on me. I just thought he might've been in trouble."

"I'm sorry to hear that," Nate says. The conversation makes no sense to me; Nate knows I wouldn't cheat on her, he's always looked so knowing around me and Marianna. *I know love when I see it,* he told me after a family dinner once.

"Whatever. It's not like I can kill him if he's cheating on me. I knew what I was signing up for here," she says, and Colton's amusement at the conversation grows ever more. "Anyway, go ahead and call off Leo and Santi, too. I think I just need to go to the penthouse, take my nausea medicine, and sleep."

"Good plan," he agrees. "Hey, will I see you for pickleball tomorrow?"

"Wouldn't miss it."

I've never heard of pickleball, much less heard of her partaking in whatever it is.

"And Nate?" she gets out before Elise can try to end the phone call.

"Yeah, Mar?"

"Thank you. For being willing to come on such short notice. You are. . .my best friend."

Elise hangs up then, and Marianna closes her eyes for the span of a big inhale. When she opens them, she meets mine and nods.

I think if I were one of her sisters, with the secret long-spoken language, I would know what message she means to convey with that look. But if there's anyone to help us, they're called off now.

She wants to protect them, I know, but who will she let protect *her*? If not me, and not Sasha, or her family, then who?

I don't currently see a way that I survive this, and I can only pray to any holy entity that will listen that Marianna will. And that the people she just spared will recognize what she did and protect her where I cannot.

I believe they will. I have to believe they will.

"The code, Maxim."

"It's not a code," Marianna says. "He's not a fool, you think he would have anything less than bio-sensors on his safes? And only one?"

"Careful," I murmur about her sharp tone. I have two dozen shallow cuts to show how Colton feels about what he deems as disrespect.

"He married a Morelli," she says by way of explanation at Colton's blank expression. "We wouldn't let him have old tech. You need Maxim to open the safes. And you need him alive."

This surprises both him and Elise, their heads tilting in opposite directions as they try to detect the lie. It *is* a lie, but God is she convincing.

Their expressions mirroring each other, Elise and Colton Tenneson bear a striking resemblance. One I can't help but wonder how I never saw it before.

"Except for the one at home, which you need both of us for," Marianna says with a sort of tired sigh. "What, you thought it was a locker combination? A simple touchpad with a six digit code?"

That's exactly what it is, but I won't say so.

"Why didn't you mention this?" Colton barks at Nikolai.

"I don't know shit about tech safes, Dad used to say there was only the one and that the code had to be changed every ninety days," he defends.

"I haven't seen one in the house," Elise adds.

"Oh, when you were snooping around our bedroom you didn't

think to look for false panels?" Marianna says, like Elise is the most stupid woman in Boston. "I mean, what kind of operation do you think Maxim is running? He's not an amateur."

"Where are they?" Colton demands.

Marianna shrugs, pushing him. The tick of her jaw is the only thing giving away to me her apprehension when she looks like a bored brat.

Colton loses his patience, lifting his gun and shooting it once, the bullet slicing through my right foot with a white hot agony. I grunt and tumble over, the chair and cuffs the only thing keeping me up.

"Okay!" Marianna screams. "One at the club, one in the house, and another at my sister's."

"Little Mary, why must you make things so difficult? That was easy, wasn't it?"

Blood is pouring from my throbbing foot, a fresh puddle joining the dried spots from my other wounds. The blood loss and pain threatens to take my consciousness again, but I stay as focused as I can manage.

"Well, get them up then. We've got some safes to open."

Marianna holds my gaze, an apology of sorts in hers, and then they start to move us.

39

———

MARY

EVEN WITH MY BOUND HANDS, I try to help Maxim get to the car via extremely unbalanced hobbling. His arms are not cuffed, which would feel like an oversight if there weren't six men with guns trained on us as we walk. No way in hell could any of them carry Maxim and he can't very well walk with the hole they put through his foot. I feel horrible about that, but I couldn't let Tenneson think I was *too* cooperative, not when I was just being so helpful calling off the backup and telling them about the safes.

The safes that are very much not real.

My heart plummeted when the gunshot sounded, echoing everywhere in the abandoned concrete dungeon, but of all the places Tenneson could've shot Maxim, I am pretty confident that he will survive the foot injury.

If we can survive this at all.

Calling Nate and saying all that shit I would never in my *life* say was a gamble. If it doesn't pay off, we will be facing inevitable death when we get to the Brickyard to find, indeed, the old key code safe that Nikolai remembered. I have told Nate no

330

less than thirteen times that I would die before I played organized sports with him, so I *think* he got the memo.

They stick us in the back of Samuel's town car, the fucking traitor looking haunted by the whole of the situation. Nikolai is in the front seat, a gun slightly shaking but trained on me in the back in case one of us decides to try something.

Of all the seating arrangements, this one is the most ideal— like I *can't imagine my fucking luck* ideal, because Nikolai is the weakest little bitch of a man I have ever had the displeasure of meeting, and Samuel looks like he is sick with guilt over betraying his beloved Maxim.

This, I can work with.

First, though, the cuffs.

While Samuel drives the tense car out of the lot behind two much larger vehicles, I take a deep breath, and prepare to do something I loathe. On a sharp exhale, I dislocate my right thumb, biting down on my cheek so as not to grunt while it pops down and out of place. Leo's dad taught me this trick, and he and Dad bought me ice cream the first time I did it successfully. I was sixteen.

Doing this now gives me exactly enough room to wiggle my hand out of the metal cuff, though it hurts like a bitch.

When I can get my hands in front of me I brace myself and pop the thumb back into place. Maxim watches with trepidation and anguish in his tired eyes.

While Nikolai is barking orders into a cell phone, gun still held in my direction, I decide to risk stripping out of my sweater. I make Maxim lift his leg as much as he's able so I can take off his bloody shoe and use the sweater to tie as tight of a wrapping around the bullet wound as I can.

"Mary," Maxim mutters, his voice weak.

"I know it hurts, baby," I say, pulling the fabric tighter. "You just have to trust me, okay?"

"Darling." His hand falls on mine and I look up at him, his handsome face, dark blue eyes, blood caked on his cheeks and jaw.

"I love you," he says, so unbearably sad.

"I know," I say. "I know."

"I wish you hadn't come for me."

"I'm not letting them kill you." I close the gap between us and press my lips to his gingerly to not upset the wounds. "Okay? You're old but you're not that old. I need you for like fifty years at least, we can revisit you sacrificing yourself for me when you're ninety."

"I—"

I kiss him again, more insistent this time, before I pull away looking at him, imploring him to try to trust me.

"I could've sworn you were a lesbian," Nikolai says, phone call over. His gun is still pointed at me, still slightly shaking. I refrain from rolling my eyes and turn to look at him. "I seen you kiss a girl before at Leroy's last year."

"Yeah, well I contain multitudes," I snipe. I reach across Maxim's chest and pull the seat belt out until I can buckle it across his body. I do the same for me before turning back to Nikolai who is looking at the cuffs dangling from my wrist like I must be a magician of some kind.

He must decide that me having use of both hands isn't that much of a threat when he has a gun pointed at me, because he says nothing.

"Safety first," I muse. He scoffs before reaching back and wrestling his own seatbelt on.

We're still twenty minutes from the Brickyard at least, more if we take the bridge.

"I knew you were a weak snake, Niko, but I didn't think you were stupid enough to let Elise string you along." It's another gamble. When she said she would be married to the boss and that boss wouldn't be Maxim, I used the process of elimination to land on the only other Orlov the Russians would accept.

"Oh please," he says. "Like you know anything."

I smile, though my entire insides are tense with the act I'm putting on. "I know she's using you as a pawn of epic proportions."

His forehead crinkles with his glare. "She's not."

My smile morphs into something genuine, because he sounds *too* defensive. He's shown his hand—his festering insecurity given a name, an outsider confirming his suspicions.

"Not that it's any of your business, but we're getting married."

I laugh out loud, a sharp, high thing, and hope it doesn't sound forced. "Oh, Niko."

Samuel is shooting me nervous glances in the rearview mirror, and I glare at him before looking back at the target of my needling. "Is that what she told you? Get your guys to stage a coup and you'd be in charge with her, your doting wife? You'd even have a rich backer behind you?"

Nikolai's eyes widen and *wow* I really didn't think that would be as spot on as it appears to be. Makes sense, though. Elise is the mastermind behind all of this; she's a sore loser about Maxim not marrying her, and decided to take matters into her own hands?

"Tenneson is her father," Maxim says, but his voice is strained.

"What?" Nikolai and I say in unison.

"I just put it together. Her mother and Tenneson divorced when she was young. Her mom became one of my father's girlfriends, it's how she and Sasha knew each other. He put their moms up in the same apartment building."

Nikolai stews on this news in the front seat, eyes not even on me where the gun is still pointed. I take the opportunity to go after Samuel.

"And what the fuck is all this about, Samuel?" I ask. "Elise promise you an empire too?"

His shoulders slump as we roll through a yellow light.

"They swore they would leave you out of it," he says. "They have my son."

I sigh. Absolutely classic move, holding-a-loved-one-captive to sway loyalties. Nothing quite so effective for a soft-hearted man than attacking his family. I'm one to talk, though. It would probably work just as well on me.

"I'm very sorry, Mary."

"Mrs. Orlov," I correct, though the words are as sour as the broken trust between us. "Your apologies mean nothing to me."

I feign annoyed dismissive glances out the window, eyes searching for familiar black vehicles. It's dark outside, almost too dark to see the cars next to us with the tinted window, but I spy Elise in the passenger seat looking at me through the window. I lower mine enough to see my face and flip her off.

Normally I would love an evil woman going after what she wants. Unfortunately in this instance, that thing is the lives of me and my husband, so I cannot abide.

"Hey, close that," Nikolai snaps and I do as he says, but not before slipping a remaining shred of my sleeve over the glass, pinching it between the car door and window so it'll flap against the car. It won't do much, but if someone in my family can find our convoy maybe they'll see it and know not to try their luck on the bulletproof glass.

"You know, you could be nicer to people who could kill you at any time," Nikolai snips and I force another smug smile.

"Niko, did you think I was nice?"

It's his turn to roll his eyes in annoyance, but before I can quip anything else, an unmistakable crunch sounds outside to our right and everyone recoils, turning to look at where the car of one of the goons is swerving between lanes, having just been rear ended.

"What the hell is—" Nikolai is cut off as Samuel swerves the car sharply left to avoid another black SUV slamming the brakes in front of us.

It's Leo's car.

Thank God.

I breathe my first exhale, and grip Maxim's thigh while Samuel rights the car and steps on the gas.

"What was that?" Nikolai asks, his voice shrill. Both his eyes and the gun are no longer pointed at me and I jump on the chance, unbuckling my seatbelt and lunging forward to grab the weapon from his grip. He's too distracted to put up a fight, and I get the gun easily before training it on his head. When he tries to grab it back from me, his seatbelt auto stops him from getting too far.

I take the opportunity to shoot him in the arm, and at the sound, Samuel swerves the car, narrowly missing the one next to us which honks.

"Keep driving," I shout.

"You shot me!" Nikolai sounds incredulous. I almost laugh at the audacity he has to feel betrayed by this.

I would've killed him, but I am attempting not to be so hasty in murdering people before they can help give us information. Think first, kill later, instead of my usual.

"The next shot goes in your head, do not *try me*, Nikolai."

He looks to Maxim as if he'll help him and even pale and injured as he is, Maxim gives a lopsided smile that's almost proud.

Someone is hanging half out of the window of the SUV that holds Elise and Tenneson, shooting a gun behind them at a baby blue Prius. *Nate's.*

I curse, lowering the window and taking two shots at the man trying to brain Nate, one missing, the other hitting him in between the shoulder and neck.

"Drive faster," I yell, and Samuel does as I say, breaking away from the pack. "Lose them or I will kill you, Samuel, don't think I won't."

"Wouldn't dare, think that, Mrs. Orlov," he says, and if I'm not mistaken, he sounds almost relieved. Behind us, we hear more screeching tires and gunshots, but Samuel pulls the wheel in a quick maneuver to the right, cutting in front of a semi onto an off ramp.

"I still can't believe you shot me!"

"Never been shot before?" I ask. My eyes search out the back window for sign of one of Tenneson's cars.

Samuel turns right, sending me careening into the car door again, and I think we might be clear when the third of Tenneson's SUVs drives over the sidewalk to get past the semi.

"They're on us." I curse, and lower the window again, reaching the gun out and shooting three shots, only one hitting the windshield of the SUV.

Their car narrowly avoids clipping a light pole, but stays on us, speeding up and shooting shots of their own. I grab Maxim's neck and pull him down, him groaning as he leans sideways toward me.

"Fuck this!" Nikolai screams. "Why are they shooting at us?!"

He's in the process of pulling a phone out of his pocket and I thud the butt of the gun on the side of his head, not hard enough to knock him out.

"Ouch," he whines, and protests when I take the phone.

"Do you want to die?" I ask, exasperated by him.

"Mary," Maxim warns with a groan, and I follow his eyes to where the SUV is gaining on us to our left.

I curse and shoot three more rounds into the car, the first two missing the gunman, and the third landing on his hand, making him drop the gun he was just aiming at us.

Samuel swerves the car into theirs, the vehicles colliding against each other with a horrible clatter and demolishing both cars' shiny exteriors. I slide as far away from my damaged door as possible.

We swerve apart from each other to avoid a motorcyclist, and then Samuel goes for a third collision like we are fucking bumper cars, and this one pushes the SUV into oncoming traffic. We hear the loud sound of their collision as we speed on.

It appears we're in the clear of enemy vehicles when, of course, sirens sound off behind us. It's Samuel's turn to curse as we speed up, weaving through traffic.

I hastily type Leo's number into the cell and he answers with a sharp, "Mary?"

"Are you hurt?"

"I'm good, Nate too," Leo says, yelling. "I lost Santi though. He followed one of the cars off the road toward the bridge." I slap Samuel's shoulder and point in the general direction of said bridge. We're not far from it now. "Are you hurt?"

"Max is in bad shape, but—" I cut off as our town car is hit from behind, lurching us forward with that too-loud crunch. Nikolai screams, and when I look back it's a cop car, bright blue and red lights flashing in the window.

Samuel speeds up.

"Call Willa," I shout. "Get her to call her cops."

I can only assume Leo is doing as I say, because he hangs up as Samuel jerks the car again, this time down an alley. The cops lose time in missing the sharp turn and we gain distance. Barely any breathing room, but enough. I lean forward and reach into the center console where Samuel has a handgun and an extra cartridge of bullets.

"Get to the bridge," I command and turn to look at Maxim who is so, so pale. My strong man looks weak, his breath coming now in shallow pants, his eyes terrified. I use the hand that's not gripping the gun and gently cradle his cheek, careful not to press the wounds on his jaw.

We reach the end of the alley and burst onto the street without stopping, narrowly missing an oncoming car that lays on its horn as we pass. The disturbance gives us more time to break away from the police, but we've met up again with the last of Tenneson's cars, this one smaller than the others.

Shots immediately start pelting our car and Nikolai screams that we aren't the enemy here.

"I love you, Maxim," I say, because every time a bullet hits the car, I am more certain it will be the one to slice through my brain or his and I can't die not having said these words. "I've loved you for longer than I could admit to myself, and I tried so hard not to, I really did. But you are the most perfect man, frustratingly loyal, and intensely forgiving."

More shots hit the front of the car, and Samuel shouts as one breaks through the window and hits him.

I lean closer to Maxim in the chaos, needing to say this. "You're impossible not to love, and I was a fool to think I could fight you off."

"*Marianna*," he tries.

"I love you," I say again, and press my mouth to his in a desperate kiss.

"Bridge ahead," Samuel says with a pained voice, his foot slamming on the gas as he tries to pass the other car. Half of it is closed for construction tonight.

I sit up and scan the area for Colton's car, missing it entirely when it races in front of us. Samuel brakes, but the other car is too busy shooting at us and when they try to stop, it's too late. Their car slams into the side of the SUV, crunching the first half of their vehicle and flipping the larger one onto the bridge's entrance, sending it over lanes of traffic while our car spins out from the sudden stop.

When things finally stop moving, and the incredible noise quiets, I catch my breath and look first to Maxim. He's slumped in his seat, but when I put my face in front of his, he blinks awake. Alive.

A sigh of relief slices out of me and I press my lips hard against his forehead, undoing his seatbelt and mine before kicking with both legs on my bent door until it creaks open.

I get out of the car and tug Maxim out with me, using all my strength to hold him up and shuffle him across the street, far enough from the car that if it were to explode, I think he'd be safe. I help him get on the ground, his shallow breaths panting against my head. I put Nikolai's gun in his palm and close his fingers around it.

"Stay with me," he says.

I smile and shake my head. We wouldn't have gotten this far without help from everyone and I refuse to stumble at the finish line and let Colton Tenneson walk free.

"I love you," I say again.

"Marianna, please don't," he starts, but the sirens are near and I'm running out of time. I spin around, Samuel's gun in hand and jog the short distance to the bridge.

Tenneson's car is upside down, and as I sneak toward it, someone emerges from the open passenger window. It's Elise. She bleeds from her forehead and looks crazed as she stumbles to standing in front of me.

"*You,*" she yells, already charging in her unbalanced way. A gunshot goes off behind me, and I duck to avoid another, but it's the only one. I glance back to see Maxim's arm still raised, pointed at the SUV.

He meets my eyes, and then nods.

When I turn to continue, Elise no longer charges for me, instead she lies unmoving on the asphalt. I see as I get closer that her eyes are now vacant, the life drained out of her body.

On the far side of the car, I hear the crunching of glass against the road and when I peer around it, I find Tenneson crawling away from the car using his arms and one leg, the other obviously broken, pulled behind him.

He looks like the weak, miserable man he is, someone who would sell children and people, robbing them of their lives.

"Tenneson," I yell, and he halts before looking over his shoulder with a sneer.

It's unceremonious, the lifting of my arm, shooting the final bullet into him. He falls dead before he can speak any of his nonsense at me, choking on his own blood as it pools beneath him.

He deserves worse.

Sound finally reaches me, shouts from behind me, a helicopter spotlight pointing down on the bridge. I squint up at it and let the gun clatter to the ground before putting my arms above my head.

40

—————

MAXIM

WHEN I WOKE up in the hospital to find that Marianna was sitting in a jail cell, Willa doing everything in her power to get her in front of a judge, I was inconsolable, trying to free myself from the various cables and IV to get to her. I wasn't conscious of the pain, the broken ribs, the hole in my foot where a bullet had been lodged, only consumed with getting to her and getting her out of there.

They had to sedate me.

When I wake again, the spare light through the window tells me that it's evening and I'm in my bed, still hooked up to machines but in my own room this time. I must've been out of it for a long time, because Marianna is asleep next to me, her body pressed against the side of mine over the covers. Greta sleeps between our legs.

My relief is palpable and I exhale before pressing a kiss against her head, inhaling the scent of her hair until I believe she's real and alive and I didn't slip into death while I slept.

"She's in good health," a quiet voice says. Lev. The old doctor closes the book he was reading and returns it to my nightstand. He stretches and stands from the chair at the side of the bed.

I pull her closer to me, ignoring the ache of my ribs. She yawns and slides her leg higher up mine, but stays asleep.

"Between your chest, arm, and face, you needed one hundred and forty stitches," he says. "You have three ribs broken and the bullet could've done more damage to your foot, but all things considered, the surgery was easy enough. You needed a lot of blood."

"Where is he?"

"Nikolai?"

"Tenneson."

A small smile turns up Lev's lips and he nods at Marianna. "She killed him. That's why she was held overnight."

I startle, remembering another detail from the mess of the day. "My brother?"

Elise had said Sasha was on his way to bleeding out, and that news was excruciating to me. He never got the respect he deserved as the Orlov bastard—my father never claimed him, and even when I had, many didn't respect him enough to care.

"Alexei is recovering," Lev says. "He's in rough shape, but I believe he'll get through it."

My eyes fill at this news and I press my nose again into my wife's soft hair. Alive and well, both of them, and me too.

Lev presses a plunger on my IV, administering something that immediately makes me feel softer around my swollen edges.

"Sleep, son," the old doctor murmurs, and I let myself drift off.

41

______

MARY

WILLA IS EXCEPTIONALLY PERSUASIVE, which is maybe
what makes her such a damn good lawyer. I had to spend a night
in jail after half of the cops in Boston found me with a gun
pointed in the direction of a dead Colton Tenneson. I would still
be in said cell if Willa hadn't called in fifteen favors to get me in
front of a judge before lunch the next day.

The cops wanted to get me on murder, but my story spoke
more to kidnapping and self-defense—especially with my
husband in surgery at the hospital. Willa made a case for me, and
apparently Nikolai's testimony helped a great deal. At least my
refraining from killing him had been good for something.

At some point in this long night, Nessa's government agent
friend got her shit together and took over the investigation from
the local police, barging in and waving her badge around. Agent
Louisa Portillo and her partner asked me a long list of questions
about my involvement with Tenneson, the events of the night, and
my knowledge of what he planned. I told them what I could, and
most of it was the truth.

I said that I hadn't heard from Maxim and was able to track

his phone to the old factory, where, as soon as I arrived, Sasha was shot and I was apprehended by Elise. I told them that Maxim was already cut up when I got there, that Colton Tenneson held a gun to my head until Maxim promised to comply with their demands, and that Tenneson swore to kill us once he got what he needed from Maxim.

They let me have a few quiet hours to myself in the cell and even brought breakfast before Willa returned. She escorted me to a courthouse where we stood in front of a female judge who ruled that I could go free until the trial—a nonnegotiable, since I shot a man point blank in front of a dozen cops.

Reasonable enough.

When I was finally free to go with a *murder trial* looming over my head, Leo took me home. I had no sleep and no shower, and came to learn that Maxim almost had a damn aneurysm when he found out the police were holding me. Willa, once again the most persuasive person on the planet, was able to get an unconscious Maxim transported to the penthouse where she promised our private physicians would look after him.

I showered, ate the food Nate brought for me, took more of my sister's nausea medicine, and promptly knocked the hell out next to Maxim and the cat. Nate, Vanessa, Leo, and my mom hung around presumably the entire day, because when I wake again, I hear the chatter of their voices downstairs.

I rub my eyes and groan, stretching out before looking up at Maxim who is already awake, watching me with that steady intent he has. His hair is a mess, his jaw unshaven, and there are bandages covering the many wounds that I know will leave scars once they heal.

He will be just as handsome, even then.

"Hi," I say, when a long minute of studying him passes without a word spoken.

"Hi," he echoes.

The last words I'd spoken to him were my hurried proclamations of love. I was so afraid he would die, and if not him, then me, and I wanted to protect him but I needed him to know where I stood more. It's where I still stand.

I like to think that when my father died, he knew where I stood, knew I cherished him. We were playing cards when he had a heart attack, and even through his anguish, he told me I was a good girl, told me he loved me between his pained breaths, thanked me for always helping him while I screamed out for anyone in the house to come help him. I performed chest compression for thirty-seven minutes while waiting for the ambulance. He never regained consciousness.

"Don't cry," Maxim soothes, wrapping his arm around me and pulling me closer to him. I didn't think I was crying, but when I wipe my cheeks, sure enough they're wet. "You're alive."

"*You're* alive," I say. "You looked like death when I took you out of that car."

"I felt like it."

"I love you," I say again, because maybe he didn't hear it last time, and if he were to die today I would need, more than anything, for him to know. "I'm sorry I didn't tell you before. I've been loving you, it was impossible to stop."

Maxim smiles, his eyes sparkling, and pushes my curls behind my ear.

"I know," he said, the same way I did the last time he told me. "I've known, Marianna."

"I haven't made it easy for you. Not once since demanding you marry me have I been lovely or accommodating, or even very nice," I tell him. I remember the speech I'd prepared for him in December, the laundry list of reasons he shouldn't want to marry me.

"I think you're nice," he says and I shush him.

"Let me say this. I *know* I am hard to love, hard to be around sometimes, but please don't stop loving me. Please stay when I'm rude and off-putting and impulsive."

"Darling—"

"No, listen. Maxim, you are the most excellent man I have ever known. You are thoughtful and smart and more understanding and patient than anyone would ever expect from you. You are so thoroughly good that you make me want to be better, kinder, less murderous every day. You are too good for this world of organized crime and blood and sabotage, but you do it anyway because you don't have a choice, and I'm so unbelievably selfish because even if you *did* have a way out, I would beg you to stay with me."

Maxim's thumbs wipe under my eyes, and I babble on.

"I know I'm not. . .easy. I know that. And I used to think you'd be better off with someone like Elise, or like who we thought Elise was, but the truth is, I would do terrible things to keep you. I'd kill fifteen Colton Tennesons, I'd rob a bank, or I'd promise to never kill again. I'd get a desk job."

Maxim laughs at this last one, and I do too.

He pulls me to him and kisses me so sweetly before cradling my face in both hands so I can look nowhere but at him.

"Nothing has ever been so simple as loving you," he says. "Nothing is so natural or inevitable. There's nothing about you that's hard to love, not a single thing, Marianna."

I don't know how to believe his words, but *he* seems to believe them, which is enough.

"You are so treasured, not just by me, but by everyone who you let in. Your sister's children worship you, your family adores you. You are so full of light, I didn't stand a chance."

"I'm a shadow of a person," I whisper and he kisses me again.

"You have never been a shadow."

As we kiss and smile and laugh and kiss some more, I decide

that maybe there's not a limit to how much love one person can hold.

Maybe it doesn't matter if it comes with more stress, more hurt. Maybe love expands your very capacity to love more until it's all you are.

I think I'd like to believe that.

42
———

MAXIM

OTHER THAN MY brief stint in the hospital last month, I haven't been inside an honest-to-God doctor's office for years, and this one is different than any I can remember. It's inviting instead of sterile, everything about it designed to be soft, light, and optimistic.

There are parenting guides and cardboard children's books on the tables, photos of brilliantly smiling families on the walls, and two other couples in the waiting room. I look again at Marianna's abdomen, covered by the black overall dress she's wearing, but if I press the fabric to her front, I know I'm not imagining the bump that's visible there.

Marianna is a small, incredibly muscular woman. I admittedly know very little about gestation, but it seems early still for her belly to be rounding.

She bites the skin around her nail before stopping suddenly and stuffing her hands under her thighs. She's been nervous about today, concerned that when they finally do an ultrasound, they'll find nothing there.

"What if it's a false alarm? Like maybe it's been just a para-site making me sick instead of a fetus," she said in the car ride

348

here. She drove us since my foot is still wrapped in a hard cast for a few weeks more and Samuel, while still alive, is no longer in our employ. I miss him more than I like to admit.

"A parasite that stops your period and gives you positive pregnancy tests?" I asked.

"Exactly."

I didn't tell her that she was wrong to worry, only put my hand on her thigh and lightly squeezed.

"Marianna Orlov?" a nurse in pink scrubs calls now from the door into the back. My wife pops up from her seat mechanically and I follow behind her. We're overdressed for this little family practice, me in my button-up and slacks, her in all black, but the nurse doesn't look surprised. I'm still on crutches, after all, and that's really what gives her pause.

"How are we feeling today?"

"Sickly," Marianna says as she drops into one of the rolling chairs instead of on the exam table. I take the chair next to her. "But much less nauseous than I was this time last month."

"That's a good sign. Improvement!"

She gives Marianna a cup to pee in, draws her blood into three vials, and then instructs her to get undressed with the blanket draped over her waist and another across her chest in preparation for the ultrasound.

When the nurse leaves the room, Marianna unbuttons the metal clasps that hold up the overall straps and steps out of the dress left only in her long sleeve and bright red underwear. I refuse to get an erection in the doctor's office, so I keep my eyes on her face while she folds the clothing and sets it in a pile on the chair next to mine.

She settles a bit stiffly on the bed, first sitting, then laying down, half sitting up, then sighing and reclining back again. I scoot my chair to the side of the table and she doesn't look at me, instead staring at the ceiling, her thumb spinning her wedding ring around in circles on her finger.

"Are you nervous?" I ask.

She turns her head to look at me. The height of the table puts her just about my eye level.

"What if it's—" A knock on the door cuts her off and she calls out a "yeah" before the door opens to reveal the nurse and now an older woman with slight shoulders and a kind smile. Dr. Simone Judd, who delivered Angel, Artie, and Clara, and is set to deliver Vanessa's baby in the next couple of months.

"Mary Morelli," she says, so pleasant.

"It's Orlov now," Marianna says, and nods in my direction.

"Of course," the doctor amends, and offers her hand for me to shake, which I do. She turns to wash her hands at the sink, which I do not take as a personal slight. "Good to meet you Mr. Orlov. And based on the urine sample, congratulations are in order."

"Thank you, it's—" I exhale, unsure how to finish the sentence. That it was a surprise to me? The thrill of my life? That I've never been so concerned for the health of a human as I am of my wife who is so strong, yet so mortal? "Thank you," I settle on instead.

"Shall we get started then?"

We both agree and she wastes no time getting to it. I hold Marianna's hand and she squeezes mine while Dr. Judd gets the machine set up for the ultrasound.

She presses a tool at the bottom of Marianna's stomach, moving it a few times while listening to the gentle whooshing sound of the machine. And then we all hear it.

Unmistakable and fast, an urgent sort of galloping.

"And we have a heartbeat!" she says, and Marianna looks at me with wide eyes, the same look I'm sure is mirrored on my face.

"It's so fast," Marianna says. The doctor smiles and nods, but she's leaning to the monitor to listen closer to the sound. Her mouth is closed in a tight line, eyebrows slightly together while she does.

Dr. Judd opens her mouth but then closes it before she clicks a few buttons on the machine until the screen populates with an image I can't begin to make sense of.

"Let's take a look then," she says before either of us can inquire if she thought something was wrong. The heart sounded normal enough to me, though Marianna was right it sounded like a fast little thing.

Dr. Judd moves the wand around Marianna's abdomen, pausing, clicking a button, smiling like she can't help it and repeating the process.

"Alright, here we have the baby," she points at a spot on the screen before making it bigger by clicking a few buttons on the machine. I do not see a baby, per se, but more of a blob in a black sack. As she moves the view slightly, though, the blob looks more human-shaped than I anticipated, albeit wrapped up like a tadpole.

"What's next to it?" Marianna asks and the doctor smiles.

"Well, that's another baby."

We both freeze, staring at the screen and waiting like the doctor might say "just kidding" at any moment.

"Breathe," Dr. Judd reminds us with a slight laugh, and Marianna shutters in a breath and looks at my face. "It was sounding so busy because you've got two heart beats in there. Well, three including yours."

She freezes the image on a view of them next to each other, the outlines of both of their tiny heads visible.

"Oh my God." Marianna exhales, and squeezes my hand tighter. I look between the screen and her face, unsure which sight is more magnificent to me. Her eyes go glassy, and I have to blink because the same can be said for my own.

"Twins do run in families," the doctor chimes. She smiles as Marianna laughs.

It is profound, watching the ultrasound, getting up close to the little blobs that are the not one but *two* tiny fetuses that we made.

I could watch it all day, but after the doctor has all the scans she needs, she has Marianna get all cleaned up and dressed again. As soon as Dr. Judd leaves, I kiss her half a dozen times, both of us astonished at the surprise.

"We made a baby?" I ask, though obviously we did.

"Two of them," she says, and gives no protest when I pull her against me, peppering her mouth and face with more kisses.

"Careful, you look a bit too happy about this," I murmur with my lips still against hers. "Someone is going to think you like me."

"Didn't you hear?" she asks, and rests her forehead against mine. "I don't just like you, I'm terribly in love with you. Disastrous, really."

"Say it again," I say, and she smiles against my mouth.

"I love you, Maxim."

I let out a long, wistful sigh. "I know," I say.

When she pinches my arm, we both laugh.

43

MAXIM

Five Months Later

MY VERY PREGNANT wife gives testimony before a court room full of people. Her hair is pulled into a braid, tied with a ribbon, and she wears a pale pink maternity dress. She was styled by Willa to look as innocent and lovely as possible. The image she paints is so sweet that even I would be hard pressed to believe she'd killed anyone out of anything other than self-defense.

Marianna was charged for the voluntary murder of Colton Tenneson, to which she pleaded not guilty. Willa, unconcerned by any conflict of interests, represents Marianna in an attempt to prove, beyond a shadow of a doubt, that this was self defense, not premeditated.

Marianna didn't know this when she shot him, but it turned out that in his hand as he crawled away from his vehicle, Colton Tenneson held a gun. Fortuitous. Middle of the night as it was, it wasn't a stretch to say that he was going to shoot her with it, and both Nikolai and Samuel swore up and down that they saw him about to do it with their own eyes. Testified under oath, even. Key witnesses.

Whether this was true is not for me to say, since I was half-unconscious at the time.

Their testimonies aren't enough to forgive either of them for what they did, but nonetheless, their loyalties in this trial have been firmly with Marianna and me. It's a start, I suppose, and I can't kill them now, not with all the press.

When the paramedics took Nikolai to the hospital the night of it all, gunshot wound in his arm, he demanded to talk to the police straight away. He wanted to give his statement.

So, while Marianna was in a jail cell, being questioned, and waiting overnight to see a judge, Nikolai told them everything about Tenneson's operation. He told them about how he'd captured me, tortured me, and even had plans to *sell* Mary.

I don't know if Nikolai was afraid of what I would do to him or genuinely repentant, but by the time my wife was able to stand before the judge the next morning, there was a solid enough case for self defense that they were willing to release her pre-trial. It wasn't enough to get the charges dropped entirely—this is homicide after all, but there was enough evidence that the judge didn't deem her a terrible danger.

Being pregnant helped, I'm sure.

Marianna chews on her lower lip while her sister asks one rehearsed question after another in front of the jury. Her face is rounder thanks to the pregnancy, less sharp edges all around. She remains the most beautiful woman I have ever had the great joy of laying eyes on.

"I had just found out I was pregnant and I was really excited to tell Maxim, but he hadn't come home. I have his location shared to my phone, so I thought I'd go see where he was, and wound up at the old clothing factory by the shipyard."

"And you didn't think to call the police?"

Marianna shrugs, and then rubs a palm absent-mindedly over her stomach. It's not actually mindless, but instead carefully planned. "Well, I knew he was thinking about developing it, so it wasn't raising any red flags. I was with Alexei, Maxim's younger brother, and we just thought we'd check it out to see if he was still there."

"And did you see any signs of trouble when you got there?"

"No, but there were a bunch of cars. That's when we ran into Elise. She had a gun and shot Alexei before I could call anyone."

"And from there?"

Marianna looks uncomfortable, her lower lip wobbling. This version of her is so different from the one we know. Nearly every member of the jury is leaning forward in their seats, absolute putty in her hands.

"Take your time," Willa says, in her sharpest suit for the occasion. It's not every day you get to represent your sister in court.

Marianna takes a big breath and her voice is a bit shaky when she speaks. "It was awful. Maxim was tied up, really bloody and cut *everywhere*. He had to get like 200 stitches after, it was horrible. Colton Tenneson was there with a knife and he was screaming at me about Maxim's money, saying he was going to sell me—that a lot of men would pay a lot of money for the pregnant wife of Maxim Orlov." She sniffles and wipes under her eyes before sitting up straighter, the picture of a woman who's gone through a lot but is being really brave about it. Christ, she's good at acting.

Her story is mostly true, and it really was very traumatic for her, but sometimes I'm surprised at how well she plays this role.

She's brilliant.

They go back and forth like this, Marianna explaining in detail the trauma of the night. She looks pale when recounting Tenneson shooting me, and by the end of her story, I am sure the jury's decision has already been made. Their minds are made up, I think.

"He was on the ground, but he had a gun pointed at me and he looked so. . .full of hate." She looks off, a haunted expression crossing over her face. "I knew he was going to shoot me. So I shot him first."

"Have you ever shot a gun before?"

"Yes, my dad used to take me target shooting sometimes. Family time."

Willa smiles a sad, patient sort of smile, playing her own part.

"I have no further questions, your honor."

The deliberation is short, and while we wait I wrap an arm around her shoulders and tug her into my side, my palm on the side of her pregnant belly, lightly drumming the pads of my fingers on it until I feel the press of one of the baby's feet against my hand. Our already perfect, tiny boys.

She's ruled not guilty in the murder of Colton Tenneson and, two days later, Marianna goes into labor.

EPILOGUE
MARY

The Following Summer

I DON'T KNOW what variables must come together for two people to fall in love. There's a myriad of things that have to line up just right, a million coincidences leading people to the exact right place and moment even to have the opportunity for love to grow.

When I consider all of the ways a person can miss it—one different decision, one missed connection—love feels like nothing short of miraculous.

And yet, it happens every day.

It happened to me even, when I least expected it to. And then it happened again when I went through the horrible ordeal of birth, only to be met with the greatest surprise of my life: more love than I could imagine.

Love is still as mysterious to me as it has ever been, even now as I overflow with it.

I've been trying to unravel the invisible string through my whole life that led me here, to him, to this life with the two tiny babies that have just started to say "mama."

I had to work today, just a few rounds with Leo, no violence or promise of violence, and only for a couple hours, but by the time I make it back to the penthouse, I miss my little family so much I can't imagine being gone a moment longer. When I get inside, I find Sasha and Maxim playing with the boys in the living room. Greta sleeps on the couch, her tail lightly swishing against the cushion. As a rule, she likes to be wherever the babies are.

Sasha bounces Iliya while Maxim helps Enzo roll over on the quilt his mother made for them.

I drop my keys and bag on the counter and my husband turns to me with a smile lighting his face. The wounds from Tenneson have healed into thin white scars that disappear into his short beard. As expected, just as handsome as he's ever been.

"Is that your mama?" Sasha asks Iliya, already bringing the smiling baby toward me. I will never get over the way his grin takes up his whole, chubby face and how he offers them so easily to anyone who will smile at him, but especially to me. Enzo makes us work harder for them, but Maxim can always get him laughing in a way so infectious and special, I want to hear it every day.

"Hi, tiny." I take Iliya from Sasha and kiss all over his plump cheeks until he laughs, and then give him another kiss for good measure. Maxim stands, bringing Enzo with him and I repeat the greeting with the both of them, saving an extra long one for Maxim, who looks down at me like I'm the center of the universe when I pull away.

"Any drama today?" he asks.

"None," I report. I'm not usually on jobs that beget much drama these days. Maxim either. We've been practicing the art of *delegation*. "Nate called and told me it was unkind to say I didn't want to go bowling with him, though. Says he's pulling the birthday card so we all have to go with him."

"Afraid you'll score less points than him?" Maxim asks.

"Absolutely," I respond solemnly.

Sasha steps back into the living room, though I hadn't noticed him leave, and stuffs his phone in his pocket. "I'm off to the Brickyard. Need anything?"

"No, but thank you," I tell him. He smiles at me and the kids, shaking Illya's little hand before heading for the elevator. He's still single, still has a roster of dates he can call at any time, none of them serious. It's so obvious to me that he craves a family. Leo is the same. I think they probably just spend too much time around a small army of babies—that would make anyone either want their own, or never want one at all.

"I missed you," I tell Maxim.

"I always miss you," he says. "Has anyone ever told you how easy it is to love you?"

"Rarely," I whisper, and smile against his mouth as he kisses me again. "Which is a surprise, because I am just so friendly and approachable."

"You are," he mutters against my mouth. It's then that both boys determine they've had enough of this. Well, Enzo decides first, and Iliya follows what Enzo does, so within seconds they're both fussing.

"Alright, alright, food time," I say, bouncing the baby until he settles. "If you make E a bottle, I'll nurse Iliya."

"Deal." Maxim kisses my nose and heads for the kitchen after clipping Enzo into his bouncer. I settle on the couch with Iliya and Greta bumps her head against me before plopping down next to my leg. Today is a good day, though not all are.

My fear and anxiety hasn't decreased since birth, and in some ways it's worse. My mind still trips over every what-if and those are threefold now that I have two little lives I brought into the world.

But I manage it, and I never have to manage it alone.

I started going to see a therapist after everything went down last year. The nightmares were getting bad again and Maxim's little sister recommended a trauma therapist in the city. It took me two months to finally agree to see someone, and then three weeks to finally start opening up to the kind woman Vera recommended. It's helped immensely.

She diagnosed me with OCD, which I resented at first. I didn't want to believe her, didn't want to label myself in such a tangible way, but she was exceptionally patient with me. With every subsequent session, I learned more about the way I think, about why I might feel the ways I do. I unpacked trauma, wrestled with thought patterns I've had for years, and complained to Maxim when it was hard.

I've learned that nothing is broken about me, I'm not damaged goods, and above all, I don't have to bear the weight of things on my own.

So when the what-ifs come, I let them. I haven't had a panic attack since the boys were born, and when my mind is insistent on imagining the horrors that could befall them, Maxim listens.

I think that part of me must've known that Maxim would be the perfect partner for me; patient, strong, and so unbearably tender. When I went to his club on Christmas Eve and panicked in the alley, and he crouched in front of me, I must've known. Or maybe it was luck. *Fate*, Sasha would say.

I'll never not be grateful for the invisible string that led me there, and for him for picking up the other end.

"My mother wants to visit," Maxim says as he sits on the other side of the couch with Enzo. "Maybe to stay longer this time."

I raise my eyebrows at the news. His mother hates this city, and braved a visit for a week after the twins were born. I liked her immensely.

"I hope she does," I say. I used to fear getting too close to any of his family. *Too many people to care about, not enough mental capacity to do so effectively.*

But I've learned that loving people doesn't make you fragile; if anything it grows your capacity to love *more*. I won't pretend to understand it.

We feed the babies, each telling the other about our days, then rock them to sleep. When they're both set into their bassinets and both asleep (a rare, miraculous occasion), I rest my head on Maxim's shoulder. He reads, I doze off, and the cat races around the house like a demon.

Everything is exactly as it should be.

BONUS EPILOGUE
MAXIM

"THIS PLACE IS LIKE A DAYCARE," Sasha says. He's softly bouncing one of the boys, Enzo, who drools on Sasha's shoulder, fast asleep.

He's right, Vanessa Morelli's backyard is overrun with children, Willa's little girl in a floaty in the pool with Vanessa's baby, both splashing as their moms pull them around in their circular floaties.

Marianna is in the pool, clapping and making the little ones laugh by splashing water in her face and acting shocked every time. It's their favorite game.

Angel and Artie are swimming too, taking turns trying to tackle Leo, who is twice either of their size. Nate saunters up to where Sasha and I stand in the shade, holding my other son, Iliya, who's got curly brown hair and eyes like his mother. He reaches for me when he sees me, and I take him, my heart growing three times its size when he babbles and rests his head against my chest in what I would like to call a hug. I pepper his head with kisses and snuggle him back, my precious boy.

I didn't know I could love something as much as I love these two, a consuming protectiveness and adoration only rivaled by the love I feel for their mother.

I think sometimes it must be genetic, since I don't love any other baby as well as I love these two. But I do love Vanessa and Willa's babies, and would do anything to protect them. So if not genetics that makes me adore them so, maybe it's the fact that the love of my life painstakingly grew them, sick most days of her pregnancy, and then labored and birthed them one after the next on a cold December evening, just before my birthday. Maybe it was the eight days they spent in the NICU growing stronger before we could take them home, Marianna and I visiting as often as we could, holding them against our skin at every chance.

Maybe it's their smiles, their laughs, the way they can have personalities already—I don't think I realized they could have personalities yet.

Whatever it is, my love for them shows me that whatever my father felt for us, it wasn't love. Not even some twisted version of the love I feel—it was something foreign and broken, a shattered, fucked up man creating offspring for his ego and legacy more than anything else.

I will protect them in ways he never cared to protect me.

"Does Enzo seem bigger this week?" Sasha asks of the sleeping child in his arms. "Like these little thighs might have doubled in size."

"He wants to be as tall as his uncle," I muse, and Sasha smiles. He sees the babies every day, the short elevator ride the perfect commute for an uncle as doting and obsessed as him. He rivals only Nate in his desire to be holding an infant at all times. Sasha's recovery wasn't a short one, but he's fully healed now with a scar like Mary's to show for it.

As if thinking of her draws her attention toward me, Marianna pushes herself out of the pool and, without first grabbing a towel, crosses the backyard to where we stand in the shade. She drips water onto my legs and blows raspberries on Ilya's stomach as he screams and giggles.

"Your cheeks are sunburnt, love," she says, and presses up on her toes to kiss each side of my face and then my mouth. Ilya laughs his screaming laugh and continues to do so while we kiss either side of his head.

The noise rouses Enzo, who blinks groggily awake. Seeing his mother, his single favorite person on the planet, Enzo reaches for her. She coos, taking him from Sasha's arms and cradling him as she rocks side to side. Her hair still drips down her back, but Enzo doesn't seem to mind her damn skin or the smell of sunscreen.

Nate calls Sasha over to help him and Sean with something on the grill, because I suppose it takes two mafiosos and a math teacher to have a successful barbecue. It warms my heart that they've accepted my brother so seamlessly into their family. It's what I wish I could've had with him growing up.

"You're looking all wistful again," Marianna remarks, smirking.

"Maybe I'm feeling wistful again," I say. "Sue me."

I never dared wish this kind of joy for us, for myself. With Marianna, hope for this kind of contentment was dangerous; it threatened to bury me alive beneath the weight of my desire.

And yet, here she is, and here I am. Two sons, a precious menace of a wife, and more joy than any one person should rightfully have to themselves.

My father raised me to believe I'd never have this, that it wasn't feasible nor even desirable. She teaches me the opposite, just by being who she is.

"I love you," she says, as she always does. "Even with the sunburn."

For someone who promised to never love me, she says it constantly now, an easy refrain and frequent reminder. Passing me a mug for tea: *I love you.* Sleepily rolling over when I get up with the babies: *love you.* Besting me in a fight with her cunning and skills: *I still love you.*

"I love you," I say in English, and then Russian, Italian, every language I know, swaying with her and our boys as the rest of our family laughs and plays, perfectly content on a late summer day.

THE END

ACKNOWLEDGMENTS

It was with no shortage of anguish that this book came to be, and, per usual, I couldn't have done it without the unending support of so, so many people. If I listed everyone, this Acknowledgements would be a veritable tome, but here are a handful of specific Thank You's:

First, to every person who read *A Love Most Fatal* and connected with these characters. Your overwhelming support, enthusiastic messages, and generous reviews helped me stay excited to keep writing.

To my street team for the posts, messages, enthusiasm, and love for my characters.

To the many new friends I've made online since the launch of *A Love Most Fatal,* ILY.

To PA Kylie, for keeping me organized when I am sometimes very, very not.

To Sam, Sophie, and Lilitherie for making the book covers of my dreeccams.

To my agent Bethany for your steady confidence in me and your expertise. I feel lucky to know you.

To Ellie for once again being a thoughtful editor, great friend, and an absolute joy to work with.

To the first readers of *Brutal*, Kat, Lauren, and my sister Jackie. Your feedback and unhinged comments pushed me through edits and made this book better. Also, Kat, I think this book was written over the course of hundreds of writing sprints with you, so fifty thank you's for always answering my "you up?" texts with "yep let's get to work."

To the Plot Heads. Reading your writing over the years has made me a better writer.

To my brunch squad, Shayla, Paul, and Devon for the forever giggles.

To The Slumber Party: Cynthia, Evelyn, and Giuliana, your friendship over the last year has been a steady, meaningful presence in my life. Writing and publishing isn't lonely with friends like you.

To Rachel. I am grateful for monster romance and twitter dot com every day for bringing us together.

To my Lizzie. Your daily encouragement from across the country keeps me plugging away.

To Rebecca for your infinite cheerleading, astute feedback, and for everything else (way, way too many things to list here, I just love you).

To my family. You make writing the Morellis easy.

And finally, to my husband. I can't even list all the ways this book wouldn't be possible without you. I love you, I love you, I love you.

ABOUT THE AUTHOR

Kath Richards is a romance writer living and writing in Utah. She graduated with a bachelor's in technology engineering and an MFA in creative writing, both from BYU. She writes poetry, short stories, and romance novels, and has a fascination with relationships, connection, and love stories of all kinds.

She is represented by Bethany Weaver at Weaver Literary.